One Perfect Summer

One Perfect Summer

Labor of Love

Thrill Ride

RACHEL HAWTHORNE

HARPER TEEN
An Imprint of HarperCollins*Publishers*

HarperTeen is an imprint of HarperCollins Publishers.

One Perfect Summer
Copyright © 2015 by Jan Nowasky
All rights reserved. Printed in the United States of America. No part of this
book may be used or reproduced in any manner whatsoever without written
permission except in the case of brief quotations embodied in critical articles
and reviews. For information address HarperCollins Children's Books, a
division of HarperCollins Publishers, 195 Broadway, New York, NY 10007.
www.epicreads.com

ISBN 978-0-06-232134-3

Typography by Lissi Erwin
15 16 17 18 19   CG/RRDH   10 9 8 7 6 5 4 3 2 1
❖
Originally published separately as *Labor of Love* and *Thrill Ride*
First edition, 2015

Contents

Labor of Love

For my dear friend Nancy Haddock
who dances on the beach . . .
and who told me about the red hat.
It changed everything.

"I see a spectacular sunrise."

An icy shiver skittered up my spine, and the fine hairs on the nape of my neck prickled. I know my reaction seemed a little extreme, but . . .

When Jenna, Amber, and I walked into the psychic's shop, we didn't tell her our names. So Saraphina had no way of knowing my name is Dawn Delaney.

Sunrise . . . dawn? See what I mean? It was just a little too spooky. It didn't help that I thought I saw ghostly apparitions in the smoky spirals coming from the sharply scented incense that was smoldering around us.

Although I certainly didn't mind that the psychic considered me spectacular. If the sunrise she mentioned was really referring to me—and not the sun coming up over the Mississippi River. Her words were vague enough that they could apply to anything or nothing.

I'd never had a psychic reading before, so I wasn't quite sure how it all worked. I was excited about discovering what was going to happen, but also a little nervous. Did I really want to know what was in my future?

My hands rested on top of hers, our palms touching. Her eyes were closed. I figured that she was trying to channel whatever it was that psychics channeled. I'd expected the psychic to be hunched over and old—wrinkled, gray, maybe with warts. But Saraphina didn't look much older than we were. Her bright red hair was barely visible at the edges of her green turban. She wore a flowing green caftan and an assortment of bright, beaded necklaces. Her colorful bracelets jangled as she took a firmer grip on my hands and squeezed gently, almost massaging my fingers.

"I see a very messy place. Broken. Boards and shingles and . . . things hidden," Saraphina said in a soft, dreamy voice that seemed to float around us.

Okay, her words calmed my racing heart a little. We were in New Orleans, after all. I didn't need a psychic to tell me that areas of it were still messy, even a few years after some major hurricanes had left their marks.

"I hear hammering," she continued. "You're trying to rebuild something. But be careful with the tools. You might get distracted and hurt yourself—more than hitting your thumb with a hammer. You could get very badly hurt. And worse, you could hurt others."

Not exactly what I wanted to hear. I wasn't even sure if I truly believed in the ability to see into the future, but I was intrigued by the possibility.

If you knew the future, should you accept it or try to change it?

"Lots of people are around," she said. "It's hot and dirty. There's a guy . . . a red and white baseball cap. The cap has a logo on it. Chiefs. Kansas City Chiefs. I don't get a name, but he has a nice smile."

I released a breath I hadn't realized I was holding.

For Jenna, Saraphina had seen "fire that doesn't burn." The fire part sounded scary, but the not burning was just confusing. And that she saw her at a fair, or something equally mystifying. Jenna's brow was still furrowed, and I knew she was trying to figure it out. She didn't like unsolved mysteries. She couldn't pass a sudoku puzzle without stopping to fill in the empty boxes.

But a nice smile I could live with, as long as that was all he offered, because I was taking a summer sabbatical from guys.

Amber, skeptic that she is about all things supernatural, had tried to mess with Saraphina. She'd been the first one daring enough to ask for a reading. When Saraphina had touched Amber's palm, she'd said she saw color. We'd all been weirded out, amber being a color and all.

Then Amber had asked if she'd find love this summer. Since Saraphina's eyes were closed, Amber had winked at Jenna and me, because she has a boyfriend back home. She's been crazy in love with Chad ever since winter break when they first started going out. He's the first boyfriend she's ever had, and she's been a little obsessive about being with him as much as possible. Quite honestly, I was surprised that she'd come to New Orleans with us, leaving Chad back home in Texas. Glad, but surprised.

Saraphina had said, "Not this summer."

Amber had rolled her eyes and mouthed, "See, I told you. Bullsh—"

"But college . . . one better than you already have," Saraphina finished.

That had been just a little too *woooo-woooo* and had pretty much shut Amber up. Once Saraphina released her hands, Amber started gnawing on her thumbnail. And she was still at it. She had a habit of worrying about things and expecting the worst.

Now, it got really quiet, and Saraphina was so still that it was eerie. How could a person be that still? Was she in a trance?

Sitting on either side of me, Amber and Jenna didn't seem to be breathing. Neither was I. Was Saraphina seeing something horrible? Was she debating whether or not to tell me?

With a huge sigh, as though she'd just finished pushing a heavy boulder up a huge hill, Saraphina released my hands and opened her eyes. They'd creeped me out at first, because one was blue and one was brown. But once I got used to them, I realized they somehow belonged together—with her face. With her. It just seemed like a psychic kind of thing.

"I see nothing else," she said.

Although she didn't look old, she seemed ancient. I think she had what my grandmother refers to as "old soul eyes."

"Oh, okay," I said, wiping my damp palms on my shorts. "Thanks."

"My pleasure."

Maybe she was older than I thought, because she also sort of sounded like my grandmother.

"If you know something really awful is going to happen, you'd tell us, right?" Jenna asked.

Saraphina smiled. "I tell only what I see. I don't interpret it."

"Yeah, but a fire that doesn't burn. What does that mean exactly?"

"I don't know."

"But it's the nature of fire to burn, so do you mean it's not actually burning or it's not burning me? See what I mean? It's kinda vague."

Saraphina shrugged, almost as if to say maybe we didn't really want to know anything else. And maybe we didn't.

I touched Jenna's shoulder. "Come on. We should go."

"But I need more—"

Amber and I had to practically drag her out of the shop, before Saraphina told her for the umpteenth time that there wasn't any more.

Once we were outside, the heat pressed down on us. Until that moment, I hadn't realized how cold I was. My fingers were like ice. I shivered again and rubbed my hands up and down my bare arms.

"Well, that was certainly . . . interesting," I said.

"Do you think she means Chad isn't my forever guy?" Amber asked. "Because I was thinking he was *it* for me. You know—my first, my one, my only?"

"Don't get all freaked out," I said. "None of it means anything. Not really."

As we started walking down the street, I slipped on my sunglasses and adjusted my "Life Is Good" cap over my shoulder-length dark hair. The humidity and my hair weren't going to get along, but that was nothing new. After all, I lived near Houston, so humidity was a way of life.

I'd come totally prepared for New Orleans—also known as the Big Easy. I was wearing red shorts, sneakers, a white lacy tank, and lots of suntan lotion. My mom's parents are from Italy—the old country, as my grandma calls it—so I tend to tan easily, but I still take precautions. I'd known we'd be doing a lot of outdoor walking today because we had so much to see and do in the French Quarter.

"Then why'd we do it?" Jenna asked, looking back over her shoulder, as if she thought maybe something was going to jump out at us.

"We thought it would be fun, and we're in New Orleans," I reminded her. "Visiting a psychic is something you should do when you're here."

We'd arrived a few hours earlier, so we had some time to play today. But tomorrow we'd start working. Because, okay, the psychic was right. We were here to help with the rebuilding efforts. So again, she hit the nail on the head— pun intended—with the whole hammering thing. But it was also an easy guess. Lots of students were spending a portion of their summer here, helping with the many rebuilding projects in the city.

"She got our names right," Amber said.

"Color, sunrise, that could mean anything," I pointed out. "For Jenna she was totally off. Come on, a carnival?"

"She didn't say 'carnival,'" Jenna said. "She said 'fair.' Maybe she meant fair as in pale, not dark. My name in Cornish means 'pale, light.'"

"In Cornish?" Amber asked. "You mean, like in serving dishes? That doesn't make any sense."

I laughed, while Jenna rolled her eyes. Amber's comment was just what I needed to shake off the lingering willies. Sometimes she was a little out there.

"Look, y'all, it was something to do for fun. But there's not going to be a fire, Amber isn't going to break up with Chad, and there's definitely not going to be a guy with a red Chiefs cap in my life."

"You never know," Amber said.

"Trust me, I know. I'm taking time away from all things male."

"Why? Because of Drew?" Jenna asked.

"Why else?"

"You really have to get over what happened prom night," Jenna said.

She was right. I knew she was right. But still, it was hard.

Prom night was unforgettable. And that made it a huge problem. Because I totally wanted to forget it.

It was the night I caught my then-boyfriend making out with another girl in the backseat of his car. It had been almost midnight, the dance winding down. I'd gone to the restroom. When I came back to the dance area, I couldn't find him. I was going to text message him, but I realized that I'd left my phone on the front seat of his car.

A few minutes later, it was where I left my broken heart.

Wouldn't those make great lyrics for a country song?

"I'm over it," I said with determination, trying to convince myself as much as my friends. "Totally and completely. But I don't see the point in getting involved with anyone right now."

I'd put my heart on the line with Drew. He was fun to be around. He made me laugh.

He also had what I guessed you called star quality. He was in drama class, and he'd been given the lead in our school's production of *Beauty and the Beast*. He'd made a great beast because he has black hair but startling blue eyes.

His performance had made me cry. He'd been so good! I'd been over the moon. My boyfriend had brought the audience to their feet for a standing ovation.

Now I wondered, probably unfairly, how much of our relationship had been a performance.

The aromas of chocolate and warm sugar brought me back to the present. They wafted out of the bakery we were passing.

"Let's stop," Amber said. "Maybe a sugar rush will wipe out the worries about our future."

"I'm not worried," I stated.

"Yeah, well, I am."

It smelled even better inside—vanilla and cinnamon added to the aroma.

At one end, the long glass-encased counter had all sorts of pastries. At the other end were pralines, fudge, divinity, and an assortment of chocolates. Several people were in line ahead of us, so we had plenty of time to make a decision. And I needed it. I'm totally into sweet stuff.

"I think I'm going for the carrot cake," Jenna said. "It's healthy."

"How do you figure that?" Amber asked.

"Carrots."

Amber and I grinned. Jenna is a pseudo-health nut. Her

dad owns a fitness center, her mother is a nutritionist, and her older brother is a personal trainer. But Jenna claims she's allergic to exercise. And when she's away from home, she eats every unhealthy thing she can find. Not that you can tell, because she's also on the swim team. She doesn't consider swimming exercise, just fun. Plus she's tall, so she has long arms that give her an advantage in the pool.

But her height gives her a disadvantage when it comes to guys. Jenna is slightly shorter than six feet tall, like an eighth of an inch shorter, which most people would probably just ignore, but she cares about the tiniest fractions because she really doesn't like her height. If someone asks her how tall she is, she'll say, "I'm five feet eleven and seven-eighths inches."

Me, I'd just say six feet.

Or at least I think I would. Having never been that tall, I can't say for sure, and like my dad is always saying, don't judge until you've walked in the other person's shoes. And I could never walk in Jenna's shoes because her feet are a lot bigger than mine.

She's taller than most of the guys at our school. Her mom keeps telling her not to worry about it so much—that boys grow into their height after high school. But get real. She wants a boyfriend now.

Because she spends so much time in the pool—with

practice and competition—she keeps her blond hair cropped really short—a wash-and-fluff-dry style.

Amber, on the other hand, wears her dark brown hair in a layered chin-length bob. It never frizzes. She's also the shortest of our group. My dad calls her stocky—which I've never told her because it doesn't sound very flattering. Not that my dad meant to insult her or anything.

Amber's family has a ranch just outside of Houston, and she's used to hard work, which I guess helped her to develop muscles. She's really strong, which will come in handy over the next six weeks as we build a house.

"What can I get you?" the guy behind the counter asked. He was wearing a big smile, and I figured he was a summer employee, still new enough at the job to think it was fun.

My parents own a hamburger franchise, and I've spent way too much time learning that the customer isn't always right and is usually a royal pain in the butt, but you have to act like you're glad they're buying your burger and not someone else's.

Since I know the truth about waiting on people, I always try to be a good customer.

"Chocolate éclair," I said, smiling.

"To go or to eat here?"

They had a small section nearby with a few tables. Sitting

in air-conditioning for a while sounded like a great idea, so I said, "Here."

Jenna ordered her carrot cake, and Amber ordered a pound of pralines. Okay, so maybe working the ranch wasn't the only reason she was stocky.

"A pound?" Jenna asked.

Amber shrugged. "I'll have one here and take the rest back to the dorm, so we can snack later."

Our volunteer group was living in a college dorm, along with other volunteers. Our group is officially H⁴—Helping Hands Helping Humans. Or as its organizer, Ms. Wynder, calls it: H to the Fourth. Ms. Wynder thinks of everything in numbers. She is, after all, our math teacher. And it was her idea to bring several of us to New Orleans.

According to her, voluntourism—"people doing volunteer work while on their vacations"—is becoming increasingly popular. She'd even shown us an article about soap opera actors who'd spent time here, staying in a dorm like normal people and working during the day. Not that the possibility of running into celebrities had influenced my decision to come here—although, yes, I did plan to keep an eye out.

No, my coming here had more to do with putting distance between me and home. Getting away, far away, worked for me. I had no desire to run into my ex-boyfriend. I was hoping that before school started his family would move to Alaska or Siberia. Never seeing him again would totally work for me.

Nudging me, Amber whispered, "He has a really nice smile." She nodded at the guy behind the counter.

Okay, great. Amber, the skeptic, was suddenly a believer. I touched the brim of my white cap. "No hat."

I was a little taller than she was, and I wasn't at all stocky. I wasn't as tall or thin as Jenna, either. If we were in a fairy tale, I'd be the one who was just right—hey, it's my fairy tale.

"Maybe he just doesn't wear it when he's working," Amber said.

Maybe.

"Are you a Kansas City Chiefs fan?" Amber asked the guy as he set our order on the counter.

He scowled, as if he'd been insulted. "Are you kidding? Saints."

"Oh, right." She gave me a look that said, *What's his problem?*

His problem was probably that he was working and we weren't. I knew the feeling.

We ordered sweetened tea, paid for our order, and sat at a nearby table.

"Okay, so he wasn't the one," Amber said.

"There is no 'the one,'" I assured her, before sipping my tea. Nothing is better than sweetened tea on a hot day. I took a bite of my éclair. The filling was a combination of custard and cream, with a wicked amount of chocolate on top. Really good.

"Ohmigod!" Amber exclaimed, after taking her first bite of praline. "This is the best I've ever tasted. It just melted in my mouth."

"I think New Orleans is famous for its pralines," Jenna said.

"Its pralines, its music, its voodoo, its beads. We're going to have so much fun," I said.

"It'll be the best summer ever," Jenna admitted.

"Although I think you're wrong to swear off guys," Amber said. "It's like my dad is always saying: When you fall off the horse, the best thing to do is get back in the saddle."

I started shaking my head. We'd spent hours discussing the unfairness of it all. All I really wanted to do now was escape into summer.

"I think Amber's right," Jenna said. "Look, we're going to be here for six weeks. We're bound to meet guys, guys who are available. Why not hook up with one? Just for fun, just to have someone to do something with? Have a summer fling?

Get Drew out of your system, completely and absolutely."

Why not? Because it was scary to think about liking someone new, knowing how much he could hurt me. I didn't know if I could do a casual relationship, if I could keep my heart from getting involved. I'd fallen for Drew really fast. And who could blame me? I mean, how many guys these days bring a girl flowers on their first date? And, okay, it was only three flowers, and I think he'd plucked them from my mom's garden, but still—the thought counted.

"Look, Drew was a jerk," Amber said. "Chad would never hurt me like that. And I don't care what the psychic said. He's the one. I totally love him."

"Because you totally love him, I should hook up with somebody?" Amber is one of my best friends and I love her, but sometimes I can't follow her thought process. Like the comment about the CorningWare.

"No, I'm just pointing out that not all guys are going to do something to hurt us."

"Just don't say absolutely not," Jenna said. "Keep yourself open to the possibility that you could hook up this summer—temporarily anyway."

"But we're not here to hook up. We're here on a mission."

"But I don't see why we can't combine guys and good works. I mean, think about it. Wouldn't it be the sweetest revenge, to post pictures of you with a hottie on my Facebook page? Drew would know you were totally over him."

"I don't care what he knows." Okay, a part of me still did. Yes, he was a jerk; yes, he'd broken my heart. But for a while he'd been everything. He was the one who sat with me in the hospital waiting room when my grandma was sick—even though my parents were there. He was the first one I called when I passed my driver's test. He was the one who got up at five in the morning to be first in line at the electronics store when their weekly shipment came in so he could give me a Wii for my birthday—because I wanted one so badly. Unfortunately I couldn't play it now without thinking of him, so I'd stopped using it. Drew and I did so much together, he was a part of so many things that the memories formed a web, connecting everything and making me feel trapped.

"I'm not hooking up with anyone. That's final," I said.

Jenna shrugged. "Fine. Don't. But I plan to." Having finished her carrot cake, she reached into the box and took out a praline. "I mean, I've never even had a date."

"The guys at school are so stupid," Amber said.

Jenna smiled. "I guess."

"I think you both should get boyfriends while we're here," Amber said.

How many times did I have to say no?

"If we did, you'd be hanging out alone," I felt compelled to point out.

"Don't worry about me," Amber said. "I'll always find someone to hang with. As my dad says, I've never met a stranger."

"I've got a crazy idea." Jenna leaned forward, her blue eyes twinkling. "We should go to a voodoo shop and have a hex put on Drew and get a love potion for me."

"No thanks. I'm still freaked out about the psychic reading," Amber said. "I'm not sure if I'm ready for voodoo rituals."

The bakery door opened and three guys wearing sunglasses sauntered in. They looked a little older than us. College guys, probably. It looked like they hadn't shaved in a couple of days. Scruffy—but in a sexy kind of way.

They were wearing cargo shorts, Birkenstocks, and wrinkled T-shirts. They grinned at us as they walked by our table. The one in the middle had a really, really nice smile.

He was also wearing a red cap.

A red cap with a Kansas City Chiefs logo on it.

CHAPTER 2

"Ohmigod, that's your guy!" Jenna whispered excitedly.

It couldn't be. It just couldn't be.

I was trying not to hyperventilate, trying not to lose it. There were probably a hundred guys in the city wearing that hat. Maybe a Kansas City Chiefs' fanatics convention was going on. Or a preseason game. Was it time for preseason games yet?

I shook my head fast. "No, he's not."

Amber leaned across the table and said in a low voice, "Is anyone else totally freaking out here?"

"Don't you think he's her guy?" Jenna asked.

"Well, yeah! Absolutely."

"It's just coincidence." I sounded breathless. My heart was pounding hard.

"I'd buy into that if he was wearing a Saints hat. But Kansas City? Why would he be wearing that?" Jenna asked.

"Maybe he's from Kansas City."

"But what are the odds—"

"Look, people visit here from all over. Saraphina probably saw him at some point, and he stayed on her mind and when she was tapping into things, she tapped into her own memory, not my future."

That was the logical explanation, and I liked logical.

"He'd sure stay on my mind," Amber said. "He's totally hot."

Her brown eyes widened. "Oh gosh, don't tell Chad I noticed another guy. He would so not understand."

"You don't think guys with girlfriends notice other girls?" Jenna asked.

"Once you're with someone, that should be your focus," Amber said, but she didn't sound as though she was totally convinced—and she was still eyeing the guys at the counter, with almost as much interest as she had for the pralines.

"My brother says even though he's ordered the entrée, he can still look over the menu," Jenna said.

Her brother—the personal trainer—was five or six years

older than she was and living with his girlfriend. If a guy was living with me, I would *not* want him still looking over the menu.

"Yeah, well, sometimes that can make you change your order. Just ask Drew," I said.

"I guess, but still it seems a shame not to be able to look at all," Jenna said. "And I'm crushing on actors all the time. Does that count?"

"That's just fantasy," I said.

And I didn't want to admit it, but the guys who'd just walked in were sort of fantasy, too. I mean, I couldn't see a college guy really being interested in me, and these three were definitely not in high school. They seemed too confident, cocky almost, but not conceited. Hard to describe.

I looked toward the counter. With one smooth motion, Red Cap removed his sunglasses. Our eyes met. From this distance, I couldn't tell the color, but they looked dark. He smiled. He really did have an inviting smile—a smile that promised fun and maybe . . . more. As though suddenly embarrassed, or maybe he was shy, or not impressed with me, he turned away and said something to one of his friends. The guy he was talking to was amazingly tall.

"How tall do you think that other guy is?" Jenna asked.

"Which one specifically?" I asked.

She glowered, because I was giving her a hard time. It was obvious which one she was referring to.

"Over six feet. Easy," I said. "Maybe close to six six."

I could hear the guys talking in hushed tones, not what they were saying, but I was pretty sure they weren't discussing the pastry options. Maybe I'd picked up some of Saraphina's psychic abilities.

"I think we should probably go," I said.

"Why?" Jenna asked. "We're not on a schedule."

She was making eye contact with the tall guy. He'd removed his sunglasses, and his eyes were definitely a light color, blue or green.

"Stop that," I whispered. "What if they come over?"

"What if they do?"

Okay, this was embarrassing to admit because I had at one time, after all, had a boyfriend, but the truth is, I didn't have a lot of experience flirting. Drew and I got together pretty soon after Mom gave me permission to start dating, and you don't flirt with your boyfriend. I mean, I never flirted with Drew.

I was tutoring him in math after school—part of a program sponsored by the National Honor Society—when he said he was having trouble with a really complicated formula. Then he wrote out Dawn + Drew = x.

He'd looked at me with those gorgeous blue eyes of his and asked, "Could x equal date?"

And yep, as corny as it was, I'd fallen for it. Totally. That was the middle of my sophomore year, and we'd been together until our junior prom when I'd realized the answer wasn't an absolute constant—that the equation contained hidden variables.

"Look, I'm really not ready to deal with this." I shoved back my chair and stood.

Jenna rolled her eyes and did the same, while Amber closed up her praline box.

"Whoa! You're tall." Tall Guy had walked over and was smiling at Jenna.

Jenna smiled. It was the first time she didn't seem embarrassed by her height. I had a feeling if he asked how tall she was, she'd tell him six feet. No problem.

"So are you," she said.

Tall Guy shot an air ball at an imaginary hoop just over Jenna's head.

"You play basketball?" Jenna asked.

He nodded. "You?"

"Swim team."

He grinned really broadly. Nice smile. Really nice smile. Maybe all guys had nice smiles, and Saraphina's prediction meant nothing.

"I like those uniforms better," he said. "A whole lot better."

"They're not uniforms. They're swimsuits."

He just winked at her, and I could see her cheeks turning red.

The guy behind the counter, oblivious to the flirting going on, rapped his knuckles on the glass case. "Hey, big guy, you want something or not?"

I sort of expected Tall Guy to point at Jenna and say, "Yeah, I want her."

But he didn't.

All three guys turned their attention to the clerk.

I could tell Jenna was disappointed that the flirting session had so easily and swiftly come to an end. With her cheeks turning even redder, she headed toward the door. Amber and I hurried to catch up.

"See ya!" Tall Guy called out.

Smiling, Jenna looked back over her shoulder and waved. Once we were outside, she said, "Was he interested or not?"

"I think boys always choose food over girls," Amber said. "It's a caveman mentality of survival."

"Do you even know what you're talking about?" Jenna asked.

"Not really, but it was getting a little intense in there."

"I thought you were okay with Dawn and me hooking up with someone, that you never met a stranger?"

"I am okay with it; I just wasn't ready for it to happen five minutes after we started talking about it."

"So maybe we should have stayed."

"But we were finished eating," I pointed out.

"So? Would it have been a bad thing to be obvious that *I* was interested?"

"Do you want to go back in?" I asked. "Because if you really want to—"

Jenna shook her head. "Nah, no reason to go back in now. It would make us look fickle or something. Maybe desperate. Besides, it'd just be a one-night thing, and we're supposed to be in front of the gate to Jackson Square at eleven tonight so Ms. Wynder can pick us up. Not sure I want to admit I have a curfew to an older guy. But he was certainly tall."

"And cute," Amber said.

"The curfew isn't really a curfew. I mean, Ms. Wynder is providing transportation, because we don't have a car," I said.

"She's responsible for us. Chaperone. Sort of," Amber said.

There were three other volunteers, six of us in all. Because Ms. Wynder had organized our group, she'd promised to look out for us, but it wasn't a school trip and no one had signed any binding contracts, consent forms, or legal documents.

She'd driven us here in her minivan and arranged for us to stay in the dorm. She'd provided transportation to the French Quarter with the promise to pick us up later and the warning to not get into any trouble. Although I wasn't exactly sure what she'd do if we did get into trouble. Call our parents, I guessed.

But was she really a chaperone? If she was, wouldn't she have stayed with us, kept an eye on us, instead of cutting us loose to find our own entertainment? Although to be honest, I was glad she hadn't tagged along. I think she's, like, thirty.

"You girls are going to be seniors in the fall. I trust you to be responsible," she'd said when she dropped us off.

Telling us she trusted us was tricky on her part, because it made us feel like we had to behave. Not that we were known for getting into trouble or walking around with fake IDs, but still. Away from home, parents, and anyone who knew us . . .

I think we'd planned to do a little misbehaving.

I thought of the inviting smile in the bakery. I was probably crazy to have walked away. Why was it so scary now to even think about getting together with a guy?

I hated Drew. He made me question everything.

"So what *are* we gonna do tonight?" Jenna asked as we crossed the street after a horse and carriage rattled by.

I almost said that I wanted to ride in a carriage, but it

seemed like such a touristy thing to do. Of course, we were tourists, so I supposed it would be okay.

Pointing to a door where a sign proclaimed TAROT CARD READINGS, Amber said, "Maybe we should pop in there. You know, verify what the psychic told us."

"Or maybe we should have our palms read," Jenna suggested. "See if Tall, Dark, and Handsome back there is in my future."

"If he was, don't you think Saraphina would have said something?" I asked.

"I guess there's no way to interpret 'fire that doesn't burn' as applying to him," Jenna said.

"Maybe if he had red hair," Amber suggested.

But his hair had been dark, buzzed short.

"Could 'fire that doesn't burn' mean passion that doesn't happen?" Jenna asked.

I was totally confused.

"What?" Amber asked, obviously confused, too.

"Maybe there would have been passion between us, but I walked away."

Actually, I thought, that sort of made sense.

"If that's the case, then you were supposed to walk away," I said.

"So why predict it? So I live with regret?"

"Who knows? I bet people go insane after a reading, trying to interpret what everything means," I said.

Jenna laughed. "I am obsessing, but you know me and puzzles. I'll stop thinking about it now."

"Sure you don't want to have a tarot reading?" Amber asked.

"I'm sure. Let's just walk around. We've got six weeks to explore things, and I'm not really sure I want the future confirmed. I mean, in theory, it sounds like a good idea, but it's just not nearly as reassuring as I thought it would be."

The French Quarter had been spared most of the devastation that had hit the other areas of New Orleans. There wasn't much traffic, other than foot traffic. I think it was because the streets were so narrow that cars barely missed swiping other passing cars and everyone had to drive so slowly. I wouldn't want to drive here. Better to park at the outskirts and walk or catch a streetcar.

The buildings revealed interesting architecture, kind of romantic. A lot of brick with wrought-iron balconies decorated with flowers. It reminded me of the Lestat vampire novels. I was a huge Anne Rice fan. Before the summer was over, I wanted to see her house in the Garden District. I could imagine vampires walking these streets. And we hadn't even been here at night yet.

By the time we hit Decatur Street, the sun had dropped behind the buildings and dusk was settling in. We were really hungry, our afternoon snack a couple of hours behind us. Even finishing off Amber's pralines while we'd explored various avenues and shops hadn't ruined our appetite.

"Hey, Bubba Gump Shrimp Company," Amber said, pointing to a restaurant. "I love the Forrest Gump movie. Let's eat there."

"Works for me," I said.

We walked inside. To the right was a bar area and to the left was a gift shop with all sorts of Bubba Gump restaurant and Forrest Gump souvenirs. RUN, FORREST, RUN signs. DVDs of the movie. A suit that Tom Hanks had worn in the movie was on display.

"Three?" the hostess asked.

"Yeah," Jenna said.

"Please come with me."

We followed her through the crowded restaurant to the back and up a set of stairs into a smaller dining area. Booths rested along the wall and tables were in the center. We were the only ones sitting up there.

"Wherever you want," the hostess said.

We took a square table near the window, with Jenna and me sitting on either side of Amber.

"The server will be up in a minute. Enjoy." The hostess walked out of the room.

"Do we stink or something?" Jenna asked as she opened the menu. "That we have to be isolated from the other customers?"

"Well, we have been walking around most of the afternoon," Amber said.

"Still."

"I like being up here," I said. "It's quiet, and we can hear ourselves talk. It seemed kind of noisy downstairs."

"It was noisy because people were down there. Maybe we'd see something interesting."

"Are you saying we're not interesting?" I teased.

"We're away from home. It just seems like we should meet other people, experience things."

"You're still thinking about that tall guy," I guessed.

"Yeah. Missed opportunity." Jenna sighed. "So, okay, I'm fine now. I've vented. What are y'all gonna order?"

That was the thing about Jenna. She never stayed angry, never held grudges. She probably would have even forgiven her boyfriend if he had ruined her prom night. I was discovering that I held a grudge awhile longer. I wasn't certain if it was an aspect of my personality that I really liked, but at the same time, I thought being too forgiving could be a fault, too.

I just really didn't understand where I went wrong with Drew. We'd always gotten along. We'd never fought. We'd never gotten on each other's nerves. I'd thought he was the one . . . until he wasn't.

"Well, duh?" Amber said. "Shrimp. We have to order shrimp. Boiled shrimp, fried shrimp, sautéed shrimp, shrimp scampi, shrimp cocktail, butterfly shrimp—"

I laughed. "Enough already. We get it."

We heard the footsteps echoing on the stairs.

"I think we're about to have company," Jenna said.

"Unless our server is an alien with multiple legs," I teased.

"Very funny."

"Well, at least putting us up here wasn't personal," Amber said.

The hostess walked into the room, three guys following behind her.

"Hey, we know them!" the tallest guy said.

Amber gasped. I felt my mouth drop open. Jenna's eyes widened.

They were the guys from the bakery.

What were the odds? That with all the different restaurants in New Orleans, they'd pick the same one as us?

Astronomical.

The hostess told them the same thing she told us, to sit anywhere they wanted, and I halfway expected them to say they wanted to sit with us. They didn't. They took a table at the far end of the room. Once they started talking, we could hear only a low rumble.

"Bummer," Jenna said under her breath. "I thought maybe they'd ask to sit with us. Maybe we should—"

"Are you ready to order?"

The server stood there, and I hadn't even seen him come

in. I'd been paying too much attention to Red Cap and trying not to freak out. Maybe they were stalkers. Maybe they'd
been following us all along and we'd been too distracted
looking at petunias on balconies to notice.

"Who wants to go first?" the server prodded, obviously
in a hurry. He crouched down, put his pad on the table, and
started tapping his pencil impatiently against the pad.

We each ordered fried shrimp. When the waiter walked
over to the guys' table to get their order, Jenna leaned in.
"What do you think it means?" she asked.

"What?" I asked.

She rolled her eyes to the side, toward the guys. "That
they're here."

"Either they like seafood or they're huge fans of *Forrest
Gump*."

"I think it's a sign," Amber said. "We should have done a
tarot reading. Then we'd know for sure."

"You don't even believe in stuff like that," I reminded her.

"Maybe I'm starting to believe. You have to admit that
Saraphina got more things right than she got wrong. I mean,
really—did she get anything wrong?"

I wasn't exactly sure how we could judge that. We were
assuming a lot of things . . . like this Red Cap was my Red
Cap. Maybe he wasn't.

I jumped when I heard a chair scrape across the floor. I'm not usually easily spooked. Nerves of steel, like Superman. But, okay, maybe I was just a little unsettled by how our day was going.

I looked over. The server had left. The guys walked to our table.

"We were wondering," Tall Guy said, looking at Jenna as he spoke, "do you know how much a polar bear weighs?"

Jenna looked at us, looked back at him. "No."

"Enough to break the ice." He grinned, and Jenna grinned back at him.

The other two guys were shaking their heads.

"Seriously," Tall Guy said. "We were talking. We're new to town, don't know anyone, and fate seems to be working here. Three of you, three of us. Running into one another again. What can I say? It seems like destiny."

Did he really say destiny?

"So what say we share a table," he suggested.

"Okay," Jenna said, nodding so rapidly that her head was almost a blur.

The guys moved a chair out of the way, then shoved the closest table against the empty side of ours. Without hesitation, Tall Guy sat next to Jenna. No surprise there. Red Cap and the remaining guy exchanged glances. Finally Red Cap sat next to me, which left Amber sitting across from the third guy.

"I'm Tank," Tall Guy said.

Jenna released a laugh, then slapped her hand over her mouth. "Sorry. It's not a funny name. It's just, were you—are you—in the military or something?"

"Nah, not even close. It's just a nickname, better than Theodore."

Her eyes widened. "Your parents named you Theodore?"

"Yeah, what were they thinking, right? Family tradition. You gotta hate 'em, though." He pointed to Red Cap. "That's Brady. And Sean."

Jenna introduced our group.

Looking at me, Brady touched the brim of his cap. "Like your hat."

"Like yours, too."

"I thought I noticed you looking at it earlier. You a Chiefs fan?"

I shook my head. "Texans." I wasn't really into football, but I believed in hometown loyalty.

"You from Houston?"

"Yeah. Well, actually, Katy, but most people don't know where—"

"We know where Katy is. We go to Rice."

Okay, so they *were* college guys. Rice University is in Houston, and Katy is about thirty minutes west of Houston.

"Talk about your small world," Brady said, smiling.

"Yeah, really."

He looked past me to Amber. "You know, we should change seats. That way you can talk to Sean."

Amber looked startled, probably because Brady had already stood up.

"Oh, yeah, sure, okay, yeah."

Brady dropped into the chair that Amber vacated. Jenna didn't even seem to notice that she had a different person sitting on the other side of her. She and Tank were talking really quietly, with hushed voices. It was strange seeing Jenna with a guy who seemed totally into her. I mean, I'd never understood guys not giving her attention, but still . . .

"So, you're from Katy," Brady said, drawing my attention back to him.

"Yeah," I said. Did he ever stop smiling? And why did it irritate me? Because I didn't want to like him. This summer wasn't about hooking up with someone. It was about doing good works.

Although I had to admit I was flattered that he was showing interest.

"Where do you go to college?"

I released a self-conscious laugh. "Actually we're high school juniors . . . or we were. We'll be seniors in the fall. I'm never sure what to call myself during the summer. You know? Am I what I was, or what I'm going to be?"

Why was I going on and on about nothing? That wasn't like me. But then, what was these days?

His smile grew. I wanted to reach out and touch the corner of his mouth. Strange, really strange. I'd never wanted to touch Drew's mouth. I'm sure it was only because the psychic had mentioned Brady's smile—correction. She'd mentioned a guy with a nice smile. I didn't know for sure if it was this guy. There were probably hundreds of guys who wore red Chiefs caps over their sandy blond hair.

He removed his cap and combed his fingers through his hair, before tucking his cap in his back pocket. Drew's hair was black, short. Brady's curled a little on the ends, fell forward over his brow. It seemed to irritate him that it did, because he combed it back a couple of more times, then shrugged. "My dad would get after me for wearing a hat indoors," he said. "So, anyway, I'll be a sophomore in the fall."

Even though he was blond, he was really tanned. I figured he liked the outdoors. Drew, even though he was dark, was pretty pale. Not vampire pale or anything, but he much preferred staying indoors.

"At Rice," I reiterated.

"Yep. We're practically neighbors, and here we meet in New Orleans. What are the odds?"

"Five million to one."

His brown eyes widened slightly. The psychic didn't mention that he had really nice eyes. A golden brown, sort of like warm, fresh pralines.

"Really?" he asked.

"No, I was just throwing out numbers. I have no idea."

He laughed. Need I say it? His laugh was nice. Everything about him was nice. And it made me uncomfortable because I didn't want to like him, not even for just one night. Because if we spent time together tonight and I never saw him again, if he didn't ask for my phone number . . . quite honestly, it would hurt. And it would add to all the insecurities that I was already harboring, because I had to have at least one flaw, maybe more. There had to be some reason that Drew abandoned me for someone else. Something had to be lacking in me.

If I'd been brave, I would have asked Drew. Why'd he do it? What was wrong with me? But part of me didn't want to know the truth, wasn't ready to face whatever it was that was wrong with me.

I actually hadn't talked to Drew at all that night after I

discovered him cheating on me. I just took my cell phone off the seat, walked away, and called my dad to come pick me up.

"You okay?" Brady asked now, jerking me back to the present—which was a much nicer place to be.

"Oh, yeah. I couldn't remember if I left the iron on." It was something my mom said when she didn't want to talk about whatever it was she'd been thinking about. It made absolutely no sense and was a stupid thing to say. Still, I said it.

"You iron?" he asked incredulously.

"It's obvious you don't."

He looked down at his wrinkled shirt. "Yeah, my duffle bag was pretty stuffed, and we wanted to get in as much sightseeing as we could today."

"So you're just here for the day?"

"Nah, we're here for the summer. Volunteering, building a house, I think. Tank's got the details, I'm just along for the ride."

"That's the reason we're here, too."

There were lots of volunteer and rebuilding efforts in the city. The odds that we were going to be working on the same project could've *really* been five million to one. I was sure it wasn't happening.

So I began to relax a little. What was wrong with having fun—just for tonight?

* * *

"Do you believe in love at first sight, or should we walk by again?"

We all groaned at Tank's corny pickup line.

Sometime between the time that the server brought our food and we finished eating, we all seemed to have become friends. Or at least comfortable enough with one another for Jenna to tell Tank that she thought his line about us being their destiny was pretty corny. So the guys had started tossing out their repertoire of worst pickup lines—just to prove that Tank's hadn't been that bad.

"I hope you know CPR, 'cuz you take my breath away," Sean said. He had a really deep baritone voice that sounded like it came up from the soles of his feet.

Jenna and I laughed, but Amber looked at him like maybe she was wondering if he was serious.

He wasn't very tall. But that worked. Because neither was Amber. Not that it needed to work, because she had a boy-friend.

"Do the police have a warrant out for your arrest?" Brady asked. "Because your eyes are killing me."

I laughed.

"No, seriously," he said. "You've got really pretty brown eyes."

"Oh, that wasn't a line?"

"Well, yeah, it's a line, but I do mean it."

"Oh, well, in that case, thanks. I think."

Were we moving into flirting territory?

"You must be tired," he said, "because you've been running through my mind ever since I first saw you."

"Is that a line?" I asked, not certain if I should laugh again.

"Not really," Tank said before Brady could answer. "We were kicking ourselves for not introducing ourselves to y'all earlier. I'm glad we ran into you again."

I watched as Jenna's cheeks turned pink. "Yeah, we're glad, too," she said.

When the server brought our bill, the guys insisted on paying for everything. Which was so nice and unexpected. I mean, they looked more like starving students than we did.

As we left the restaurant, Tank said, "We're going to hang out on Bourbon Street. Want to come?"

Jenna didn't hesitate. "Absolutely."

Even Amber seemed up for it, which left everyone looking at me. What choice did I have? I shrugged. "Sure."

No way was I going to wander around New Orleans at night alone. And it had gotten dark while we were eating. Besides, I'd heard about Bourbon Street, and I wanted to experience it.

It was obvious Jenna was really interested in Tank. They were even holding hands already. I'd expected Amber to walk with me, but she was still paired up with Sean, talking to him as we headed over to Bourbon Street. Apparently she wasn't worried about what Chad might think, or maybe she was okay with being with a guy as a friend.

Maybe she was right. What would it hurt if tonight—just tonight—I was a little wild and crazy? If tonight, I had fun with a guy? If tonight, I pretended my heart hadn't been shattered?

Brady took my hand. His was large, warm, and comforting. But still, I jerked a little at the unexpected closeness.

"So we don't get separated," he said, as though he wanted to reassure me that nothing heavy was going on between us. "There's usually a crowd on Bourbon Street."

"I thought you were new to town."

"I am, but I know things."

Several blocks of Bourbon Street were closed to traffic. The area was a mash of bodies, noises, and smells. I hadn't expected one of those noises to be the *clip clop* of horses' hooves or one of the smells to be manure.

But the police were patrolling on huge horses, and big horses left behind big business.

"Watch out," Brady said, slipping his arm around my waist and hauling me to the side before I stepped in something I absolutely didn't want to. He laughed. "I think my shoes just became disposable." Although we'd missed stepping into a big mess, the street was trashed.

"Mine, too. Definitely."

I smiled up at him, not sure why I suddenly felt very

comfortable around him. Maybe it was the revelry surrounding us. Maybe it was everyone shouting and laughing and having a great time. The attitude was contagious, something I wanted to embrace.

I was suddenly very glad to be sharing all this with a guy. Not even Brady particularly, just a guy. Because it seemed like the kind of partying that required holding hands and being part of a couple.

People were acting wild, crazy, totally uninhibited. Dancing, yelling, hugging, kissing, laughing. It wasn't all because of the drinking going on. Sure, some people were drinking freely in the streets, weaving in and out of the crowds. I'm certain a lot of them were drunk on booze, but many were simply drunk on having a good time.

When everyone around you doesn't care what anyone else thinks, why should you?

A guy bumped into us, staggered back, and raised his fist in the air. "Rock on!"

He swerved away, hit a lamppost. "Rock on!"

Brady drew me nearer. "That dude's going to be seriously hung over in the morning if he already can't tell the difference between a post and a person."

"Are you speaking from experience?"

I didn't know why I asked that. It was rude. But I think I

was looking for a flaw. He couldn't be this perfect. I wanted him to be not so nice.

He grinned. Obviously he didn't take offense at what I'd said.

"I refuse to answer that question on the grounds that it might incriminate me."

"What are you—a law student?"

"Architecture. We're all architecture majors. It's part of the reason we're here."

"To help rebuild."

"That, and to appreciate what remains."

He made it sound so noble, so . . . un-Drew. The only thing Drew had appreciated was the spotlight, which hadn't bothered me at the time, because it had made him—made us—seem special. I'd never considered him self-centered or selfish, but now I wasn't so sure.

Brady and I walked in tandem, following Tank and Jenna. Their height made them easy to keep in sight.

The street didn't have a shortage of bars, which you'd probably expect of a street named Bourbon, although the name didn't really refer to booze. At the time New Orleans was founded by the French, the French royal family was the House of Bourbon and *Rue Bourbon* was named to honor them. Yes, I'd spent a lot of time on Wikipedia, looking up facts that were probably only interesting to me. Which is why I didn't share that one with Brady.

We stopped just outside a corner daiquiri bar. The huge doors were wide open. People walked in, got their drinks, and strolled out. Behind the counter were several huge vats of frozen drinks, so it didn't take very long to get served. The tables inside were crammed with people watching a baseball game on the TV hanging on the wall.

"I don't get that," Brady said.

"What?"

"You've got all this stuff happening out here, and people are in there watching TV. I can watch TV at home. Why come here if that's what you're going to do?"

"Maybe New Orleans is their home."

"Maybe."

"Or maybe they're huge baseball fans."

"Still. I believe you gotta experience life, not watch it."

He looked at me like he thought I should agree. I didn't know what to say. Up until this summer, my experiences were pretty limited. I didn't want to get into an experience-listing competition.

"I'm making a run," Tank suddenly said.

He went inside, leaving Jenna on the sidewalk. She had her cell phone out, pointed it at me, took a picture, and winked. For her Facebook page, no doubt. As proof to Drew that I'd totally gotten over him. Moved on.

Who knew pictures could lie?

It was only then that I realized I was still nestled snugly against Brady's side. I didn't want to be obvious about easing away from him, which meant that I stayed beside him because there was no way to move away without being obvious.

So, okay, maybe I was just looking for an excuse to stay close. The weight of his arm around me felt really nice.

"You're not going to get something to drink?" I asked.

He grinned and winked. "I'm not going in to *buy* something, but yeah, I'll have something. Tank's the only one who's twenty-one. I might get carded if I tried to buy it, but I don't usually get carded once I'm holding it."

I wondered if that was part of the reason he kept stubble on his chin, so he'd look older. It was considerably darker than his hair. It gave him a rough, dangerous look. Which gave me a thrill. To be with someone older, someone who looked like he could be trouble, someone who wasn't Drew.

"Sounds like you have a system," I said. There I was again, being snide, trying to find that elusive flaw. What *was* wrong with me?

"I believe in partying hearty. And tonight we're pedestrians, so the only crashing that will take place is when we hit the beds." He gave me his sexy grin. (Did he have any other kind?) "Who am I hurting?"

Tank came out with a frozen red drink.

"Strawberry daiquiri," he said. "They give a free shot of Sex on the Beach, but I couldn't bring it out, so I was forced to drink it myself."

"But you're always willing to make the sacrifice," Brady said.

"You bet! Let's party!"

We started walking up the sidewalk, stepping into the street when the crowds were thick on the sidewalk outside the bars that had entertainment. Music wafted out through the open doors. I wasn't familiar with the tunes but hearing them live made me want to follow their rhythm. I thought I could probably become a fan. Expand my musical horizons.

When we passed through some shadows, Tank passed the drink back. Brady took it and offered it to me. Okay. I wasn't old enough, but I didn't want to seem like a prude, either. I compromised and took a very small sip. It was tasty, so I took another. I was pretty sure all the alcohol was on the bottom and I'd lifted the straw up some, so I was drinking from the middle. The alcohol-free zone. Sounded reasonable to me. Not that a cop would buy into my reasoning.

A vision flashed through my mind of having to call Mom and Dad to bail me out of jail. Wouldn't that be just great? I wondered if that was how things worked for Saraphina. Pictures just flashed through her mind and they could mean nothing, something, everything. How did she know which ones mattered?

Brady didn't bother with a straw. He just gulped down some frozen concoction. We passed another bar, and Tank went inside.

I looked around. "Where's Amber?"

Jenna turned in a slow circle, then shrugged. "I don't know."

"She and Sean ducked into one of the bars we passed back there to listen to the music," Brady said, jerking his thumb over his shoulder.

How had I missed that? I hadn't seen Amber and Sean slip away. I guess maybe I was paying too much attention to Brady. But sitting down and listening to a band sounded like a terrific idea. One way to keep my shoes semiclean anyway. But then, I also wanted to see everything there was to see out here, too.

"We can go back there if you want," Brady said.

He didn't say it with much enthusiasm. I didn't know

him well enough to read between the lines, but I had a feeling that he wanted to keep walking. I didn't know how I knew that. I just did.

"No, I'd rather explore."

"Great! Let's at least go to the end of what they've got blocked off. See what other stuff they've got going on. Then we can head back, find the bar they're in."

"Sounds like a plan."

"I'm known for my plans."

"Really?"

"Oh yeah. That's what architects do. Draw up plans."

He gave me a smile that seemed to say I was part of those plans. Or maybe I was just reading things into his expression that I wanted to be there. Maybe he was really talking about blueprints. Although part of me was hoping for the more personal meaning. We were having a good time. And I suddenly wanted to have a good time. A really good time. Show Drew that I was finished moping about him. Have Jenna post a hundred of those pictures for him to see.

Tank came out of the bar with a yellow frozen drink. "Banana," he said, boldly offering it to Jenna.

She took it without hesitating.

We started walking up the street again.

"More?" Brady asked, holding the strawberry daiquiri toward me.

"Uh, no, but thanks."

I felt like a total downer, but my parents had let me come here because they trusted me not to get into trouble. Trust was a heavy burden, a double-edged sword. Too many clichés to name. But I didn't want to do something the first night that would have me back home the second.

Brady finished the daiquiri, crumpled up the plastic cup—why do guys always feel a need to crumple whatever they've been drinking out of?—and tossed it in a nearby trash can.

"We need to get you some beads," he said.

I was pretty sure he wasn't talking about buying me any that were hanging in the windows of the many shops.

Guys stood on balconies, dangling beads, and yelling at girls walking by. Whenever a girl lifted her top, a guy would toss her a strand or two. Unless he was totally wasted, in which case the beads landed on nearby trees or shrubbery. Beads were pretty much all over the place.

"I've decided not to do *everything* the first night," I said. "I want to leave something for later in the summer."

Brady chuckled, leaned near my ear, and whispered, "Chicken."

Okay, maybe I was. I'd never even lifted my shirt for Drew.

"Don't look so serious," Brady said. "I'm just teasing."

"I guess I don't know you well enough—"

"To share what's underneath that tee?"

"To know when you're teasing," I corrected.

"There is that."

He released his hold on me, which I realized felt strange. Not to have him holding me. I almost felt bereft. But that didn't make sense. I'd just met the guy.

He moved so he was standing near a balcony. Waving his arms, he was yelling up at the people leaning over the railing. I'd seen only guys on the balconies, but this one had girls, too. Probably in college. When Brady got their attention, he laughed and pulled his T-shirt up and over his head, then he swung it around like a lasso.

Someone bumped against me. I barely noticed.

Brady was buff. Nothing at all like Drew.

I'd tried to interest Drew in various charity runs. He'd always been willing to sponsor me if I was participating, which I'd thought was nice, but I had a feeling that Brady actually ran. And worked out, and engaged in outdoor activities. Based on the bronzed darkness of his back, I had a feeling he spent most of his time in the sun.

I watched as dozens of beads dropped through the air. Brady snagged them. He was hamming it up, dancing around, strutting his stuff. The party girls were whistling, dropping more beads, inviting him up.

Brady was being crazy, dancing around, having fun, not caring what anyone thought.

I started laughing. He hadn't struck me as being quite so uninhibited, but it was all in the spirit of New Orleans. I think everyone around him was having as much fun as he was.

I was really, really glad that I was there, involved, part of the madness.

Brady turned toward me, holding up all the strands of beads, smiling like some returning explorer who was delivering gold to his queen or something. He dropped them down over my head.

Then, grinning broadly, he wrapped his fingers around them, pulled me toward him, and kissed me.

Right there in the middle of Bourbon Street, with people pushing past us and music filling the night.

CHAPTER 5

Brady tasted like strawberry dai-
quiri, and I thought his mouth should be cold from the frozen
drink, but it wasn't. It was hot. Very hot.

He brought the beads and his knuckles up beneath my
chin. He tilted my head back slightly and started kissing me
more thoroughly.

And the thing was—I was kissing him back.

I told myself that the sip of daiquiri had gone to my head.
I told myself that it was simply the craziness of Bourbon
Street.

But I think part of it was that I wanted to hurt Drew.
Like me kissing a guy as though my life depended on it would
somehow make us even.

Which was crazy. Because Drew would never know. And it wasn't fair to Brady. And I knew, I knew, I *knew* that I should stop kissing him. That my reasons for kissing him had nothing at all to do with him, but was some convoluted sense of revenge.

Brady was such a nice guy, with a terrific smile. And he kissed me like Drew never had. Part of me wanted to stay there forever.

But it was wrong.

I drew back.

Brady gave me a broad smile. "Oh yeah."

He leaned back in. I put my hand on his bare chest. His skin was warm and my fingers tingled. I almost moved back toward him. Instead, I said, "I've gotta go."

He looked like I'd just told him that he'd stepped in something gross. "What?"

"I have a curfew."

"A curfew?"

"Yeah, our chaperone is picking us up at the gate to Jackson Square." I looked at my watch, preparing to lie about the pickup time, but it really was almost eleven. How had that happened? Time had completely gotten away from me. "She's picking us up at eleven. I really have to go. Thanks for the beads, for dinner, for . . . everything."

The kiss, I thought, *really, really thank you for the amazing kiss.*

Turning, I hurried back the way we'd come. Or I tried to hurry. It was a little hard when I had to wedge myself between people. "Coming through. Excuse me."

"Wait, you can't just . . . go off by yourself!" I heard Brady call out.

Only I wasn't planning to go off by myself. I was planning to go with Jenna and Amber. I just had to find them.

Brady caught up with me. "Hey, come on. Slow down."

I had my phone out, trying to call Jenna. I didn't know if she'd be able to hear her cell ringing over the saxophones and horns playing their upbeat music and the din of all the people.

"Hey, Dawn, wait up." Brady grabbed my arm.

I spun around. "You're a nice guy, but—"

"It's okay. I didn't realize . . . a curfew. Wow. Do your friends have one?"

I nodded, wishing I'd used some other excuse. I suddenly felt like such a kid. "It's not really a curfew; it's just that she's picking us up at eleven, so we need to go. Otherwise, she might give us a real curfew."

That sounded worse. Why didn't I just shut up already?

"Okay, I just wish you'd said something sooner."

If I had, he probably wouldn't have brought me to Bourbon Street at all. He probably wouldn't have kissed me.

It took us nearly twenty minutes to find everyone else. Brady didn't say anything the entire time. Didn't hold my hand, although he did keep brushing up against me when the crowds thickened. He'd put his shirt back on—thank goodness. He placed his arm around my shoulders only once and that was when some drunken guy almost stumbled into me—Brady pulled me out of the way, trying to protect me.

I kept thinking I had to be insane for not holding on to this guy with both hands. I probably could have called Ms. Wynder and . . . what? Our first night here and we couldn't meet up for the rendezvous because we were partying too hard? I was pretty sure that wouldn't go over well.

After we found everyone, we headed for Jackson Square. Tank and Jenna were in the lead again, holding hands. Amber was with Sean, talking. Brady and I trailed behind.

"Look, about that kiss—" Brady began.

"Don't worry about it. It was no big deal."

"Ouch!"

I grimaced. That had really come off sounding bad. I wanted to be cool about it, but I didn't know how. I mean, Drew and I had dated about a month before he ever got up the courage to kiss me. I think it had been his first kiss, too, and it had been, well, awkward. Eventually, we were kissing like pros. I'm not sure pro what. Are there pro kissers?

"I just meant that I know it was the craziness of Bourbon Street that made us kiss," I said.

"You think?"

"Oh yeah. I mean, we just met. It can't be more than that."

"I guess."

"I mean, this wasn't even a date or anything. It was just hanging out."

"Okay. Yeah."

I couldn't tell if he was disappointed or relieved.

When we got near the gate, I saw the other three girls Ms. Wynder had dropped off earlier. They went to my school, too, but I didn't know them very well.

"There's our group," I told Brady.

I turned around, walking backward. "Thanks again."

A familiar minivan pulled up to the curb. Amber, Jenna, and I started running for it.

We were all eerily quiet in the minivan after Ms. Wynder asked how our day was and we all responded "Great." As though a one-word answer would suffice when it most certainly didn't.

It had been one of the most up-and-down days of my life. I'd run through the entire gamut of emotions. I was exhausted. And wondering about the psychic's prediction. Was Brady the guy? Had I seen him for the last time? Was my last memory of him going to be watching him fade into the shadows of the night?

Once we got to our dorm room, we all let out collective sighs and started preparing for bed. Even though it seemed like something needed to be said, none of us was saying anything.

I plugged in the pump and pressed the button to inflate the AeroBed that I'd be sleeping on. Each dorm room had only two beds. I had the choice of an air mattress or a roommate I didn't know—Amber and Jenna had already agreed to bunk together before I realized that I wouldn't be doing a summer tour of Texas water parks with Drew. Yeah, that had been our plan. To be together as much as possible. Slipping and sliding the summer away. It had sure sounded like fun at the time.

Since my life seemed to be a series of adjustments lately, I hadn't wanted to adjust to living with a stranger, so I'd decided to go the air mattress route.

Besides, the summer would be a lot more fun if we were all together. Every night would be a sleepover.

Amber sat on the edge of her bed. "Okay, guys, I need y'all to promise that you'll never tell Chad what I did tonight."

Crouching on the floor by the mattress, I twisted around. "What did you do?"

"Where were *you*? I hung out with another guy!" Her voice went up a bit; it had an almost-panicked sound to it.

I know after my prom night experience, I probably should have been all over her case, but Amber was innocent. She hadn't done anything wrong, which I felt a need to point out. "Yeah, but you—what? Listened to music?"

She nodded and looked miserable.

"It's not like you were all over him, or sneaking around."

"Still, he's a guy."

"But you can have guy friends."

"Just don't say anything to Chad. Ever."

"We won't tell," Jenna said.

"Of course, we won't," I assured her. "You don't even have to ask."

"Thanks. He just so wouldn't understand." She looked at Jenna. "What about you?"

"What about me?"

"You and Tank. Are you going to see him again?"

She shrugged. "I gave him my cell phone number, but we

were in such a rush at the end, we didn't really say good-bye or make any plans—"

Her cell phone rang. She took it out of her shorts pocket and just stared at it.

"Answer it," I prodded.

"It's Tank. What do I say?"

"Hello?" I suggested.

She took a deep breath, opened her phone, and answered, "Hey."

With a big smile, she said, "Oh yeah. We're fine. I know it was crazy there at the end. I didn't realize it was so late until Dawn found us." She laughed. "No, we don't turn into pumpkins at midnight."

Rolling onto her side, she curled up and started talking really quietly.

"Should we leave the room?" Amber whispered.

"Nah. We can't head out every time one of us gets a phone call." I turned off the pump and tested the firmness of my bed. It worked.

"What are we going to do if she keeps seeing him?" Amber asked.

"What do you mean?"

"Well, the other two guys will probably be there. I just

don't know if it's such a good idea for all of us to hang out together. I mean—"

"Why don't we worry about it if it happens?"

She jerked her thumb toward Jenna. "You don't think his calling means it's going to happen?"

It probably did.

"I'm too tired to solve this right now," I told her. I just wanted to go to sleep. We'd been running around all day.

"I know I'm probably worried about nothing. Gawd, I wish we hadn't decided to visit a psychic." Amber got her stuff together and went into the bathroom.

I fingered the beads dangling around my neck. I didn't know why I'd freaked out when Brady kissed me. Yes, I did. Brady was nice and that scared me. I didn't trust him not to hurt me. Even for one night. It was a lot easier leaving him than it would be having him leave me.

Jenna had talked about having a summer fling, but I'd never had a casual relationship. Drew had been my first date. I didn't know how to date a guy without caring about him. And why would I want to?

Why spend time with someone I didn't like? And if I liked him, well, the more time I spent with him, it seemed like the more I'd start to like him, and the next thing I'd know . . . I'd be vulnerable again.

The best thing for me to do this summer was to just hang out with Jenna and Amber. And if Jenna was with Tank all the time, then Amber and I would buddy up.

I was probably worrying for nothing.

I'd never see Brady again, anyway. Even if Jenna saw Tank, it didn't mean that Amber and I would hook up with the other guys.

Brady was no doubt going to be just a one night . . . whatever.

Okay, I've blogged day one of what I'm calling our Amazing Summer Adventure," Jenna said, leaning away from the desk where she'd set up her laptop.

It was the next morning. Ms. Wynder had knocked on our door shortly after the sun made its appearance. When I'd volunteered for this, I hadn't considered that I'd be sleep deprived the whole summer. Even when I worked for my parents, I didn't go in until just before the lunch crowd hit.

Although I suppose I wouldn't have been dragging so much if I hadn't stared into the darkness for most of the night, thinking about Brady. Reliving the kiss. Wondering if he'd decided that I was a total nut.

What did I care what he thought? I'd probably never see him again. Saraphina's predictions were no doubt all jumbled up. Visions weren't an exact science. Just because she'd mentioned hammering and a red cap didn't mean they were in proximity. Last night was probably it.

Of course, Amber, who was used to getting up with the cows—literally—was her usual perky self. She seemed to be totally over all the doubts she'd had the day before about the psychic encounter.

She and I peered over Jenna's shoulder. Jenna wanted to be a journalist, so she was all about reporting what was happening in our lives—with posting photos and all. And there was the photo of me and Brady.

I looked . . . happy. And he looked . . . sexy. And together we looked . . . cuddly. An item.

And I thought, *Drew, eat your heart out.*

"So Drew is still on your friends list?" I asked, trying not to sound as interested as I was.

"Oh, sure. He's bound to see this."

"Why?"

"Because I write interesting stuff, and he knows it. And he'll be interested. I mean, face it. What we're doing here is way different from what anyone else is doing over the summer. He'll want to know all the delicious details."

She got up from the chair and I sat down. The room didn't have much furniture except the beds, two dressers, a desk, and three chairs—two of which we'd raided from a lounge down the hall.

Amber pressed up against my back as she tried to read what Jenna had written. "You didn't mention Sean, did you?"

"Of course not."

Jenna had written about our visit with the psychic but glossed over her prediction for Amber—no doubt because Chad was on her friends list, too, and he didn't need to know that Amber might find someone better.

Jenna hadn't revealed anything incriminating. Still, it always unsettled me a little to see the intimate details of my life shared with others.

"Oh, by the way," Jenna said as she started getting dressed, "I might see Tank tonight."

I could hear the excitement in her voice.

"Where?" I asked, trying to sound casually interested, instead of anxious to know if that meant that I might see Brady. Did I want to see him? I did. Scary.

Amber moved away to start getting dressed, too. I decided I'd better follow or I'd be left behind. I pulled on the Helping Hands Helping Humans T-shirt that Ms. Wynder had designed for us to wear the first day to identify our group.

It had hands all over it. What can I say? She was more into numbers than art.

Jenna shrugged. "I'm supposed to figure out exactly where the dorm is and call him later with directions. He has a car. Said he'd come get me."

"That's awesome!" Amber said at the same time I said, "Aren't things moving a little fast?"

I never would have asked that question before prom night. Sometimes I missed the old me.

"I mean—"

"I know," Jenna said. "You got hurt and now you don't trust boys, and you're worried that I'll get hurt, too."

"I trust boys." I trusted them to hurt me. Drew had really messed me up. I hated that I was giving him that power.

I sat on a chair and started lacing up my hiking boots. We'd been warned to wear sturdy shoes and jeans because we didn't know what we'd run across in the debris. No exposed legs. No sandals.

"You don't trust boys," Jenna repeated.

What was I supposed to say to that? Do, too? So we could get into exchanging meaningless comebacks like two-year-olds?

"Uh, y'all, do we *have* to wear these T-shirts?" Amber asked.

I looked over at her and saw that the hands on her T-shirt were rudely placed. I dropped my gaze to my own chest. Yep, those little hands were sending a message that I didn't want to send.

Jenna started laughing. "Oh my gosh. I never thought I'd be so glad for a tall body. At least my hands aren't exactly where they shouldn't be."

"Considering the message, I don't think we do need to wear them," I said. "At least I'm not."

I jerked off my T-shirt and scrounged around in my suitcase until I found a faded T-shirt from a vacation my family had taken at Thrill Ride! Amusement Park.

Amber and Jenna changed their shirts, too.

I welcomed the distraction from what might have turned into an argument with Jenna. I was really happy for her, glad she'd met a guy who wasn't bothered by her height. And I really, really hoped . . .

I didn't know what I hoped. That she didn't get hurt, of course, because we were only here for the summer, and he was only here for the summer, and even though he went to college in Houston. . . . I suppose their relationship could last past our time in New Orleans. As a matter of fact, before prom night, I probably would have *believed* in it continuing after we got home. But I used to believe in a lot of good things, like love was forever and boyfriends were neat to have.

Pancakes and sausages were waiting for us in the cafeteria. Several of the volunteers were already eating. Our little group of six, along with Ms. Wynder, gathered at one table. While we ate, Ms. Wynder went over the safety rules again: Watch out for critters, stay alert, don't get in a hurry, haste makes waste, the usual stuff. When we were finished eating, we headed outside, climbed into her minivan, and caravanned with the other volunteers to the site.

We were silent as we drove along, looking out the windows at the devastation. Walking through the French Quarter yesterday, having fun, it was easy to forget how ruined other parts of New Orleans still were. But we could also see the areas that had already been rebuilt. They spoke to the strength and determination of the people of the city.

As my admiration for them was growing, my cell phone rang. I pulled it out of the case attached to my belt. My dad had given me the case because he thought it would make it easier to keep my phone handy and he didn't want me to be without quick access to it. "In case of an emergency."

So maybe he and Mom *were* a little worried about me

being away from home—at least, that's what occurred to me when I saw Mom's name pop up in the window.

"Hey," I said, after answering.

"What's going on?" Mom asked curtly.

Her question wasn't at all friendly. Not a *what's happening?* It was more of a *what trouble are you getting into?*

I was sitting on the backseat between Amber and Jenna. They must have heard her through the phone because they both looked at me.

"What do you mean?" I asked.

"Drew e-mailed me a picture of you with some guy—"

"He did what?" That jerk! Why would he do that?

"He sent me—"

"Sorry, Mom," I interrupted again. Mom hated being interrupted, but she was almost four hundred miles away. What could she do, other than growl? "I got you the first time. My question was more of a 'what was he thinking.'"

"So who is this guy?"

"Just someone I met."

She was quiet for a minute. It was never good when Mom was quiet.

"He's a student at Rice," I felt compelled to explain. "He's here for the summer doing the same thing we are."

"Does Ms. Wynder know him?"

Define know, I thought. She'd seen him if she'd been looking out her window last night at the precise moment needed to see him before he disappeared.

"Yes."

I squeezed my eyes shut, hoping she wouldn't ask to speak with Ms. Wynder.

"It's just that I know you're still not over Drew—"

"I am over Drew," I interrupted.

"—and I don't want you doing anything stupid," Mom finished.

"I won't. Don't worry."

Of course, do we ever *plan* to do something stupid? It's not like I wake up in the morning and think, "Today would be a good day to do something stupid."

"It's a mother's job to worry," Mom said. "I just need reassurance there isn't any craziness going on."

"None whatsoever. Please don't worry, Mom. I'm fine. We're in the van now, heading to the site." I thought trying to distract her would be a good move on my part. "We're looking forward to helping to clean things up."

"Yet you don't seem to care about cleaning your room. What's wrong with this picture?"

I could tell that she was teasing and had gotten past whatever had been bothering her. We talked for a little while longer, then said good-bye. I told Jenna and Amber what Drew had done.

"Why would he do that?" Jenna asked.

I shrugged, surprised that he cared what I was doing. I hadn't *really* thought that he'd read Jenna's blog. Why would he? We were so over. Why would he care?

"He's definitely coming off my friends list," Jenna said.

I didn't say anything, but I thought he should have come off sooner.

"Everything all right back there?" Ms. Wynder asked.

"Yes, ma'am. Just my mom missing me."

And my ex-boyfriend trying to stir up trouble.

Our caravan pulled to a stop in a neighborhood that still reflected the aftermath of the storm. The street had been cleared of debris, but what remained of the houses littered the yards.

No one said anything as we climbed out of the van. I thought I was prepared for this, but I wasn't. It seemed like an impossible task, and yet I was also filled with a sense that we could make a difference. We could get this done.

"Hey!" a guy called out in a welcoming way. "Everyone over here!"

He was standing on a ladder, near the first house on the block, urging us over. He was older, much older. Probably as old as Ms. Wynder. He wore a black T-shirt with the French fleur-de-lis on the front above the words "Rebuild New Orleans." He had curly red hair that fluffed out beneath his white cap and made him look a little like a clown. All he needed was the red nose—only his was very white, covered in zinc oxide.

Another caravan of vehicles pulled up. I found myself standing on tiptoe, trying to see if I recognized anyone from the dorm or breakfast that morning. Okay, that wasn't exactly true. I was searching for someone I'd seen yesterday, last night to be precise. I was pathetic. I didn't really know what I wanted. To see him again, to never see him again.

I knew he probably wouldn't be at the site, but there was one irritating little spark of hope that wouldn't have been disappointed if he showed up.

And then I saw someone I recognized, the very last person I'd expected to see here.

"Hey, is that—" Amber began.

"The psychic," Jenna finished.

"Hey, Sara! Bring your group over here," the guy on the ladder yelled.

Waving at him, she herded her little group over. Wearing jeans and a tank top, with her red hair pulled back in a ponytail, she looked like a normal person. Her group was mostly guys, which was pretty understandable because she was really pretty—gorgeous actually. It took me a minute to realize that, because I was scanning the guys following her.

Okay, I was doing more than scanning. I was seriously searching for the familiar red cap, the nice smile. Which was dumb, because if I wanted to see Brady again, all I had to do was tell Jenna and she'd call Tank and he'd tell Brady and Brady could call me . . . only I didn't know if that's what I wanted.

But I didn't see anyone I recognized.

"Why is she here?" Amber asked. "Is she going to do psychic readings?"

"Based on the way she's dressed, she's probably here for the same reason we are," I said.

"That's weird," Jenna said.

"Not really," I said. "I mean, people who live in New Orleans are working to rebuild it, too."

"Still, a psychic," Jenna said. "Do you think she'll let us know if she gets bad vibes?"

Before I could respond, the guy on the ladder clapped his hands. "All right, people! I need your attention!"

Everyone stopped talking and edged up closer.

The guy clapped his hands again. "I'm John. And this house is our project." He pointed toward the house behind him. "Working together, we're going to gut it, then rebuild it."

Gut it. That sounded so harsh.

"Gutting should take only a couple of days. We're going to move everything out, put it at the edge of the street so we can haul it away. We're going to remove the walls, the windows, the doors. The only thing we'll leave is what remains of the frame."

We'll be able to do all that in a couple of days? I thought. Amazing.

"The woman who lives here is staying with her parents right now. She's already taken all that's salvageable, so anything else—just move it to the curb. Be sure to gear up. We have hard hats, safety goggles, and dust masks over there. Work together and be really careful because you don't know what you're going to find hidden beneath all this stuff."

Hidden? A shiver went through me. Saraphina had said I'd find something hidden.

"Any questions, people?" Without hesitating a beat, he clapped his hands three times. "Then let's go!"

"I had a question," Amber said.

"Did you really?" I asked.

She smiled. "No, but he didn't even give us a chance to ask one if we did."

"Guess he's anxious for us to get started." I caught a glimpse of Jenna off to the side, talking on her phone. I took out the work gloves that I'd stuffed into my jeans pocket earlier. Ms. Wynder had given us tips for how we needed to prepare for this summer of labor. She'd done it last year as well, so she knew what was useful and what to expect. I tugged on the gloves, grateful that I had them. Jenna came back over. She and Amber tugged on their gloves.

Then we walked over to get the rest of our equipment. A line had already formed. Probably two dozen people were here, many already starting to walk by with their gear in place.

"Does a hard hat leave a hard-hat line around your head when you take it off?" I asked.

"What does it matter?" Jenna asked. "You're not trying to impress anyone."

"Still, with all the gear, we're going to look like we're going into a contaminated zone."

"We probably are—with the mold and stuff," Amber said.

Once we were properly geared up, we grabbed one of the wheelbarrows at the edge of the property and rolled it closer to the house.

"Why don't you girls pick up some of the loose debris that's still around the house?" John asked.

I saluted him. He grinned.

"You okay with us just tossing stuff off the porch and letting you take care of it?" he asked.

"Works for me," I said.

"Good. I love a can-do attitude."

He walked into the house and several people tromped in after him. Amber, Jenna, and I began gathering any broken and rotting pieces of wood that hadn't yet been hauled to the curb. Beneath one board, we found a doll's head, which made us sad thinking of a little girl without her doll.

John came outside and tossed what looked like molding cushions onto the ground.

"Did a little girl live here?" I asked.

He glanced over at me. "Yeah, she's fine. There are two girls, actually. They're with their mom."

"How old are they?" I asked.

"Four and six, I think."

"I guess they have new dolls now."

"Yeah, but little girls can never have too many, right?"

I smiled at him, wondering how he knew what I was thinking. "Right. If I bought something for them, would you be able to get it to them?"

"You could give it to them yourself. When we're finished, we'll welcome them home. You'll get to meet them then."

"Oh, cool."

I hadn't realized we'd be doing that. I went back to work, picking things up. I was carefully placing the remains of a clay jar in the wheelbarrow when I heard, "Smile!"

I looked up. Jenna snapped a picture and then laughed.

"You look like someone doing something she shouldn't," she said. "Let's try this again."

"Why do you need a picture? I'm all scruffy looking."

"For one—my Facebook page. But I also want to send a pic to your mom so she can see you're hard at work and it'll calm her worries. So smile."

"I'm wearing a mask. You can't even see my mouth."

"So smile, anyway."

Smiling while picking up trash was kind of like those people who smiled in commercials selling exercise machines. It wasn't natural. Still, I pulled down my mask, gave a big fake smile, and a huge thumbs-up.

"That'll do it," Jenna said. "I'm going to see what else I can document."

She walked away. I pulled up my mask and returned to my task. I was reaching down, wrapping my hands around what looked to be a massive table leg attached to a small section of dining table, when I heard a deep voice I recognized say, "Need help with that?"

I jerked up, stepped back. My foot landed on an old board that wobbled. I teetered and would have fallen, except strong hands wrapped around my arms, steadying me.

"Careful," Brady said in a voice that fell between concerned and amused.

"What are you doing here?" I asked.

He was wearing sunglasses so I couldn't read his eyes. Some sort of white powder was sprinkled over his burgundy T-shirt. *Maybe that's his flaw*, I thought. *Maybe he does drugs.*

And how had he even realized it was me, with all my gear on? Had he noticed me when I'd posed for the camera?

"I told you yesterday. I came to volunteer," he said.

"But this site?"

He shrugged. "It's where they sent me."

"So you're into snow?" Wasn't that what they called it? Or was it blow?

"Love snow. Went skiing over spring break."

"I was referring to the powder." I pointed to his chest, trying not to remember how nice it had looked last night without a shirt covering it.

Glancing down, he started dusting off his shirt. "Oh, that. Powdered sugar. We went to Café Du Monde for beignets. Place was packed. It's the reason we're late." He looked up. "You thought it was drugs?"

I felt so silly. Talking to him through the mask. Looking at him through the goggles. Accusing him of dumb stuff.

"I was teasing."

And if you believe that, I have some swampland I could sell you.

He grinned, like he knew I was out of control, but he was willing to tolerate it.

"You eaten there yet?" he asked, taking the conversation back to his breakfast.

"No."

"It's a must-do."

"They feed us breakfast in the dorm."

"Doesn't mean you have to eat there."

Why was I discouraging a hot guy from showing interest in me?

And why was he interested in me?

Why not?

I felt like the before-Drew me and the after-Drew me were on the debate team. And doing a pretty lousy job at substantiating arguments.

"Are you staying at the dorm?" I asked. It would be totally weird if he was, that everything—fate, the dating gods, whatever—was putting him in my path.

"Nah, we've got some cheap rooms in a small hotel in the French Quarter. Tank knew some people who knew some people." He shrugged.

"Is he in charge of your group?"

"We're not official, not really organized. As a matter of fact, very unorganized. Tank asked if I wanted to come to New Orleans for the summer and do some volunteer work, said he'd secured some beds, and since I had nothing better to do—here I am." He made a grand sweeping gesture. "At your service. So let me help you with this."

"But you're not geared up."

"I'll gear up in a minute. Let's get this done."

Squatting, he grabbed the end of the table leg that was still attached to part of the table.

I bent over—

"It's better for your back if you use your legs to lift stuff," he said.

"My toes don't hold things well."

He laughed. "Funny. You grab with your hands, but lift with your legs. See?"

He demonstrated, his legs doing a smooth pumping action, like a piston. He had really nice thighs. Even covered in jeans, they looked firm. Very firm.

"So, you're what? A lifting coach?" I asked.

"Nah. I worked for an overnight package deliverer over winter break. Had to watch safety videos." He shifted the table leg so he was able to carry it by himself and drop it in the wheelbarrow.

It was only then that I noticed Tank and Jenna working together to remove a screen from a window. How it had managed to remain attached, I couldn't imagine. Most were gone, or hanging lopsided.

"Where's Amber?" I called out to Jenna.

"She went to talk to Sara/Saraphina. I think she wants another psychic reading."

"Now?" I asked.

Jenna shrugged as she walked over to me. "She's still bummed about what Saraphina told her yesterday."

"You had a psychic reading?" Brady asked.

Now it was my turn to shrug. "It's like eating at Café Du Monde. Something you have to do when you're in New Orleans."

"What did she tell you?"

"Nothing that made any sense. Do you believe in that sort of thing?"

"Not really." He reached down, picked up a brick, and dropped it in the wheelbarrow.

Apparently, I had a new partner for the day—whether I wanted him or not.

"Okay, so her real name is Sara, and Saraphina is, like, her stage name or something. She said it all has to do with marketing," Amber said.

It was a little past noon, and we were all sitting on the curb, eating deli sandwiches called po'boys that one of the local eateries had sent over. Apparently some of the restaurants provided food for the volunteers, which made it really nice on our budgets. It also gave us such a sense of being appreciated—not that we were doing any of this for kudos, but still, it was nice.

"So, did she give you another reading?" I asked.

"No. She doesn't give freebies, and she doesn't do readings when she's outside the shop. She's just a normal person today—or as normal as she can be with two different colored eyes, but whatever. She said I'm trying too hard to interpret what she saw. I don't know how I can *not* interpret"—she darted a quick glance at Sean, who was attacking his ham sandwich—"what she told me."

I wondered if she thought that since Sean was in college, he had the potential to be the better love.

"It's not like psychic-ism—or whatever you call it—is an exact science," I reassured Amber. "She puts a thought in your mind and then when something similar—"

"Similar? Red Kansas City Chiefs hat is pretty specific," she interrupted.

"What?" Brady asked, taking off his cap and looking at the logo on the front, like he was trying to confirm that it was there.

Before lunch, we'd all taken off our gear and washed up with a water hose. He'd put his cap back on then. I'd put mine on too, because of course I had hard-hat hair.

"Saraphina said Dawn would meet a guy—" Amber began.

"She said she saw a red cap—" I interrupted.

"Close enough."

"What happens with you and the red cap?" Brady asked, settling it back into place.

"Nothing. And look"—I turned my attention back to Amber—"nothing that she saw for Jenna has shown up."

"Maybe it has and we just haven't recognized it."

"You know, I heard a story once about a guy who went to see a fortune-teller," Tank said. "He wanted to know how he was going to die. She told him that cancer would kill him. So he's looking in the mirror one day and sees this strange-colored lump on the end of his nose. He's sure it's cancer and he panics. Jumps in the car, heads to his doctor, and on the way, he's hit by an eighteen-wheeler. Game over."

"So the fortune-teller was wrong," Jenna said.

Tank shrugged. "Maybe, but in a way, cancer *did* kill him."

"That's kinda convoluted," Amber said.

"Exactly," Tank said, "but that's the way all this mumbo jumbo works. You can read anything into it that you want, and practically force what was predicted to happen."

"So you're saying that I'm overreacting," Amber said.

"I'm saying you're letting her mess with your head."

"You don't believe in psychics?"

He grinned. "I didn't say that."

"I just really wish we hadn't gone there at all."

I knew Amber was a worrier, but she'd never believed in

stuff like this before. Why was she so troubled now? It made no sense.

I took a long sip of water. I was drinking water like there was no tomorrow.

"I can't believe that y'all were assigned to the same site we were," I said. "What are the odds?"

"Five million to one," Brady said, grinning.

I'd known him less than twenty-four hours and already we had a private joke. I couldn't remember what private joke Drew and I had—or if we'd even had one.

"Are you kidding? The odds were stacked in our favor. Jenna called and told me where y'all were working," Tank said.

I didn't know whether to stare at Jenna or glare at Brady. Jenna was leaning against Tank's shoulder like he was the only thing supporting her, and Brady was studying his sandwich like he was trying to determine what lunch meats they'd stuffed between the French bread.

"You called them?" I said.

"Oh yeah," Jenna said. "They're not with a group like we are. They're like freelancers or something. Just helping where needed, so I called him this morning right after we got here to see if they wanted to help out."

"John was a little freaked that we were here and not on his list. That guy is way too tightly wired," Tank said. "Apparently there are people you're supposed to contact to be an official volunteer, but"—he shrugged—"John decided having our muscles was more important than following the rules."

"It'd be insane to turn away someone wanting to help," Jenna said.

"Exactly the point we made. Who'd have thought we'd even have to argue?"

"John's Sara's brother," Amber announced.

"Really?" I asked.

"According to Sara."

"Guess she wouldn't say it if it wasn't true. Now that you've told me, I can see the resemblance, sort of," I said.

"I asked him if he could see things, but he said no," Amber said. "He said that's Sara's burden."

"I imagine it would be hard to see things, to know things," Jenna said. "It's hard enough just knowing the little bit she told us."

"All right, people!" John yelled. "Five more minutes and we need to get back to work!"

"So much for the Big *Easy*," Sean said.

We all smiled.

"You got that right," Tank said.

Amber smiled at Sean, then dropped her gaze to watch a centipede walking between her feet. Her cheeks turned red, like she was embarrassed to have Sean's attention. Or maybe it was just the heat, which was turning us all red.

The day was only half over and I wanted a shower already. With lots and lots of soap. A bubble shower. I smiled at the thought of filling a shower all the way up with water and swimming in it.

"A dip in a pool would be nice right about now," Brady said.

And I had a vision of him in the water-filled shower with me, and we were cavorting around like seals or something. Way too much imagination.

"Ookay!" I said, standing. "Think I'm ready to get back to work."

I started the exodus from the curb. Everyone crumpled up the sandwich wrappers and tossed them into a nearby trash bin. Then we went back to picking up the debris brought out of the house and putting it into a wheelbarrow. When it was full, the guys hauled it over to the curb and dumped the stuff there.

"I think we've got the absolute best team out here," Jenna said.

She was using the time when the guys went to empty the

wheelbarrow to catch her breath. Okay, we all did. But her gaze followed them a little more closely.

"So you really like Tank," I said, although my voice went a little high at the end, and it came off sounding like a question.

"Yeah, I do. And I think Brady might be the one Saraphina was talking about for you. It's obvious that he likes you."

"Or I could just be convenient. You like Tank. He hangs out with Tank. I hang out with you. It's just serendipity."

"Come on. He's here, helping us, just like Saraphina predicted."

"Actually, you sort of orchestrated that, by inviting them. And Sara didn't say anything really happened with me and the guy. She just said she saw him."

"*Whatever*. We could all have so much fun together!"

I know she thought I was being difficult, stubborn. And maybe I was. But I'd learned the hard way that you can't tell by looking if a guy is destined to hurt you. From the outside, they all look nice.

By about two o'clock, I was hot, sweaty, and ready for another break.

"All right, people," John called out, from atop his ladder.

"Can I have your attention?" He made sweeping arm gestures, trying to get us all to come closer.

Jenna, Amber, and I sort of migrated together.

"Wonder what's going on?" Jenna asked.

I shook my head. I didn't have a clue.

"We're making great progress, people," John said. "But we worry that if we work you too hard, you won't come back."

Everyone laughed.

"Soooo . . . you have the rest of the afternoon off."

Applause, a few roars of approval, and some whistles followed that announcement.

John waved us into silence. "For anyone who's interested, Sara arranged a swamp tour! The bus will be in front of Sara's shop in about"—he made a big production of looking at his watch—"forty-five minutes. Whether you go to the swamp or just hang loose, enjoy your afternoon. Tomorrow morning come back ready to hit it hard again!"

People began to disperse.

"Hmm. Swamp," Jenna murmured. "What do you think? Do we want to go to a swamp?"

"I watched an old movie called *Swamp Thing* with my dad once. That's all I know about them," I said.

"A swamp seems like such an icky thing," Amber said.

"Okay, so what do we want to do?" Jenna asked.

I shrugged. "Maybe we could go down to the French Quarter—"

"Hey, Jenna," Tank called out, walking toward us. "We're going on the tour. Are you?"

"Yeah, we are," Jenna said.

Okay, I guess our plans changed.

"Great! See you at the bus."

She waved at him as he walked away. I watched as he joined up with Brady and Sean, said something to them. Then they headed to his car.

"Hope you don't mind," Jenna said.

"I'm good with it," Amber said. "I mean, we're here to work *and* have fun."

They both looked at me, like they thought I was going to argue with the fun part. I guessed there was no reason why I *had* to go. But I didn't want to spend the rest of the afternoon alone either.

"It'll be interesting," I said enthusiastically. I didn't see how, but I was trying to be a good sport. "But I have an important question here—what *does* one wear to a swamp?"

Ms. Wynder took us back to the dorm so we could clean up—fast. She wasn't going on the tour, but she was willing to drop us off at Sara's.

I changed into shorts. I decided to double layer two tank

tops that I had, putting a red one over a pink one that peeked out just a bit. I slipped on my red sandals.

"You know a swamp is probably squishy," Jenna said.

"Yeah, you're right." I changed into sneakers. I didn't want muck getting between my toes.

Quite a crowd was at Sara's when Ms. Wynder dropped us off. The other three girls in our group immediately headed toward three guys who'd shown up at the site with Sara that morning.

"Wow, that didn't take them long," Amber said.

"Looks like a lot of people are pairing off," Jenna said.

"Here we go, everyone!" Sara said as the bus pulled up.

"I guess we can all sit together," Jenna said.

She said it like it was a fate worse than death, obviously worried that Tank wasn't there yet. And then suddenly there he was, grinning broadly, Brady and Sean right behind him.

"Hey," Tank said, taking Jenna's hand. "This is going to be awesome."

Maybe swamps were a guy thing.

Brady and Sean were both standing there with their hands in their back pockets, like they weren't exactly sure what to do. Like maybe they were wondering if we were all going to pair up again like we had last night.

I remembered how worried Amber had been about how

things would play out if Jenna was seeing Tank. I hadn't wanted to deal with it then. I still didn't.

We headed onto the luxury bus. Each row had two seats. Sean was leading the way. Amber was following him. I was behind her. Sean dropped down onto a row, reached out, took Amber's hand, and pulled her down beside him. I felt a small spark of panic. Where was I supposed to go now?

I went a couple of rows back and took a seat by the window. Jenna slid onto the seat in front of me, and Tank sat beside her. That was cool. I could sit alone.

But suddenly Brady was there. He eased down beside me.

"I think the bus is going to be packed," Brady said. "Tight fit for everyone, so I figured sitting by someone I knew beat sitting by a stranger."

"These are all people from the site. Don't you know them?"

"Some of 'em, sure, but not like I know you."

What exactly did that mean?

"So should I move?" he asked.

I shook my head. "No, you're fine."

He grinned, wiggled his eyebrows. "Some would say I'm better than fine."

I couldn't help myself. I laughed.

Sara took a head count, and then the bus headed out.

"So . . . Sara predicted I'd walk into your life?" he asked in a low voice.

"Uh, no, she predicted a red baseball hat was in my future. Not exactly the same thing."

"That's weird, though."

"Yeah."

"I mean, how many Chiefs caps could be in the city?" Before I could answer, his grin broadened. "Let me guess. Five million?"

I smiled, shrugged. I didn't want to be unfriendly. But I didn't want to be too friendly.

"What else did she say?" he asked.

"Not much. That things were a mess. There'd be hammering. Pretty vague."

"And pretty general. That could pretty much apply to anyone."

"That's what I thought. It was interesting, but not something I want to do on a regular basis."

"Well, I'm all about interesting and having fun."

I scowled at him. "But a swamp? Really. How much fun can we have at a swamp?"

"As much as we want."

CHAPTER 9

Honey Island Swamp. I liked the
name—the Honey Island part at least sounded sweet—but
I still couldn't get past my image of a swamp being, well, a
swamp.

It was located almost an hour from New Orleans. I wasn't
sure what I'd been expecting. Maybe taking a look at slime-
covered water from a dock and moving on. Swatting at a few
mosquitoes, shooing away flies. Heading back to the Big Easy.

But no, we were getting out *on* the swamp, in a boat.
And I soon discovered that the sounds out there were a different kind of music than what we'd heard in the city. Here
it was the croak of bullfrogs—some were disgustingly huge
and ugly—and the chirp of crickets. There were mysterious

knocks and pecks and little trills. Luckily Sara had brought lots of insect repellent for anyone who wanted it. I'd slathered, sprayed, and squirted it on. I was taking no chances. I was not into bugs.

And we were at a very bug-infested place.

We climbed aboard a large, covered boat, like the kind I'd ridden once at a safari ride at a theme park—except this one was real. It didn't run along a rail. It had a motor and a captain, who steered it through the swamp.

Benches lined all four sides of the boat. We all worked our way around the deck. I managed to get a seat near the front of the boat. Brady sat beside me.

I was turned sort of sideways on the bench, so I could see clearly things that approached our side. Brady was twisted around, too, which almost had us spooning.

"You smell really nice," he said in a low voice.

"It's the insect repellent."

"It is?" Out of the corner of my eye, I could see him sniffing the back of his hand. "Oh God, it is. How sick is that—to like the smell of insect repellent?"

I laughed. "Pretty sick."

"But admit it. You were thinking I smelled good, too."

Okay, I had been, but I wasn't going to admit it. "Maybe."

The motor cranked to life and the boat glided away from

the dock. I was surprised that the water looked more like what you'd find in a river than what you might expect to find in a swamp.

Our guide was native to the area, and he shared a lot of the history—especially about pirates and Big Foot sightings—as we journeyed deeper into the swamp. Because so much of the area was protected, he explained, Honey Island Swamp was one of the least-altered river swamps in the country. It probably looked the same more than two hundred years ago when pirates were hiding out there.

"Wow," I whispered. There was an awesome beauty to the place. Huge cypress trees rose from the water.

And I'd expected the marshes to smell . . . well, like stagnant water. There was a little of that, but there was also the scent of wild azaleas. I hadn't expected the sweet fragrance.

"Look," Brady said, pointing.

At first I thought it was a log, resting at the edge of the bank, barely visible through the tall grasses. But it was an alligator. A very large alligator.

"We have more than a million alligators in Louisiana," the guide said.

"Imagine if they ever decided to band together," Brady said. "They could take over the state."

"I think I've seen that in a movie."

"Me, too. I can never get enough of giant alligator movies."

"Really?"

"Oh yeah, the bigger the creature the better. *Night of the Lepus.* A classic."

My dad was a huge creature-feature watcher, so I'd pretty much seen them all.

"Now, see, I didn't get that one. What's scary about a bunny rabbit?" I asked.

"It's a big, big bunny rabbit."

"Still, not scary."

The guide warned us to keep all our limbs inside the boat. Then he began making a sound I'd never heard before. Alligators—the ones I'd spotted and ones that had been hidden—began slipping into the water and gliding toward the boat.

"Ohmigod!" I couldn't help it. There were so many. I imagined them tipping the boat over. I'd definitely watched too many bad movies with my dad if I really thought that was going to happen.

"It's okay," Brady said, putting his arm around me, squeezing my shoulder.

He was so comforting. But this wasn't a date. It was a

group outing, and we were all sitting close together. It was just natural to reassure each other that we weren't about to become alligator dinner.

The guide began tossing something toward the alligators and the *clack* of their mouths snapping shut filled the air.

"Is he tossing marshmallows?" I asked.

"Looks like."

"How did anyone find out that they like marshmallows?"

"Beats me."

Every now and then we'd come in close to the shore, and we'd see other animals: deer, red wolves, raccoons, beavers, turtles . . . and always the alligators.

"I don't think I'd want them for neighbors," I said quietly.

"Me either."

We saw an egret and other birds. It was an untouched paradise. I knew New Orleans had once been swampland, and I wondered if it had looked like this at one time. Hard to imagine.

I looked over my shoulder to see Sara sitting near the captain. I figured we were safe. She wouldn't get on the boat if she saw danger, would she? On the other hand, her visions were so cryptic. Maybe she just saw herself swimming and didn't realize it meant she'd be swimming with the gators.

Amber and Sean were sitting together. He was pointing

stuff out to her. She was smiling. They were just being friendly. Having fun. Like me and Brady. No big deal.

Jenna and Tank were sitting close, his arms around her as they looked out at the swamp. There was no doubt that Tank was really interested in her.

I turned my attention back to the alligators. Sometimes nature was so powerful, you had no defense against it.

It was early evening when we got back to Sara's, and Ms. Wynder was there, waiting for us. Before anyone could say anything, she said, "I've made reservations for eight o'clock. We need to get moving."

Jenna didn't bother to hide her disappointment as she waved good-bye to Tank. I thought Amber looked relieved. I knew I was. It gave me time to think, to try to figure out what, if anything, was happening with Brady and me. We all got along, so I could see our little group hanging out together. But at the same time, did I need to explain to him that more kisses weren't in our future?

On the other hand, did I really want to give that up?

After we were seated at the restaurant and had given our orders to the waitress, Ms. Wynder folded her arms on the table. She looked incredibly serious.

"All right, girls, we need to talk," she said.

I wondered what we'd done wrong. Everyone looked guilty.

"I know some of you are developing . . . friendships." She paused and looked at each of us.

I wanted to raise my hand and say, "Not me!"

But the truth was that maybe I was. A little.

"During the week, curfew is midnight. On Saturday, two o'clock. I already have all your cell phone numbers"—she held up her phone as though to demonstrate—"and I want phones to be kept on at all times."

"What about when we're at a movie?" one of the other girls said.

"Vibrate. I will be making room checks. Or stop by my room and let me know when you get in. Are there any questions?"

It sounded pretty straightforward to me.

She smiled. "All right then. Tell me about the swamp."

The next day, it seemed like the sun had moved a million miles closer to earth. How else could it be so much hotter?

Or maybe it was just that we were working harder. We were actually beginning to see progress. John had given crowbars to some of the guys to start ripping off the outer walls.

Jenna had muttered, "Sexist!"

So Tank had given her his crowbar. Or let her work the crowbar with him. He'd put his arms around her and together they'd ratchet off boards. Boards that Amber and I would pick up after they were tossed to the side, put them in the wheelbarrow, and haul them to the curb.

I caught Brady watching me a time or two. Today he was geared up so much that the only thing that gave him away was when his head was turned in my direction. It felt as if he was studying me, trying to figure me out.

What was there to figure out?

We'd had fun at the swamp yesterday, but it hadn't been anything serious. And it hadn't ended in a kiss like the first night. Actually it hadn't had any type of real ending.

There had just been stepping off the bus and Ms. Wynder ushering us away like a hen going after her chicks. And all of us too surprised to say anything other than "See you tomorrow."

And even though we'd seen each other earlier today, our greeting had been a little cautious. Just a *hey*. Like we were both trying to figure out if yesterday had been more than just hanging out together because of convenience.

Do you like me?

Should I like you?

Where do we go from here?

Should we go from here?

I really wasn't sure. Last night, when I'd asked Amber why she'd hooked up with Sean, she'd said, "Everyone was pairing up. It would have been rude not to."

But if you kept pairing up with the same person, didn't you eventually become a *couple*? I didn't want to be part of a couple. I didn't want expectations.

Hooking up one night when I didn't expect to see him again was one thing. Hooking up twice was creeping toward dangerous territory.

I thought maybe Amber was feeling the same way, too, because she was staying pretty near me today, helping me haul the debris to the curb.

It kept getting hotter and hotter, and by late afternoon, it was miserable.

John announced that we could quit for the day, but we were so close to being finished with the gutting that everyone protested. We all wanted to stay and get the job done.

Brady, Tank, and Sean walked to their car—a black Honda Civic—pulled their tees off, and tossed them inside. Not that I blamed them. All our shirts were damp from the humidity and our efforts. I thought about how nice it would feel to have the breeze blowing over exposed, damp skin.

They tossed their gear onto a table. I guess they'd had

enough of being safe. They wanted to be not so hot.

Carrying their crowbars, they headed back toward the house. I really tried not to stare at Brady's chest. It had looked nice in the shadows of Bourbon Street, but now there were no shadows. And he was definitely in shape.

Tank walked past us, touching Jenna's shoulder as he went by. "Jenna, help me out over here, will you?"

Only Jenna didn't move. Neither did Amber. Neither did I, for that matter. We were staring at Tank's back. His right shoulder, to be precise.

A shoulder that sported a tattoo of a blue and green flying dragon.

A dragon breathing fiery red and blue flames.

Fire that didn't burn.

CHAPTER 10

"I know you must think I'm insane, but I just can't help it."

Following an afternoon that seemed to have way too many hours—and surprises—in it, we were back at the dorm. Jenna and I were standing in our room, speechless, watching as Amber tossed all her stuff into her suitcase.

"I mean, red Chiefs cap"—she pointed at me—"fire that doesn't burn?" She pointed at Jenna. "I don't care what you say, there is something to that psychic reading. I've got to go home and figure out if things between Chad and me are real or over."

She'd freaked out when she'd seen Tank's tattoo. She'd

told Ms. Wynder that her mother called and her grandma had died.

That afternoon, her mother *had* called, to see how things were going, after Amber had left a panicked message on her voice mail saying that she was homesick and wanted to fly home—immediately, that night, the first flight out that she could get.

And her grandmother *had* died—five years ago.

"She didn't say you were going to break up with Chad," I pointed out.

"She said I was going to find something better."

"Well, if there is something better, isn't now the time to find out?" Jenna asked. "You're only in high school—"

"Who are you—my mother? Always thinking that I'm too young to know what I'm doing? I know what I'm doing."

"We've been planning this summer adventure for months!" Jenna exclaimed. "You can't just pack up and leave. We just got here!"

"This is a free country. I can change my mind about what I want to do."

"But we're only going to be here six weeks," I reminded her. "Chad will still be there."

"I'm not going back for Chad. I'm going back for me. You

don't understand how I feel about him."

I stepped in front of her, trying to stop yet another mad dash between her dresser and the suitcase on the bed. "I know you're crazy about Chad—"

"Not Chad. Sean. I really, *really* like Sean." She dropped down on the bed, scrunching her clothes between her hands. "That first night when we were listening to the band at that bar, I was leaning into him and he had his arm around me, and I wasn't thinking about Chad at all. I was just thinking about how nice it was to be with Sean. And then yesterday at the swamp—I knew I should have been hanging around with you."

"What could you do? He took your hand—"

"He took my hand because he thinks I really like him. He doesn't even know about Chad."

"He doesn't know you have a boyfriend?"

"How do you tell a guy that?"

"'Oh, by the way, I have a boyfriend?'"

"But what if I shouldn't?"

"What?" Jenna asked, while I said, "Huh?"

I was afraid Amber was about to veer off into one of her strange thoughts that we couldn't follow.

"Look—Chad? He's the only one I've ever wanted to date. I've been crushing on him since I was a freshman. When he finally asked me out over winter break, I thought he was it. Forever. And now, all of a sudden, it's like all I can think about is Sean. And that's so wrong. I know it's wrong. He's like that extra scoop of ice cream that you know you shouldn't have, but you can't resist it. I need to get as far away from the ice cream as possible. I need to go home."

Okay, some of what she was saying was making sense. I wanted to try to convince her that she should stay, but I couldn't anymore. I couldn't without fearing that she'd cheat on Chad—and I'd be encouraging it. She was right. It was better to leave and figure out what was going on.

"I know if we hadn't gone to see the psychic that I wouldn't have all these doubts. Or maybe I would. I just don't know anymore. I mean, what was I thinking to even consider going away for most of the summer? I have a boyfriend and nothing should be more important than him."

Jenna sat on the edge of the bed and drew her long legs up beneath her. "You know, what you're doing is sort of self-fulfilling Sara's prophecy. You're going to make happen exactly what she predicted. Just like Tank was talking about."

"You can't tell me that you weren't a little freaked out when you saw that tattoo."

"I was surprised," Jenna admitted. "But it could be that we're taking her words and seeing things that apply. We're assuming she meant the tattoo because it fits. But it could mean something else."

"Like what?" Amber challenged.

Jenna sighed. "I don't know."

Okay. I thought it was a little difficult to read anything else into that tattoo, but I understood what Jenna was saying—or trying to say. You see what you expect to see, and Saraphina had influenced what we expected to see.

Amber turned to me. "Look at the bright side. You don't have to sleep on the AeroBed anymore. You can have a real bed."

"The bed isn't an issue. I'd rather have you here."

"I can't, guys. I'm sorry, but I just can't stay."

An hour later, Jenna and I hugged Amber good-bye and watched her climb into the minivan. Ms. Wynder, after repeatedly clucking about how sorry she was that Amber's grandmother had died, drove Amber to the airport where she could catch her flight back to Houston.

"Whose idea was it to visit the psychic, anyway?" Jenna asked as we trudged back to our room.

"I think it was Amber's."

"Talk about a fun idea going bad."

"It is a little . . . eerie, though."

"Yeah, but at least I didn't see the tattoo until after I'd

fallen for Tank, so my feelings about him are my own. Do you ever worry that what you feel for Brady is because of the reading? I mean, would you have noticed him if you hadn't been looking for a red Chiefs cap?"

"I wasn't looking for a red Chiefs cap."

"Okay, you weren't looking, but when you saw it—I saw your jaw drop, so I know he caught your attention. Would you have noticed him without the reading?"

"Yeah, I think I would have." I sighed. "But I might not have shot up my defenses so fast. Or maybe I would have. I don't know, Jenna. I just really don't want a guy in my life right now."

"At least you're not totally avoiding him and flying back home."

"That would be a bit extreme, especially since I really do want to be *here*."

Jenna smiled at me. I gave her a weary smile back. To say I was exhausted was an understatement. We'd worked harder and longer today than yesterday. On top of that, dealing with Amber's hysterics—

"Dibs on the shower," I muttered.

I wanted the shower first, last, and always. It felt so wonderful to get all the grit and grime off. Amber had hit the shower as soon as we'd gotten back to the room. When she'd come out, she'd gone immediately into frantic I've-got-to-get-out-of-here mode. And Jenna and I had gone into intervention mode. A lot of good that had done.

I guess, being alone with her thoughts, Amber hadn't liked where she and Sean were going.

I was too tired to think of anything except how great the shower felt. And if Jenna wasn't a friend, I probably wouldn't have cared about using up all the hot water.

The bathroom was steamy by the time I was finished; the mirror fogged. Not that I needed a mirror when I only planned to comb the tangles out of my hair. When that was done, I massaged my peach-scented body lotion on my legs, arms, and hands. I'd picked up a few scratches on my arms, even though I'd tried to be careful. But nothing serious.

I slipped on cotton boxers and a tank. I was ready to fall into bed and fall asleep.

When I opened the bathroom door, the only light in the room came from the bathroom behind me.

Jenna rolled off her bed and walked toward me, holding her cell phone out. "Here."

"What's that?"

"Phone."

"I know that. I mean, who is it?"

"Brady."

"You were talking to Brady?"

"No, I was talking to Tank, but Brady wanted to talk to you when you finally got out of the bathroom. Did you even leave me any hot water?" She took my hand and wrapped my fingers around her phone. "He doesn't have your phone number. Keep talking until I'm finished with my shower."

She closed the door, leaving me in the dark except for the phone's little bit of indigo glow. I stumbled to the bed, sat down, and stared at the phone for a minute like it was the snake that had slithered out from beneath one of the boards we'd moved that afternoon. Some guy had used a shovel to kill it, and we'd all heard a lecture from Sara about how we should live in harmony with all creatures. The dead snake had upset her. Personally I didn't have a problem with killing anything that slithered and stuck its tongue out at me.

And why did I have to talk to Brady until Jenna got out of the bathroom? It wasn't like she didn't already have Tank's number programmed into her phone, so she could call him back. What about *I really don't want to get involved with anyone this summer* did she not understand?

I moved the phone to my ear. "Hello?"

"Hey."

His voice was as sultry as the Louisiana night. I could almost hear the crickets chirping and the bullfrogs croaking in a bayou. Oh, wait. That could have been them outside the dorm window, since quite a bit of water surrounded the Crescent City.

"You okay?" he asked. "You sound kinda dazed."

"Nah, just totally relaxed after a hot shower."

Which suddenly seemed like a really personal thing to say to him. Maybe he was thinking the same thing, because he didn't say anything. It was definitely a conversation stopper.

"So, uh, Jenna said you wanted to talk to me?"

"Yeah. I, uh . . . this is awkward."

"What?"

"Well, Sean said that Amber's heading home because she has a boyfriend."

"How does he know that?"

"She called him from the airport. Upset. It was strange."

I imagined it was. But Amber was my friend. I wasn't going to call her strange.

"Well, anyway," Brady continued, "I just—it's just that I didn't even think to ask, but do *you* have a boyfriend?"

My heart thudded, because why would he ask unless he was interested? Who was I kidding? He'd kissed me. And we'd hung out a little.

All I had to do was say yes, and he'd move on. Instead, I heard myself telling him the truth. "No."

"Okay."

What did that mean? I wished we were talking face to face so I could see what he was thinking.

The silence stretched out between us. Finally I couldn't take it anymore.

"Okay?" I repeated. "What do you mean by that?"

"Just okay. Now I know you don't have a boyfriend."

"Do you have a girlfriend?"

"Why do you care?"

"I don't," I responded quickly. I felt like I'd been tricked into revealing something, but I didn't know what. "I mean why would I care? We're just here for the summer, working, having a little fun."

"Okay."

"Okay."

But I felt like something had shifted, and I wasn't sure what.

The door opened. Mist, light, and the scent of strawberry shower gel wafted out.

"Jenna's ready to take back her phone," I said, hating that I sounded so relieved. Hating even more that I wasn't relieved at all. Should I give him my number? Should I ask for his? Did I even want to continue this conversation?

"See you tomorrow," Brady said.

"Yeah."

I held the phone out to Jenna. "Thanks."

She took the phone, reached back, and turned off the bathroom light. She was whispering quietly as she crawled into bed.

I slipped beneath the sheet and blankets. We'd turned the thermostat on the air conditioner way down and now that I didn't have Brady's voice to keep me warm, I was feeling the chill of the room.

Maybe it was because I was sleeping in the bed that Amber had been sleeping in, but I kept thinking about her telling me that I needed to climb back in the saddle. And I kept thinking of climbing in the saddle with Brady.

Because it was going to be a very long and lonely summer if I didn't take some action. Now that Amber was gone and Jenna was practically glued to Tank, I was going to be spending a lot of time alone. Unless I wanted to hang out with Ms. Wynder. And I wasn't sure that was even an option because I'd seen her near the porta-potties laughing with John. And no one laughs near porta-potties, so I had a feeling something was going on there.

Suddenly I realized that it was really quiet in the room. That I couldn't hear Jenna whispering anymore. I heard her bed creak as she shifted on it.

"Dawn?" she whispered.

"Yeah."

"You still awake?"

I smiled in the dark. "Nah, I'm talking in my sleep."

She released a small laugh. "You're so funny."

No, not usually.

"Listen," she began, "in the morning I'm going to go have breakfast with Tank at Café Du Monde. Wanna come? It's one of those places you should eat at once in your life."

"Did Tank tell you that?"

"No, actually, my dad told me that he wanted me to eat there. He said Jimmy Buffett mentions it in one of his songs and Dad's a huge Jimmy Buffett fan, so he told me to go eat some beignets on him." She laughed. "Actually everything I eat is on him since he's the one who gave me the money for this trip. So, anyway, do you want to come?"

"Is it going to be just you and Tank?" Not that her answer should really affect my decision but still—

"No, Brady will be there for sure. Maybe Sean. So what do you think?"

I rolled onto my side. I couldn't really see her because of the darkness, but it made it easier to talk to her. "Jenna, if I keep doing stuff with him, he's going to think I'm interested."

"I'm going to keep seeing Tank."

It wasn't like Jenna to be this determined.

"But I want to spend time with you, too," she said. "I'm just talking about you going to get a doughnut with *us*. So what if Brady is there? Big deal."

"I thought it was a beignet."

"Beignet, doughnut—same thing. We wanted to have fun this summer, didn't we?"

Yeah, we did. We'd wanted to do some good, but we'd also wanted some adventure, some laughs, some memories. It was our first summer away from home. Where was my adventuresome spirit?

"Okay," I said. "Yeah, I'm in. Totally."

She didn't take offense that I sounded resigned instead of overjoyed. She just said, "Great."

Yeah, I thought, as I rolled back over and closed my eyes. *Great.*

I'd expected to sleep like a rock, or a log, or something heavy and inanimate. Instead I woke up while it was still dark and couldn't go back to sleep.

I crawled out of bed, grabbed my clothes from the chair where I'd left them the night before, and crept into the bathroom. Once I closed the door, I turned on the light and got dressed as quietly as I could. Today I was going to wear coveralls over a tube top. Coveralls had seemed like a building-house-kinda-thing to wear, but now I was wondering if maybe they'd be too hot. At least my shoulders would be cool.

And bare. Maybe a little sexy.

Oh no, I was thinking about Brady again. I didn't want

to do things to get his attention.

I don't know how long I sat on the edge of the tub and worried about how I could spend time with Jenna, without getting in over my head with Brady. A sudden rap on the door startled me. I nearly fell backward into the tub. Just what I needed—to start the day with a concussion.

"You okay in there?" Jenna asked.

"Oh yeah, I'm fine." I got up and opened the door. "I couldn't sleep and I didn't want to wake you."

She yawned. "Ow. I can barely move this morning. Working with a crowbar was harder work than I thought."

She stumbled into the bathroom as I walked out.

"Call Ms. Wynder and tell her we're going to breakfast with some friends," she said before shutting the door.

"You think she's up?" I called through the door.

"Oh yeah."

I called Ms. Wynder. She was indeed up, sounding way too bright and cheery for that time of day. She said she was fine with us doing breakfast elsewhere, and she'd see us at the site.

When Jenna came out of the bathroom, we grabbed our backpacks and headed outside.

The dorm was a square, uninteresting brick building, part of a campus that had survived the storm. It was early morning but humidity already hung heavy in the air.

Parked at the front of the drive, in a no-parking zone, was the black Civic. Our two guys were leaning against it— one against the hood, one against the trunk—arms crossed over their chests. Totally sexy pose. Rebels, I thought, and my heart did a little stutter. What was I getting myself into?

"Hey," Tank said as we got nearer.

"Hey, yourself," Jenna said, practically skipping to his side.

He grinned at her. No kiss. No hug. But it seemed to be enough for her as she slid into the front passenger seat, and it probably was. After all, he hadn't tattooed her name on his arm yet. I suddenly wondered if he would someday.

Then I wondered if maybe that was where I'd made my mistake. I always wanted things to happen fast. Drew and I were a steady item after that first date. I'd never questioned where the relationship was going; I'd just followed where it had seemed to lead. Now I was trying to question everything.

Brady just grinned at me, tapped the brim of my "Life Is Good" cap. "You ever not wear that thing?" he asked.

I touched the brim of his. "Same goes."

"Yeah, but I use mine to hide a bald spot. You got a bald spot under there that I need to know about?"

"No. Do you? I mean really? Bald?"

He laughed. "Nah. At least not yet. Someday. If I take after my dad."

"I think bald men are sexy."

I don't know what made me say that.

"Really?" he asked, opening the door to the backseat.

"Really." I climbed inside, scooted across, and he got in.

"Like who?" he asked. "Give me a name."

"Bruce Willis."

"Is he shaved or bald?"

"Is there a difference?"

"Oh yeah. Shaved you have a choice. Bald you don't."

"How bald is your dad?" I asked.

"Pretty bald."

"Bet he's pretty sexy."

"Yeah, and what do you base that assumption on?" His grin was cocky, almost a dare.

And I almost responded with "you." But that would have taken the flirting to a whole new level, and I wasn't even sure that I should be flirting.

Instead I looked out the window as Tank drove along the street. "Looks like it's gonna be another scorcher today."

It was my dad's equivalent of Mom's "I think I left the iron on." A detour in the conversation.

Brady laughed and leaned back in the corner. I could feel him studying me, and I wondered what he was thinking. The easiest way to find out would be to ask. But I didn't.

We couldn't find a parking spot near Café Du Monde, so we parked several streets over and walked. Although it was early, people were queued up on the sidewalk. A very small portion of the restaurant was indoor seating. Most of the seating was outdoors, some beneath a roof, some beneath a large green-and-white striped canopy.

As we waited in line, Jenna was nestled against Tank's side, and they were doing that quiet talking thing they did. I couldn't figure out how two such tall people could talk so quietly. And Tank wasn't only tall, he was broad. He was wearing a tank top today and the muscles of his arms rippled and when they did, so did the dragon on his shoulder that was peering out beneath his shirt.

"Like his ink?" Brady asked.

"Oh, gosh, I was staring, wasn't I? That was rude."

He shrugged. "It's an unusual piece. He goes to a guy who does original artwork, so nothing he's ever tattooed on anyone has ever been put on anyone else."

"That's cool. I've never heard of that. I thought you just

looked in a catalogue and picked out the one you wanted."

"You can do it that way. But Tank—he never follows the crowd."

"Do you have any tattoos?" Was that question too personal? If he did, they were well hidden because I hadn't noticed any the couple of times I'd seen him without his shirt.

Brady shook his head. "Nah. Been thinking about it, but I don't know if there's anything I'd want forever. I mean, how do I know I won't change my mind? How 'bout you?"

"I did a temporary one once. A peel-on wash-off."

He grinned. "How did that work for you?"

"Not too bad, except I got it out of a machine, like a bubblegum machine, and so I just had to take what it dispensed. It was a skull with a snake coming out of the eye socket. Gross. But I was fourteen, and for a quarter, it was a great deal."

"Where'd you put it?"

"On my wrist."

He looked disappointed, like maybe he'd been fantasizing about it being someplace really personal. And that made me feel very unadventuresome.

"Hey, I had to put it someplace I could reach," I explained.

"Very unimaginative," he said. "Next time you want a tat, I'll help you put it someplace you can't reach."

I narrowed my eyes. "Like where?"

"Your hip, maybe. Someplace so it just peeks out over the waistband of your jeans."

I got warm just *thinking* about him applying the tattoo. I couldn't imagine what would happen if he was actually putting it on. I really wanted—needed—to talk about something else.

"So where's Sean?"

"He hooked up with Sara."

I stared at him. "The psychic?"

Brady grinned. "Yeah. Is that a problem?"

"No, I just"—I shivered—"I don't know if I'd want to be involved with someone who could read my mind."

"Do psychics read minds?" he asked.

"I don't know. They read something. All that paranormal stuff just seems to mesh together. I don't know if there's a line that distinguishes what a person can or can't do."

"She seems nice anyway."

"Oh, well, yeah. I mean, she doesn't seem evil or anything." Then something else occurred to me. I scoffed and muttered, "She didn't have to leave."

"Huh?"

"Amber—she, well, she didn't have to leave. If she'd known Sean was interested in Sara—"

"I don't think he was interested. He was just bummed out because Amber left, so we hit some bars last night." He shrugged. "Sara was at one of them."

"Oh."

So had he turned to Sara because he'd been heartbroken? That made me sad. Why did love—or even just liking someone—have to be so complicated?

We finally got to the front of the line. It was an unorganized type of organization, and I wasn't at all sure how the staff remembered who had been waited on and who hadn't.

As soon as people got up from a table, people sat down at it—mess and all. Then the server would come clean up the mess, take the order, and head over to another table and do the same thing.

"Over here," Tank said and led us to a just-vacated table.

It was covered in plates, cups, and loads of powdered sugar. We dusted off the chairs before sitting down.

"This is something that just has to be experienced to be believed," Tank said.

The server came over and began clearing the table. "Order?"

"Two orders of beignets and four café au laits," Tank said. Then looked around at us. "Any objections?"

"Sounds good," I said.

Jenna just smiled.

"We're going to be sticky after this, aren't we?" I asked.

"Oh yeah," Tank said. "But it's worth it."

I couldn't believe how crowded it was. And how fast the servers were taking care of people. Apparently Café Du Monde was a tradition for tourists and locals alike.

The waiter brought over our two plates of the little fried squares of dough smothered in confectioners' sugar. He also set down our mugs of café au lait—half coffee, half milk. It all smelled really good.

I picked up a beignet. It was still hot, very hot, just out of the fryer, and the powdered sugar floated around me. There was a jar of more sugar on the table. Not that I could imagine anyone ever needing to add any to the beignets. I bit into the fried dough. Was it ever good!

We made an absolute mess as we ate, leaving powdered sugar all over our faces, our hands, our clothes, but no one seemed to mind.

I kept sneaking peeks at Brady, only to discover him looking at me. It was starting to get awkward. I was afraid I was sending a message I didn't want to send, like that I was obsessed with him or something—when I wasn't. I wasn't going to let myself be.

Even though it seemed like he might be interested in me.

Sean had tried to hook up with Amber, and then he'd hooked up with Sara. While Brady, as far as I know, hadn't tried to get together with anyone except me.

So was he interested?

I was pretty sure he was, but he was keeping it cool. Casual. I thought maybe I could handle that.

Maybe.

"I'm sorry your friend left," Sara-phina—oops, she was Sara when she wasn't at the shop—said.

I was in the backyard, sawing off the dead branches of an uprooted tree. The tree itself was dead as well, rotting, and nothing more than an eyesore. But it was also huge. I could imagine the wondrous shade that it had provided for the nearby house. I could certainly use some shade now. It was late morning, and we were waiting for the truck with the lumber and supplies to arrive, filling in the time with odd jobs.

"She just got a little freaked," I explained.

"Sometimes people do that," Sara said, picking up scattered smaller branches and tossing them into the wheelbarrow.

I stopped sawing for a moment and took the red bandanna Brady had given me earlier and wiped my brow. When he'd given it to me, it had been wet and cold and he'd wrapped it around my neck to help cool me down. It had felt so good that I hadn't even been bothered that it was such a boyfriend kind of thing to do. Now all the water had evaporated, and I was using it as a towel to mop my face.

"How long have you been able to see things?" I asked.

"As long as I can remember."

"Do you see your own future?" I thought that would be pretty weird. Would you know what days not to get out of bed?

Hmm. That might be advantageous.

"I see things, but I don't always know who they apply to. Sometimes the visions are stronger when I'm touching someone, but it doesn't necessarily mean it's for that person. It's hard to explain."

"But the things you predicted, they've all sort of happened."

"Sometimes I get them right."

"Do you like being psychic?"

"It has its moments."

"Have you ever helped the police?"

She laughed. "At least you don't think it's a parlor trick. I tried to help them once, but they're as skeptical as your friend was."

I placed the saw on the branch and started moving it back and forth. "I think she's an actual believer now."

"She'll be back here before the end of summer," Sara said quietly.

I stilled the saw and looked over my shoulder at Sara.

She shrugged. "I see her here, but all this looks less messy."

"I didn't think you gave free readings."

"This isn't really a reading. It's just conversation."

But that didn't make it any less spooky.

"Is she just visiting or coming to help?" I asked.

"That I can't say."

"You can't or you won't?"

She smiled. "I don't know why she's here. I only know that she's here. And I see someone else . . . a guy with black hair. I see things getting broken."

Chad had black hair, but how could things get broken if he was here with her? That meant everything was fixed. Didn't it?

"What exactly does that mean?" I asked.

Again, she shook her head.

"I know, I know. You can tell me only what you see, not what it means. You must have been wildly popular at sleepovers."

She laughed. She had a light, lyrical laugh. It seemed to suit her.

Reaching out, she wrapped her hand around mine. "Don't be afraid to rebuild."

I started sawing diligently. "Does this look like I'm afraid?"

"No, Dawn, it doesn't. But looks are often deceiving."

"No offense, but I'd like to have a conversation with you sometime when you didn't tell me the things you were seeing."

"That would be nice. Normal, even," she said, smiling.

"Have you ever seen the endings of movies that you're watching?" Jenna asked as she walked over and handed each of us a bottle of water. "That would be a total bummer."

She'd missed the rest of our conversation, having gone on another water run. We were trying to drink as much as we could. One girl had fainted yesterday. They called EMTs who had taken her to the hospital. She was going to be fine, but it was a reminder that we needed lots of fluids throughout the day.

"No," Sara said. "And I don't know any winning lottery

numbers or who's going to win the Super Bowl. I can't control what I see. It just happens. Anyway, I didn't come over here to discuss my visions. I'm organizing a group to go on a ghost tour Saturday night, and I wanted to see if you were interested in coming."

"That would be fun," I said. I looked at Jenna to gauge her reaction and knew what she was going to say before she said it. Sara's psychic ability was rubbing off on me.

"I'm sort of leaving Saturday night free for now, in case something . . . well, maybe you already know. Am I going to have other plans?"

"No, you won't have other plans."

"Oh." Jenna's face fell. "Then I guess I'll say yes."

"She could be wrong," I told Jenna. "Not everything she sees is an absolute."

"This is," Sara said smugly.

"So you saw her on the ghost tour?"

"No, Tank told me that he and Jenna were coming. So I was just asking you, Dawn, because I figured Jenna's answer was already yes. Are you interested?"

Was I, or did I want to keep Saturday night open? Open for what? A better offer? I wasn't looking for a date. So what could be better than getting up close and personal with ghosts?

"Sounds like fun," I said. "I'm definitely there."

"Good. We'll meet outside my shop at nine." She turned to walk away, then stopped. "And just so you know—I'll be matching people up into pairs. You'll be with Brady."

"He's going to be there?"

She gave me a secretive smile. "I'm pretty sure he is. He asked if you were going, so I just assumed . . ."

Her voice trailed off. I wasn't sure I liked what she was assuming.

"What if I'd said no?" I asked her.

"I knew you wouldn't."

"How did you know?"

She smiled all-knowingly. "Because I'm a psychic."

She could be really irritating, but I liked her.

She walked away, humming a song that sounded strangely like the theme from *Ghostbusters*. Sometimes I didn't know whether to take her seriously. But how could I not?

"She gives me the creeps," Jenna said, picking up branches and tossing them into the wheelbarrow. "I don't care how nice she is, she gives me the creeps. She just knows too much."

"At least we have something to do Saturday night."

"Are you okay with having a date?"

"It's only a date if he asks, and he didn't," I pointed out.

Jenna held up her hands. "Okay, I guess. It's not a date."

Still, it felt like maybe it was.

And if it was, could I get hurt?

"Ow!"

"Hold still," Brady commanded—like a drill sergeant or something—as he studied my palm and the large sliver of wood that had slid under my skin.

"You're not the boss of me," I grumbled.

He looked up and grinned. "That's real mature. I thought only guys were bad patients."

Just before noon, lumber had been delivered on a long-bed truck. We'd been unloading it, carrying it into the yard, and stacking it up. Brady had been there helping me.

We'd been carrying some boards across the yard when I'd tripped and lost my balance. I'd landed hard, and in trying to not drop the wood, I'd ended up with a wickedly long splinter.

I should have been wearing my gloves. But they were hot, making my hands all sweaty, and I was tired of being hot and sweaty. Stupid, I know. But I'd thought I'd be okay. They'd told us we didn't need to wear our hard hats or goggles while unloading the truck.

It didn't make me feel any better that Brady had wrapped his hand around my arm and hauled me across the front yard. He'd grabbed the first-aid kit from Sara and then led me to a picnic table where the blueprints for the house had been spread out earlier. He'd set the first-aid kit down. Then he'd put his hands on my waist, picked me up, and set me on the table—like I couldn't have gotten up there by myself.

I didn't even know why I had to be sitting down. I wasn't going to faint. I could probably take out the splinter myself.

I knew I shouldn't be irritated, but I was.

"About Saturday night," I said.

He looked up again from studying my hand. I didn't think even a palm reader would look at a hand that much.

"The ghost tour? It's not a date," I told him.

"Okay. I didn't think it was."

"You didn't?"

"Nope."

"But you asked if I was going to be there."

He shrugged—like that was an answer. I suddenly felt bad for being snappish and was worried that I might have hurt his feelings.

"Look, don't take it personally. I'm just not dating this summer."

He studied me for a minute, then said, "Okay."

"I mean, you're nice and all—"

"Nice *and all*? Please. You're going to make me blush with the compliments."

I scowled. "You know what I mean."

"Actually I don't. What's included in 'all'?"

Terrific smile, great shoulders, strong arms—

I shook my head. "You're missing the important part of what I'm trying to say here."

"You're not dating."

"Right."

"But if I get scared on the ghost tour, can I hold your hand?"

I stared at him a minute. Was he teasing? "You're going to get scared?"

"I could. Ghosts. They're frightening." He rolled his amazing shoulders dramatically. "I get goose bumps just thinking about them."

"Do you believe in ghosts?"

"Oh yeah. Especially when they help me get babes."

I smiled. Did he take anything seriously? Other than a splinter in my hand. That he seemed to take way too seriously.

"You don't believe in ghosts," I said.

"Hey, I believed in Santa Claus until I was seventeen."

"Really?"

"My mom told me if I stopped believing, no more presents on Christmas morning. So, yeah. I believed."

"Why stop at seventeen?"

"Got tired of getting toy fire trucks."

I laughed.

He opened the first-aid kit and took out a pair of tweezers. They looked so tiny in his large hand. Had I ever noticed how large his hands were? How tanned? How steady? How strong?

Was I suddenly developing a hand fetish?

"Do you even know what you're doing?" I asked.

He furrowed his brow. Suddenly he seemed to realize something. He jerked off his sunglasses and hooked them in the front of my coveralls.

"No wonder I couldn't see," he said.

He spread my palm wide, shifted around so he wasn't creating a shadow over my hand.

"It's really in there," he said.

"Let me look."

"I've got it, but this is probably going to hurt."

No surprise there. It did.

But as far as hurts go, it wasn't too bad. And I couldn't help but be relieved. I'd been careless. I'd gotten hurt. Just like Sara had predicted. And that irritated me, too. Even knowing the future, I hadn't been able to change it.

Brady poured alcohol over my palm.

"Ow!" I jerked my hand free and waved it in the air to get the stuff to evaporate.

"Sorry." Then he laughed. "You're such a baby."

"Am not."

"Are to." He moved near, put his hands on my waist, and leaned in. "But that's okay. Because I have a thing for babes."

I thought he was going to kiss me, but he just lifted me off the table.

"Be careful. I don't like it when you get hurt," he said.

"You think I do?"

I stepped away, thinking I might get hurt again—worse— if I stayed close to him. I handed him his sunglasses. We took the first-aid kit back to Sara.

"You okay?" she asked me.

"Oh yeah, just a little hurt." I smiled. "Which you predicted."

"I predicted a splinter?"

"You predicted I'd be careless and get hurt."

She furrowed her brow and a faraway look came into her eyes.

Oh God, maybe the splinter wasn't the hurt. It probably wasn't. It couldn't be that simple.

"Whatever it is," I said hastily, "I don't want to know. Thanks just the same."

I started walking away, and Brady hurried to catch up.

"Hey, that was kinda rude," he said.

"I really don't want to know what she sees. She says things like they're all innocent, but—" I shook my head. "I just really don't want to know."

That night John arranged for us to have reserved tables at a local restaurant and club—for crawfish étouffée and blues music. The blues originated in the African-American community. To me, it sounded as though the notes themselves were melancholy.

As soon as we walked into the restaurant, he snagged Ms. Wynder and led her over to his table. A table for two away from everyone else.

Jenna waved at someone, and I didn't need to look around her to know who she was waving at. I was slightly disappointed when we got to the table to discover it was a small one, with only four chairs. Tank and Brady were sitting in two of them.

Jenna sat beside Tank, then looked at me as if it was a foregone conclusion I'd sit between her and Brady, so I sat. And then wondered if I should have asked Brady if it was okay.

"John reminds me of a cruise director," Jenna said. "Making sure everyone has something to do."

Tank nodded. "That's one of the great things about volunteering here in New Orleans. You can work during the day, but party at night. The tourist part of voluntourism. And the businesses here need the tourist dollars as much as the people need help getting their homes rebuilt."

Then he leaned toward Jenna and they started that low talking that they did. Drew and I hadn't whispered that much to each other in the entire year and a half that we were together.

Don't compare them to you and Drew, I scolded myself. *Just don't.*

Because they were nothing like us. I didn't want them to be anything like us. But in a way they were. When Jenna was with Tank, he was all that mattered to her.

Just the thought of ever feeling that way again made me nervous.

On John's recommendation, we all ordered the étouffée,

a spicy Cajun stew served over rice. Cajuns were descendents of Acadian exiles—French Canadians. Their influence was strong in the city.

"I think John has a thing for your chaperone," Brady said.

He was leaning near so I could hear him over the music being played. His breath wafted over my ear. It sent a shiver, a very nice shiver, down my back.

I looked at him and smiled. "She's not really our chaperone, she's more like our sponsor, I guess."

"Sponsor? Makes it sound like you're in a rehab program."

"No, I'm in a cleaning-up-New-Orleans program." I tapped the table, trying to decide if I should give him the option of having someone else sit here. Was it fair to him for me to take a seat beside him when I wasn't going to spend the night whispering low?

"Listen—"

"You're not wearing your Life Is Good hat," he said. "Is life suddenly not good?"

"What? Oh." I touched my head, as though I needed to verify that I hadn't worn it. I usually tucked it into a pocket so I could put it on as soon as I took off my hard hat. But tonight I'd clipped my hair back.

"No. Life is great. I don't *always* wear it. You're not wearing your hat."

"True."

And his hair kept falling forward. I wanted to reach out and brush it back.

"So you're sitting here," he said. "Coincidence or intentional?"

That was a hard one.

"It had to be intentional; I mean, I didn't just discover the chair beneath my butt."

He smiled. So maybe I was going to get off easy, without having to actually explain anything about what I was feeling.

"You said you're not dating this summer," he said.

Okay, maybe I was going to have to explain after all. "Right. I'm planning on this being a dateless summer."

"Dateless summer? Wasn't that a movie?"

"You're thinking of *The Endless Summer*."

"A summer without a date would seem pretty endless—or at least it would to me."

I smiled again. And maybe he even had a point. I didn't want to think too much about that.

"The movie was about surfing," I said.

"So we're really talking about the movie here?"

No, we weren't, but it was a more comfortable topic than my whole not-dating thing. Before I could say anything else, he said, "You don't have a boyfriend."

"No."

"So is there someone you're interested in?"

Was he hoping I'd say him? I swallowed hard. This was so hard to say, embarrassing even. "Look, there *was* a boyfriend."

He studied me for a minute and finally asked, "Bad breakup?"

I nodded.

"When?"

"About six weeks ago."

"Okay."

"What do you mean okay?"

"I get it now."

"What's to get?"

"You don't want to date. And I'm okay with that. I don't want to date either."

"Really?" Was I relieved or actually a little hurt? Yes, I think I was—hurt.

"Look, just because you don't want to date, and I don't want to date, that doesn't mean I wouldn't like to hang out," he said. "Or even that we couldn't hang out. I mean, look around. Everyone's pretty much paired up already."

I did take the time to look around then. Yeah, I could see what he meant.

"So, you're saying we're kinda stuck with each other?" I asked.

"Is that such a bad thing? You're fun. I'm fun. We could double our fun."

"You had better pickup lines the other night."

He grinned. "Yeah, but this isn't a pickup." He shook his head. "I'm not sure what this is. Maybe just trying to define what we've got going on here."

What was going on? A casual romance? A summer fling? Summer buddies?

Tonight my thoughts were being influenced by the blues. The thrill definitely wasn't gone. It was fun to have someone to share things with, and Jenna was clearly no longer available.

So I could hang out with Brady. Nothing serious. Nothing permanent. At the end of the six weeks, we'd each go our separate ways. And in the meantime, we'd have fun.

And wasn't that the reason I was here?

I mean, besides helping to rebuild, I wanted to have a great summer.

"I'm not looking for anything serious," I told him.

"Not a problem. I know a thousand knock-knock jokes."

I smiled. "Seriously—"

"Didn't think you wanted serious."

"Look, nothing long-term. Just a New Orleans thing," I said.

"Okay."

I moved closer to him and moved my shoulders in rhythm to the music.

"Then while I'm here in the Big Easy, only while I'm here"—I bobbed my head to the rhythm and blues—"we could hang out together. A friends-with-benefits kind of thing. The benefits being"—I couldn't believe I was being this bold, but if he wanted the relationship defined, I wanted to make sure we were using the same dictionary—"occasional kissing."

That really nice smile of his spread across his face. Reaching out, he wrapped his large hand around my neck and brought me nearer. "I'm good with that. Definitely good."

And then he kissed me.

Yeah, definitely good.

"So . . . you and Brady," Jenna said quietly later that night as we were lying in the dark.

"Yeah. Me and Brady." I went to sleep smiling.

The next morning I woke up feeling . . . good. Really, really good. Great, in fact, not only in body but in spirit.

Some of the soreness and stiffness had finally worked its way out of my muscles, mostly I think because Brady and I did a lot of dancing the night before. Dancing to the blues. Although it hadn't really been any kind of dancing I'd done before. We'd just moved with the music and had a great time.

I'd always thought the blues meant depressing music, music determined to make you blue, but I'd been happier last night than I'd been in a long time. Being with Brady was a lot of fun. He didn't seem to take anything seriously, and that was what I needed right now. Someone who lived in the moment, someone who was all about fun.

He laughed a lot. He was always smiling. He was nothing at all like Drew. I decided Drew had been a downer. I wasn't certain what I'd ever seen in him.

I thought I actually might be on my way to recovery. And I was loving it.

I'd just pulled on jeans and was working my way into a ratty T-shirt—one I normally wore on laundry day, but decided I should wear for work because who did I want to impress anyway? Brady was already impressed—when my cell phone rang.

I snatched it up, looked at the number, and answered. "Hey, Amber."

Jenna looked up from tying her shoes, a question in her eyes.

"How's it going?" I asked Amber.

"Awesome! I wanted you guys to know that I panicked for no reason. Everything is totally cool between me and Chad. I feel like such a dummy for worrying."

"I'm glad everything's okay."

Jenna rolled her eyes and went back to tying her shoes.

"Things between us are stronger than ever. I just love him so much."

"Great." I didn't see any reason to remind her that the psychic hadn't questioned Amber's current boyfriend. She'd simply said that in college she'd find something better. Of course, that didn't meant she wouldn't find it with Chad. He could be even better as he got older. Or they could break up and another guy would be in Amber's life. Who knew?

"So what's happening with you guys?" Amber asked.

I filled her in on the fact that Jenna was definitely with Tank and I was sort of with Brady.

"Any chance I could borrow your AeroBed if I decide to head on back to New Orleans?" Amber asked.

My knees grew weak and I sat on the edge of the bed. Would Amber freak if I told her that Saraphina had seen her back here? Yes, she'd definitely freak.

"Absolutely," I said, pushing past my own discomfort with the fact that Sara could, in fact, see into our lives. "Are you going to come back?"

"I'm thinking about it. Next week maybe. Or the week after. I don't know for sure. I was telling Chad about how satisfying it was and how it made me feel good, so he's sort of interested in maybe coming with me. I mean, we haven't worked out all the details. But he has a car, so he'd drive us. I don't know if we'd stay the whole summer, but maybe a couple of weeks. A couple of weeks are better than nothing, right?"

"A couple of weeks would be awesome," I told her. "Every little bit helps."

"Are y'all to the fun stuff yet?"

"What fun stuff? Eating, dancing, shopping?"

"The house. Aren't you going to rebuild it, decorate it?"

"We're rebuilding it. I don't know about the decorating part."

"If you'll measure the windows, I'll sew some curtains before I come back."

Amber was the only person I knew who could—and loved to—use a sewing machine.

"That'd be great. I'll see if I can get that information for you."

We talked a little more and then I said good-bye.

"What information do you need to get?" Jenna asked, slipping on her backpack.

"Measurements for the windows. She wants to make curtains."

"She's feeling guilty."

"Probably. Although maybe she's just embarrassed that

she totally overreacted to the psychic reading."

"Could be. So things are okay with her and Chad?"

"Apparently. The whole breaking up was a false alarm."

"We'll see what happens when she goes off to college," Jenna said. "Although we probably shouldn't point that out to her. She might not apply to any colleges."

"You want to know something freaky? Yesterday Sara told me that Amber would be coming back."

"You're kidding?"

I shook my head.

"Wow."

"Yeah. I didn't tell Amber, though, because her reaction to the other prediction was so out of control."

"Unlike ours. I mean, we took it in stride, right?"

I grabbed my backpack. Had I taken it in stride?

"Well, at least we don't have to worry anymore. All the predictions have been met," I said.

"Have they? Or do we just think they have?"

Goose bumps rose on my skin.

"Is there a statute of limitations on how long after a reading something will happen?" I asked.

"I don't know. Could check with Sara."

"Nah, I'm sure we're in the clear."

And checking with her might result in her having another

vision. I'd definitely become a firm believer that seeing the future wasn't all that it was cracked up to be.

It's just a fact that hard-working guys are sexy. Incredibly so. Especially when the afternoon sun beat down unmercifully and they decided it was time to ditch the shirts.

Oh yeah.

It was funny in a way, because when the guys started heading to their cars, the girls stopped hammering. It was like we took a collective breath, and held it, and then released an appreciative sigh. Then we all smiled at each other, a little embarrassed, maybe, and went back to work.

I couldn't believe how fast things were going up. Brady, Tank, Sean, and a couple of other guys were working on the roof. Jenna and I were rebuilding the porch flooring. We'd ripped it up earlier because it had been rotting. I discovered that hammering was an extremely cathartic experience. I just pretended every nail was Drew's tiny, little, stupid head.

Bang, bang, bang.

It was actually fun.

We still wore the hard hats and safety goggles, but we no longer wore the masks.

"Listen," Jenna said.

I stopped hammering, looked around. "For what?"

She rolled her eyes. "To me."

"Okay. What's going on?"

She sighed. "What if Tank stops liking me?"

"He's not going to stop liking you, unless he's an idiot. And if he's an idiot then you want him to stop liking you."

Bang, bang, bang.

I moved up to put the next nail in place.

"Did you just compliment me?" she asked.

"Of course."

"Did you insult him?"

"Only if he stops liking you."

"How do I stop that from happening?"

I pounded Drew's head—I mean, the nail—into the board.

"Jenna, you're worrying for nothing. He's crazy about you. You've never had a boyfriend. Enjoy it."

"Did you worry when you were dating Drew?"

I gave one more nail a hard pound and sat back on my heels. Had I worried? Good question.

"No, I don't think I did."

"Do you worry about Brady?"

"No. What I have with Brady is perfect. We both agreed it's only while we're in New Orleans. It's finite. No worries."

"What if you decide that's not enough?"

"It's enough, Jenna." I started hammering again. A summer thing with Brady. That's all I wanted. It was nice and safe.

I liked nice and safe.

CHAPTER 14

"We should have done this days ago," Jenna said.

We were sitting in the hot tub beside the pool at the guys' hotel. It was early Friday evening, and it felt wonderful to have the heated water swirling over my aching muscles.

The hotel was a small one with a very historic feel in the French Quarter. The guys had called that morning and told us to pack bathing suits, so we could stop by before hitting the clubs. Jenna and I had changed in Tank's room while the guys had changed in Brady's room. I thought it was generous of the hotel to give them their own rooms. According to Tank, the owner was married to a cousin of a cousin or something.

I was wearing a bikini and when we'd come out of the

room, Brady had wiggled his eyebrows at me and said, "Know what you need?"

"A bubblegum machine tattoo?"

And he'd laughed.

I liked making him laugh, liked watching him smile. Liked watching the way he watched me now as the water swirled around us.

"I've had enough," Jenna said and stood.

"Not me," Brady said, and his eyes held a challenge.

A challenge to me. Was I going to choose him or Jenna?

Tank had also stood up, and I wondered if maybe Jenna wanted to be alone with him.

"I want a few more minutes," I said.

"Okay. Great," Jenna said. "I'll see you in a bit."

She wrapped a towel around her waist, and Tank wrapped his arm around her. I watched as they walked off.

"He's been dying to get some time alone with her," Brady said.

I snapped my attention back to him. "Yeah, it just occurred to me that they haven't really had much of that."

We'd gone to listen to jazz last night, but it had been another group outing. Group outings were safe. I liked them.

Brady glided through the water until he was sitting by me. "But then, neither have we."

I shook my head. Probably a little jerkily. Not being alone with him had seemed like the smart thing to do. And now that I was alone with him . . . I probably shouldn't have been.

"Go out with me tonight," he said.

I stared at him for a minute. "I *am* going out with you tonight."

"No. You're going out with me, Tank, and Jenna. I'm asking you to go out with just me."

"What—you mean like a date? You said you didn't want to date."

"I said *that*?"

"Yeah. The night we had étouffée."

"Are you sure? Maybe I was talking about the fruit, date. I don't eat fruit . . . or vegetables, for that matter."

Why was he giving me a hard time about this? We had an agreement. I shoved on his shoulder. "No, you weren't talking about fruit. You were talking about dating."

"Okay, then, I changed my mind. Is that illegal?"

It could be. When the thought of it made my heart pound so hard that I thought I could die. When we were hanging out with other people, it was easy to find things to talk about—we could always talk about the people around us. If it was just us—

The thought of being with only Brady, with no buffer, no

other people, was scary and thrilling. And I suddenly realized that it was something I wanted. I wanted a lot.

I took a deep breath. "Okay."

He grinned at my use of what seemed to be a word that he thought explained everything—when it really explained nothing.

"Just okay?"

I nodded. "Just okay."

We went to House of Blues. Just the two of us. Brady and me. It was in the French Quarter, close enough that we could walk. I never walked as much at home as I walked here—but I was starting to appreciate the fact that we didn't have to get into a car to go everywhere.

Especially when Brady held my hand. He'd changed into jeans and a snug black T-shirt. He looked so hot and smelled so good. And it wasn't insect repellent, this time. The guys had gotten ready in Brady's room, while Jenna and I had showered and changed in Tank's. I was wearing white shorts and a red halter-neck top. I'd left my hair down, brushing my bare shoulders.

"I think it's great that you and Brady are going on a date," Jenna had said, as she ran her fingers through her hair.

"It's not a date."

She'd looked at me, her lips pursed.

"Okay, it's a date."

"We'll meet back here in the lobby at eleven-thirty so Tank can drive us back to the dorm in time for the bed check."

"Sounds like a plan."

She'd hugged me. "Have fun."

"You, too."

"Oh, I will. Definitely."

Now Brady and I were being seated outside in the voodoo garden. My sandals clicked over the bricks as we followed the hostess to a round table covered in a blue tablecloth. A live band was playing—what else?—blues.

Whenever I thought about voodoo, I thought of scenes from shows or movies where voodoo was used for evil. But I'd learned that, like everything, it has two sides, and here was the peaceful, tranquil, bringing-everything-into-harmony side. Lots of lush, green plants surrounded us. It was simply a place that made me glad to be there.

Brady scooted his chair closer to me. "So I can see the band better," he said.

I smiled. "Yeah, right."

"Okay, so I want to be closer to you. Is that a bad thing?"

"No, it's nice, actually."

Very nice.

After dinner, he moved his chair even closer, put his arm around me, and we settled back to enjoy the music—drinking virgin daiquiris so we wouldn't get kicked out for taking space from paying customers.

It felt right. And was no longer scaring me. Or at least not scaring me as much as it had. As long as I kept everything in perspective.

When the band took a break, I said, "This hanging out that we're doing, it's only for the summer."

I needed to be sure that I wasn't expecting more than I was going to get. And that *he* wasn't expecting more than he was going to get.

"Right," Brady said. "That's what we both wanted. Just for the summer, just while we're here."

"I just want to make sure that you understand that it's *only* while we're in the Big Easy, even though we've sorta moved into actual dating territory."

"I get it."

Did he?

"I mean, it's a set period of time. When one of us leaves New Orleans—whoever leaves first—that's it, it's over. No good-bye. Good-bye is understood."

"What? You want me to sign a contract? I get what you're saying. And it's what I want, too. A hundred percent."

"I just don't want another breakup. I just want an 'it's over' but without either of us saying it's over."

"And you think that'll make it easier?"

"Knowing that it's coming, being prepared? Yeah, I do. We'll be together five weeks, and then that's it. We move on."

"Okay."

I released a long sigh. "Okay."

It would be easier. I was sure it would be.

He absently-mindedly traced his finger across my bare shoulders, back and forth. It felt delicious.

"Where are you going to go to college?" he asked.

"I haven't decided for sure."

"Okay."

"Why do you say that so much? Just 'okay.'"

"So you know I heard you, but don't have anything else to add." He nuzzled my neck. "And sometimes just so you know I understand."

We were in the shadows. No one was paying any attention to us. He kissed my shoulder, and I thought I might not wear anything that covered my shoulders ever again.

"You understand a lot without me saying much," I said.

"I have three sisters who think I'm Dr. Phil. I've heard about every rotten thing that every guy they've dated has ever done to them. And they always end with, 'If you ever do that to a girl . . .'"

His voice had gone prissy at the end.

"As though I would," he finished in his normal voice.

"What would they do if you did?"

He shrugged. "They never say. But knowing them, it'd be a fate worse than death—forcing me to sit through a marathon of romantic comedies or something."

Brady had a way of always making me smile.

"Still, I bet you make a great Dr. Phil."

He pointed up. "Especially once I get the bald thing going."

I laughed. "You're really bothered about losing your hair."

"Yeah, I think I am. Vain, I guess."

I leaned into him. "You really shouldn't worry about it."

"No?"

"No."

"Okay."

Then he leaned in and kissed me. Being with him without Jenna around wasn't nearly as uncomfortable as I'd expected it to be. Actually, it seemed natural.

He told me funny stories about his sisters. Two were older, one younger, and he finally admitted that he was offended that they'd think he'd ever do any of the jerk stuff guys had pulled on them.

"Why can't relationships be easy?" I finally asked.

He shrugged. "Would they be worth it if they were?"

"I just wonder how you ever know . . . this is the one." I told him about Amber's reading and the reason she'd bugged out on us.

"Sean liked her," he said.

"You want to hear the really weird thing?" I asked.

"There's something weirder than a psychic's prediction and your friend freaking out because Tank has ink?"

"Well, maybe not weirder, but . . . well, the thing is, Amber has always talked about going to Rice. It's her first choice, and there's Sean . . . at Rice."

"Mmm. So maybe in another year or so . . ."

"Maybe."

"I'll let him know."

"No." I leaned back. "You can't do that. Then you're influencing it and making it happen."

"I've got something else I want to make happen."

And then he was kissing me again. I stopped thinking about Amber and Sean or Jenna and Tank. Or Sara and her predictions.

I was only thinking about how much I liked kissing Brady.

We left the restaurant at ten, which gave us an hour and a half before we had to meet up with Tank and Jenna and head back to the dorm. Neither of us was in the mood for the madness of Bourbon Street, so we just walked along the river. We could see the lights of the riverboats as they traveled along the Mississippi. It was all so romantic.

"You know, I don't even know your last name," I said, when we began walking back to the hotel.

"Miller."

I smiled at him. Brady Miller. I liked it.

"And yours?"

"Delaney," I responded.

"I thought you'd have an Italian-sounding name."

I grinned. "That's my mom's side of the family."

When we got to the lobby, Jenna and Tank were waiting for us. Tank drove us back to the dorm. While he walked Jenna to the door, Brady and I lagged behind.

"So being alone together wasn't so bad," I said.

He chuckled. "You really know how to stroke my ego."

I groaned. "I'm sorry. I just, I don't know, I just feel like I can say what's on my mind when I'm with you. That's a good thing, right?"

"Yeah, I guess."

"Seriously, though, I had a great time," I told him.

"Yeah, me, too."

Then he kissed me good night.

CHAPTER 15

Saturday we only worked until noon.

Tank drove us back to the dorm with the promise he and Brady would be back to get us in an hour. No way were we going to spend time in the French Quarter without getting cleaned up first. I was going through clothes like crazy. Tomorrow I definitely had to make time for laundry. Or else buy some more clothes.

Hmm. Buying more clothes might be the way to go.

I dressed in a denim miniskirt with cargo pockets on the sides so I could carry money and an ID without having to lug around my backpack. I put on a tank with skinny straps, slipped on sandals, and used a banana clip to get my hair up off my shoulders. I picked one string of red beads to wear. I didn't think I'd be adding to my stash tonight, but I wasn't completely saying no to the possibility.

"Nice," Brady said to me when he and Tank picked us up.

We parked at their hotel, then started making our way through the French Quarter.

"I know just the place for lunch," Tank said. "The home of the original muffuletta."

Central Grocery had been housed in the French Quarter for nearly a century. As we walked inside the red emporium, the tantalizing aromas of salami, cheese, and garlic wafted around us. The worn floor creaked as we made our way around the aisles—displaying various containers of olives, pickles, and spices—to the counter where they took the food orders. The menu was pretty simple. Only one thing was served—the muffuletta. We ordered two to share, because the round sandwich is huge and piled with salami, ham, provolone, olive salad, and other special ingredients.

"Want to split a Barq's root beer?" Brady asked.

"Yeah. Thanks."

"Why don't you grab us some chairs?"

Off to the side was a counter with stools where people could eat. The store was small, the eating area even smaller, but we found four seats together.

"It smells really good in here," Jenna said.

"Yeah, it does."

"I am *so* hungry."

Brady took the stool beside me and unwrapped the sandwich. It was huge, cut into quarters. I had a feeling that one piece was going to be enough for me, and I wondered if we should have just ordered one for the four of us to share.

But Brady and Tank had monstrous appetites, and in no time the sandwiches were gone. They were delicious, and the root beer just topped it off.

I felt incredibly stuffed as we walked out of the store. I didn't think I could have eaten a pecan praline if it was given to me free. Okay, I could have. My theory is that sugar melts, so it doesn't fill you up.

Once we were outside, Jenna pulled me aside.

"Tank and I were thinking of going off and doing our own thing, but I wanted to make sure you were okay with that, with being alone with Brady."

"That's cool."

"You sure?"

"We've been alone before," I reminded her.

"I know. I just didn't know if you wanted a lot of alone time, because I was thinking we wouldn't hook back up until later tonight."

"I'm fine, Jenna."

"Okay, then, we'll catch up with you at the ghost tour."

She took Tank's hand and led him away.

"What was that about?" Brady asked.

I shrugged. "Just Jenna being silly. They want to do their own thing."

"I'm not surprised. He's got it bad for her." He suddenly looked guilty. "Don't tell her I said that. I mean, it should come from him."

"But it would give me a chance to play psychic," I teased.

"Don't. Please."

I pretended to think it over for a bit. Then finally I said, "Okay."

"You were never going to tell her, were you?"

Smiling, I shook my head.

Holding hands, Brady and I walked to the French Market. It's a covered flea market, so we were at least out of the sun. There were so many vendors.

"This probably isn't the place to be if we're going on a ghost tour tonight," I said, thinking of hauling anything I bought around all day.

"If you find something you want, we can always take it back to my room," Brady said.

"Do you like shopping?"

"Not particularly, but I really like people-watching, and this is a great place for that."

"So you're okay if I stop and look at stuff?" The one time I'd taken Drew shopping with me, he'd moped around and totally spoiled the day. He said guys had a gene that prevented them from having patience at a mall. I didn't buy into it, though, because my dad always went shopping with my mom.

"Look all you want," Brady said. "I've got no appointments to keep."

"Except for the ghost tour," I reminded him.

"Well, yeah, but that's not for a while yet."

We strolled up and down the aisles. A lot of the vendors were craftsmen, displaying various items they'd made. Some of the vendors had really inexpensive products—knockoffs, trinkets.

Like Brady had said, the most fun was just watching the people, seeing their excitement when they discovered a find, listening to them haggling over prices.

"Hey, I was wondering if you'd do me a favor," Brady said after a while.

I gave him what I hoped was a sultry smile. "Depends what it is."

"I want to find something to take back to my youngest

sister. I was hoping you could help me figure out what would be a good thing to get her."

Did he think all girls liked the same things? I didn't have a clue what his sister might like.

"How about a box of pralines?"

He shook his head. "She'd yell at me for screwing up whatever diet she's on when I get home."

"She yells at you?"

"Oh yeah."

"And you want to buy her something?"

He shrugged. "It's what brothers do."

"Not mine."

"You have a brother?"

"Yeah, but he's twelve."

He grinned. "He's probably too young to appreciate you."

"Maybe." I squeezed his hand. "There's so much we still don't know about each other."

It was weird, because we hadn't grown up in the same town or gone to the same school. I didn't know all the details of his life, but I felt like I knew him.

"What's there to know? I have a mom and a dad and three sisters, one who likes to get presents. I go to Rice, majoring in architecture. And I like you. A lot."

He made it all seem so simple, and I knew that he probably wanted me to say back that I liked him . . . a lot. But I couldn't. Even if it was true. So instead I asked, "Why the Kansas City Chiefs?"

"What?"

"Your hat." He wasn't wearing it today. "Why that team?"

"My oldest sister lives in Kansas City now. I went to visit her, went to a Chiefs game."

"So you're not necessarily a fan?"

"Nope, Houston Texans all the way. So, you and I have something in common."

"Uh, actually we don't. That first night at dinner, I just said that to have something to say. I'm not really into football."

"That's just un-Texan."

I knew what he meant—in Texas, football is king.

I grimaced. "Yeah, I know."

"Might have to do an intervention here. Take you to a Rice game."

It was the first time he'd said something—anything—that hinted at us seeing each other when our time here was finished.

My concern must have shown on my face, because he

said, "Sorry. Forgot. We're just summer buddies, right?"

I nodded. "Yeah, just for the summer. That was our agreement."

He studied me for a minute. "Okay. Let's go souvenir shopping."

We stopped at a table of handcrafted jewelry. He spent about twenty minutes looking over the various selections, asking me my opinion. My favorite piece was a delicate silver chain threaded through a fleur-de-lis charm.

He decided to buy it for his sister.

"I trust your judgment. If you like it, she will, too," he said.

"She might not."

"She will."

"Do I remind you of your sister?"

He scoffed. "No. No way."

"So our tastes might not be the same."

"I can tell you they're not. You have better taste."

He always made me feel good about myself.

"My pockets are a little roomier," I said. "Want me to carry it for you?"

"Sure. Thanks. Good thing I didn't get her a box of pralines, huh?"

I laughed. "Yeah."

We spent some more time walking by the stalls, looking at the various offerings. Then we slipped on our sunglasses and walked back into the sunshine.

It was hot and muggy so we went to the aquarium, to cool off in the air conditioning as much as to view all the exhibits. When we were walking, we'd hold hands. When we were simply standing, looking at something, Brady would slip his arm around me and hold me against his side.

Needless to say, I found an excuse to stand and watch a lot of things.

I loved the way that I fit up against him. My head nestled right into the little curve of his shoulder. His arm would come around me and he'd rest his hand on my stomach or my hip. And sometimes he'd kiss the curve of my neck and shoulder.

It all seemed so natural. So right. I couldn't imagine not being with him.

We rode the streetcar down to the Garden District, famous for its mansions. We got off the streetcar at one end and began walking back up toward the French Quarter. The nice thing about walking through the Garden District was that the area had so many trees we were almost always walking in the shade.

"I think that's Anne Rice's house," Brady said when we got to the corner of First Street and Chestnut.

It was a white two-story house with a balcony on the second floor.

"She lives in California now," I said.

"But doesn't this seem like the perfect place to write about vampires and witches?" Brady asked.

"Yeah, it does."

"Wonder if it'll be on the tour tonight."

I shrugged. "Have you ever been on a ghost tour?"

"Nope. How about you?"

"No. I'd say I was skeptical, except after Sara's reading, I have a feeling that after tonight, I'll believe in ghosts."

Brady chuckled. "Yeah, I know what you mean."

We were walking along, holding hands again.

"I didn't think you believed in psychics," I said.

"I don't . . . or at least I didn't. But yours seemed to be right on and the one I had—"

I stopped walking and pulled him back to face me. "You had a reading? You didn't say anything. When was this?"

"The day I met you."

"Was it with Saraphina?"

"No, someone else."

I grinned broadly. "Come on! Spill it! What did she tell you?"

He removed his sunglasses and held my gaze. He looked

so serious that I got a little worried. What could she have told him? Was it bad news?

He cleared his throat, took a deep breath. "She said, 'For you, I see life is good.' Which didn't make any sense at the time, because some stuff was going on in my life that wasn't good, so I figured it was a con, something she probably said to everyone, but then . . ."

His voice trailed off, and I realized where this was going.

"My 'Life Is Good' hat," I whispered, goose bumps erupting along my arms, in spite of the heat of the afternoon.

He grinned. "Yeah."

"Spooky. Way spooky."

"Oh yeah."

I furrowed my brow. "What was bad in your life?"

He shook his head. "Nothing important, nothing that matters anymore, anyway. Now, life *is* good."

And he drew me close and kissed me. No doubt a ploy to stop me from prying into his past.

It worked, because when he kissed me, I could hardly think at all.

CHAPTER 16

We caught up with Tank and Jenna

a little before nine in front of Sara—Saraphina's. It was hard to think of her with her psychic's name now that I knew her as a normal person. Almost normal, anyway.

As long as she didn't give me any secretive, off-the-record readings.

Amber was coming back, just as she'd predicted. But she'd also predicted some hurt when that happened. I didn't like the idea of that. Not at all. Although maybe it would be something simple, something not too painful—like another splinter, or a sunburn. Something small. But then, why bother to mention it?

Palling around with a psychic had its drawbacks. It was

one thing for her to give me a reading when I was paying for it, but when she told me something she saw because she felt compelled to tell me—well, quite honestly, it made me worry.

Nearly a dozen people stood around, waiting for our hostess or tour guide or whatever she would be calling herself tonight.

"I don't believe in ghosts," Jenna said—three times—like a mantra.

Which made me think maybe she did believe in them. She sounded nervous. I knew she didn't like scary things.

"I have a feeling Sara will have us convinced before the night is over," Brady said.

"Yeah, well, just don't let go of my hand," I ordered. "And hold me close if I get scared."

"I hope you get scared," he said in a low voice near my ear.

"Me, too." A delicious shiver went through me. "I can practically guarantee it."

He was standing behind me, and he tightened his arms around my waist, pulling me closer. He dropped a kiss onto my bare shoulder.

Oh yeah, I might get scared, but it would be the good kind of scared, where we held each other close and laughed. Or maybe just kissed. I was starting to like him so much—and that scared me most of all.

When she finally arrived, Sara was dressed all in black, a black, hooded cloak swirling around her. It seemed like the fog was trailing in behind her. Her vibrant red hair was the only visible color. She was wearing it down and it flowed past her shoulders.

"Good evening," she said in a very melodramatic, haunting voice. "Does anyone not have a partner?"

Everyone was already paired up.

"Good," she said. "Now, I want you to hold your partner's hand and no matter what happens, don't let go. People have been known to disappear on the streets of New Orleans and never be seen again."

A chill went through me. Yeah, she was going to have us believing in ghosts.

"We are known as the most haunted city in the country," she continued. "And sometimes the spirits get jealous of the living. If you listen closely as we walk through the streets, sometimes you'll hear them crying, sometimes you'll hear them singing, sometimes you'll hear them dying."

I squeezed Brady's hand and rose up on my toes, so only he would hear me. "Are we sure we want to do this?"

"Oh yeah. And if you get so scared you need someone to sleep with you tonight—I'm there."

I didn't think I was going to get that scared, but who knew?

And okay, quite honestly, snuggling up with Brady appealed to me. It was frightening how quickly and how hard I was falling for the guy.

He was nice, he was fun, and he was hot. I just liked the way I felt when we were together. Like we were part of something.

"Follow me as we seek out the lost souls of New Orleans," Sara said in that spooky voice she'd perfected. It sent more chills over my flesh.

Must have sent chills over Brady's, too, because he put his arm around me, like holding hands wasn't enough to keep us from getting lost. We headed up Royal Street.

"New Orleans history is rich with hauntings. Some of the spirits are here because of something left undone. Some feel compelled to remain and re-create the circumstances of their death until justice has been gained. Most spirits are playful, causing mischief. Especially those who died as children. There are rare accounts of spirits causing harm, but rest assured that you'll all be safe tonight. The spirits know me, and they know we mean them no harm. That we mourn their passing, and that we're here to remember."

"That doesn't sound too bad," I whispered, starting to relax.

I felt something brush against my bare calf. I looked down, but there was nothing there. I shivered.

"You okay?" Brady asked.

"I thought I felt something."

"Like what?"

"A cat maybe. A very, very soft cat. It was just a light touch."

"Probably nothing."

"Probably."

But it hadn't felt like nothing.

"Over here we have a mansion that reflects our city's dark history," Sara said.

We stopped in front of a large gray building as Sara told us about Delphine Lalaurie and her physician husband. Wealthy, they were known for their lavish parties until it was discovered that they were monsters, performing surgical experiments on their slaves.

"Within the manor," Sara said, "there have been reported sightings of a man walking about carrying his head."

A shudder went through me.

"Is that what she calls being playful?" I whispered.

Brady chuckled. Did I sound spooked? I thought I sounded spooked.

"And on foggy nights, you can hear the screams of those who were abused within those walls. They are still crying out for justice."

Sara took us down Orleans Street, where on rainy nights the ghost of a priest who'd led a funeral procession to bury the remains of wrongly executed men could be heard singing.

Brady tightened his arms around me and rested his chin on my shoulder. I felt breath whisper across my neck. I told myself it was his. It had to be his.

"Thank goodness it's not raining," he said.

"Really."

"Are you believing this stuff?" He sounded totally stunned.

I twisted my head around. He was grinning.

"Don't you?" I asked.

"No. This is all bogus."

Was it? I didn't know anymore.

At 716 Dauphine Street, Sara told us about the ghost of a sultan who was murdered along with his wives and children and now haunted the four-story house.

"One of my favorite spirits remains here," she said. "I'm fairly certain it's one of the sultan's children. It likes to tickle necks."

I felt a light prickle over my neck. I hunched my shoulders and turned to Brady. "Don't."

"What?"

"I know you're trying to scare me."

"What are you talking about?"

What *was* I talking about? Because he was holding my hand, and no way he could have touched my neck without twisting around—and that I would have noticed.

Maybe it had been a moth or a mosquito. Some little insect of the night.

Every street she walked us along had tales of horrific murders—a man had killed his wife and the ghost of his wife had killed his mistress. What was that she'd said earlier about ghosts not causing harm?

Although the night was warm, I felt chilled. At one point, I thought I saw an apparition—a woman in a white nightgown—but it was gone so fast that I couldn't be sure.

When we'd circled back around to Sara's shop, she seemed really pleased with herself. Maybe because it looked like several people were pale. I probably was, too.

"In two weeks, John and I will take you on a vampire tour. He loves fresh blood! Sleep well," she said, before whipping her cloak around her and walking off. It seemed as if she disappeared from sight sooner than she should have.

"Okay, that was creepy," Jenna said.

"You mean the tour, or John liking fresh blood?" I asked.

"All of it. Sara was a little out there at the end."

"I can't see Ms. Wynder with a vampire," I said.

She laughed. "Me either."

I figured they'd laugh if I told them that I thought I'd felt something. So I kept quiet, but I couldn't stop thinking about it. New Orleans was definitely a city for those who believed in the supernatural. And even those who didn't could have their skepticism challenged.

"Anyone hungry?" Tank asked.

I wasn't, but I welcomed anything to take my mind off the tour.

We went to McDonald's. Not very New Orleans-ish, but it was late and they were open. And the lights were bright—I suddenly had a love of bright lights—so there were no spooky things lurking about.

And actually, once I bit into my burger, I realized that I was hungry. Very hungry. Apparently ghost hunting works up an appetite.

"I don't know if I'm going to do the vampire tour," Jenna said as she swirled a fry in the ketchup. "I mean, I don't believe in vampires, but then I didn't believe in ghosts either, but that was before tonight. I think I saw one."

"Saw what?" Tank asked.

"A ghost."

He laughed so loudly that several other late-night customers looked over at our table.

"I saw something, too," I said, feeling a need to support Jenna. And okay. I *had* seen something.

"Probably just someone walking by," Tank said.

"If they want to believe in ghosts, I'm down with that," Brady said, scooting closer to me. "As a matter of fact, I'm not certain I want to sleep alone tonight."

"You're scared?" Tank asked.

Brady glared at him, and I laughed.

Then Tank widened his eyes. "Oh. Right. Right. Babe, if you're scared—"

"I might be," Jenna said, "but not if you're going to make fun of me."

They started talking low again, like Brady and I weren't even there.

"Did you really see something?" Brady asked.

I shrugged, popped a fry into my mouth. "Maybe. I don't know. Could be the power of suggestion. I definitely felt something. On my calf, on the back of my neck."

"Me, too. On the back of my neck."

"Really?"

"No. But if it'll make you not want to sleep alone—"

I shoved playfully on his shoulder. "Get over it. That's so not happening."

We left McDonald's and started walking toward Bourbon Street, as though it was a given that that's where we wanted to end the night.

Since it was Saturday, Ms. Wynder had said she wouldn't do a bed check until two, and I wondered if she'd even bother. What if things got hot and steamy between her and John?

Tank and Jenna were behind us. Brady turned, walking backward. "Hey, we'll catch up with y'all later, at the hotel."

Then he quickened his pace, pulling me along with him. "Come on."

"Where are we going?"

"You'll see."

The guy was nothing but surprises, which I liked. Because every surprise was better than the one that came before.

He brought me around a corner, where a horse and carriage were waiting. The driver wore a top hat, very high society.

"Do you go down to the Garden District?" Brady asked him.

"Yes, sir."

"Hop in," Brady said to me.

Once he paid the driver, and we were settled against the leather seats with Brady's arm around me, I asked, "How did you know I wanted to do this?"

"It's a chick thing. All girls want to do it."

"Your sisters trained you right."

He laughed. "Yeah, but don't tell them that. I'll never hear the end of it."

And I wondered if I'd ever meet his sisters. It didn't seem likely. I mean, why would they come here? And in a few weeks, Brady and I would go our separate ways.

He wound his finger around my beaded necklace. "So, are you planning to get more of these tonight?"

"I don't think so."

"Yeah. That's what I figured. So I didn't think Bourbon Street would be *that* much fun."

"Watching *you* get beads is fun."

"Yeah, but we should take turns."

That sounded like such a couple thing to say.

"I really had fun today," I said.

"Yeah, me, too."

I nestled my head against his shoulder.

"So tell me about your breakup," he said quietly.

I eased away from him a little and met his gaze. "What does it matter?"

He tucked my hair behind my ear. "I like you, Dawn. I think this guy, whoever he is, is still messing with you."

I looked at the driver. His back was to us. He wasn't paying any attention. And we were talking low. I sighed. "Drew. His name is Drew and he—" I shook my head.

"He what?"

It hurt to think about it, hurt even more to say it. "He cheated on me."

"Okay."

"Okay? That's all? Aren't you going to tell me that he's a jerk?"

"You already know that."

Yeah, I knew that, but I still found some comfort in hearing it. And while I was usually okay with his single okay, right now I wanted more.

"What you need to understand," he said quietly, "is that I'm not him."

Then, with his hand cradling my cheek and his thumb stroking near the corner of my mouth, he leaned in and kissed me. Something about the kiss seemed different. Like all the others had been for fun, but this one was meant to be more.

It was kind of scary, but at the same time, I realized that

it was something that I wanted.

I felt like I had on the ghost tour. Doubting what I was feeling. Wondering if it was real.

Or would it—like an apparition—disappear, and leave me wondering if it had truly ever been there?

It wasn't until Jenna and I were back in our dorm room—with thirty seconds to spare before the two o'clock curfew—and I was getting ready for bed that I remembered the necklace I'd put in my pocket for safekeeping.

I sat on the edge of the bed and looked at it again. It was really pretty. I wished I'd bought one for myself. Next week, I would. I was sure the vendor would still be there.

"What's that?" Jenna asked.

"Oh, a necklace Brady bought for his sister."

"He buys things for his sister? Wow. My brother doesn't know the first thing about buying me something."

"I helped him pick it out." Saying that sounded weird.

Like maybe we were shopping for something much more important.

"I'm really glad you're hanging out with him," Jenna said.

"Only because it means he's not hanging out with Tank all the time, and you have some time alone."

"Well, there is that. I'm so crazy about Tank, Dawn. It's scary sometimes."

"Tell me about it."

"But it's exciting, too. It's everything." She sat in the middle of her bed and brought her legs up beneath her. "Did you feel that way about Drew?"

Did I? Gosh, it was suddenly hard to remember. All I could remember now was being hurt and angry at him. Like that moment of seeing him with someone else had totally destroyed any good feelings I'd ever had for him. Had I been scared when he asked me out? Nervous? Excited?

"I can't remember, Jenna. That's so weird."

"You know, sometimes I think about what Sara said about you rebuilding. I thought she was talking about New Orleans. But what if she was talking about your heart?"

"She didn't know my heart needed rebuilding."

"She doesn't need to *know* stuff. She just sees things. She said you had to be careful with the tools. I thought she meant hammers and saws. What if she meant Brady?"

I flopped back on the bed. "You're really giving too much thought to all this."

"It's the puzzle solver in me. I can't help it."

I rolled my head to the side and looked at her. "She said I could get hurt. If I wasn't careful. Jenna, I don't think I've been careful. I think I've fallen for him."

"That's a good thing, Dawn. It means you're over Drew."

"No, it means I've set myself up to be hurt again. We agreed this was a Big Easy–only relationship."

"So, change the terms of your agreement."

"What if he doesn't want to?"

She sighed. "Do you have to doubt everything?"

I sat up. "Me? Doubting? You're the one trying to figure everything out, trying to solve the puzzles, wanting all the answers."

She came off the bed. "Well, I've never been in love before, and I don't know if I like it. I thought having a boyfriend would stop all the questions, but there's just more of them."

I smiled. "Yeah, it's a bummer, isn't it?"

"The future is just so"—she threw her hands up—"vague. There are just so many possibilities."

"And going to see a psychic sure doesn't help."

"No, it doesn't." She sat back down on the bed. "So what are we going to do?"

"You think *I* know?"

Laughing, she shook her head. "No, actually, I think you're probably more confused than I am."

"Well, thanks a lot."

Her cell phone rang and we both jumped. Then mine rang.

"Time for good-night calls," she said.

Okay, I guessed tonight we'd moved to a new level. I mean, we'd spoken that one night before I went to bed, but it had been on Jenna's phone, so it didn't really count. Oh, heck, maybe it did.

I answered, "Hey."

"Did I wake you?"

"No." I stretched out, rolled onto my side, and my knee touched the sack the necklace had been in. "I forgot to give you your sister's necklace."

"It's yours."

My brow furrowed. "What? No, I'm not talking about the beads, I'm talking about—"

"The fleur-de-lis."

"Yeah."

"I bought it for you. Why do you think I let you pick it out?"

"But you said it was for her."

"I thought you'd go all weird on me if I bought you something."

"Weird?" I said, offended. "I don't go weird."

"You go weird. You worry about what I really feel or what you really feel or what we're thinking. You're expecting me to hurt you, and I don't know how to make you stop expecting that."

I wrapped my hand around the charm. "I'm a mess. I don't know why you hang out with me."

"I hang out with you because I like you. You're funny and fun and you believe in ghosts—"

"I don't believe in ghosts. I just had some weird stuff happen tonight."

"Are you sleeping with the light on?"

I hated to admit it, but—

"Yeah, we probably will. Jenna wants to." When in doubt, blame it on your friend. I figured we'd at least keep on the light in the bathroom with the door partially opened.

"About the necklace," I said.

"Yeah?" I heard the impatience in his voice, maybe even a little bit of anger. I couldn't imagine Brady being angry.

"Thank you. I really wanted one for myself, and this one

will always be special. Remind me of my time here. My time with you."

"Good."

"But, you were very sneaky having me pick it out."

"I thought it was clever. If I'd known you longer, I might have known what to get, but we're on the short-term plan here. Right?"

"Yeah. Short term."

"End of summer."

"End of New Orleans." And that made me sad.

"Okay, then. See you tomorrow."

"What are we going to do?"

"I figure the least you can do is my laundry."

"What?"

He laughed. "No go, huh? I don't know what we'll do, but it'll be sometime in the afternoon. I do have to get my clothes washed. Maybe we'll just hang out by the pool."

"I like that idea. I could use a day of not doing anything."

"Okay. Then. Tomorrow."

"Yeah. Night."

I ended the call, set my phone aside, sat up, and looked at the necklace. I could feel myself smiling. It was the smile of someone who was totally and completely happy. It was the smile of someone who wasn't worried about getting hurt.

I put the necklace on. It felt right. Suddenly everything did. I wasn't even worried about Saraphina's prediction.

But maybe I should have continued to worry about being careful.

Things were coming along nicely on the house. We were getting to the details. Jenna and I were hammering the trim around the windows that had been replaced.

The four of us had spent last Sunday at a lake near where we were staying, just relaxing. Sometimes we got together after we were finished building for the day. Sometimes it was just Brady and me. It seemed like we could always find something to talk about. And when we weren't talking, we were kissing.

"Hey, catch!" Brady yelled.

I looked over, dropped the hammer, and caught the bottle of water he tossed my way. He'd set his watch to go off every hour and he brought me a bottle when he grabbed one for himself. I sat down on the edge of the porch, removed my safety goggles and hard hat, and set them aside. I twisted the cap and took a long swallow of the cold water. It tasted so good.

Brady leaned against the beam. I watched a droplet trail down his bare chest. A silly thing to be fascinated watching, but fascinated I was. Just about everything about him fascinated me.

"Do you have a sec?" he asked.

I felt my cheeks warm as I lifted my gaze to his, certain my brow was furrowed and a question was in my eyes. We'd been really good about not sneaking off for stolen kisses. I wasn't sure Jenna could say the same. From time to time, she disappeared. Tank was usually AWOL at the same time.

Brady jerked his head to the side. "I want to show you something."

"What?"

He grinned. "If I could tell you, I wouldn't have to show you. Come on."

I got up and walked beside him as he headed toward the street, then sauntered along the line of cars that was parked against the curb. He had a lazy stride—which was odd because I knew he wasn't at all lazy. He was probably one of the hardest workers here. Me, I took a break every fifteen minutes just to catch my breath, dip a towel into ice water, and wrap it around my neck to cool down. I couldn't imagine what it would be like around here come August. Next year, I thought, I'd do this volunteer work over spring break, when it wasn't quite as hot yet.

Yeah, I was already making plans to come back. I really liked New Orleans. It had so much to offer, and we hadn't even explored everything yet.

When we got to Tank's car, Brady stopped, reached into his back pocket, pulled something out, and held it toward me. It looked like white cardboard, folded in half.

"What is it?" I asked.

"Open it."

I set my water bottle on the trunk of the car, took the cardboard, and unfolded it. It was a colorful butterfly. A temporary tattoo. I laughed.

"I saw it at the convenience store where we stopped to get coffee this morning," Brady said. "It reminded me of you."

I squinted up at him. I hadn't put my sunglasses on. The sun was bright, but his smile was brighter.

"I see."

"I could put it on you if you want."

"What? Right now?"

His grin, if at all possible, grew wider. "Yeah. Why not? Lean on the trunk."

He took the towel from around my neck and poured some water from his water bottle on it. I glanced around. It seemed kind of wicked in a way, and sort of silly, too.

"Why not?" I repeated, handed him the tattoo, and leaned against the car. I lifted my T-shirt slightly and pushed the waistband of my jeans down just a tad, near my left hip.

I felt him lay the piece of paper against my skin, felt the damp towel against my back. "That's cold!"

"Bet it feels good, though," he said.

In no time at all he was peeling back the paper. "Perfect."

I moved around him and looked in the sideview mirror, twisting around slightly, so I could see my backside. All I could see was part of the wings peeking out above the waistband of my jeans.

"Sexy," Brady said.

His voice dropped a notch or two, and it sent a shiver along my spine. I'd never had a guy tell me I was sexy before. I liked it. I liked it a lot.

He put his hands on either side of my hips and drew me closer. "I had an ulterior motive in giving you the tattoo. Now I can say something innocent like, 'I'd like to see the bottom half of that tattoo.'" He wiggled his eyebrows. "And it might not be innocent at all."

"Yeah, well, you should have taken a good look at it when you were applying it, because that was probably the last time you'll see the bottom half." I stood on tiptoes and nipped his chin. He had a really nice chin. Strong, sturdy. It matched his strong jaw.

I'd always thought a guy's eyes were his best feature, revealed the most about him. But the truth was, there wasn't anything about Brady that I didn't think was darn near perfect.

"We'll see," he said in a low voice, like a challenge. I knew he was still talking about the tattoo and wanting to see all of it again.

Then he was kissing me, and I thought—

Yeah, we'll see.

A week later, I moved from hammering outside to painting bedroom walls.

I'd called Amber and given her the measurements for the windows and told her that I was going to paint the little girls' rooms pink. Brady had borrowed Tank's car to take me shopping for the paint. I'd bought it myself, because the builder who was donating the supplies had brought only cream-colored paint. And while cream is a nice neutral color, little girls should have something special.

I dipped the roller into the pan, then began rolling it over the walls again. When we'd first started working on the house it smelled of mildew and rot. Now it smelled of paint, of new. It smelled wonderful.

I'd never been involved in something that made me feel this good about myself.

"Hey, guess who just got here?" Jenna asked from the doorway.

I turned around, but before I could answer, she said, "It's Amber. Come on."

I'd known that, of course. Just as Sara had predicted. Back from her doubts.

I was so ready to see her again. I hurried through the house—in Jenna's wake—and stepped out onto the porch. And there Amber was, running across the yard that when we'd first arrived had been littered. Now the house was almost completed.

I hopped off the porch and rushed to her, reaching her at the same time that Jenna did. We did a three-person hug, laughing. Hopping up and down. Going in a circle. I had so much to tell her. So much to share.

I wanted to hear about everything that had happened at home, too. She'd hardly called, so I knew she'd been wrapped up in Chad. That's the way it is when you have a boyfriend. You spend so much time with him. I wanted to hear it all.

She leaned back, and her smile dimmed. "I didn't come alone."

"I know. Saraphina told me you wouldn't," I said.

She frowned, worried, so typical. "She knew I was coming back?"

I nodded. "With a guy with black hair."

I looked past her. At the black-haired guy standing a few feet away.

Drew.

The very last person I wanted to see.

I spun on my heel and walked back into the house, back to the bedroom I'd been painting.

Without saying a word to Drew. Without even acknowledging his existence, his presence, his intrusion on my life.

I picked up the roller and started rolling it over the wall in a frenzy—almost insanely. It was a little frightening really. But I thought the problem was that painting wasn't nearly as cathartic as hammering.

I really wanted to feel a hammer in my hand right now.

This place, this city, this house in a demolished neighborhood, had been my paradise. My sanctuary. It had been untainted. No memories of Drew. This was a Drew-less place.

I'd been happy. I'd been really happy.

I'd stopped thinking about Drew before I went to sleep. I didn't want to see him, didn't want to talk to him, didn't want him to creep back into my life.

I heard footsteps. If it was Drew, I was going to pick up the can of paint and throw its contents on him.

"Dawn?"

It was Amber. I set down the roller, faced her, and crossed my arms over my chest. Jenna was standing beside her. Was she there to support Amber or me? I'd lost my boyfriend. Was I going to lose my friends?

"What were you thinking?" I asked. It was all I could do not to shout.

And knowing Amber, she probably hadn't been thinking.

"Chad and I broke up," she said.

"You're kidding?" Jenna looked dumbstruck.

"Why would she kid about that?" I asked. "And how does that even remotely begin to explain bringing Drew here?"

Ignoring me, Jenna asked, "Why did you and Chad break up?"

"Because I wanted to do something meaningful with my summer, and he wanted to rent DVDs for TV shows he hadn't seen and do season marathons. All the different seasons of *24*. All the different seasons of *Monk* and *Lost* and *Scrubs*. I just wanted more."

"But you told me that he was interested in coming," I reminded her.

"He said he was, but he really wasn't. He was just humoring me. He didn't really care about what I wanted."

"So you broke up with him?" Jenna asked.

Amber nodded. "Plus, I couldn't stop thinking about Sean."

"He's with Sara," I said.

I knew it was mean, but I took some satisfaction in telling her that. I was upset that she'd brought Drew here.

I know sometimes she says things that are out there, but this was beyond out there. This was plain stupid.

"Well, Sean's not *with* her, with her," Amber said. "I mean, I know they've been hanging out together, but they're just friends. She's way older than he is. And he's called me."

I couldn't believe this. Everything was such a mess.

"You broke up with Chad so you could get together with Sean?" Jenna asked.

Jenna still wanted details. I wanted Drew out of there.

"I broke up with Chad because watching TV isn't enough for me. And if Sean isn't the one Sara was referring to—what

I'll have better in college—I'm okay with that. I just knew Chad was wrong."

"But you loved him."

Amber nodded. "I know it seems all screwed up, but I know I did the right thing."

"Maybe you did the right thing about Chad," I said, "but Drew? Why bring him?"

"Because I needed a way to get here, and he has a car," Amber explained.

"You could have flown, your parents could have brought you, you could have hitchhiked." Although I knew that was a dangerous option and really didn't want her to risk it—I was upset. Anything was better than seeing Drew again.

"He wanted to help out, though, so it seemed like a perfect solution."

I couldn't believe this. "Amber—"

"I know you're still mad at him, but you should at least talk to him. He's sorry—"

"Oh, he's sorry, all right."

"Prom night was a moment of weakness."

What a crappy excuse. I wasn't buying it. And while she wasn't usually good at figuring things out, she read the expression on my face perfectly.

"Look, he wants to get back together with you," she said.

"Ain't happening."

"But you need closure."

"I hate that word. I had closure. I slammed his car door *closed* and walked away."

"And never talked to him again?"

"There was nothing to say. There still isn't."

"I think you're wrong. I think there's a lot more to say."

No, there wasn't. There was nothing. Absolutely nothing. I didn't care about Drew anymore. I didn't care about him at all.

I headed for the door.

"Where are you going?" Amber asked.

"To take care of something."

I walked into the kitchen where Brady and some other guys were supposed to be working.

And there was Drew.

The guys were standing around talking to him, but I knew that nothing he said was important. Everything was a lie. Especially when he said he loved you.

Brady stepped out of the circle just a little bit when he saw me.

Drew turned around and took a step toward me, his hands out, his smile . . . God, it looked so fake, so stupid. How had I ever trusted it?

"Dawn—"

I walked right by him. Totally ignoring him. I went up to Brady, wrapped my arms around his neck, and kissed him.

Energetically, thoroughly. Maybe even a little desperately.

He pulled back and gave me a funny look. Then he took my hand. "Come on."

He led me past Drew, whose mouth was hanging open.

Good, I thought. *Now you know how it feels.*

"What was going on back there?"

Brady was leaning against Tank's car, his sunglasses on, his arms crossed over his chest.

"I was missing you."

"Dawn, I deserve better than that."

I looked down at the grass and could see some shards of broken glass. Would we ever get everything cleaned up?

"He was your boyfriend, wasn't he?"

Nodding, I looked up.

"You were trying to make him jealous."

Well, okay, maybe I was. Maybe I wanted him to see what he gave up.

"Which means you still feel something for him," Brady finished.

"I don't! Not at all. He's such a jerk!" I felt tears burn my eyes. "I hate him."

"Hate's a feeling."

"It's not a good feeling. It's not like I care."

"Why's he here?" Brady asked.

"He gave Amber a lift. He wants to help."

"That's it?"

His voice dripped with skepticism. This was a side of Brady I'd never seen. Impatient.

I shifted from one foot to the other, while I decided whether to confirm what he suspected. "He wants us to get back together."

"Do you?"

I stared at him. "No. No way."

"Are you sure?"

"Yes."

"I'm not."

"You're not what?"

"Not so sure you don't want to get back together with him."

"Are you saying I'm a liar?"

"I think you were using me back there. Maybe I've been using you, too, but you need to figure out how you really feel about him."

Using me? How had he been using me?

"Because if you want to make him jealous," he continued, "it's because you want him back. I've been there, done that, and I'm not doing it again."

"I don't know what you're talking about. What are you saying?"

"I'm saying that we're over."

Brady walked over to Tank, talked to him, then they came back, got in the car, and drove away.

Just like that.

It was just as I suspected: All guys eventually turned into jerks.

It was the opposite of the frog turning into the prince. Eventually, no matter what you did, the prince turned back into a frog.

"Dawn?"

Drew. Behind me.

Even his voice grated on my nerves. Without even looking at him, I started walking toward the house.

"I'm really, really sorry," he said.

I kept walking.

"Won't you even talk to me?" he asked.

Nope.

I just kept walking.

I saw Amber leaning against the new wall of the house, talking to Sean. Smiling. Laughing. He was tucking her hair behind her ear.

At least she'd broken up with Chad, before getting more involved with Sean. I was sure it had been hard to break up with him, and he was probably hurt. But it was easier to get over a breakup than a betrayal.

Or at least I hoped it was.

Right now I was still reeling from Brady's outburst.

What was up with that anyway?

He'd broken our bargain.

Creep.

I felt tears sting my eyes. He wasn't a jerk or a creep. Not by a long shot.

But where had the guy who'd always been "okay" with everything gone?

Jenna came out of the house, hopped off the porch, and came over, stopping me from going wherever it was I was going.

I had no idea.

I was in shock.

"Are you okay?" Jenna asked.

"Brady left. He just left."

"Yeah, I know. Tank called to let me know."

"I don't get it. He's been so understanding—this whole time. And now, when I really need him, he just goes ballistic."

It was a little scary to realize how much I'd come to depend on him being there. That was so not what I'd planned for the summer.

Amber had left Sean and joined us.

"I'm sorry," she said. "I thought you'd be happy to see Drew."

"How could you possibly think that?" I asked.

"I just thought since he wanted to be with you again—"

"But I told you I was with Brady."

"Yeah, but I thought it was just for the summer."

It was. It was. But still.

It was hard to stay mad at Amber. She just didn't think, and I knew she hadn't meant to mess things up for me. But still, she had.

"Brady didn't even give me a chance to explain," I said. "He just said it was over."

Jenna sighed. "Probably because of Melanie. Don't you think?"

My heart did a little stutter. "Melanie? Who's Melanie?"

Jenna looked surprised. Startled, even. "He didn't tell you about Melanie?"

Shivers went all through me. This was worse than thinking I felt a spirit tickle me on a ghost tour.

"Nooo. What's this about?"

She grimaced. "Oh, I don't know if I should tell you, then."

"Jenna! I need to understand what's going on here."

"Let me call Tank and see if it's okay for me to tell you."

"You need Tank's approval to help your friend?"

"He told me, but I don't know if I can tell you."

"Jenna."

She sighed. "Oh, all right. Melanie was Brady's girlfriend."

"He had a girlfriend?"

She nodded.

Why was I surprised he'd had a girlfriend? Honestly I would have been surprised if he hadn't. I mean, he had way too many smooth moves never to have had one. And he was so cute and nice. Of course he'd had a girlfriend.

"When?" I asked.

"I don't know all the details. Tank just told me about how she broke up with Brady—because it was such a cold way to do it."

"What'd she do?"

"She text-messaged him. He's in class and he gets a text message: 'I'm back with Mike.'"

"Back with?" I repeated.

"Yeah, apparently, she broke up with her boyfriend, then she was dating Brady, then she got back with the other guy."

"Did Brady like her? I mean, a lot?"

She nodded. "Think so."

"This is so weird," Amber whispered. "I don't know if I should have come back."

"You should have come back," I reassured her. "You just shouldn't have brought Drew."

"No, don't you get it? Saraphina said there would be things hidden. I thought she meant that stupid snake," Amber said.

Another shiver went through me.

Secrets were things hidden. And Brady had one.

Why hadn't he told me?

Then I remembered him saying how he hadn't believed the psychic because life wasn't good. But he hadn't explained why.

I'd finally discovered his flaw.

My old boyfriend showed up and Brady just assumed I'd get back together with Drew.

He was as untrusting of girls as I was of guys.

Weren't we a terrific pair?

I'd never questioned why he'd been so agreeable to the terms of our agreement. Why a New-Orleans-only-no-breakup-predetermined-good-bye had been okay with him. Now I knew.

He was as scared of getting hurt again as I was.

"So what are you going to do?" Jenna asked.

"I don't know. I just . . . I just need to take some time." I looked at Amber. "Go talk to Sean. That's the reason you came back. And Jenna, go finish painting the bedroom. I'm just going to . . . I don't know."

I walked away, walked across the yard to where we kept the ice chests. I opened one, searched through the icy water until I found a bottle. I closed the chest, twisted off the cap, took a long swallow.

It didn't help. My knees still felt weak. I sat on the chest.

Maybe I'd just go home. Who needed this aggravation?

Drew being here when I didn't want him to be. Brady believing that I'd get back together with Drew—just because he'd shown up.

Only I didn't want to go home. I wanted to be here. I wanted to build a house. I wanted to be with my friends. I wanted to explore the city more.

I'd run away once before because it had hurt too much to

stay. But now, no matter how much it hurt to be here, I wasn't willing to leave.

I was vaguely aware of someone opening one of the other ice chests, the pop of a top being twisted off a bottle, the moan of the chest as someone sat on it.

"Sometimes I hate it when the things I see really do happen."

I looked over to find Sara sitting next to me.

"Amber's back," she said quietly. "And the black-haired guy with her? He broke something, didn't he?"

Oh yeah, big time.

Sara looked sad. As sad as I felt.

I nodded. "He used to be my boyfriend. And Brady was just so un-Brady about it. Do you happen to know any voodoo?"

A corner of her mouth quirked up. "Voodoo?"

"Yeah. I was thinking maybe a spell that would send Drew away and bring Brady back."

"You take three hairs from each of their heads, bury them in a backyard"—she jerked her thumb over her shoulder—"like this backyard, and jump up and down on the spot three times."

I looked at her, my eyes wide. "Really?"

She smiled. "No. It's never that simple, Dawn."

"Brady probably wouldn't give me three strands of his hair anyway. He's kind of protective of his hair. He has this fear of going bald."

She shook her head. "Huh. I don't see him without hair."

I straightened up. "You mean, he's not going to go bald?"

She laughed. "Oh no, I don't *see* him, see him. I just can't imagine him bald."

"Oh. I thought if I gave him some good news . . ."

What did it matter? It didn't.

I sighed. "I don't suppose you see how all this is going to end."

She slowly shook her head. "Sorry."

I nodded. "That's okay. Sometimes it's probably better not to know."

"Yeah, sometimes it is."

And the way she said it made me think she knew more than she was letting on.

"I hate leaving you alone," Jenna said.

We were back in the dorm. I was sitting on the bed.

"I'll be fine."

Amber shifted her weight from one foot to the other. "You sure?"

Tank and Sean were coming to get them for a night of

listening to bands. I wondered what Brady was going to be doing. I was a little afraid to ask.

So I didn't ask.

So typical of me. Not wanting to face the truth.

I could see him dancing shirtless on Bourbon Street, gathering beads. I wondered whose neck he'd put them around.

I wondered why he didn't tell me about Melanie.

It was strange, so strange, that all I could think about was him. How much I wanted to be with him.

After Jenna and Amber left, I just looked at the ceiling and thought about him.

When my phone rang, my heart gave a little jump—until I saw who was calling.

Drew.

I almost didn't answer. Mostly because, suddenly, nothing was there. The anger that I'd felt earlier—it was just gone.

"Hey."

"I didn't think you'd answer," he said.

"Then why did you call?"

"Just in case you did. I really want to see you, Dawn."

"Okay."

"Okay? You mean it?"

"Yeah." I gave him the address for the dorm. I changed into jeans and a knit top.

I was waiting outside the dorm when he drove up.

It was kind of funny. There was no excitement. No antici-pation. It wasn't at all like waiting for Brady.

I walked over to his car and got in.

"Where do you want to go?" Drew asked.

"McDonald's."

"Seriously?"

"Yep."

I told him there was one near the French Quarter. As he drove, neither of us talked. There seemed to be so much to say and nothing to say.

I showed him where to park.

"Seems like we ought to eat someplace, I don't know, Cajun, I guess," he said as we crossed the street.

"I like this place because the lights are bright. I want to see you."

That seemed to please him. Maybe it sounded like a romantic thing to say, but romance had nothing to do with it. I just wanted to be able to see him clearly when we talked. Wanted him to see me, so there'd be no misunderstanding about what was being said.

Sometimes in the dark, you can misunderstand things.

He ordered a burger and fries. I ordered a soft drink.

"That John guy, he's nice. He found me a place to stay,

with some other volunteers," Drew said once we were sitting in a booth.

"Amber said you came here because you wanted to help."

"Yeah. That, and to see you."

I really, really, really wanted nothing more than for him to go back to Katy. But at the same time, I couldn't help but think of him as an extra pair of hands. And New Orleans needed all the helping hands it could get.

So I wasn't here to tell him to leave. I was here to figure out how I could work with him. I didn't think it was going to be as hard as I'd envisioned.

"I thought you wanted to spend the summer doing water parks," I said.

"Yeah, me, too. But I was reading Jenna's blog—"

"Thanks for sending my mom that picture, by the way."

He blushed. "This afternoon, it looked like you were still seeing the guy."

"Yeah, I am." Or I would be, once I figured that part of my life out. I wasn't going to give Brady up nearly as easily as I'd given up Drew. I wasn't going to walk away without talking to him.

"How serious?" Drew asked.

"Serious enough." My arrangement with Brady wasn't any of Drew's business. "I just want you to know that I'm fine with you being here. I'm fine with you helping. I just need you to understand that you and I are over."

I thought about asking what had been wrong with me because I'd always thought it was somehow my fault. But now I knew there was nothing wrong with *me*. There had just been something wrong with *us*.

There wasn't much else to say after that. He drove me back to the dorm.

It may seem cold, but I didn't even bother with good-bye. I just got out.

I heard his door open.

"Dawn?"

I looked back over my shoulder. He just stood there.

"I'm really sorry. About prom night. You have to believe that. I was just getting so much attention from girls after being in the play that I let it go to my head. You were the one."

"Actually, Drew, I wasn't. If I was, you probably wouldn't have kept looking at the menu."

"What?"

I smiled, shook my head. "Just something Jenna said once."

"Are you sure you don't want to give it another shot?"

"You broke my heart, Drew."

"Dawn—"

"You. Broke. My. Heart. We're over. Completely and absolutely."

Now all I had to do was figure out what I was going to do about Brady.

I was lying on the AeroBed reading when Jenna and Amber came back to the room, just before midnight.

"You can have the bed," Amber said.

"Nah. Our original arrangement was that you got the bed, I got the air mattress."

"You don't sound mad at me anymore."

I sat up straighter, folded my legs beneath me. "I'm not. I saw Drew tonight."

They both sat on the floor.

"What happened?" Jenna asked.

I told them about our trip to McDonald's.

"You're not going to get back with him?" Amber asked.

I didn't know how many different ways to say it, so I just said, "No."

She looked confused.

"Are you going to get back together with Chad?" I asked.

"Absolutely not."

"There you are."

"But I left Chad on my terms."

"And tonight I left Drew on mine." Maybe in her spacey sort of way, she'd been right. I had needed some closure where Drew was concerned.

"So you're back with Sean?" I asked.

She nodded. "Yeah. I can't believe how much I missed him. And how much I missed you guys. I even missed the work. I'm thinking about going into construction after I graduate."

"Seriously?"

She nodded.

"But you left before we got to the really hard stuff."

"I know. But just the idea of it, of building. It's something I really want to do. Besides, there are women builders."

"I think that's great," Jenna said. "I'm glad you're back."

"Me, too," Amber replied. She peered at me.

"I am, too." I smiled at her. I knew what it was to worry about what someone thought about you.

"So what are you going to do about Brady now?" Jenna asked.

"Do some rebuilding."

Much to my surprise, Drew was at the site the next morning. I hadn't really expected him to stay. He was wearing shorts, a T-shirt, and flip-flops. Like maybe he was on his way to a water park. So maybe he wasn't staying.

He walked up to me.

"Hey," he said.

"Hey."

In a way, it was sad that I felt so little for him.

"So what do I do?" he asked.

"What?" Did he still have hopes of us getting back together? Had I not been abundantly clear last night?

He flapped his hand around. "Around here. How do I help?"

"Uh, well, you should probably go talk to John." *And John is going to tell you to go home and change into jeans and boots*, I thought. Drew really seemed clueless about what was involved in working here.

"Can't I just help you?"

"It doesn't work that way." Usually. Well, okay, if Brady had wanted to help me, I would have welcomed him. "John gives the assignments."

And I'd totally kill him if he assigned Drew to me.

"Okay. I'll see you around, then."

"Yeah."

It was only after Drew walked away that I saw Brady standing a short distance away, watching us.

He turned and went into the house, and I wondered what he thought he'd witnessed.

I went to the bedroom to finish painting. Amber had brought curtains and rods. As soon as we were done with the walls, we were going to hang everything up.

We still had a way to go with the last wall when I decided to take a water break. I went out the front door to the ice chests and grabbed four bottles of water. I walked back into the house, went into the kitchen, and waited while Brady and a couple of other guys finished putting up a cabinet. As soon as he turned around, I said, "Brady, catch."

I tossed him a bottle of water. He caught it, no problem. He had good reflexes—which I already knew.

He studied me, like he was trying to figure out what I was doing.

I just walked out and went back to painting the bedroom.

An hour later, I did the same thing—taking him a bottle of water like he'd always brought one to me.

When we finished painting the bedroom, I went back to the kitchen.

"You guys finished with the ladder?" I asked.

"Sure," one of them said.

I closed it up, tried to carry it—and discovered it was a lot more awkward than it looked.

I heard Brady sigh. Not sure how I recognized his sigh, but I did.

"I'll get it," he said, lifting it. "The legs, remember, it's all in the legs."

He carried it to the bedroom. "Where do you want it?"

"By the window."

Jenna and Amber were in the room, reading the directions for how to hang the curtain rod.

I took one of the brackets, some nails, and a hammer. I climbed up the ladder.

"Do you even know what you're doing?" Brady asked.

Not really, but still I said, "Oh yeah."

How hard could it be to put up a bracket?

I put the bracket against the wall, put the nail in the little hole, brought the hammer back—

"You've got—" Brady began.

And I missed the nail, slamming the hammer against my thumb.

"Ow!"

I jerked back, lost my balance, released a little shriek, fell—

And suddenly found myself in Brady's arms.

"Are you okay?" he asked.

I couldn't help it. Tears started burning my eyes and I shook my head. My reaction had nothing at all to do with the pain in my thumb. It had everything to do with the pain in my heart.

He set my feet on the floor and took my hand. "How bad is it?"

Out of the corner of my eye, I saw Amber and Jenna sneak out of the room, like partners in crime worried about getting caught. If I'd thought it was possible, I'd have thought they arranged all this. But it wasn't possible.

"Doesn't look too bad," Brady said.

I hadn't planned on hitting my thumb. I hadn't planned on ending up in Brady's arms.

"Looks can be deceiving," I said. "I know you saw me talking to Drew."

"You don't have to explain. His being here says it all." He moved away, picked up the hammer that I'd dropped.

"Actually it doesn't say anything," I said. "He's staying to work on the house. Not because of me."

"Yeah, right." He picked up the nail and bracket. He climbed the ladder and began hammering the bracket into place.

"Are you pretending that's my head?"

He looked down at me. "What?"

"I used to pretend every nail was Drew."

"So you spent the summer thinking about him."

That confession had backfired.

"Only at first. And yes, yesterday, I was mad when I saw him. It was just the shock of it. And yes, I kissed you to try to hurt him. But he doesn't mean anything to me. Not any-more."

"I can't do this." He climbed down the ladder and handed me the hammer. "I just can't do it."

My heart almost stopped. For a minute, I thought he was leaving. Permanently. Going back to Houston.

But I found him in the kitchen, working on the cabinets. Not that he saw me.

I just peered in the open doorway, saw him, and thought, *Okay.*

Then I went to find Sara.

Saturday, Jenna and Amber spent the day shopping with me and walking around the French Quarter.

I told them that they didn't have to. I was okay with them spending the day with their guys. But they didn't want me hanging around the city by myself.

Besides, the three of us hadn't had much time together since that first day.

At least that was their reason. But I knew the truth. They were worried about me.

The past couple of days at the site had been a strain. To say the least. Mostly because I wasn't giving up on Brady.

I took him water every hour. Sometimes I'd just toss the bottle to him. Sometimes I'd stop and talk with him for a minute. Not about anything important. Not about us. Not about Drew.

He'd hold up the water bottle. "You don't have to do this."

"I know. I want to, though." And I'd decided that wanting to do something was enough reason to do it.

And tonight I was going on the vampire tour. Because I wanted to.

I wanted to because Brady was going on it, too.

Sara had confirmed that for me earlier in the week—after the falling off the ladder incident. I hadn't asked her for a reading. I hadn't wanted her to confirm my future. Or not confirm it. Or give any hints. All I wanted her to do was pair me up with Brady.

And I'd take care of the rest.

Tank and Sean were going to be there as well. Jenna and Amber were going to meet up with them then. And hopefully, if my plan worked out . . . well, I just hoped it would.

So after a day of shopping and talking, we headed to Sara's.

I hadn't expected Drew to be there. I really needed to put a hex on the guy.

He smiled brightly when he saw us. "Hey!"

I just wiggled my fingers.

"This is going to be fun," he said.

"Yeah, it is."

Sara came over—dressed in her black cape again—and

took his arm. "You're going to be with me."

"Really?" he asked.

She winked at me. "Really."

She led him away.

"That was close," Jenna whispered.

Too close. I figured if Brady had seen Drew talking to me—he probably would have walked on by. But the guys weren't there yet.

"They are coming, aren't they?" I asked.

"Absolutely," Jenna said, looking at her phone. "Tank just texted. They're on their way."

I took a deep breath and adjusted the tote bag on my shoulder. "Okay."

Then I saw them crossing the street. They were heading right for us. Brady wasn't trying to avoid me, probably because Tank and Sean were leading the way and he was just following, not really looking the group over. I was standing a little behind Jenna and Amber, so he didn't see me until it was too late.

"Hey," I said.

"Hey."

Sara walked through the group, matching people up. "Brady, you and Dawn."

She didn't even give him a chance to object.

"Your boyfriend's up there if you want to switch partners," Brady said.

"He's not my boyfriend. He *was*. Past tense. No more."

"You really think you mean that, don't you?"

"I don't *think*. I know." Had I been this obstinate in the beginning about wanting to have a dateless summer? Yeah, I guess I had been.

"Okay, everyone, shh . . . ," Sara said.

John suddenly appeared. It was like one minute he wasn't with us, the next he was.

I don't know how he did that, but I jumped. Brady snickered.

"Are you going to hold my hand if I get scared?" I asked.

He looked at me. He wasn't holding my hand now. I really, really missed him holding my hand.

"I believe in vampires," I said. I'd believe in just about anything if he'd hold my hand again.

"All right, people," John said. He was dressed in a flowing cape. And yes, he had fangs. And he looked pale—bloodless even. "Tonight, I'm going to give you an experience you'll never forget. Follow me."

He started walking down the street, and everyone fell into step behind him.

Everyone except Brady and me.

"Do you really want to do the tour?" I asked.

"Not really. You?"

I shook my head. "I'd rather go sit by the river." I lifted my tote. "I brought a blanket."

"Okay."

We turned and headed toward the Mississippi. He took my hand.

It was a start.

It was late, and night, and dark, and sultry. Even the breeze coming across the water was warm. Sometimes we could hear people laughing or music coming from the decks of the lighted riverboats.

Brady and I were sitting on the blanket. We'd stopped at one of the many tourist haunts and bought a bottle of water. Just one. For the two of us.

Another step in the right direction.

We'd been sitting there for a while, though, neither of us saying anything. It wasn't uncomfortable. Or at least, I didn't feel that way.

I brought my knees up and wrapped my arms around my legs. "I went to a voodoo shop today."

"A voodoo shop."

I heard the skepticism in his voice. I turned my head, lay

my cheek on my knees. "Yeah. Want to see what I got?"

"You bought something?"

"Uh-huh." I reached into my bag and brought out a candle. "If you light this, it keeps the bad mojo away." I set it down near my feet.

Then I brought out another candle. "And this one brings in the good mojo."

"Do you even know what mojo is?" he asked.

"Not really. I think it's like karma. Do you want to light them and see what happens?"

"Sure."

I struck a match, lit one, and then the other.

Brady lifted the first one, studied it. "This smells like peach."

With the flame flickering so close, I could see his face more clearly now.

"Is this really a voodoo candle?" he asked.

I shook my head. "No. But I've learned that sometimes what you believe is more important than what is real. I mean, if I believed that ghosts were really touching me, it didn't matter if it was a moth. And if you believed that I'd get back with Drew, it didn't matter that I wouldn't. You believed it. But you have to understand. I'm not Melanie."

He blew out the flame. "Who told you about Melanie?"

"Tank told Jenna. She told me. Why didn't *you* tell me?"

"What was there to say?"

"I don't know. But you were asking about Drew. So it seems like you should have said something about her."

He sighed. "She doesn't matter."

"Neither does Drew."

And maybe he'd been agreeable to my only-while-we're-here terms because they made him feel as safe as they made me feel. No commitment. No breakup. No heartache.

"We had an agreement," I said quietly. "I'm still in New Orleans. So unless you're planning to leave—"

"I'm not leaving."

"Okay then. I've got you for three more weeks."

"And what's-his-name?"

"I'm not interested in him at all."

He shook his head. "I don't usually overreact to things. But all I could think was that the boyfriend was here and you'd hook back up. I guess I wanted to get out first, on my own terms."

Which I understood completely.

"But our terms are . . . as long as we're in New Orleans," I reminded him.

"And we're still in the Big Easy," he said.

I nodded.

"Okay then."

He leaned in, touched my cheek. "I'm sorry if I was a jerk."

I smiled. "Even Dr. Phil has a bad day now and then. Besides, the reason I was kissing you in the kitchen was wrong. You were right about that."

"I've really missed you," he said.

He leaned in closer and kissed me.

I couldn't have been happier. Not only were we back on speaking terms, we were back on kissing terms.

CHAPTER 21

I couldn't believe that we'd completed our first house.

The hammers were silent, the rubbish carted away. We'd planted two spindly trees.

The house itself was painted. Inside, it was sparsely furnished. But it did have curtains hanging from the windows to give it a welcoming touch. I had bought some dolls and put them in each of the pink bedrooms.

All the many volunteers stood on the lawn, near the front porch, waiting for the residents to return.

Brady was holding my hand, but then he usually did. He knew that I wasn't going to leave him for Drew. And not only because Drew was no longer there.

Drew had decided to go back home after only a week in the Big Easy. At least he'd helped for a while.

I couldn't say I particularly liked him, but I did know that I didn't hate him anymore.

The funny thing was—after that first day, having Drew around really didn't bother me. He was not a part of my life any longer.

Brady was.

Things between us were . . . well, developing. We spent most evenings together, going somewhere to listen to a band or a musician.

I was noticing everything about him. I knew he put his sunglasses on two seconds before he stepped into the sun. Always.

I noticed that he looked great in wrinkled T-shirts. And all his T-shirts were wrinkled. Even right after he washed them, because his sorting system was one pile for clean clothes, one pile for dirty clothes.

"Folding, hanging stuff up—not how I want to spend my time," he'd told me.

Yeah, I'd been in his room a couple of times. To watch pay-on-demand movies. And cuddle without everyone in New Orleans looking on. He never pushed, but he hinted that he was interested in seeing the bottom half of my tattoo—even though it was long gone.

I was thinking about getting another one. A permanent one. One that would be there when I was ready to share it with him.

Now, Jenna and Tank were standing near us. So were Amber and Sean. It was kind of funny that so many couples were around, that so many of us had bonded while building.

A car pulled up in front of the house, and a thrill shot through me. I couldn't believe how excited I was that the family was coming home. That we'd done what we could to ensure that they were able to come home.

John went to greet them. Holding her daughters' hands, the woman walked to the house and stepped up on the porch. She was younger than I'd expected her to be and pretty. She turned to face us, with tears in her eyes.

"Thank you," she said. "Thank you . . . so much."

We clapped and cheered, acknowledging her—that she was home again. That we were all glad.

John opened the door for her, and she walked inside. I could hear the patter of her daughters' feet as they raced through the house.

"Mama! My room is pink!" one of the girls shouted. "I love pink!"

Brady put his arm around me, hugged me. "Good choice," he said.

My throat was tight. All I could do was nod, as tears filled my eyes. I felt a little guilty that I'd originally planned to spend my summer going to water parks. If Drew hadn't been such a jerk, that's what I would have done. And I would have missed out on this sense of accomplishment.

John stepped out on the porch and clapped his hands. "All right, people! Your job is done. Enjoy the rest of the day. We start on the next one in the morning!"

Tank, Jenna, Brady, and I walked to Tank's car. Sean and Amber were catching a ride with Sara. We seldom rode with Ms. Wynder anymore. But, then, she was usually with John.

As we were driving away, I looked out the back window and watched the mother and her daughters waving at us from the front porch. Her daughters were clutching the dolls I'd left in their rooms. I felt . . . happy.

Wiping the tears from my eyes, I leaned my head back on the seat. "One down, and about a thousand to go."

"I think there's more than a thousand," Brady said.

I rolled my head to the side and looked at him. "How

many houses do you think there are that need to be rebuilt?"

He shrugged. "A lot."

"Even after all this time?"

"Oh yeah. It takes a long time."

Yeah, I thought, looking at him, rebuilding does take a long time. But it was worth it. It was so worth it.

"I am so glad we decided to spend part of our summer here," Amber said, later that night, as we were holding our own celebration.

She, Jenna, and I were sitting on a park bench. A jazz band was playing nearby. The guys had decided to take a walk around, do some people-watching.

I think they knew that we wanted some time alone.

"Yeah, me, too," I said, fingering the fleur-de-lis on the necklace that Brady had given me. I wore it all the time.

"This has been the best summer ever," Jenna said.

"And it's not over," I pointed out. "We've still got another week to go."

"Now that we know what we're doing, maybe the next house will go faster."

"Maybe."

"You want to hear something crazy?" Jenna asked.

Amber and I looked at her.

"I've been thinking about asking Sara if Tank and I will get married."

"You want to marry him?" Amber asked.

Jenna lifted her shoulders. "I've thought about it."

"And what if Sara gives you a cryptic answer like, 'Yes, you'll both get married'?" I asked.

Jenna scowled. "That's the only thing stopping me. I'd worry about whether that meant to each other or to someone else."

"You know, Jenna, it doesn't really matter what she sees. You have to decide what's best for you. Even though she saw things, we were the ones who made them happen," I said. "You were crazy about Tank before you saw the dragon. Amber's reasons for coming back had nothing to do with Sara's predictions. She came back because she wanted to do good things. Have some purpose. And I'm with Brady because I want to be. Not because he has a red hat."

"Are you saying we'd be where we are, even if we hadn't had a reading?" Jenna asked.

"Yeah, I think so. It was fun, but we didn't make any of our decisions because we thought we had to make what Sara saw happen. We determine our destinies."

"That is so corny," Jenna said. "As corny as what Tank

said that first night. But I like it. I like it a lot."

I looked up and saw the guys walking toward us.

I grabbed Jenna's and Amber's hands and closed my eyes. "I see a night on Bourbon Street in our future."

They laughed.

"That was an easy prediction," Jenna said. "It's Friday night!"

We got up from the bench.

"We thought we'd head on over to Bourbon Street," Tank said when they got to us. "See what's happening there."

Jenna smiled. "We figured."

I kept myself nestled against Brady's side as we walked along the now-familiar street. We strolled slowly, listening to bands, watching the people, and celebrating the completion of the house.

"You know what you need?" Brady asked.

I laughed, because I knew where this was going. Sara had definitely rubbed off on me.

"Beads," he said.

He grabbed my hand, and I let him drag me farther into the craziness that's Bourbon Street.

CHAPTER 22

It was our last night in New Orleans.

We'd finished gutting another house and were halfway completed with its rebuilding. I wanted to stay and finish it, but we needed to get home, needed to start getting ready for school to begin. Another group of volunteers was going to finish the house. John said he'd let us know when the job was completed, in case we wanted to come back and welcome the family home.

I thought I probably would.

John and Sara had arranged for us to have an all-night party on a riverboat, their way of thanking us for the help we'd given them over the past six weeks. Even though none of us thought thanks were needed, we weren't going to say no to a party.

Brady and I were standing by the railing on the upper deck watching one of the paddlewheels churn through the water of the Mississippi. There was a romantic element to it, but then, New Orleans is a city of romance. Since I'd been here, I'd come to appreciate what it had to offer: its history, its ghosts, its food, its music . . . its love of life.

Sometimes I think it takes almost losing something to realize how very precious it is.

Like what happened with Brady. I almost lost him. And in the losing, I'd finally discovered what I'd found. During the last few weeks, we'd grown closer, but I felt like I still had so much to tell him, so much he needed to know.

I needed—wanted—to tell him everything tonight, because tomorrow we'd be going our separate ways.

"Feeling better?" Brady asked.

We'd been down below with the other volunteers when I'd started to feel a little seasick. Who knew you could feel seasick on a river? But I guess moving on water is moving on water, regardless of what you call it. So we came up top. I was fine as long as I had plenty of fresh air to breathe. I guessed that was why the swamp hadn't bothered me. We hadn't been enclosed.

"Yeah, I'm okay now."

"Then let's go get something to eat," he said. "I'm starving."

He always was. Still, I nodded. The moment wasn't right

for what I wanted to say. Or maybe a small part of me was still afraid—afraid of being hurt again.

But being hurt is part of life. And you learn to rebuild.

New Orleans had taught me that. I figured there would be other storms . . . more rebuilding. The city would shift, reshape, and change, but the heart of it would remain the same.

With Brady holding my hand, we walked past some benches and said hey to the volunteers who were sitting there. Then we went down the stairs that led into the dining room. Jenna, Tank, Amber, and Sean waved at us from a cloth-covered table near a window.

Jenna and Tank—they were tighter than ever. Definitely in love. They were going to keep seeing each other when we got back to Houston. Jenna was going to apply to Rice, so she could go there next year after she graduated. And if Rice didn't accept her—it had pretty tough academic requirements—well, there was another university in Houston and there were community colleges. They'd find a way to be together. I had a feeling Tank was it for Jenna. The real deal. Forever.

I wasn't quite as sure about Amber and Sean, but then neither was she. She didn't know if he was the college love that Sara had predicted. What she did know was that meeting Sean had shown her that Chad wasn't the right one. And maybe Sean wasn't, either. Time would tell. But I had a feeling there was someone else in Amber's future.

After all, Sara had said Amber wouldn't find love this summer.

Not that I believe in all that mumbo jumbo.

Well, okay, maybe I did a little. It was hard not to after everything that had happened. Even if I did believe we were in charge of our own destinies.

"Wow. They've got quite a spread," Brady said.

And they did. Red crawfish—piled high on a platter and on Brady's plate. Plus there was gumbo, étouffée, fried alligator, an assortment of shrimp and fish and chicken. I went with the fried shrimp and a bowl of étouffée.

We carried our plates and bowls over to the table where our friends were waiting.

"Sara's over there doing readings," Jenna said once Brady and I were settled. "Twenty dollars a pop. The money goes toward the rebuilding efforts."

I glanced over my shoulder. Sara was in a corner with a large window behind her. The sun was setting and the river visible through the window almost glowed red.

She was also holding Ms. Wynder's hand. I could see Sara talking, but of course she was too far away for me to hear what she was saying.

"Think she's telling her that curly red hair is a permanent part of her future?" Jenna asked.

Watching and grinning, John was sitting beside Ms. Wynder. They were always together. Ms. Wynder had even stopped doing bed checks. I think maybe it was because she wasn't always back in the dorm on time to make them. Not that I was going to tell my mom that. She might not let me come back next summer if she thought there was "craziness" going on.

But then how could there not be? This was New Orleans.

"Maybe," I said.

"That wouldn't be much of a prediction," Amber said. "Ms. Wynder already told me that she's going to organize a group to come back over winter break."

"I think there is definitely something going on with those two," I said.

"That is just so . . . I don't know what it is." Jenna sighed. "But I just don't think of older people as falling in love."

"She's not that old," I said.

"Still. She's a . . . teacher."

I laughed. "Teachers fall in love. I think it's terrific. I just wish Sara had ended up with someone."

"Do you think she's seen him? Do you think she knows who he is?" Jenna asked.

We all looked at Sean. He was the one who had spent the

most time with her—before Amber had come back.

"What are you looking at?" he asked.

"Did she ever say anything? About her future, about her falling in love?" I asked.

He cracked open a crab claw. "She's married."

I was sure my eyes grew as wide as Amber's and Jenna's. "*What?* But you and she—"

"Friends. That's all. She's fun. Interesting."

"And her husband didn't mind?" Jenna asked.

"He's in the military, overseas." He held up a hand. "But she sees him on their porch, playing with a little boy, and they don't have kids yet, so—" He shrugged.

For the first time, I really, really, *really* hoped there *was* something to what she could see.

"So are we going to ask for another reading before we leave?" I asked.

"No way," Amber said.

"Uh-uh," Jenna emphasized. "From now on life is a surprise."

"'A box of chocolates,'" Amber quoted. "It's the only way."

On the top deck, a small jazz band—friends of John's—was playing, and the music drifted down to us. It kept everything festive and fun. I was going to miss all this when we left.

I was going to miss Brady most of all.

We danced some, visited with the other volunteers, and said good-bye to the numerous friends we'd made. We all promised to keep in touch, but I didn't know if we would. Maybe at first. But then we'd all get busy. And we'd all just become memories.

That's what was going to happen with Brady.

It was our pact, our understanding, our agreement. We were together only as long as we were in New Orleans. And our time here was ticking away much faster than I wanted it to.

It was getting close to dawn as we stood on the top deck of the riverboat and watched the lights of New Orleans drift past. He'd had his arm around me a good part of the night.

But right now he was leaning forward, his elbows on the railing, his hands clasped, as the riverboat began heading back to the dock.

"So . . . I guess this is it," he finally said. "The end of our arrangement."

"About that . . ."

He turned his head around and met my gaze . . . and waited.

And waited.

While I tried to figure out if I was willing to risk having my heart broken again. Because I'd fallen for him—hard. And it could break—easily. And this time, it would hurt worse than before. So much worse. Hard to imagine, but I knew it was true.

"I was wondering . . . ," I began.

"Yeah?"

"You were really patient with me in the beginning, when I was so guy shy."

He shrugged.

"Did the psychic see more than life is good?"

"Maybe."

"Tell me."

"What does it matter?"

"It doesn't. I'm just curious."

He sighed. "'I see life is good, but I see hurt. You're trying to rebuild something, but don't build too fast or it'll crumble.' So I decided to go slow."

"But you told me you didn't believe in psychic stuff."

"I don't. But when I met you, I thought, why risk it?"

So he'd gone slow, and been patient, and been understanding. Maybe he'd thought he was rebuilding a house.

But he'd rebuilt my heart.

And maybe I'd helped, just a little, to rebuild his.

"I want to keep seeing you," I blurted. "When we get home."

A slow smile eased across his face. "Okay."

That was all he said, but it was everything.

And then he was kissing me. And that was definitely *everything*. I wrapped my arms around his neck and pressed my body against his. It felt so right. It all felt so incredibly right.

Brady drew back, kissed my nose, my chin, my forehead. Then he turned me around, put his arms around my waist, and held me close while we watched the sun easing over the horizon in the distance.

Sara had told me that she didn't see how things would end for us. But the truth was that she *had* seen the ending. It was the very first thing she'd seen when she took my hand.

With Brady kissing my neck, I watched as the last of Saraphina's predictions came true. That morning, the sunrise was indeed . . . spectacular.

It always is, when you're in love.

AUTHOR'S NOTE

In June 2006, I went to New Orleans to sign books at the Romance Writers of America's exhibition booth at the American Library Association Conference. According to numerous newspaper reports, it was the first conference held in New Orleans following the devastation of Katrina. We were welcomed with open arms.

Friday night, my husband and I ate dinner at Bubba Gump's Shrimp Company. We were seated on the second floor. At another table was a large group of teenagers from out of town. They were laughing, cutting up, having a great time—after a long day of helping with the rebuilding efforts. While I didn't talk to them, after they left, our waiter explained who they were and what they were doing.

They served as the inspiration for this story.

—Rachel Hawthorne

Thrill Ride

In memory of Fargo,
who always kept me company when I wrote.
We'll meet again at the rainbow bridge.

CHAPTER 1

Summer job possibilities . . . decisions, decisions

<u>Work at Hart's Diner</u>
<u>Pros:</u> Weekly paycheck, Nick, my new boyfriend, works there;
chance to kiss in the cooler in between serving customers?
<u>Cons:</u> Aching feet, aching jaw from continually smiling to get
better tips, living at home while Mom and older sister, Sarah, go
through the insanity of planning Sarah's summer wedding (They
can't agree on anything! Mom? <u>Hello?!?</u> Sarah is twenty-three,
old enough to plan her own wedding. Note to self: Stay out of it!)

<u>Work at the local movie theater</u>
<u>Pros:</u> Weekly paycheck, watch the latest blockbusters for free, eat

complimentary no-limit-on-the-butter popcorn until I pop.
Cons: Aching feet from standing behind the concession counter, sweeping up spilled popcorn, sticky floors, see less of Nick, live at home while Mom and Sarah . . .

Work at amusement park near lake far, far away
Pros: Weekly paycheck, get on all the rides for free, gone all summer, dorms are available, being totally absent from home while Mom and Sarah . . .
Cons: Share a dorm room with someone I've never met, never seeing Nick, and okay, I have roller coaster issues . . . like, I totally don't get what is so great about the whole queasy-stomach, heart-in-throat, up-and-down, faster, faster, higher, higher experience.

Decision: No brainer. Living with a stranger has got to be better than living with Mom and Sarah while The Wedding is being planned. I don't have to ride the big roller coasters. It's only three months. True love can survive that, can't it?

And that's how I, Megan Holloway, a life-in-the-slow-lane, carousel-ride type of girl, packed up the essentials of my life following my junior year in high school and headed to the Thrill Ride! Amusement Park, vacation destination extraordinaire on Lake Erie.

That afternoon I'd flown into the airport. With my back-pack dangling off one shoulder, I pulled my large wheeled suitcase to the passenger pickup area outside the main terminal. An impossible-to-miss bright red Thrill Ride! shuttle bus was parked nearby, motor running.

So I headed over to it and peered in the door.

"Going my way?" I asked the driver.

He wasn't exactly what I was expecting. White-haired, wrinkled, slightly hunched. Still, he laughed and climbed out of the bus. "You here for the summer?" he asked.

"Yep."

He wore a red shirt, cargo shorts, and his name tag read PETE (SANTA FE, NM).

"You from Santa Fe?" I asked.

"Before I retired. Got tired of playing golf so came up here to work. Being around young people keeps me young."

He took my suitcase and put it in a holding bay at the back of the bus. "Climb aboard," he said.

I settled onto a seat. I heard laughter and two other girls clambered onto the bus.

"Hi!" one said.

"Hiya!" the other chirped.

"Hi." Not exactly an original response, and maybe part of the reason that our conversation didn't last longer.

They sat in front of me and immediately started talking to each other like long-lost friends. Pete returned to the driver's seat, closed the bus door, and headed away from the airport.

I figured the two girls were returning summer employees. Maybe a little older than me. Definitely friends. They were giggling, talking, and screeching periodically.

I looked out the window, trying really hard not to feel ignored and lonely. I *so* did not want to be lonely.

I was already missing Nick. We'd only been dating for three months, and he was totally bummed that I'd applied for a job at the park, and even more bummed that I'd been hired to work there for the entire summer.

"That sucks," he'd said.

Not exactly what I'd wanted to hear when I told him. I wanted him to be ecstatic about my good fortune. I mean, a thousand people had probably applied. I'd had to fill out an extensive application and submit an essay about the reasons that I wanted to work there. And I'd gotten in just under the wire on the minimum age requirement of seventeen. My birthday was yesterday.

So I'd been feeling pretty good about myself when I received the letter telling me that I'd been hired.

After I'd shared my good news with Nick, he'd moped

around most of the evening. I'd shown him a video of the amusement park that my dad had ordered for me. My dad is really into watching the Travel Channel, so he was the one who discovered Thrill Ride! and told me about it. It sounded like it would be an awesome experience.

But Nick was less than impressed with the rides, the park, and all the facilities that the tour guide on the video walked us through. The video was geared toward enticing teens to come work there and making parents feel comfortable sending their kids off into the scary unknown. There were dorm moms and curfews and all kinds of safety features.

"It's just the same as Six Flags," he'd said. "You could have worked there over the summer, commuted from home, and been a lot closer to me."

"It's not the same. It's the thrill ride capital of the world. It's in another state. I want to live away from home. I'll be more independent. On my own. Or pretty much on my own. I mean, I'll live in a park-sponsored dorm, but gosh, Nick, no parents."

I'd tried to talk Nick into applying, so we'd be together, but since he worked at Hart's Diner during the school year, he didn't feel like he could leave for the summer and expect to have a job when he got back. I admired his dedication, and totally understood his reasoning, even if I was a little hurt because it showed lack of dedication to our love.

But I didn't say anything to him about it, because I figured he could argue that my not hanging around showed *my* lack of dedication to our relationship. And while it would be a valid point, since he didn't live in my house, he had only an inkling of how insane it had gotten around there.

So I let the whole dedication-to-our-relationship thing slide.

Besides, I'd be gone only three months, and I was certain our love could sustain a short separation. People did it all the time.

All these thoughts were going through my mind as the shuttle bus took us out of the city and down a lonely road that seemed to lead into the heart of nothingness. But then the theme park became visible—or at least its tallest rides did. The roller coasters and vertical drops and Ferris wheel. Why anyone would want to go up that high was beyond me. It made me dizzy just to think about it.

Beyond all the rides, I could see the lake. The park compound included all the rides, a huge hotel, and bungalows nearby. At the far edge, back a little way from all the tourist accommodations, was the employee dormitory.

The driver pulled to a stop in front of the large brick building. Compared to the hotel it was downright plain, but

I didn't care. I didn't plan to spend that much time there, anyway.

I slung my backpack over my shoulder and disembarked. The two girls followed me off the bus, but then they released an ear-splitting squeal and were loping toward two other girls. More friends from summers past, I guessed. Great. I hoped I wasn't going to be the only one who didn't know anyone here.

I walked around to the back of the shuttle and took my suitcase from the driver. "Thanks," I said.

"Have a great summer," he said, with a smile and a wink. He reminded me a little of my granddad.

"I plan to," I assured him.

I pulled my suitcase along behind me as I headed to the dormitory. I went through the sliding glass doors and saw registration to my right.

I swallowed hard, the excitement mounting. I walked up to the desk and smiled at the girl behind it. Her name tag read MARY (BALTIMORE, MD). They hired students from all over the country, and I figured they felt like where you were from was as important as who you were.

"Welcome," she said, smiling brightly. "Are you here to check in?"

"Yeah," I said. I sounded a little breathless, part of my excitement and nervousness, not knowing what to expect, hoping everything was going to be okay. "I'm Megan Holloway."

She turned to a computer and began typing. Stopped. "Megan Holloway of Dallas, Texas?"

"That's me."

She searched through a drawer, pulled out a blue folder, and handed it to me. "You're assigned to room 654. Orientation begins at eight thirty in the morning. Don't be late. You'll get your picture taken for your employee pass at that time." She winked at me. "I like to warn people because my first year here, I didn't know and I hadn't put on makeup. No retakes on the pictures. Not my best moment."

"I appreciate the warning," I told her, even if I wasn't heavy into makeup. Living in Texas blessed me with a permanent tan, so mascara and a touch of lip gloss were about all I ever used.

"Breakfast starts at six thirty," Mary continued. "A layout of the dorm is in your packet." She reached into another drawer. "And here's your name tag and a key to your room."

She placed a sheet of paper on the counter. "I just need you to sign that you received them."

My hand was actually shaking as I picked up the pen and signed my name. Everything was happening so fast. I couldn't wait to get to my room and calmly look through everything.

Get oriented. Of course, I guess that's what morning orientation was for.

Mary took the sheet from me and dropped it into a wire basket where a stack of pages was already waiting. She gave me another one of her dazzling smiles. "Elevators are down that hallway to your right."

"Thanks."

"If you have any questions, there's an advisor on your floor. First door on your right."

On my right, on my right, on my right. Easy to remember. I had about a thousand questions, but I didn't even know where to begin, so I just nodded. "Thanks, again."

"Anytime." She looked past me. "Next?"

Oh, gosh, I hadn't realized that people were forming a line behind me. I moved away from the desk, giving the four girls and two guys an apologetic smile. I wondered if any were my roommate. Only one of them looked as nervous and apprehensive as I was.

I pulled my suitcase behind me, heading for the elevators. Off to my left, through double doors and plate glass windows, I could see the dormitory cafeteria. That was one of the neat things about working here: a room and food were provided at bargain-basement prices. I would have very little in the way of expenses, so I could save most of my paychecks through the summer and have money to get me through my senior year. I wouldn't have to work my last year of high school and could just enjoy the final months before I graduated.

I got to the elevators and pressed the button, my excitement mounting. And my apprehension. I could have requested a specific person to be my roommate—the only problem was, I didn't know anyone else who was working here.

I thought of getting to know a complete stranger as an adventure. It would be fun. I was sure of it.

The elevator arrived and took me up to the sixth floor. It didn't look that different from any of the hotels I'd ever stayed at. A long narrow hallway, doors on each side. Just as Mary (Baltimore, MD) had told me, the first door on my right had a sign:

FLOOR ADVISOR

ZOE (LONDON, ENGLAND)

How cool was that? I hadn't realized that the theme park was international, but why not? My excitement ratcheted up a notch. I thought about knocking on the door, introducing myself, but I was anxious to get to my room, see what it looked like, meet my roommate—if she was in.

At the end of the hallway I found room 654. Two pictures of Ferris wheels were taped to the door. On one was written MEGAN (DALLAS, TX) and on the other was JORDAN (LOS ANGELES, CA).

I tried to picture what a Jordan might look like, but decided the best way to satisfy my curiosity was to meet her.

I started to knock, then realized it was my room, too. I didn't have to knock. Might as well begin the way that I planned to continue. At least, that was my mom's favorite motto, especially when it came to guys and relationships. Be up front, be honest, be yourself. Basically, be who you were supposed to be.

The problem was that sometimes I wasn't quite sure who I was supposed to be. I mean I know who I am, but I am still trying to define myself, especially as a girlfriend, because every now and then, I do feel a twinge of guilt that I'd chosen working at an amusement park over Nick.

"Don't be silly," Sarah had said. "You're young! You have to explore options. Plenty of time later to put him first." Which, in retrospect, seemed odd advice from someone who was about to make a permanent commitment to a guy.

I slipped the electronic key into the slot, watched the green light come on, turned the knob, opened the door, stared in disbelief . . .

And wondered what in the world I'd gotten myself into.

It was unmistakably obvious that Jordan had moved in already. It was equally obvious that she didn't realize we'd only be here for three months or that she was sharing a room with someone. I gingerly made my way through the quagmire of crap that she'd left in the room: discarded boxes, strewn clothes, inline skates, tennis racket— did she think we were on vacation here?

A single bed was on either side of the room. On the far wall, a desk—one for me, one for my roomie—sat on either side of the window that looked out over the lake. The blinds were raised and I had a spectacular view of the water.

My desk had a phone. Hers had a computer, a television, and an iPod speaker setup. I assumed since the bed on the right was covered in clothes that Jordan had claimed that side of the room. The dresser beside it was cluttered, the accordion door of her closet half open.

Sitting on what I perceived to be my bed, my solitary suitcase and backpack on the floor beside me, I wondered if I should try to find Zoe (London, England) and ask for a room transfer. My roommate was a slob. Not that I was a neat freak or anything—I mean, my mom had to threaten me with withholding my allowance to get me to clean my room—but let's get real here.

At home, the entire room was my domain. Here, we were supposed to learn about living with someone new, giving and taking equally, sharing, respecting the other person's space.

Jordan had three-fourths of the space already.

My impression of her had formed: slob, inconsiderate, disaster—

The phone rang.

I knew it couldn't be for me. I hadn't given anyone the number yet. Besides, I had a cell phone in the front pocket of my backpack that anyone who knew me would use. I thought about letting the phone on the desk go unanswered, but it goes against my nature. There's just something about the ringing of the phone that calls to me to pick it up. Even when I know it isn't going to be for me. So I did what any self-respecting girl would do. I snatched up the receiver.

"Hello?"

"Hey! Is this Jordan's room?"

"No, this is her *roommate*." I don't know what possessed me to toss out a smart comment, but the guy laughed.

"Pretty funny! Is she there?"

"Nope."

"Can I leave a message?"

"Sure."

"Just tell her, 'Cole loves ya.' "

"Okay."

"Thanks."

He hung up. I reached down, grabbed my backpack, set it on my bed, and pulled out my decision-maker. Compared to modern technology, my decision-maker was pretty old-fashioned: a spiral notebook where I list the pros and cons for any major decision, so that I always make wise and informed choices. It's kind of an obsession with me. Sarah is always telling me that I take it to the extreme, but I believe in looking at all the options.

I turned to the last page, jerked out a blank sheet of paper, and wrote, "Cole called." No way was I going to get into delivering really personal messages about love. I folded the paper in half and set it on the edge of her desk, tucking a corner beneath her iPod speakers.

Obviously, my roomie had a boyfriend. I wondered if he was here. I thought about how nice it was that he'd called her, and it made me miss Nick more.

Nick was the absolute best. We had so much in common—went to the same high school, excelled in the same subjects, had the same friends. One night we'd all gone to the movies together. As usual Nick was sitting beside me. And, I don't know. The movie wasn't that good. Okay, it was really pretty terrible. And Nick leaned over and said exactly what I was thinking: We'll never get these hundred and twenty minutes of our lives back. And when I turned to reply, his face was so close to mine . . .

I didn't remember moving toward him, or him moving toward me. But suddenly we were kissing, and we'd been an item ever since. And we were going to remain an item even though we would be far apart. Me, up north on a great lake. Him down south in Texas.

We had e-mail and instant messaging and text messaging and our cell phones—we could manage.

Couldn't we? Sure we could. No sweat.

I was reaching for my cell phone to call him when the phone on the desk rang again. I almost let it ring, but in the end, I didn't have the willpower to deny the siren's call.

"Hello."

Silence. Great.

"Helllloooo?" I repeated.

"Sorry. Are you Jordan's roommate?"

Okay, I was starting to hate my roomie now. Another guy? And this one . . . oh my gosh, he had a voice like Brad Pitt, Orlando Bloom, and Colin Farrell all rolled into one. It just sent a shiver of pleasure through me. Really strange. I never reacted that way to a guy's voice. Not even Nick's. But this one . . . deep, smooth, just a little—

"You still there?" he asked.

I was totally embarrassed. I swallowed, cleared my throat. "Sorry. I got distracted watching the boats on the lake."

Yeah, right, Megan. "Uh, yes, I'm her roommate. She's not here. Did you want to leave a message?"

Even though my roommate was obviously an inconsiderate jerk, I wasn't going to stoop to that level. Sarah would be proud of me. She was always advising me not to get caught up in pettiness. Although I'd learned long ago that what she usually meant was, *don't argue with me.*

"Has anyone ever told you that you have an incredibly sexy voice?"

I held the phone away from my ear and stared at it. Had he said what I thought he had? First of all, my voice is not sexy. It's kind of raspy-sounding. Nick told me once that I sounded like his aunt Carolyn who smoked cigarettes. Hardly flattering.

I knew this guy must be a major player. He was coming on to me and he didn't even know me. What a creep! The fact that I was thinking the same thing about his voice only seconds earlier didn't lessen my irritation with him. What kind of guy calls for one girl and flirts with another?

Jerk!

"Do you want to leave a message?" I asked, impatiently.

"What's your name?"

"My name?"

"Yeah. I bet it's as intriguing as your voice."

"Hardly."

"Let me be the judge. What is it?"

"Is that the message you want to leave for Jordan? That you want to be a judge?"

He laughed. Big mistake to make him laugh because the deep rumble shimmered down to my toes and made them curl. Laughter never made my toes react. This was too totally strange.

"Come on, what's the big secret? Is it something embarrassing maybe? Millicent?"

I rolled my eyes. "No."

"Bambi?"

I ground my teeth together. "No."

"Come on. There's no way it's as bad as my name."

"What's your name?" I asked.

"I thought you'd never ask. Parker."

I scowled. His name wasn't bad at all. Had he tricked me into expressing an interest in him?

"So I can tell her Parker called?"

"Who's going to tell her?"

I swear I heard him smile. I know that's impossible, but it sure sounded like a smile in his voice. I relented.

"Megan."

"I like it."

"My mom would be thrilled to know she has your seal of approval."

He laughed again. It was an infectious laugh. It made me want to laugh with him, but I was so not going to play his game.

"Look, I'm really busy here," I said.

"Watching the boats?"

"Unpacking."

"We could watch them together."

"Do you not listen? I'm unpacking."

"So you just got there?"

"Yeah."

"Met Jordan yet?"

"Not in person, no."

"But you see evidence of her personality?"

"Definitely."

"Let me guess. Clothes everywhere. Looks like a tornado ripped through the room."

"Sorta. Look, I really need to go."

"Gotcha. It was nice to meet you."

"We didn't actually meet."

"Close enough. Just tell Jordan I called."

"I will."

I hung up, grabbed the piece of paper with her previous message, scrawled another name, and set it back in place. I was obviously rooming with Miss Popularity.

Already, I regretted taking my chances with a roommate. Not that I really had any other choice. I didn't know anyone who was working at the amusement park, and even if I had managed to convince Nick to join me, the dorm policies prohibited girls and guys from sharing a room.

The questionnaire I'd completed requesting a room had asked only one question regarding roommate preference: Do you smoke?

So all I really knew about Jordan was that she didn't

smoke, and she was a slob, a guy magnet, and from Los Angeles. Not exactly resounding endorsements.

I walked to the window and looked out onto the lake. I could see the boats that I'd fibbed about watching: sailboats and speed boats. People were spread out on blankets and beach towels on the sand near the water, absorbing the last rays of the late May sun. The next weekend would kick off the summer and the theme park would go into high gear. Right now the park opened late in the morning and closed at seven in the evening. This week was training for the new employees.

The door suddenly sprang open. I whipped around.

And there was my roommate. Had to be. She was way shorter than me, maybe five-five to my five-nine. She had short, cropped hair the color of a midnight sky and sapphire blue eyes.

"Oh, gosh! I'm so sorry!" she exclaimed, moving into the room like a strong wind was pushing her. "I'd planned to get back and get everything cleaned up, but then Ross wanted to go to the lake, and I couldn't find my bathing suit."

And who was Ross? Guy number three?

She dropped two large shopping bags on her bed. "Can you believe that I didn't pack my bathing suit? *Hello?!?* We're on a lake! How dumb was that? Totally. So we had to go to the mall, and wouldn't you know it? They were having a beginning of summer sale, and no way could I buy only a bikini. You know?" She hopped over a box and grinned at me like she'd won something. "I'm Jordan, by the way. In case you didn't figure that out." Her eyes got really big. "Which I'm sure you probably did. Because you look like you're really smart."

I just stared at her. I'd never had anyone talk nonstop for so long. Was she on some sort of drugs? And what did really smart look like?

She laughed. "You're Megan, right?"

"Right."

"Well, it'll only take me about fifteen minutes to get everything picked up." She jerked her thumb toward the door that led into the bathroom and whispered, "Our suitemates are total slobs."

Our room had a bathroom that connected to the room next door. I hadn't even thought to check it out, but I was also totally stunned that she'd think anyone was a slob. My mom told me once that people never see their own faults but will see them in other people. That was certainly true of my roomie.

Although she *had* spoken the truth about cleaning up quickly. It wasn't taking her long at all, mostly because she was just closing up boxes and stacking them in the closet, tossing clothes in drawers. She definitely took the minimalist view on tidy.

"So you're from Dallas, huh? We've been there a couple of times for vacation and stuff, mostly at the airport, passing through, you know? On our way to someplace else. Is this your first time working here?"

I was getting dizzy. "Yep."

She laughed. "Yep? That sounds so Texan. You don't have much of an accent. I thought Texans had slow drawls."

"Depends on which part of Texas you're from." I was anxious to get the conversation turned away from me. "By the way, you got some phone calls while you were out." I pointed at her desk.

"Oh, gosh, I didn't think anyone would ever call me here." Jordan snatched up the sheet of paper and scanned it. "Cole called! That was so sweet of him. Did he say anything special, why he called?"

I shrugged, shook my head. He could tell her when he saw her that he loved her. "Not really."

"Huh. He usually leaves a 'love ya' message, as his signature. I've never figured out why, but that's Cole. Lots of love. How about Parker?" Her voice softened with the mention of his name. "He didn't leave a message either?"

Again I shook my head.

"I'm surprised he called. He hates talking on the phone."

Could have fooled me. The guy was a regular chatterbox.

Jordan picked up the receiver and began pressing numbers. She gave me a wink as she waited.

"Hi! I know! I know!" She bobbed her head from side to side. "I went shopping and I had my cell phone with me, but I'd forgotten to recharge it . . . I know, I know, I'll charge it tonight. Yeah, she seems really nice. So I was worrying for nothing. Just like you said. I'm going to come over later. Okay . . . See you in a bit. Love ya . . . Bye."

Jordan hung up. "Parker . . . he is just so cool. He's worked here two summers already so he knows everything and everyone. I'm going to have him give me some tips for tomorrow."

"Does he live in the dorm?"

"No way! He's nineteen, already had a year away at college, totally out on his own. No way would he live somewhere with a curfew. He's living in a little house on the lake down the way."

I understood why Jordan was a short person. Any energy her body would have needed to expend in growing had been used up talking. She didn't even stop to breathe.

A knock sounded on the door. She bounced over and flung it open. A tall, slender guy with brown hair hanging past his ears was leaning against the doorway.

I could only hope that this wasn't guy number four.

"I'm starved," he said. "We gonna eat or what?" The hint of irritation in his voice didn't match the sparkle in his brown eyes.

I wasn't surprised to see a guy in the doorway. I knew both guys and girls lived in the dorm. Some on the same floors, just not in the same rooms or suites.

Jordan pointed her fingers between us. "This is Ross. Ross, this is my roomie, Megan."

Ah, we were back to guy number three.

Ross gave me a warm smile. "Hi. Newbie?"

"Yeah."

"Me, too." Ross's gaze went back to Jordan. "I'm really hungry."

"Wanna come with us?" Jordan asked me. "They don't serve dinner in the cafeteria on Sunday night."

Decisions . . . decisions . . .

Go to dinner with Jordan and Ross . . . or finish unpacking and call Nick. No-brainer. I really needed and wanted to talk with Nick.

"Thanks, but I need to take care of some stuff here."

"Okay, cool. We'll catch you later." She drew a circle with her finger. "I swear before we go to sleep that I'll have everything put away."

"Not a problem." A little lie, maybe, because I didn't want to spend the summer putting my life at risk in this obstacle course of a room. But I didn't want to start out as a difficult roommate, either.

She and Ross left, and I began putting away my few belongings. I didn't need that many clothes because I knew I'd have a uniform to wear while I was working. As for TV, stereo, etc., I had my own iPod—no speakers—and my laptop and that was about it.

My cell phone rang. With my luck, it would be another boy calling Jordan. Ridiculous thought. So she had boys coming out the wazoo. Big deal. I took my phone out of my backpack, looked at the number, and smiled. My sister. "Hey, Sarah!"

She groaned melodramatically. "Are you ready to come home?"

I laughed. "I just got unpacked. Too late now!"

"So what's it like?"

"I've been here only an hour, but first impressions? It's going to be totally cool." I didn't want to tell her my doubts about my roommate. Otherwise she'd start hounding me to come home. She was almost as thrilled as Nick about my coming here. According to her, I'd abandoned her in her hour of need.

"Mom is driving me absolutely crazy," she said.

"Why do you think I took this job way up here?"

"Chicken! Maybe I'll go up there and move in with you."

"Thought you were going to move in with Bobby."

"Yeah, but not until after we're married, and that's not for several more weeks—if I survive. The latest is that Mom thinks my wedding dress is too daring for church. You've seen it. What do you think?"

The neckline *was* low.

"Do you have to get married in church?"

"You agree with her?"

"The gown is pretty revealing. I mean, it wouldn't be on me, because I don't have that much to reveal, but you are an entirely different story." It was hard to believe we came from the same gene pool. We both had brown eyes but that was about where the similarity ended. I was tall, slender—okay, I'm being generous. I had to run around in the shower to get wet. I really got tired of hearing girls complaining about their excess weight, when no matter what I ate, I stayed thin. And hopelessly flat-chested. I had brown hair, highlighted, that was presently clipped to the back of my head. Sarah was a tad shorter, had blond hair, highlighted, too, and she was one of the people who always complained to me about her weight, but of course she's gorgeous and has amazing curves. Gag, gag, gag.

"Why didn't you say something about the neckline when I was ordering it?" she asked now.

"Number one, you were looking in a three-way mirror, so I figured *you* could see that half your boobs were showing, and number two, because it's your wedding. You should wear what you want."

"You're doing your usual exaggeration thing, right? I mean, half my chest isn't exposed."

"Almost."

"Shoot. I hate for Mom to be right."

I smiled. That was part of the reason that so much yelling was going on at the house right now. Mom and Sarah are both stubborn, convinced that her way is the only way. For

Sarah to even hint that Mom might be right was major.

"So what are you going to do?" I asked.

"Guess I'll see about changing out the gown, except that my one and only sister abandoned me for Canada—"

"I'm not in Canada."

"You might as well be. Just cross the lake and you're there."

"Do you have any idea how big Lake Erie is? It's like looking out on an ocean. You can't see the other shore."

"That's not the point. The point is, how can I go shopping for a gown without you to help me make a selection? You're my maid of honor."

"Take Lena with you."

Lena is her best friend and one of the six bridesmaids.

"I will, but I like having you there, too. Maybe you could fly home for the weekend."

I laughed. "Sarah, I had to sign a blood oath that I would ask for only one weekend off all summer. And I'm taking it to go to your wedding."

"That sucks. You being there sucks. I never thought I'd say this, but I miss you, Megan. What were you thinking when you took a job so far away?"

"I was thinking it would be a lot better than a summer of listening to you and Mom fight all the time."

"We don't fight. We just don't ever agree."

"You fight."

"Okay. We fight. I'll send you a picture of the new gown that I pick out and you can tell me what you think."

"Okay."

"Okay," she said, sadness in her voice. "What's it really like there?"

"I'm not sure yet. Ask me tomorrow."

"Okay. I gotta go. Love ya."

"You, too."

I hung up. I sometimes thought that the reason that Mom and Sarah fought so often was because they were so much alike. Headstrong, determined, bossy. I was more like Dad: laid-back, quiet, didn't let too much bother me. Which was the reason that I'd thought I wouldn't have much trouble adjusting to living with someone I didn't know.

And maybe Jordan wasn't that bad. I mean, she'd realized that she needed to pick up her mess and she'd done it . . . almost. It could work between us.

I went back to unpacking. Like I said. I didn't have that much. My clothes went into the closet or in the dresser beside my bed. My toiletries went into the bathroom. I didn't think our suitemates were slobs, but four girls, two sinks, and one counter did make for a lot of clutter. My laptop went on my desk. I put a few odds and ends on shelves nailed to the wall over my desk and placed my alarm clock on my desk next to the computer so it was near my bed for easy reach.

I looked at my watch. It was already seven. The sun was setting. I thought about calling Nick, but I guess I was being a little stubborn, hoping he'd call me.

This was insane. I grabbed my phone, slipped it into the pocket of my cargo shorts, along with my key, and headed out the door. A few people were in the hallway, and I sorta felt like I was walking a gauntlet.

"Hey!" girls said, as I passed.

The conversations were all the same. Name. Town. State. Laugh. First time? Yes. No. Just the facts, ma'am. And on I walked.

I got to the end of the hallway where the advisor's room was. A girl with spiked black hair was standing in the doorway.

"'Ello!" she said. "And who might you be?"

No doubt. She was Zoe (London, England).

"I'm Megan."

"Meg! It's great to meet you."

"Megan."

"Oh, a purist, eh? I'm Zoe." She pointed to the sign. "Floor advisor. Come to me if you have any problems, luv."

Her accent was delicious.

"I was going to take a walk by the lake."

"Brilliant! It's lovely out. Just don't forget about the curfew. One o'clock and we lock everything up."

I laughed. "No way will I be out until one."

"Don't be so sure; it gets addictive. Especially when a hottie catches your fancy."

She was probably only a couple of years older than I was. I thought I could have been content to spend all night talking with her, but I did want to take that walk, so I headed out.

Down the elevator, through the lobby, out the front door. I walked along the sidewalk that went around the building until it ended at the sand. I kicked off my sandals and walked toward the water. I touched the water's edge with the tips of my toes. It was freezing!

And Jordan had gone out to buy a bathing suit? My roomie was a crazy girl.

I sat down on the sand, drew my legs up to my chest, and wrapped my arms around my knees. I hadn't expected to be homesick after just one day. I was sorta wishing Sarah hadn't called. Who would have thought that I'd miss her squabbling with Mom?

I took my cell phone out of my pocket and willed it to ring. Now I was being as stubborn as my sister, but I guess the truth was, Nick had hurt my feelings a little bit. I mean, here I was going on an adventure, and he didn't want to share it with me.

Not the actual coming here. I really did get why he couldn't just pack up and leave his job. But when I'd gone shopping for the things I'd need, like new clothes, he had no interest in going with me. When I researched on the Internet to figure out how inconvenient it would be not to have a car, he didn't care about my findings. It was like Thrill Ride! or anything to do with it was totally off-limits, as far as a topic of conversation.

Surly. That's how he'd get. I'd read the word in novels, but had never actually seen anyone who was surly. Nick had been.

"This sucks big time," he'd said last night.

We were sitting in his car in my driveway. He'd taken me to dinner at Outback to celebrate my birthday.

"Let's not say good-bye tonight," I said. "Take me to the airport in the morning."

"Why? It's just putting off the inevitable."

"But it's more romantic at an airport."

"I don't see how. I wouldn't be able to go to the gate with you because of all the security stuff. We'd have to say good-bye outside the metal detectors. What's romantic about that?"

I'd sighed. "Well, then, I guess we'll say good-bye now."

"Yeah." He'd put his arm around me, drew me up against his side. "I'm sorry, Megan. It's just that I had plans for this summer, plans that included you and me, getting really close." He touched his forehead to mine. "You know?"

And I did know. He'd been pushing for us to take our relationship to the next level, but I wasn't ready yet. I mean I loved him, I was sure I did, but right now I was happy just kissing and snuggling.

I angled my face for easier access and kissed him. His arms tightened around me.

"God, I'm going to miss you, Megan. I don't know how I'll survive."

That's what a girl wanted to hear. Deep devotion. But it was only three months, and not all at once. I'd be back halfway through the summer for the wedding. And didn't absence make the heart grow fonder?

Then Nick was seriously kissing me, hard, our teeth clicking, like he thought he could save our kisses or something. I pulled back. "Nick! Don't be so . . . eager."

"Most girls would like to be wanted as much as I want you."

"But you were bruising my lips."

"Sorry. Do you have to go?"

"You know I do. I gave them my word."

And that's when he started to sulk. It suddenly got really cold in the car, a drop in temperature that had nothing to do with the air surrounding us, and it frightened me a little to think that I might lose him, but it also frightened me to think that I was making my decisions based on what was best for Nick, rather than what was best for me.

"Look, I'm not begging you to leave Hart's," I said. "I understand that you have a commitment there. Well, now I have a commitment."

"Thought you were committed to me."

I groaned. "Nick, it's only for the summer."

"You don't even act like you're going to miss me."

"Of course I'm going to miss you."

I was already missing him. It was like he'd gone away from the moment I'd first told him about my summer plans.

Maybe that's the reason I was now sitting on the shores of Lake Erie feeling lonely. We hadn't kissed good-bye. We'd barely *said* good-bye.

This was supposed to be a fun, exciting excursion. I didn't want to feel guilty about being here.

Bad news. I did.

On the way back to my room, I stopped off at the vending machines and bought some peanut-butter crackers and a Mountain Dew, my favorite snack.

But my first night away from home, out on my own, and this was how I celebrate? Vending machine?

At least it was cheap, leaving me lots of money for another night. By the time I got to my room, it was almost nine o'clock. I didn't realize that I'd sat by the lake for so long. Jordan was back, the room was tidied up, but it was no less crowded. We had guests.

"Roomie!" Jordan exclaimed as soon as I walked in. "Meet our suitemates: Alisha, Washington, D.C., and Lisa, Toronto, Ontario. Is it not totally cool that everyone is a name and a place? It's awesome to think of all the different people we'll meet. The places they'll come from. Totally wild experiences."

Alisha had short, black hair, dark eyes, and a milk-chocolate complexion. She was Halle Berry gorgeous. Lisa had curly red hair, an abundance of freckles, and an impish smile. Not to be mean, but she reminded me of a leprechaun.

"I was just telling them that they could use my fridge in the bathroom," Jordan said.

"You have a fridge?" I asked.

"Well, yeah! This is like dorm life, you know. Before I left home, Parker told me everything I'd need. I've got a micro-wave, too."

She patted the microwave sitting on her dresser. When had she moved in the appliances? I had a feeling that my roommate was going to be a constant source of surprises.

"We're all newbies," Jordan said. "None of us have ever worked here before."

"Which I think puts us on the take-what-you-get list as far as positions at the park goes," Alisha said.

"Hey, everyone, let's sit down, let's talk," Jordan said. She promptly dropped to the floor.

The dorm rooms had no chairs other than the straight-backed ones at the desks. Hardly comfortable. The rest of us sat on the rug with Jordan.

"Okay, so," she said with excitement, like someone who was in charge of a field trip, "what did everyone request as a job?"

"Rides," Lisa and I said at the same time. Then we smiled at each other. The choices were rides, concession, entertainment, mascot, gift shop.

"I put it in for mascot. Since I'm a cheerleader, I figured it was a natural spot for me," Jordan said. "What about you, Alisha?"

I was so not surprised to discover that Jordan was a cheerleader. Probably head cheerleader at that.

"Entertainment."

"Totally cool! What do you do?"

Alisha looked slightly embarrassed. "A little dancing, singing. I actually want to be an actress."

"Awesome!" Jordan said.

"You'll have to try out, won't you?" I asked.

"Yeah. I actually have an audition tomorrow afternoon after orientation."

"You'll get a spot on the stage," Jordan said, complete confidence in her voice.

"How do you know?" Alisha asked, not sounding quite as confident.

"Positive thinking. Works every time. It's all about the vibes you put out there. Just go in there tomorrow thinking, 'This spot is mine.' You'll get it guaranteed. I'm certain that I'm going to get to be Thumbelina."

Thrill Ride! had all kinds of fairy-tale characters in costume, wandering around throughout the park to entertain kids.

My stomach rumbled. The three girls looked at me, and I held up my crackers and drink. "Dinner."

"You're kidding," Jordan said. "You gave up dinner with me for that?"

I shrugged. "I ended up walking along the beach until it got dark. And since I don't have a car—"

"I do. Want me to take you somewhere?" Jordan asked.

I was grateful for her offer, but it really seemed like an imposition. "No, but thanks. I'm fine tonight."

"The hotel actually has this little mini mall, food court area," Alisha said. "Lisa and I had pizza over there tonight."

"It was pretty good," Lisa said. "They're open until eleven."

"Then let's go!" Jordan said.

Alisha laughed. "You have way too much energy, girl."

"Really, guys, thanks," I interjected. "But y'all have eaten and I'm tired. Think I'm just going to have a few crackers, give my boyfriend a call—"

"You have a boyfriend?" Alisha asked.

I felt myself blushing. "Yeah."

"Does he work here?"

"No, he has a job back home, so he couldn't come."

"Bummer."

"Yeah."

Boy, was I a conversational genius tonight or what? I just couldn't seem to get over this bout of self-consciousness I was feeling, or maybe I was simply subconsciously really upset that Nick hadn't bothered to call.

No subconsciousness about it. I was bothered.

There was still a lot of excitement in the air as our suitemates said goodnight and exited through the bathroom into their room.

"Aren't they great?" Jordan asked, but it was more an exclamation than a real question.

"Yeah." There I was, Miss-Stuck-on-One-Word.

"This is going to be the absolute best summer ever," she said.

"Absolutely." Finally, I seemed to have moved beyond my stuck word.

"So what's your boyfriend like?" Jordan asked.

"He's wonderful, he's . . ." How to describe him?

"It must have been hard to leave him."

"Definitely." My vocabulary was increasing. I lifted my phone. "I'm going to call him now."

"Oh, sure! Sorry, didn't mean to keep you from it. I'm going to get ready for bed." She gathered up her clothes and disappeared into the bathroom.

I sat on my bed and stared at my phone. We were in the same time zone. It was almost ten now. Not too late to call.

My phone rang and I nearly dropped it. My chest tightened with joy. Nick!

"Hello?"

"Hey, Megan."

"I was just about to call you."

"Really?" He sounded relieved, like maybe he was as insecure with how we'd left things last night as I was.

I settled back against my pillow, smiling. "Yeah."

"I'm sorry about last night. I'm not going to see you for almost two months, and I didn't even give you a proper kiss. I'm a total jerk."

My heart just melted. Nothing like an apology to make everything all right with the world.

"I could use a kiss right about now," I said.

He made smacking noises, and I started laughing. When he stopped, I said, "Thanks, Nick. I needed to know you weren't still mad at me."

"I actually went to the airport this morning, to say goodbye."

"You did?" My heart was expanding.

"Yeah, but since we're not related, security wouldn't let me through to the gate."

"I'm sorry."

"No biggie. I'll be waiting at baggage claim when you get back for the wedding."

"Oh, Nick." I felt tears sting my eyes. I could turn into a puddle of emotion so easily. It really didn't take much.

"Don't suppose you'll come back tomorrow?" he asked.

"I can't, Nick."

"All right. Love ya, Megan."

"Love you, too."

He made a few more kissing sounds; so did I. Then we hung up. I held my cell phone close against my chest, like it would bring me nearer to Nick. It was going to be all right, being away from him for a while. People survived long-distance relationships all the time.

Jordan came out of the bathroom. "How'd it go?" she asked.

I smiled. "Good. He misses me."

"Sounds like a perfect boyfriend."

She would know. At last count, I think she had at least three. Or maybe they were just boys who were friends. It happened.

I changed into my sleeping boxers and tank and crawled into bed. Jordan turned off the light.

Then I just lay there in the dark, in a room that wasn't my bedroom with someone who I'd only met a few hours before. It was kinda strange, and I wondered if I'd even be able to sleep with a stranger in the room.

"Are you scared, Megan?" she asked, suddenly.

"Of what?"

"I don't know. Just being out on your own."

"Yeah, a little, but I figure next year after I graduate and go off to college I'll be on my own for real."

"You're a senior?"

"Yep."

"Me, too. So what made you decide to come here?" she asked.

"Honestly?"

"Yeah."

"My sister, Sarah, is getting married July fifteenth, and it was driving me crazy to be around while she and my mom planned the wedding."

"Really?" I heard a tinge of excitement in her voice. "Like what were they doing?"

"Well, for starters, Sarah wanted to be married in a park, Mom wanted her married indoors. Mom won, since in July it's hot beyond belief in Texas."

"That's what I've heard."

"Then they were arguing about how big to make the wedding party, what color the bridesmaids' dresses should be—Sarah wanted black."

"What's wrong with black?"

"Mom says it's taboo for a wedding."

"I see people in black at weddings all the time."

"Apparently my mom hasn't. That one had them yelling. Mom said she wasn't paying for a funeral. They argue about everything. They can't agree on the simplest of things. I'm definitely eloping."

"Me, too, I'm going to Vegas and getting married by Elvis."

I laughed. "Are you really?"

"Either that or never getting married."

"I don't know that I could take my marriage vows seriously if they were overseen by Elvis, but I definitely want small and away from home."

"They marry people here."

I stared into the darkness. "I didn't know that."

"Yeah. They have this little park with a bridge. It's kinda neat." She yawned. "Probably see it tomorrow when they take us on a tour of the place. Parker says he's getting married on a roller coaster. He is so crazy."

"Sounds like."

"This is his third summer here, so he's already working. He actually oversees Magnum Force. That's the tallest, fastest roller coaster. He has to ride it every morning before the park opens. I'm going to go ride it with him in the morning. Want to come?"

Ride Magnum Force? I don't think so.

"Uh, thanks, but we have orientation."

"We're going to ride at six, so we'll be back in plenty of time."

"I can't do rides on an empty stomach. Besides, I have some things I have to take care of in the morning."

"Okay. Whatever." She yawned again. "'Night."

"'Night."

I heard her bed creak as she rolled over. I should have been tired. It was late and I'd left home early that morning. But my mind was reeling with the possibilities. I really hoped that I didn't get assigned to one of the roller coasters. There were like fifteen or so. It had never occurred to me that I'd have to actually get on the ride where I worked.

Geez. That would be disastrous because I absolutely, no way, could get on a roller coaster.

Only 55 Nick-less days to go, and counting. . . .

As it turned out, I could have slept without worries. As a matter of fact, I might have even welcomed riding a roller coaster.

I was assigned to the Hansel and Gretel gift shop, otherwise known as H & G, or as I was beginning to think of it: hell and god-awful. Because, of course, since this was a *theme* park—theme being the operative word here—I was scheduled to show up in wardrobe for sizing at two o'clock. And I didn't have to ask what my costume would be.

"At least the gift shop is air conditioned," Jordan said, swirling her French fry around in a glob of ketchup. "I mean, I'm going to be standing out in the hot sun all day saying, 'Please exit to your right. Watch your step.' Can you believe they gave me a script for this?"

They'd given everyone a script of things to say and not say. Rules and regulations to follow. We'd been given a mission statement, a purpose, and a rousing pep talk.

Then we'd walked through the entire park, while its history was revealed to us by a very energetic guy named Bill (Waterloo, Ontario).

The most fascinating of all the rides to me were the carousels: original pipe organs, original wooden horses—restored by artisans. They actually had three carousels in the park, and I wished that I'd been given one of them as my assignment. Those who took care of the rides wore cargo shorts, red shirts, white socks, tennis shoes, and red baseball caps. They could wear their hair however they wanted. Me? I was going to have to wear braids on each side of my head. I was seriously contemplating a major haircut.

Throughout the tour, Ross had stuck to Jordan like paper to glue, but not in an overtly romantic way. They realized that they were at work and not on a date, but still it made me miss Nick all the more to see them together.

The park was open but hardly crowded, since the "season" hadn't officially started.

When the tour was over, we broke for lunch. Now the

three of us were sitting at a table in the food court area of the theme park.

"So what are we going to do this afternoon?" Ross asked.

"Wanna go sailing?" Jordan asked.

He grinned. "Sure."

Jordan looked at me. "Wanna come with us?"

"You have a boat?" I asked.

She laughed lightly. "No. Down the lake a ways they have rentals."

"I'd love to but I need to go to costume."

"Oh, right. Gretel. Wonder how long it'll take."

I shook my head. "No idea, but since everyone is getting fitted this afternoon"—I wrinkled my nose—"you probably shouldn't wait on me."

"Okay, but let me give you my cell phone number in case they cut you loose quickly. We can always come back for you."

That was so nice. As we exchanged numbers, I was thinking that maybe things were going to work out with my new roomie after all.

I stood in front of the mirror in costume, fighting back my strong urge to yodel. My costume had a white blouse with short puffy sleeves, a short black skirt with a bib that came up the front and straps that went over the shoulders and crossed in the back, and a petticoat. Oh, yeah. And white knee socks and black shoes.

"The only thing that could be worse than this is to be Hansel," said Patti (Weed, CA). She was tall like me, but not as slender. Healthy, my grandmother would have called her.

I bit back my laughter. "I don't know. This is pretty bad."

"Do you think we got this gig because we have long hair? I mean, give me a break. Tomorrow we have to braid it." Her hair was long, blonde, and wavy.

"I'm thinking of buzzing mine tonight," I confessed.

She laughed. "I always thought of Gretel as being petite. We're both pretty tall."

"I think you're right—it's the hair."

"At least we'll be in air-conditioning."

"That's what my roommate says."

"What did she get assigned?" Patti asked.

"One of the kiddie coasters."

"Lucky girl."

Although I wasn't sure how lucky it really was. I mean, dealing with tired kids on a hot day? Ross would be working at Jet Scream, a ride that went straight up and spiraled down, and had a puke factor of ten. They even had a special cleanup crew for any "incident," as our tour guide had so politely referred to it.

Working inside a gingerbread-designed gift shop was sounding better all the time. And, at least, back home I would never run into anyone who saw me this summer, so the embarrassment factor was lowered.

After Patti and I changed back into our regular clothes, we took our costumes to a window. A middle-aged woman named Jeannie (no city, no state) was working behind it. She took our costumes, scanned the bar codes that were located on tags inside them, then swiped our park ID badges through the machine.

"All righty. You'll pick these up in the morning before work, change in the locker room, then drop them off after work so they can be washed for the next day," she said briskly.

"Wouldn't it be better if we took them with us and just washed them ourselves?" Patti asked.

"Weren't you paying attention during orientation, honey?" Jeannie asked. "Everything is computerized. I'll swipe your badge in the morning, and I'll know exactly where your costume is on the rack. Runs like clockwork."

"Sounds great," I said, not at all disappointed that I didn't have to wash clothes every night.

"What now?" Patti asked me as we turned away from the window.

"I don't know." I thought about joining Jordan for the sailboat ride, but I didn't feel like being a third wheel.

I ended up spending the afternoon lounging out by the pool. Nothing too exciting. I could hear the rumble of the roller coaster nearest the dorm. Magnum Force. It was a steel roller coaster, so it didn't have all that clacking noise, but still it sounded fast. And of course, I could hear people scream.

I just so didn't get that.

When I got back to the room, a note from Jordan was resting on my computer.

Dear Gretel:

Ha! Ha! Very funny, I thought.

Sorry we didn't connect.

I'm going to have dinner at Parker's.

Be back late! Don't wait up!

Your Roomie, Roller Coaster Gal

That was interesting. Dinner with Parker after spending the day with Ross. I thought Ross was her boyfriend; maybe Parker was just a friend. Not that it was any of my business.

I was in the shower when the bathroom door burst open.

"I got it!" Alisha cried.

"Got what?" I called back.

"A part in the stage production! Hurry up! Lisa and I are going out to celebrate, and you have to come with us!"

We ended up at the food court, each celebrating in our own way: me with a burger, Alisha with a chef salad, and Lisa with pizza. When you're working a summer job, celebrations are as inexpensive as you can make them.

"So what exactly will you do?" I asked.

"I'm not sure. They'll start teaching us the routines tomorrow. Basically, we come out on stage and sing and dance. You'll have to come watch a performance sometime."

"You must be really talented," Lisa said.

Alisha shook her head. "I don't think so. I think everyone else was just really bad. Some people just don't have a clue about how hard it is to perform."

"How long have you been dancing?" I asked.

"Since I was four."

"Wow! That's a long time."

"I really want to go to Hollywood someday. You have to commit early. So what job did you get?"

I stuck a French fry into ketchup, swirled it around. "I'm working in the gift shop."

"Oh, no," Lisa said. "Which gift shop?"

"Pick the worst one."

"Hansel and Gretel's?"

"Yep." I shook my head. "I got my costume today. How about you?"

"Carousel ride."

I was jealous. "That's my favorite."

"I figure after an hour of listening to that music, it won't be mine."

"Want to switch positions?"

She laughed. "No, Gretel."

Gosh, was that going to become my nickname? If so, I was already tired of it.

After dinner, we went back to our rooms. Jordan wasn't back yet. I watched a little TV, thanks to the fact that she'd brought one. Checked my e-mail. Read the joke about rednecks that Nick had forwarded to me. Sent a reply, "Ha-ha! Miss you." Then wrote a letter to Sarah about my day. Tried not to be disappointed that no one was online to flash me an IM.

I sat in my desk chair, looked out the window over the lake, and watched the way the moonlight sparkled over the water.

So tomorrow I'd pick up my costume and report to the Hansel and Gretel gift shop inside Storybook Land. It was a good thing I had a boyfriend, because the only hotties I'd be seeing were overdressed tourists who were literally hot and sweating. I might work with a Hansel, but his costume would be as bad as mine, and would definitely ruin any to-die-for factor that might have been evident before said costume was put on. We'd be surrounded by munchkins and their parents. No young cute guy tourists would ever show their faces at H & G's. Come to think of it, no girls my age would show up, either.

I told myself that it didn't matter. I was there to work, after all. But part of the appeal of coming here was the opportunity to experience new things, meet new people. And just as I was feeling really sorry for myself, I realized that I'd met a lot of new people already. So I was being silly.

The phone rang. Had to be for Jordan, but since she wasn't here . . . let it ring.

But I was too weak. I picked up on the third ring.

"Hello."

"Hey, Meg."

Parker. Gosh, I didn't like the way he sounded. Like there were secrets shared between us.

"Megan," I corrected him.

"No, that voice doesn't go with a Megan."

The nerve of this guy. He didn't even know me and here he was . . . I couldn't deny that I was flattered.

"Jordan's not here."

"I know. She's on her way back."

"Then why did you call?"

"Your voice. It's been haunting me. What do you look like?"

"Listen, I have a boyfriend."

"Does he work at the park?"

"No."

"Where are you from?" he asked.

I stared harder out the window. Why was I answering this guy?

"Dallas."

"He's there. You're here. That has to be hard."

"Are you offering to fill in for him?"

He laughed, that deep rumble that shimmied through me. "If I were that obvious, I think you'd lose all respect for me."

"You've made the mistaken assumption that I had any respect for you to begin with."

He laughed again. Then he quieted suddenly, and all I could hear was the pounding of my heart.

"Dark hair," he said quietly.

"What?"

"You have dark hair."

"What does it matter?"

"Your voice sounds exotic."

"Well, I'm not. I'll tell Jordan you called."

"No, don't tell her. Like I said, I called to talk to you."

There was a strange shift in his voice that I couldn't quite identify.

"You don't want her to know you called me?"

"Let's just say that it would be better if she didn't know."

"I hear the key going into the lock."

"Then that's my cue to hang up. Sweet dreams."

And as quickly as a heartbeat he was gone.

I dropped the phone in the cradle just as Jordan walked into the room. My hands were shaking, and I didn't know why. I hadn't done anything wrong, but I felt like I was betraying my roommate and my boyfriend. How dumb was that?

"How was dinner?" I asked.

"Great. I love Parker so much. He's the best."

She loved Parker? I thought she loved Ross. Maybe she could love more than one guy at a time.

"He called." I couldn't stop myself from saying it. I didn't owe the guy anything and if she loved him but he was flirting with me . . . but then she had Ross . . .

"Parker?"

"Yeah."

"I wonder why he didn't call on my cell. I recharged it." She pulled her cell out of her pocket and for some reason I panicked.

"He just wanted to know if you got home safe. As soon as I heard your key in the door and told him you were here, he hung up."

She closed her phone. "Crazy guy. He worries about me so much. Overprotective. That's what he is. I'm going to take a shower and go to bed. Tomorrow is going to be a long day."

I was beginning to feel like it was going to be a long summer.

Only 54 Nick-less days to go, and counting. . . .

"Remember: The customer is always right. No matter how old, how small, how grumpy."

Nancy (St. Augustine, FL) pressed the tips of her fingers against her cheeks, and twisted until her lips curled up. "And we always smile. It's hard to get upset with someone who's smiling at you."

Nancy managed H & G's. She had red hair, braided on either side of her head. Not even managers were exempt from the tortures of the theme park. And here in Storybook Land, we were all in costume. We actually had one Hansel in the store, and I decided it was way worse for a guy to be Hansel than for a girl to be Gretel. He had to be on someone's hate-this-guy list.

I cast a glance over at Patti. She rolled her eyes. I so agreed with that assessment of our situation.

"Follow me and I'll show you how to work the register," Nancy said.

Pointing a scan gun didn't require a lot of skill. Neither did making change or bagging souvenirs. This was going to be an easy gig and no doubt boring as all get out. Patti and I spent the morning doing imaginary sales, then voiding them; practiced making change; and learned to run credit cards.

Around one o'clock, Nancy cut us loose. Patti and I changed out of our costumes, dropped them off, and started walking back to the dorm.

"Hey, since we only have a couple more days before things get crazy and we're working full shifts, you want to spend this afternoon with me on the rides?"

I grimaced. "I'm not really into thrill rides."

She stared at me. "You're kidding. Why are you working here, then?"

"Because I wanted to get away from home."

"But the whole point in being here is that you can ride the rides for free."

I shook my head. "I like the antique cars. And the carousel."

"Oh my God, I've heard of people like you."

"People like me?"

"Yeah, people who are irrationally afraid—"

"I'm not irrationally afraid. I just don't enjoy doing it."

"They have a guy, some famous psychiatrist who comes here every Wednesday and helps people get over their roller coaster phobias. You should sign up for a session."

"Why? I have no desire whatsoever to ride one, so why bother learning to do it?"

"Because you're afraid and you need to conquer your fear."

"I'm not afraid." Afraid was too tame a word for what I felt at the thought of even getting on a roller coaster. I'd ridden one once, with my dad. I'd buried my face against his arm and screamed during the entire ride. I was twelve. Hadn't been on one since.

I didn't like the heart-in-my-throat feeling, the sensation of plummeting. And I absolutely hated the cranking sound as the car went up the incline.

"Then go riding with me," Patti said.

We stepped out of the building into the sunshine.

"I can't. I really have a lot of stuff that I need to do."

"Like what?"

"I need to call my boyfriend before his shift starts tonight."

She narrowed her eyes. "Yeah, right. Well, I'm going to go ride Magnum Force. The guy who manages the controls there is totally hot."

I smiled. "So it's not that you're a roller coaster fanatic. It's that you're hoping to hook up with someone."

"You know it. Later, girlfriend!"

I watched her walk away. I guess it did seem a little insane for someone who didn't like thrill rides to work at a place known for them.

I was going to head to the dorm, but then changed my mind. I would do a ride after all.

I went to the carousel. I don't know what it is about carousels. I love the old-time feel of them. The mirrors, the gold, the glitter. The music. And I always ride on a horse that goes up and down. Of course, I was probably the oldest one on the carousel that afternoon, but what the heck. I could live dangerously every now and then.

I actually stayed in the park until it closed, which for two more days would be seven in the evening. When I got back to the room, Jordan was dressed to kill in low-rider jeans, spike-heeled boots, and a clinging spaghetti-strap tank top that revealed her belly button ring. Her hair was spiked out in all directions.

"Hot date?" I asked.

She slapped her forehead. "I am such a dunce. I forgot to tell you. Parker is having a party tonight. Wanna come?"

"No, thanks."

"Why not?"

I thought about the phone call last night. The fact that he spent time with her, she loved him, then he called me . . .

"I'm exhausted. I spent the afternoon on the rides."

"Oh!" She squealed. "Did you ride Magnum Force?"

I don't know what possessed me not to confess that my rides had been the three different carousels, the taxis, and the teacups. "You bet."

"Isn't it awesome?"

"Totally."

"Did you ride in the first car?"

"No." Don't know why I chose at that moment not to lie.

"Oh, you have got to ride in the front. It is a totally different experience. No one to block your view as you're hurtling along the rails."

"I've got all summer. No sense in doing everything at once."

"That's true. Sure you don't want to come with me tonight?"

"I'm sure."

"His roomie is twenty-one. There will be booze."

"I'm not twenty-one."

"So? He doesn't card, you know."

"I have to be at costume at eight in the morning."

"So?"

"Thanks so much, Jordan, but I just can't."

"All right. Don't wait up."

She slung her purse over her shoulder and was gone.

I sat on my bed. Another exciting night.

It actually turned out not to be too bad. Zoe, our floor monitor, knocked on my door about eight.

"You the only one left on the floor?" she asked.

"I guess so. I haven't seen my suitemates, and my roomie went to a party."

"Brilliant! Come on down and join me, then. I just called for a pizza, and they delivered a large instead of a small."

Her room was awesome. Painted pink instead of white like ours. She had posters of England on the walls: Stonehenge, a guard standing outside Buckingham Palace.

"How did you end up here?" I asked, just before I bit into the mushroom pizza.

"Came on holiday with my parents a couple of years ago. Loved it! So I came back the next summer. Worked the rides. The summer after that I worked tickets. This year I'm bossing people around."

"You mean on the floor."

"No, luvie. I oversee some of the ride crews. I'm the hall monitor, so they don't take anything out of my paycheck for staying in the dorm. And I might as well be, I'm here anyway. So how are you liking your position?"

"You mean as Gretel?"

"Oh, God." She looked like she might hurl her pizza. "You're a Gretel?"

I nodded.

"So sorry, Megan."

I smiled. "It's not that bad."

"It's bloody awful is what it is. Little ones crying 'cuz they can't have a toy. It's my least favorite place."

"Thanks a lot. At least it's air-conditioned."

"It is that."

She'd left her door open, so as girls returned for the night, they stopped by. She had lots of warnings for everyone—don't look for a summer love, keep cool with the guys, don't end the summer with a broken heart.

By the time I left her room, I didn't know if I was glad or not that I'd come here for the summer.

The phone woke me. Not the soft ring of my cell, but the clanging of the dorm phone. I groaned, buried my head under the pillow, then decided that since it was after one it could be Jordan calling with an emergency.

Groggily, I scrambled for the phone. "Hello?"

"Hey, Roomie!"

She sounded totally wasted.

"Jordan?"

"Listen, I missed curfew so I'm going to sleep in Parker's bed tonight."

More information than I needed to know.

"Whatever."

"I just didn't want you worrying."

But I was worried a little. I mean what if he'd deliberately gotten her drunk to take advantage of her?

"Jordan, be careful, okay?"

"Always." She giggled. "I'll see . . . oh, wait. Parker wants to talk to you."

"Why me? Jordan, no—"

"Hey."

Okay, I *so* did not like the way that his voice sent pleasant chills through me, and I was a little angry that he had flirted with me last night. Angry for Jordan, not about me. I had a boyfriend, and I wasn't interested in Parker, but he needed to treat my roomie better.

"Did you get her drunk?" I asked pointedly.

"No, she did that all on her own. She said she invited you to come to the party. So why didn't you come?"

His voice was lazy, sultry, and quiet. I could hear people

and music in the background. Why hadn't I wanted to go to a party? Why had I chosen to spend the night eating pizza in the dorm? Because just this guy's voice had me thinking things that I shouldn't be thinking. I thought about his stupid voice more than I thought about Nick.

"I'm not into the party scene." What a lie. As a rule, I loved parties, but how could I have fun at a party when my boyfriend was hundreds of miles away? It seemed like cheating or something.

"It's not a wild party—"

"Jordan sounded pretty wild."

"Jordan is always wild. She's all about having fun."

"So I gathered."

"What about you, Megan? You like to have fun?"

"Well, duh? Yeah!"

"So why didn't you come to the party?"

"I already answered that."

"Except that you lied."

I stuck out my tongue, even though no one could see.

"Look, I need to go," I said.

"Why do I get the impression you don't like me?"

"I don't know you well enough not to like you," I said. "But shouldn't you be spending time with the people who are there?"

"Yeah, probably. The next time I have a party, you should come, okay?"

"I'll think about it."

"But you won't come, will you?"

"Probably not."

"Why?"

Because his voice intrigued me and that was oh so dangerous.

"Because I have a boyfriend."

"So? We could be just friends."

"Yeah, right. That's why you keep calling to talk to me. Because you want to be *friends*. How do you think Jordan would feel about that?"

He released a low groan. "Yeah, that could get awkward."

"That's what I thought. 'Night, Parker."

I hung up before he could say anything else. I was rooming with the good-time gal.

It took me a long time to go back to sleep. And when I did, I dreamed about Nick. Only whenever he talked, he sounded like Parker.

Only 53 Nick-less days to go, and counting. . . .

"Okay, so tomorrow is the big day, right?" Patti asked after we'd changed out of our costumes and were heading out of the building.

"That's what they say."

We stepped out into the bright sunshine.

"You sure wouldn't know it by our boring day. I hope we have more customers tomorrow."

All during our shift at H & G's, we'd stood within the circle of the counter with four cash registers, only one being used. She'd rung people up, I'd bagged the items. Totally boring.

"You should watch what you wish for," I told her.

"I'm wishing for something to make the time go faster.

Don't suppose you've overcome your roller coaster phobia."

"It's not a phobia."

"So today you'll ride with me?"

"No, today I'm going to sit out by the pool, enjoy the sunshine."

"All right, then, I'll see you tomorrow."

She walked off, and I headed toward the entrance. It was actually starting to get a little more crowded along the midway. It was Friday and people were coming in early for the weekend. The park would actually stay open until ten o'clock tonight, midnight tomorrow. Tomorrow I would start working the late shift, so I could sleep in, which was great because I am not a morning person.

I edged around a little kid who was running to get somewhere, his mother chasing after him, and knocked up against a guy.

"Oh, sorry," I said, embarrassed but continuing on.

Someone grabbed my arm and spun me around. I found myself staring into gorgeous green eyes, sparkling eyes, amused eyes.

"Megan?"

I swallowed hard, almost shook my head no, mostly because I couldn't believe who I might be staring at. "Parker?"

He slowly grinned. "Yeah. I recognized your voice."

"I recognized yours, too."

He had black hair, cut pretty short. I imagined that working on the roller coasters, he'd want to be as cool as possible. He was wearing jeans, a black T-shirt, and a yellow Livestrong bracelet.

"I got your hair wrong," he said.

I found myself self-consciously touching it. After I'd changed out of my costume, I'd unraveled my braids, brushed my hair, pulled it back, and used a clip to hold it in place off my shoulders. No way was I going to walk around off-duty looking like Gretel.

"I pegged you for a brunette," he continued. "But it's a golden brown. It suits you. The eyes, though, brown and mysterious, I got those right. So are you done with your shift?"

I nodded. "Yeah, heading back to the dorm."

"Me, too." He shook his head, his grin growing. "Finished with my shift, not heading to the dorm. Want to go get some Dippin' Dots?"

"Look—"

"I know you've got a boyfriend, but I don't know that many people around here—"

"Hey, Parker!" a guy called out as he strode by.

"Hey, Matt!" Parker cleared his throat. "Okay, I know a few people, but I believe people are experiences that we need to experience. So come on, what's ten minutes of your time?"

What was ten minutes of my time when I thought my roommate had slept with him, and he seemed to be flirting with me?

Decisions . . . decisions.

Say no and remain mysterious, have him keep calling and trying to get to know me better.

Say yes and be as dull as possible so he leaves me alone.

"Sure, why not?" I said.

I didn't think it was possible, but his smile grew even broader. "Great! Come on, it's this way."

I wrinkled my brow. "Are you sure, because I thought it was that way," I said, pointing in the opposite direction.

"This is my third year here. Believe me, I know where the Dippin' Dots cart is. I'm addicted to them."

I considered arguing, but the park was huge. He must know where the cart was and I was just confused.

"Okay, lead the way."

"So, what job did you get?" he asked, glancing over at me.

"What would be the worst job imaginable?"

"Hansel and Gretel gift shop."

I arched my brow.

He looked like he was in pain. "Oh, man! Bummer. So what, you have experience working a cash register?"

I hadn't even considered that. I had put on my application that I'd worked in a clothing store my junior year. So yeah, maybe it was my experience working in a store or maybe it was as Patti and I surmised. . . .

"I was thinking it was my hair."

"I can't tell with it clipped back. How long is it?"

"Past my shoulders." I glanced over at him impatiently. "Shouldn't we have reached Dippin' Dots by now?"

He shook his head. "Nah, it's just up here."

Only I didn't see it, and I was beginning to suspect that we were taking the long route and that I'd been right to begin with.

"Hey, Parker," another guy said in passing.

"John."

"You sure know a lot of people," I said.

"They're just my crew."

"Your crew?"

"Yeah, I oversee Magnum Force."

I remembered Jordan mentioning that he had to ride the roller coaster every morning.

"You been on it?" he asked.

"Nope."

"Want to ride it after we have our Dippin' Dots? I have a cut-to-the-front-of-the-line pass."

"No, thanks."

"Why not? It's a tight ride."

"I'm just not into roller coasters."

"What's not to be into? The thrill of the speed, the plummets, the loops—"

"It just doesn't appeal to me, okay?"

"Are you afraid?"

"I'm not afraid."

"There's a guy—"

"Who comes on Wednesday. I know. My friend Patti told me. But it's not a phobia. It's just something I have no interest in."

"How can you not be interested?"

Why couldn't people just accept my decision and let it go?

"Do you ride the carousel?" I asked.

"Not since I was about eight."

"Okay, that's your choice. My choice is to ride the carousel, not the roller coaster."

"It's not the same. If you asked, I'd ride the carousel. As a matter of fact, after we eat our ice cream, we'll ride the carousel."

I stopped walking, put my hands on my hips, and glared at him. "I agreed to the Dippin' Dots, but not a ride. And speaking of the Dippin' Dots, I don't think you know where the cart is."

"I know where it is. We're about halfway there."

I stared at him, unable to believe it. "If we'd gone the other direction, we'd already be there, wouldn't we?"

"Yeah, but then we wouldn't have had as much time to talk."

I scoffed. "I can't believe you did that."

"Why? Your voice fascinates me. It's so smoky sounding."

"It sounds like I'm a smoker."

"No, it doesn't. My Uncle Joe is a smoker, hacking cough and everything. You don't sound like him. You sound like"— he shrugged—"I just like the way it sounds, wanted to learn if there are other things about you that I might like."

I laughed lightly. "But it doesn't matter. I have a boy-friend."

Holding out his arms, he looked around. "Where? I don't see him."

"You're too much, you know that?" Turning, I started to walk away. He grabbed my arm again. I jerked free. "Look—"

"Okay, I'm sorry. I know a shortcut."

"Right. I thought *this* was supposed to be a shortcut."

"It was a shortcut to my getting to know you."

At least he was honest.

"So sue me," he added, not looking at all sheepish, but somehow managing to defuse my anger. "Come on, I'm paying for the Dippin' Dots. You can't beat that."

"The ice cream, that's all," I said.

"Scout's honor."

I narrowed my eyes at him. "And you know a real shortcut."

"Yep, follow me."

I fell into step beside him. I couldn't help but be a little flattered that he'd gone to so much trouble. Or that he liked my voice. And he did know a shortcut. We slipped into a gate marked EMPLOYEES ONLY, walked along what looked like an alley between some of the rides, and when we came out on the other side, there was the cart we'd been looking for.

I ordered strawberry, he ordered chocolate. I didn't argue when he paid. I figured he owed me.

He pointed with the hand holding the cup of Dippin' Dots, the other holding a spoon, toward a bench. "Wanna sit?"

"Sure."

I sat on the bench, and he sat beside me.

A couple of people called out to him as they walked by.

"You know a lot of people," I said.

"I'm a likable guy."

"So, Jordan said you live in a house on the lake."

"Yep, a buddy and I are house-sitting over the summer. A guy we met last year needed someone to look after his place this summer, so he made us a great deal. Couldn't afford a house on the lake otherwise."

"That's a lot of responsibility."

"I live for responsibility."

He leaned forward, planting his elbows on his thighs, dipping into his cup of tiny frozen ice cream balls. I thought about asking him exactly what his relationship was with Jordan. I mean, it seemed odd to me that she'd slept with him, but here he was spending time with me. I certainly didn't want to be the reason that they broke up. That would make for a very awkward roommate situation. Worse even than being around Mom and Sarah while they fought about the wedding.

"You like watching movies?" he asked.

"Who doesn't?"

"Some people don't. What's your favorite?"

I smiled. "Are you playing twenty questions?"

"Just trying to get to know you a little better. So what's your favorite movie?"

Seemed like a harmless question. "*Titanic*."

He cringed.

"What's wrong with *Titanic*?"

"Don't get me wrong. Loved the special effects, but it was just a little too mushy."

"Well, I loved it. Your favorite is probably *Night of the Living Dead*."

"*Blade Runner*."

I shook my head. "I thought that one was strange."

"It's kind of a tech-noir movie, and I appreciate film noir more after I sat through a class on the subject."

I shook my head again, feeling a little dense. "I have no clue what film noir is."

He grinned. "It's a style of black-and-white movies that became popular after World War II. Detective movies where the filming style seemed really dark. That semester we watched all the old classics during class."

"A class where you watch movies. Sounds tough."

"Yeah, it's a rough life. I'm majoring in film. The danger there is that you stop watching movies for the enjoyment factor, but for the critique factor. What worked, what didn't? But I discovered that if I go to a movie with a girl, I'm less likely to go into critique mode."

I was shaking my head and grinning.

"What?" he asked.

"I see where this is leading."

"Maybe we could catch a movie sometime."

"I don't think so."

"Why not?"

"Boyfriend factor."

"It wouldn't have to be a date."

"Jordan factor?"

"As much as I love Jordan she is so not a factor."

What a jerk! But for some reason I didn't say it to his face. Maybe because I was disappointed that someone as good looking as he was, someone who seemed so nice, could turn out to be a total creep.

"Sorry. But I'm not interested. At all." I tapped the bottom of my empty cup. "Gotta go."

I stood up and tossed my cup in the trash.

"Thanks," he said.

I looked over at him. He was still sitting there, elbows on his knees, his ice cream melting. He didn't look like a guy who was trying to cheat on his girlfriend. I guess it was true what they said: Looks can be deceiving.

Of course, Jordan had Parker and Ross. Plus some guy named Cole who claimed to love her. Maybe they were just all into love without commitment. I wasn't.

"For what?" I asked.

"For hanging out with me."

"We weren't really hanging out."

"Whatever. Think about coming to my place the next time we have a party."

"Do you have a lot of parties?"

"Oh, yeah, and every Wednesday night we have a hump party . . . and it's not what you think. It's to help us get through the middle-of-the-week hump."

"I'll think about it."

"Great."

I didn't know why I felt bad walking away. I didn't know if it was guilt because he was involved with Jordan and I was involved with Nick. Or if it was just leaving him there, with a lie. Because I wasn't going to think about it.

If I felt this guilty just talking to him, getting ice cream with him, how much worse would I feel if partied with him?

Only 50 Nick-less days to go, and counting. . . .

"I'm sure that my son did not eat a little gingerbread man," the woman standing in front of my cash register said.

The fact that the five-year-old monster still had crumbs at the corner of his mouth seemed to say otherwise to me, but the customer is always right, so smiling brightly, I removed the cookie from her total.

"That'll be $12.56," I said.

She began laying coins on the counter. I wanted to scream. There was a long line behind her with harried parents and tired kids, and she'd dipped into her piggy bank. I wanted to tell her to forget it, but I started helping her count.

She slapped at my hand. "Don't touch my money."

"Yes, ma'am."

An eternity later, I was finally saying, "Next!"

"When's your break?"

How could I have not noticed Parker standing in line? And how long had he been standing there?

"Not soon enough," I said.

He stepped aside without me having to prod him to get out of the way, and I took care of the next customer. At least this one was using a credit card.

It had been nonstop customers from the moment I came into H & G. Although we were open until midnight, people with kids were getting ready to leave the park, and each and every one of them needed souvenirs. It was a constant stream of customers.

I felt a tap on my shoulder and glanced back. It was Nancy. "Time for your break."

I wanted to hug her. "Great! Thank you."

I slipped through the narrow opening in between the two sections of the counter and started for the door. I barely noticed when Parker fell into step beside me.

"I have to sit down," I said, as soon as we were outside.

"Over here."

I didn't protest when he took my arm and led me to a small table, a pint-sized table—because we were, after all, in

Storybook Land—and my knees touched the tabletop when I sat in the small chair. I put my elbows on the table and dropped my head into my hands. I just wanted to go to sleep and it was only seven o'clock.

"Here."

I looked up. Parker had set a cup of lemonade and a huge salty pretzel in front of me.

"Thanks." I tore off a piece of the pretzel, popped it into my mouth, and chewed. It was heavenly. "I didn't even realize I was hungry."

"You usually don't. At least not at first."

"This is insane."

"It'll get worse before the summer is over."

I sipped the lemonade. "I don't see how it can."

"Trust me, it will."

I took another bite of pretzel. "What are you doing here, anyway?"

Shrugging, he tore off some pretzel and ate it. He was in his uniform: khaki cargo shorts, red polo shirt, name tag. Parker (Los Angeles, CA).

So he probably wasn't Jordan's summer boyfriend. They probably knew each other from school or the neighborhood or something. I remembered that first day, how excited she'd been that he'd called. Maybe she'd come here to be with him.

But then what was Ross to her?

They obviously had a connection.

"What are you thinking?" he asked.

Now it was my turn to shrug, shake my head, and lie. "That I never knew eight hours could seem so long."

He grinned, reached for the lemonade, and took a sip. The park didn't use straws because too many ended up on the ground and the maintenance crew had to sweep them up. Still it seemed intimate that we were sharing a drink, even if he wasn't using the side of the cup that I'd used.

"So how is it at Magnum Force?" I asked.

"Unbelievable. When I left, the wait in line was an hour and a half."

"I can think of better things to do with my time than wait in line."

"Me, too. Listen, some of us are getting together at my place after the park closes, just to unwind. Thought you might want to join us."

"You know, I really think I'm going to be too tired."

He studied me a couple of seconds, then said, "Okay." He did a *rat-a-tat-tat* on the table with his palms. "I need to get back to work."

He stood and stepped back.

"Thanks again for the rescue," I said.

"Sure thing."

"Maybe after I've adjusted to the schedule . . ."

He nodded and smiled. "Let me know if you think of anything that I can do to help you adjust."

Before I could respond, he'd spun on his heel and was walking away.

What in the world made me say that, made me offer him any kind of hope at all?

In the end, I was actually grateful that I had said no to the party. I was completely wiped out.

Or so I thought. But it was just my body that was exhausted. My mind was traveling about as fast as Magnum Force. I couldn't get it to slow down.

I lay in bed, staring in the darkness, the sound of the cash register still ringing in my ears.

No, wait, it wasn't the cash register. It was the phone. I reached over and grabbed it. "Hello?"

"Hey."

Parker. Why was I not surprised?

"Listen, Jordan crashed in my bed, so she's staying here tonight. I didn't want you to worry about her."

"I'm not her keeper. And listen, Parker, stop bothering me, okay?"

I hung up before he could answer. I knew it was totally irrational on my part to be upset, but could the guy be any more of a player?

I reached for my cell phone and punched a number. Nick picked up on the second ring.

"Megan? What's wrong?"

"Did I wake you?"

"No."

He was lying. I could tell by his voice. It had that just-woke-up rasp to it, but I loved him for trying not to make me feel guilty.

"I know it's late, but I needed to hear your voice," I said.

"I'm glad you called. I needed to hear your voice, too. How is it there?"

"Busy." I'd called him two nights ago and told him about the position I'd been given. "Lots of little kids wanting souvenirs, crying because they're tired. Typical stuff. My feet hurt."

"Mine, too."

"How are things there?"

"Frustrating. We got this new waitress—Tess. I'm supposed to train her, and she thinks she already knows it all, so when I try to tell her something, she won't listen."

"Then leave her to it. Let her make a fool of herself."

"But it'll fall on me and I'll get chewed out. I wish you

were here. I really need a distraction."

I wasn't certain that I liked being called a distraction.

"A distraction?"

"You know. Something to take my mind off work. I miss you, Megan. I miss kissing you, talking to you, holding you."

"I miss you, too, Nick. We can still talk, even if we can't kiss or hold."

"I know, but it's not the same when I can't look at you."

I tried really hard not to think about the phone calls that Parker had made before he even knew what I looked like. He'd been content to just hear my voice, to talk with me. So unfair. Parker was a player. The calls hadn't meant anything, other than the fact that at that precise moment when he was talking, he wasn't giving attention to Jordan.

"So?" Nick said.

I shook my head. "I'm sorry. I must have dozed off."

"What? Am I boring or something?"

"No, Nick, I'm just tired. What did you say?"

"I said that I'm counting the days until you come home."

"Really?"

"Yeah. Forty-nine to go. I'm saving up my kisses."

I laughed lightly. "You'd better be."

"I was thinking that when the summer is over we could do something special."

"Like what?"

"Like go somewhere for the weekend, just the two of us. You know?"

Yeah, I did know, sorta. "Like my mom's going to go for that."

"She let you go up there for the whole summer."

"Yeah, but there are people here watching over me, so she doesn't think I could get into any trouble."

"How close do they watch?"

"Not very."

"So . . . if I came up for a visit . . ."

"I'd see a lot of you, Nick, when I wasn't working."

He sighed. "But I don't have any vacation days. Since I'm part-time."

"It's a nice thought, though, isn't it? That we could be together up here without any parents around?"

"Yeah. Who knows? Maybe I'll go AWOL."

"If you're going to do that and risk your job, then you could have come up here with me for the summer."

"I didn't know I'd miss you this badly, Megan. I mean, I knew I'd miss you, but I'm miserable without you."

It seemed kinda mean to feel good that he was miserable. Shouldn't I feel just as miserable? Only I didn't, but it was just because I was so busy. I was working full-time. Nick had more time on his hands.

We talked for another half an hour, and when we said good-bye, he was making kissing noises, which made me laugh and made me miss him. Made me miserable.

Only 49 Nick-less days to go, and counting. . . .

Monday was my day off, and I was so incredibly ready for it. Strangely, I woke up to find my roommate sleeping in her bed. She must have come in after I'd already been asleep. I wondered why she didn't just move in with Parker. She'd stayed over twice now, and had gone to his place for dinner again last night, so they were obviously serious.

I tried to be quiet getting out of bed, but she rolled over and looked at me. Smiled. "Hey!"

I'd never known anyone who actually woke up happy.

"Hi," I muttered. First thing in the morning wasn't when I was at my best.

"I am totally bummed," she said. "It's my day off and

Ross has to work. I can't believe that his day off is tomorrow and he couldn't find anyone to swap with him—"

She was back to Ross now? Was that why she'd slept in her own bed?

"And it's so unfair. The whole point of us coming here was so we could be together."

"What about Parker?" I asked.

"What about him?"

"You slept over—"

"Yeah, so? What has that got to do with anything?"

I shrugged. "Apparently nothing."

We obviously had a different view on commitment. I mean, I didn't even want to hang around with the guy, even nonseriously, because I had a boyfriend far, far away.

Suddenly, she sat up. "So you want to go to the mall with me? They had some of the cutest little shops, and I've been dying to get back there, but it's no fun shopping alone, you know? So how 'bout it, roomie? You and me, shopping 'til we drop?"

The other option was to spend the day alone lying on the sand or by the pool. Decisions, decisions . . . what the heck? I was ready to get away.

"Sure, I'd love to go the mall." Not that I had any money to spend, but maybe I'd find something that would make a unique wedding present for Sarah, and I wanted to send something to Nick so he'd know I was thinking about him.

"Awesome!" Jordan said. "We'll have oodles of fun!"

The mall was like a thousand other malls in a thousand other cities, and the fact that it was so familiar made me feel less homesick. Though until that moment, I hadn't even realized that I *was* homesick.

Not that I had a lot of time to focus on home, not while shopping with Jordan. She was incredible. I'd never known anyone with so much energy or such shopping skills. She seemed able to take in an entire display with a single glance.

"Oh, look at this, isn't this cute?" she asked, pointing to a pink halter with "YES, IT'S ALL ABOUT ME" glittering on it. "I've got to have this." She peered over at me. "Parker is always telling me that not everything is about me. And that is just so wrong."

So she was planning to still see Parker. Otherwise, why buy it?

"We should find one for you," she said. "What sentiment fits you? Princess? Nah. Spoiled? I don't think so. Too Hot to Handle? Yeah, that would do it."

She turned to me, holding out the red top that she'd decided suited me.

I laughed. "I'm not too hot to handle."

"It's the closest thing I can find." She shook it at me. "Come on. It's just for fun. You can wear it to Parker's hump party."

"I'm not even sure I'm going."

"Why not? I know he won't mind. He told me to invite my roomie and my suitemates."

So he hadn't told her that he'd issued me a personal invitation? Wasn't that interesting? Like he really didn't want her knowing that he knew me.

Of course he didn't want her to know. He'd already hinted a couple of times not to mention when he'd called or when he'd shown up at H & G's. Although he hadn't come by yesterday, and the awful thing was, I'd kept looking for him. But he'd obviously taken the hint when I'd told him that I didn't want him bothering me anymore. So now he was going to let Jordan do the bothering.

"I think I'm working Wednesday," I said.

"Well, if you're not, you can come. And even if you are, the park closes at ten during the week. Plenty of time to party. Oh, look at these shorts. I've got to have them."

By the time we were finished, we'd eaten lunch at the food court, Jordan had bought something in nearly every store—she'd spent way more than we'd make in earnings that week—and I'd bought the Too Hot to Handle shirt only because she was going to buy it for me if I didn't, and I didn't want her spending her money on me. I had a feeling that Jordan saw money the same way that she saw guys—disposable.

Not that it was any of my business.

I didn't find anything special for Sarah or Nick.

"So how is it working at H & G?" Jordan asked as we were walking to her car.

"Not too bad."

"You hear from your boyfriend much?"

"We talk at least once a day, usually before I go to bed. And he's always forwarding me all these jokes through e-mail. Each e-mail's subject heading is like a hostage watch or something: day 3 without Megan, day 5 without Megan."

"That's sweet!"

"It's so negative, though, like looking at a glass of milk and saying it's half empty. My subject headings are forty-seven days 'til I'm with Nick, forty-five days 'til I'm with Nick."

"The anticipation, the countdown. I'm so with you. Positive vibes to get you through the separation. It's a shame he's not here. Even seeing him a little bit would be better than not seeing him at all."

She popped the trunk and dropped her packages inside. I put my single sack in there as well. Then we got in the car.

She put the key in the ignition, turned it . . . nothing.

She looked over at me like I'd done something to the car. "It won't start."

"Maybe you didn't turn it far enough."

She tried again. Nada. Zilch.

"Great! Just great!" She searched around in her mammoth-sized purse and pulled out her cell phone, punched a button, waited . . .

"Hey! I've got a problem."

I tried not to listen as she explained what was happening. It seemed kinda nosey. When she ended the call, she said, "Parker will be here as soon as he can."

Parker. Great. This could get awkward.

"Let's wait outside where it's a little cooler," she said.

We sat on the hood of her car, my stomach knotting more tightly as the minutes went by. I knew it was ridiculous to worry about what might happen when Parker finally arrived. Would he acknowledge me? Had he told Jordan that he'd called me a couple of times, that we'd shared ice cream, that he'd taken his break with me?

Did any of it mean anything? It couldn't. They'd slept together afterward. He was just being . . . friendly to her roommate.

A black Mustang pulled up beside us, and Jordan slid off

the hood. I didn't think it was possible, but my stomach knotted up even more tightly when Parker got out of the car.

They greeted each other, then he looked at me, and even though he was wearing sunglasses, I had the impression that it was an extremely penetrating look and my discomfort with the situation intensified.

"This is my roomie, Megan," Jordan said.

"Yeah, we've met," Parker said.

"When?" Jordan asked.

"Long story. What's wrong with your car?" he asked impatiently.

"It's broken."

He scowled. She shrugged and held up her key. "It won't start, doesn't make any noise."

"Great. Probably the battery."

"Probably. Why don't you let me take your car while you figure it out? Megan and I have things we need to do."

"Like what?"

"None of your business. But let's do a vehicle swap, and we'll fix you dinner tonight."

"Who's we?" he asked, but he was looking at me, probably because I was slowly sliding off the hood, wondering what Jordan was about to get me into.

"Me and Megan." She glanced over at me. "You don't mind, do you?"

How could I say no without seeming ungrateful?

"Sure." If I'd used a longer word, my response would have been a stammer.

"So see?" Jordan said to Parker. "You get a free meal out of the deal."

"I'm not sure that makes it worth it."

"Sure it does," she said. "Pop the trunk so we can get our bags out."

Hardly knowing what else to say or do, I walked around to the back of the car to get my bag. Parker opened the trunk.

"Good Lord!" he said when he saw all the bags inside.

He reached in at the same time that I reached in and we bumped heads.

"Sorry," we said at the same time, each of us rubbing our respective heads.

"I just have the one little bag," I said, pointing and reaching, but he was reaching too and somehow with us both grabbing it, the shirt fell out.

"Sorry," he said again, quicker at grabbing it than I was.

It unfolded as he was lifting it out. Then he was staring at it, a grin forming over his face, before looking at me.

I snatched it from his fingers. "It was Jordan's idea."

His grin grew. "But you're going to be the one wearing it. Are you too hot to handle?"

"You'll never know."

His grin faded and I bit my lower lip. Why had I said that? Why was I so touchy whenever he was around?

Because he belonged to Jordan, but didn't act like it, and I belonged to Nick, but had a hard time remembering that whenever this guy was around.

"Sorry," I mumbled again, but I don't know if he heard me. He was too busy gathering up all of Jordan's bags and carrying them to his car.

And now I was going to have to spend the evening fixing this guy supper?

Could life get any more complicated?

CHAPTER 10

It could.

Or if not more complicated, it was definitely beginning to feel out of control.

The reason Jordan had so desperately wanted to swap cars with Parker was because she had an appointment to get a manicure and pedicure, and since we were running late, she didn't have time to drop me off at the dorm. So by default, since they had an opening, I got a manicure and pedicure as well.

The place where we went was called the Salons of Indulgence. It was actually a lot of little rooms in this main building, and different things happened in different rooms. And of course, Jordan had appointments lined up in several of the rooms.

"You don't have to get an eyebrow waxing," she said after we were finished at the nail salon. Then she leaned toward me. "But what can it hurt? Just a little more shaping than you have now."

I stood by the doorway and watched as she laid back in the recliner and the woman waxed her brows. I'd never actually had a waxing done. But it looked relatively painless.

When Jordan was finished, I decided what the heck. Plucking my eyebrows was a tedious chore anyway, so I took a turn.

Ow! I was wrong. It *did* hurt! And the reason it hurt was because she'd removed a good portion of my eyebrows.

I stared in the mirror when she was finished.

"You have a natural arch," she said with an accent from some Scandinavian country. "You weren't taking advantage of it. See how much bigger your eyes look now? The men will be dazzled."

"I don't need to dazzle men," I grumbled. "I have a boyfriend."

"Then he will be charmed."

"She's right," Jordan said. "Your eyes really do stand out now."

"My brows are still tingling."

"That'll stop soon, and if it doesn't, you can put some ice

on them when we get back to the dorm. But honestly, next week, it'll hurt even less."

"Next week?"

"Sure," she said. "Monday maintenance is a weekly ritual for me. Since we're both off, you're more than welcome to come along, only next time we'll make appointments for you."

Monday maintenance? Geez.

"Once a month I do hair, facial, and massage," she added.

I shook my head. "Jordan, I can't afford to do this weekly. A haircut and an occasional manicure are really about all my budget can handle."

"Daddy gave me a credit card to use on anything I wanted. I can use it to pay for your stuff, too."

Was she crazy?

"Thanks, Jordan, but I'm not going to have your dad pay for my stuff."

"Why not?"

I couldn't believe she was asking.

"Because I believe in paying my own way."

"He won't mind, Megan. Money is so not an object with him."

"Well, it's an object with me. I'll join you when I can, but not every week."

"Okay," she said, a little sadness in her voice, "but if you change your mind . . . he said I was supposed to use the card to have fun, and spending time with you is fun."

"If your dad is paying for so much, why are you even working this summer?" I asked, hoping that I didn't sound rude.

"The experience. I don't want to be too spoiled. Besides, it's nice to have money of my own, you know?"

Yeah, I knew, but hanging around with Jordan, I wasn't going to hold on to it for long.

I'd barely dropped my stuff on my bed when Jordan announced that we didn't have much time to get ready.

"We need to go grocery shopping for tonight's dinner," she said before disappearing into the bathroom.

I heard the shower. What a tornado of activity!

But she was also a lot of fun, in a frenzied kind of way.

I thought about changing into the shirt I'd bought today, but decided it conveyed a message that I definitely didn't want Parker taking the wrong way. Especially since he'd already seen it.

I tried to think of an excuse to get out of helping with the dinner, without looking weird, but there was no way around it. Any excuse was a definite show of weirdness.

So after Jordan got out of the shower, I had my turn. Put on a light application of makeup, stared at myself in the mirror. Did a change to the shape of my eyebrows really make that much difference in the way that I looked?

I looked, gosh, I didn't know. Prettier?

Maybe it was the dark green of my tank top. Couldn't be the white of my shorts. But something sure made me look different. I decided to leave my hair loose, hanging around my face. Maybe it would detract from the radical change in my eyebrows. Did guys even really notice eyebrows?

On the way to Parker's, we stopped at this little grocery store. Jordan knew everything about Parker. That he only ate dark meat chicken, never white, which was important because we were going to make chicken and rice. He ate wheat rolls, again, never white. Kernel corn, never creamed. Unsweetened tea, never sweetened. Plain brownies, never double chocolate or iced or chunky chocolate.

"If it weren't for his love of roller coasters," she said, "the guy would be totally dull."

I almost told her I didn't think he was dull at all. But if she thought he was, why did she hang out with him? But I kept my opinion and curiosity to myself.

After we finished shopping, we drove over to his place. It was only about fifteen minutes from the dorm, but the setting was totally awesome. The house, like a few others that I could see, was set back along the lake, massive trees in front.

It was a log cabin with a wide porch that wrapped around the front and sides. Each side had a couple of wicker rockers.

It was an incredibly peaceful place. No wonder Jordan spent so much time here. It was far away from the madness of the theme park. I couldn't hear the roller coasters or the screaming riders or the crying kids. As I stepped out of the car, I couldn't hear anything except the water lapping at the shore and the breeze rustling through the trees.

"Come on," Jordan said.

"What about the groceries?" I asked.

"The guys'll get them."

I followed her toward the house. A tall, blond guy in a dark T-shirt stepped onto the porch.

Jordan hopped up on the porch and hugged him. "This is Cole."

Cole, who had called the first night and declared his love for Jordan, lived with Parker, whom she slept with?

"You must be the roommate," he said to me.

"Oh, I'm sorry," Jordan said. "Yep, she's my roomie. Don't you love what she's done with herself today?"

"Jordan—" I began.

"And what is that?" a deep voice asked.

I turned toward Parker. He'd come up to the side of the porch. He was wearing a black T-shirt and jeans, his hands dirty with grease. How could anyone that dirty look that sexy?

"If you can't tell, I'm not going to tell you," Jordan said. "Did you get my car fixed?"

"Yeah. I had to replace the battery. But when was the last time you changed your oil?"

My roommate shrugged, looking a little guilty when she did it.

"Geez, Jordan, it's no wonder you have so much car trouble."

"But at least I have you to fix it. Will you guys get the groceries out of the car?"

She grabbed my arm. "Come on. I'll show you around while they do that."

The house was even better inside. Lots of leather furniture and brightly colored cushions and large windows in every room so we could look out onto the lake.

By the time we got to the kitchen, the groceries had been delivered. It was an open, cheery room.

Jordan walked to the oven and turned it on. "Let's get started."

It was really a pretty easy recipe. Chicken in a casserole dish, rice over the chicken, soup over the rice. Into the oven it all went, which left us with a couple of cans of corn to heat up and some rolls to bake. She worked on those while I hand-stirred the brownie mix.

I walked to the window and gazed out on the lake. The view wasn't that different from what I saw outside my dorm window, but it was just so much lovelier here. Maybe because I could see green grass instead of a cement sidewalk that led to the sandy shore. I could see branches swaying in the breeze.

I don't know how long I stood there staring out, but the timer was suddenly going off.

"Can you get the dish out of the oven?" Jordan asked.

"Sure." I set the bowl aside, slipped on the oven mitts, opened the oven door, reached in—

"Something smells good," Parker suddenly said.

I jerked up, caught my arm on the oven right above where the mitt ended—

"Ouch!"

I jumped back. Arms were suddenly around me, hauling me toward the sink. I could smell sweat and oil and grease. Parker turned on the cold water and put my arm beneath it.

"I'm so sorry," he said. "Jordan, get some ice."

"It's not bad," I said. "Just stings."

"Still, shouldn't have happened."

He was looking at me with those green, green eyes. So

apologetic, so much concern. Had anyone ever looked at me like that?

I was sure Nick would if I ever burned myself in front of him. And I might have if I'd worked in the restaurant with him. But since I'd never hurt myself, I'd never had him look as though he'd take the pain on himself if he could.

"Parker, you probably shouldn't be touching her. You're filthy," Jordan said.

He stepped back, but I could tell that he was reluctant to do it. Jordan moved into place, turned off the water, gently patted my arm dry, and looked at the burn. "That's not too bad."

It really wasn't. Maybe an inch long, a half an inch wide. I'd been really lucky. The mitt had saved me from the worst of it. Jordan smoothed some aloe cream on the burn, then placed the bag of ice against my arm. I held it in place. It was going to be all right.

She spun around and faced Parker. "The way you were acting I thought we were going to have to take her to the ER."

"I felt responsible."

"You don't usually overreact."

"Guilt, okay? Let it go."

"Aren't we snappish?"

"I spent my day off working on your stupid car, and you

haven't thanked me once."

"You stink. Go take a shower."

"No, I want a hug."

She started moving around the island. "No way. You're sweaty and so dirty."

Grinning broadly, he pulled off his T-shirt. He was sweaty, but he was also very trim, very fit. Wow.

"Don't you dare," she warned. "Don't you dare—"

He went after her. She screeched and headed out of the kitchen. He followed.

I heard her scream. I walked to the doorway. He'd caught her and was hugging her. She broke away.

"You are disgusting," she said. "Go shower. But hurry, everything is almost ready."

He was heading to his room when he looked back, saw me standing in the doorway. "Want a hug?"

I shook my head and stepped back out of sight.

No way would I ever admit that yeah . . . I thought maybe I did want a hug.

CHAPTER 11

While Parker was taking his shower,

Jordan and I began setting up dinner on the counter.

"We're just going to serve it buffet style," she said. "Everyone can fill their plates and join us on the back porch."

"Something sure smells good," a girl said, standing in the doorway. "What's the special occasion?"

She had red hair, pulled back into a ponytail.

"Parker had to fix my car so I'm paying him back." Jordan jerked her thumb toward me. "This is my roomie, Megan."

"Hey, Megan. I'm Ronda."

"She's Cole's girlfriend."

"Allegedly," she said, smiling.

"You've been with him, since what? Middle school?" Jordan said.

Ronda smiled. "Pretty much."

"Grab Cole and get your plates ready. Food is getting cold."

The four of us were sitting at the wicker table on the back porch when Parker joined us. He pulled over a chair and set it between Jordan and me. "How's the arm?" he asked, as he set his plate on the table.

"Fine," I said. I wasn't certain I could say the same thing about my appetite now that he was sitting beside me. His hair was still damp, and I could actually see a couple of drops of water on his eyelashes.

Why are you looking that closely? I chastised myself.

"What happened to her arm?" Ronda asked.

"She burned it taking the casserole dish out of the oven. Parker has been totally overreacting," Jordan said.

"I have not. I'm showing a little concern."

"Whatever." She perked up and smiled. "Hey, Ross."

"Hey, babe."

I looked toward the doorway and there was Ross from the first night, holding a plate full of food. He walked over and set the plate on the other side of Jordan. Then he pulled a chair to the table and sat. He leaned over and gave Jordan a quick kiss.

I cast a furtive glance at Parker, wondering how he might take the show of affection, but he didn't seem at all bothered.

"So, Jordan's car had problems?" Ross asked.

Parker nodded. "Yep. It was a mess under that hood. I can't believe I spent my day off working on it."

Jordan leaned toward him, her nose wrinkled. "That's what brothers are for."

"He's your *brother*?" I asked, before I could stop myself.

Everyone looked at me like I'd just asked the stupidest question in the whole world.

"Well, yeah. Who did you think he was?" Jordan asked.

"He never said his last name, and you seemed to really like him, and you"—I swallowed—"you were over here a lot."

"Omigod! I slept over here and you thought . . . ew!" She shuddered. "He was so not in the bed with me. Omigod!" she said again. "Ross is my boyfriend, totally, absolutely. Who did you think Ross was?"

I felt like such an idiot. "I thought you had two boyfriends?" It sounded stupid even as I gave voice to my assumptions.

"So, what? You, like, thought I was a slut?" She laughed. "Omigod. This is too much."

Parker didn't say anything at all. Just studied me, like he was slowly figuring something out. Then as though he'd figured it all out, he turned to Jordan. "Common misconception. We don't look alike."

"Thank God." Jordan laughed again. "This is really too much."

She was shaking her head, grinning.

"So, Megan, what's your position at the park?" Ronda asked, as though trying to shift the subject away from my stupidity.

"Gift shop."

"Not Hansel and Gretel's, I hope?"

"Yeah. Where do you work?"

"I work on the shows, putting them together. We have one girl this year, Alisha, who is so talented."

"Omigod! That's our suitemate," Jordan said. "Is she really that good?"

"Good enough that you need to have your dad come up and watch her perform," Ronda said.

Parker leaned toward me and said quietly, "Our dad's a director."

"Of movies?" I asked stupidly.

He grinned. "Yeah."

I thought I understood now why Jordan had unlimited credit card use.

"Do you know famous people, then?" I asked.

"Other than our dad, you mean?"

"Yeah."

"Sure. Jordan and I have crashed a few of his parties. The thing about the famous, though, is that they're just regular people."

"But they're *famous*," I pointed out.

He shrugged. "I guess."

"That's the reason you're majoring in film? Are you planning to follow in your dad's footsteps?"

"I'd like to. Entertainment is my life."

"But you manage a roller coaster. I don't see how that's related."

"It's entertainment. It's fun, exciting, thrilling. It's an experience. For sixty seconds, people aren't thinking about work or worries."

"No, they're wondering if they'll survive."

"You say that like it's a bad thing," Cole said. "Don't you like roller coasters?"

Until that second, I hadn't realized that our conversation had an audience. I looked over to find everyone watching us, waiting. . . .

Why did I feel like I was at some addicts' anonymous meeting?

"I'm not a big roller coaster fan, no," I admitted.

"Why?" Cole asked, appearing truly perplexed.

I held out my hands. "It just doesn't appeal to me."

"But you told me that you rode Magnum Force," Jordan said.

I was so embarrassed. "I lied."

"Why?"

"Because I get tired of trying to explain why I so don't get roller coasters."

"Could be acrophobia," Ronda said.

Cole looked at her.

"Fear of heights," she explained.

"It's not a phobia," I assured her, although I couldn't stand to ride in elevators that were on the outside of buildings.

"Or illyngophobia, fear of dizziness," Ronda said. "Or tachophobia, fear of speed." She grinned. "I aced my psychology course. There's probably a definite phobia for roller coasters, but I don't know what it is."

"I'm not afraid of anything. I have no phobia."

"She just has no interest in roller coasters," Parker said, unexpectedly coming to my defense. "We've already discussed it."

"When did you discuss it?" Jordan asked.

Parker shrugged. "Sometime when our paths crossed.

The point being, it's not important. Different strokes, that's all, so give her a break."

"Aren't we touchy?" Jordan asked.

"I just fixed your car. I can unfix it, you know," he said.

Seeing them parrying back and forth, I realized how totally insane it was that I'd thought they were anything except brother and sister. I could even see the similarities now . . . not in the eyes or the hair or the smiles, but in the mannerisms, the confidence. They were as different from each other as Sarah and I were, but I could detect shadows of similarities. I just had to look hard, and I'd really tried not to look hard at Parker.

But the truth was that looking at him was a pleasure.

Since Jordan and I had cooked, we got out of cleanup. Parker got out of it, too, since he'd fixed Jordan's car. While everyone went inside to get a brownie, I stayed on the porch, standing at the railing, gazing out at the lake while twilight came.

"It's awesome, isn't it?" Parker said quietly from behind me.

I glanced over and he was extending a brownie on a paper towel.

"We're not too fancy here," he said, as though to apologize for the offering.

"That's fine." I took it, bit into the brownie. Like Parker, I preferred the original to any fancy variety.

He stood beside me, eating his brownie, without a paper towel.

"I'm just curious," he began. "All the cold shoulders you gave me, was that because you thought Jordan was my girlfriend?"

"Not completely. Like I said, I have a boyfriend."

He finished his brownie, hitched up a hip, and sat on the edge of the railing, looking at me. "What's he like?"

"Smart. Dependable, loyal—"

"Those are the same words I use to describe my dog."

I glowered at him.

He held up his hands. "Sorry, but look, I'm interested in you. Just trying to size up my competition."

"Read my lips. I'm not interested in you."

"You really shouldn't draw my attention to your lips."

I rolled my eyes. I couldn't really take offense, though, because he said everything like it was a joke. And somehow, as much as I didn't want to, I found myself fighting to hold back a smile.

"Does he make you laugh?" he asked.

"What has that got to do with anything?"

"My father's advice when it came to women. He said, 'Find

a woman you like being with, who views spending money the same way you do, and makes you laugh.' "

"Sounds like he's an expert."

"Totally. And you're avoiding my question."

I sighed. "Yes, he makes me laugh."

"That's good."

Thank goodness he didn't ask for examples, because at that precise moment I couldn't think of any time when Nick and I had laughed. I knew there had to have been laughter; I guess it just hadn't been memorable.

"So maybe you'll come back for the hump party," he said, with no hint of it being a question.

"Maybe."

I didn't know why I felt guilty. I'd come here to work, but surely Nick didn't expect me to have no fun whatsoever. All work and no fun would make Megan a dull girl.

Only 47 Nick-less days to go, and counting. . . .

CHAPTER 12

"She wants Aunt Vic's holy terror to

be ring bearer!"

The "she," of course, was Mom. Aunt Vic was my dad's youngest sister from my granddad's third marriage, and the holy terror was her three-year-old son, Vincent.

"Why?" I asked, beginning to think that Sarah was right and that Mom may have indeed gone off the deep end.

"Because he's cute."

"In photos, yeah, but he's like the Tasmanian Devil in person." Honestly, the kid worked up a gust of breeze wherever he went.

"Talk to her, will ya?"

"Me? This is your wedding. You talk to her."

"Come on, Megan, you're her favorite."

"Only because I'm not there."

It was Tuesday night and I'd just gotten off my shift. I was walking along the lighted sidewalk that stretched from the theme park to the dorm. To my right were the sand and the lake. People were still out on the beach, and I could hear people at the hotel pool as I walked by.

In my backpack was a wish-you-were-here postcard I'd picked up at H & G's today to send to Nick. The neat thing about a theme park is that it has lots of postcards, tiny gifts, and I'm-having-a-great-time-but-miss-you stuff. I'd actually bought a six-inch stuffed bear that I was going to send to Nick, too. Just a little something so he'd know I was thinking about him.

"It's your wedding, Sarah. You're about to become a wife. Shouldn't you be able to tell someone when you don't like something they're doing?"

"Are you saying I shouldn't get married?"

Although there were people around, especially other people walking back to the dorm after finishing their shifts, it seemed so quiet without all the rides going. I thought that unlike an hour ago, *now* someone would hear me if I screamed. And I was really tempted to do that.

"No, I'm not saying that. I'm just saying that you have to

stand up for yourself."

"It's just that I can see him running around, dropping to the floor, kicking—"

"You're preaching to the choir here."

She growled. "This would have been so much easier if you had stayed here this summer."

For her maybe. No way would it have been easier for me.

"So what are you doing?" she asked, suddenly changing the subject.

"Walking home. I really like it here, Sarah."

"You *are* going to come home for my wedding, right?"

"I wouldn't miss it. Now go talk to Mom. Tell her it's your wedding and you don't want the little monster."

"Okay. Love ya, sis."

She hung up before I could say, "Love you back." Her timing was perfect. I'd arrived at the dorm. I really hoped it would be the same for her wedding. Perfect timing on everything. Maybe I should call Mom and suggest that she lighten up.

I walked into the dorm and went to the elevators, saying hi to a couple of the people standing around.

On the sixth floor, Zoe was greeting us, like she did every night. "Hello, ladies, did everyone have a lovely night?"

There were a couple of groans, and one girl just rolled her eyes.

"It's only the beginning of summer, luvs. Wait until we really get busy," Zoe said. "Anyone want to pop in for a bit of chitchat?"

I had on other nights, but tonight I was just way too tired. "Later, Zoe," I said, as I walked past her.

I got to my room, inserted the key, opened the door—

The hallway light spilled into the room, chasing back the darkness.

Someone rolled off Jordan's bed, someone too tall to be Jordan. Ross, obviously. Still fully clothed, thank goodness. And the bed was made. So whatever I'd interrupted hadn't gotten to any embarrassing stage.

"You're home already," Jordan said, sitting up.

"It's after ten thirty."

"I just wasn't expecting you back so soon. Ross, was just, uh, Ross was just . . . you know."

Yeah, I knew.

"Hey, Ross," I said, to try to ease some of the tension in the room.

"Hey. Guess I need to go."

"Can I turn on the light?" I asked.

"Sure," Jordan said.

I flipped the switch. Poor Ross looked like he wished he was anywhere but where he was.

"Night, babe," he said, leaning down to give Jordan a quick kiss.

He edged past me, mumbling sorry as he went. He closed the door behind him. I locked it.

Jordan got out of bed, fluffed her hair that Ross had obviously already fluffed. Took a deep breath. Clapped her hands.

"We need a signal," she announced.

"A signal?" I walked to my bed and dropped my backpack on it.

"Yeah, you know, like, so we avoid embarrassing situations."

"I wasn't embarrassed." I sat on my bed and looked at her.

"It could have gotten embarrassing. I mean, Ross and me, we've been going together for two years now." She sat on the bed, folded her legs beneath her. "So sometimes, we get into some pretty heavy stuff. And okay"—she held up her hands—"part of the reason we both came here to work was so we could have a little alone time, because my dad would totally freak if he ever caught Ross in my room. You know how it is?"

"Not really. Nick and I have only been dating for three months. We're not into heavy stuff yet."

"That's cool. I'm all about not rushing into something before you're ready. But Ross, he's my one and only. My dad just doesn't get it. He keeps saying that he does get it, because he was young once, too, but that was, like, a hundred years ago. It is so not the same."

"It sounds like you're close to your dad, though."

"Oh, yeah. He's just unreasonable. What about your dad?"

"Totally cool. He was the one who suggested I work here this summer."

She gave me this look like I was really clueless. "He wanted to get you away from your boyfriend."

I scoffed. "No way."

"I'll bet you a day off that he had an ulterior motive, and it involved getting you away from your new boyfriend."

"Bet a day off?"

"Yeah. You work during the night, I work during the day, so sometime you'll work my shift so I have some extra time off."

"What? You just expect me to call up my dad and ask him?"

"No, just sometime when you're talking to him, let it slip into the conversation. We have all summer. I'm in no hurry for an extra day off."

"But you have to work my shift if you're wrong?"

"Certainly. I can dress up like Gretel. No problem."

"You're on." There was just no way that my dad was that underhanded or devious.

"All right." She got up, went to her dresser, and took out a silk scarf. "We'll keep this on the inside of the door, but if it's on the outside, then it means knock before you come in."

"Okay," I said.

"And if your boyfriend ever comes up here, then you can use it to signal me."

"I don't think Nick has any plans to come up here."

"I don't see how he can stay away. I mean, if he really loves you."

"But isn't the opposite true? If I love him, I shouldn't be able to stay here?"

"Nah. The burden of proving love is always on the guy."

So why was I the one sending teddy bears?

A thunderstorm struck late Wednesday afternoon. Which, as they'd explained in our orientation was usually bad news because all the rides had to shut down. And where do people go when the rides shut down and they want to avoid the rain?

Into the gift shops.

But what made this one worse than usual was that it struck with such ferocity and so quickly that it knocked out the power. And left people stranded at the top of roller coasters for a couple of hours before power could be restored.

It was the main topic of conversation at the hump party. I'd decided to go because I couldn't think of a good reason not to, especially since the park closed down early, due to the weather. It just didn't seem like the rain was going to let up. Even though we got our power back, an amusement park without rides isn't very amusing.

Of course, since it was still raining, our options for where to hang out at Parker's was limited. I'd decided on the back porch. So had a lot of other people, including Parker.

Although he wasn't standing right beside me, he was close enough that I could hear what he was saying.

"Everything just stopped," he said. "Except for the screams. It was totally weird. I've heard of this happening at other parks, but never here."

"I guess the one good thing was that they hadn't started their descent," Ross said.

They'd just reached the apex on the tallest roller coaster in the park when the power cut off.

"We have guys who inspect the rides every morning. They're like monkeys getting to the top and we talked about trying to get the people down but, man, do you know how high that thing is?" Parker asked.

"Three hundred and fifty feet," I said. "Taller than the Statue of Liberty."

Everyone looked at me, and I felt like a total fact geek. I couldn't help it. I liked trivia.

"I'm impressed that a roller coaster phobe would know that," Parker said, grinning.

I ignored his phobe comment. "And it travels at a hundred and twenty-five miles per hour."

"A total rush," Parker said.

It wasn't the speed that bothered me. It was the dips, the curves, the loops, the feeling of not being in control. Plus the initial descent was almost a complete vertical drop.

"Sure you don't want to try it sometime?" he asked.

"I'm sure." I would have totally freaked if I'd been on it when the power went out.

He left the group and moved closer to me, pressing his shoulder against the beam that supported the eave of the porch. "So what other stats do you know?"

"Not a lot. Those just stuck with me because they were so . . . incredible. It's like there has to be a limit on how high those things can safely go, how fast . . ."

"Designers will continue to push the edge."

He was wearing a T-shirt that said, "I love it when you

scream!" The words were superimposed over an image of a roller coaster.

"You really like roller coasters, don't you?" I said.

"Love 'em."

"Have you ridden the one on top of that hotel in Vegas?"

"Yep. I've been to more than twenty different theme parks. My dad's a big enthusiast, so he pretty much made sure that all our summer vacations took us close to some park or another."

"So why not work at Disneyland, closer to home?"

"The key words there are *closer to home*. Sometimes it's good to just get away, you know? So why aren't you working closer to home?"

"The wedding."

He looked like he'd just been dropped from the top of Magnum Force. "You're engaged?"

I laughed. "No, my sister is. I just wasn't sure I could survive two more months of listening to my mom and sister arguing about *the* wedding."

"So what are they arguing about?"

"What *aren't* they arguing about? Name something."

"The groom."

"Actually, that's the one thing they do agree on. It's the

details of the wedding that are causing the problem. Sarah doesn't exactly go for the traditional."

"No?"

I shook my head. "Her first choice was to wear a tuxedo."

He laughed. "You're kidding?"

"Nope."

"That sounds like something Jordan would do."

"How would you feel if your bride wore a tux?" I asked.

"I think it would be a hoot as long as she didn't expect me to wear a gown." He shook his head. "Nah, I don't think I'd want her to wear a tux."

"Neither did Bobby, which is the only reason that Sarah is wearing a gown, but Mom still chalked it up as a win for herself."

"She's not actually keeping score."

"Yeah, actually they both are. It's pathetic. Then Sarah comes to me and complains about Mom, then Mom will ask my opinion, and it's so awkward, because I just want Sarah to be happy, but I want Mom to be happy, too, and I sorta understand where Mom is coming from. She and Dad got married behind a grocery store—"

"What?"

I smiled. "That's how they always tell it. They got married by a justice of the peace and his office was behind the grocery store. Apparently my grandparents sat in the jury box and watched what my grandmother refuses to call 'a ceremony.' I think Mom wants Sarah's wedding to be really special because hers wasn't."

"Can't argue with the results," he said. "They're still married, right?"

"Yeah, they are. Twenty-eight years."

"My dad is on wife number three. And every wedding has been bigger and more expensive than the one that came before. There are already signs that this last one is on a downward death spiral. Mom is on boyfriend number eight. Each one younger than the one who came before." He glanced toward the lake. "So that's the reason I'm here." He looked back at me. "I just like to be far away from the madness. Talked Jordan into coming this year. Because there's going to be fallout. It's never pretty when my parents end a relationship."

"I'm so sorry—"

"Hey, it's not your fault. It happens. The sad thing is, I think Mom and Dad still love each other. They just got so busy with careers and community and one thing and another, they had no time to remember that they loved each other. It's easier to start over than to work to make something last."

"Well, my parents have definitely worked at it. I think

Sarah will be fine when it comes to the marriage. I think it's a question of surviving the wedding."

"Guess you'll go home for the wedding."

He said it like a statement, not a question, but I answered anyway. "Definitely. I'm the maid of honor."

It suddenly got very quiet beyond the house. The rain had stopped. I shivered. It was really silly of me to be standing out here in jeans and a long-sleeved shirt, because the rain had brought a definite chill to the air. Everyone else had been smart enough to wander inside where they actually had a fire going.

"Here," Parker said, shrugging out of his jacket.

Before I could protest, he'd draped it over my shoulders. It enveloped me in a cocoon of warmth. "Thanks. I guess I really should go in, but it's so nice out here."

"Feel free to come visit anytime. The beach stays a lot less crowded than the one in front of the hotel."

"Thanks for the offer, but I don't have a car—"

"You have a cell phone?"

I wrinkled my brow. "Yeah."

"Can I see it?"

"Sure, it's nothing fancy. Doesn't take pictures or anything."

I dug it out of my front pocket, handed it to him, and

watched in amazement as he began punching buttons.

"What are you doing?" I asked.

He handed it back to me with a grin. "Programmed in my number. Now you can call me when you want to come over and I'll come get you. I *do* have a car and it's a lot more reliable than Jordan's."

I took my phone, shoved it back into my pocket. "I'm not going to call you. That's too much trouble for you."

I turned away, looking out on the lake.

"It's only too much trouble if I think it is," he said. "And I wouldn't."

"You might change your mind. Maybe I'll call every day," I said without looking at him.

"I wouldn't change my mind if you called every hour."

I spun around and faced him. "I can't believe you keep flirting with me."

"Why not? I'm interested, and I think you are, too."

"No way am I—"

I don't remember him moving toward me, or me moving toward him, but we were suddenly kissing. . . .

And he was skillfully revealing that all my protests were a lie.

CHAPTER 13

Thursday Night Possibilities

Watch Alicia perform at the Summit Theater
Pros: Not have a boring night writing to Nick, telling him how much I miss him. Be with people, laugh, have a good time.
Cons: Possibility of running into Parker, who I actually ran away from Wednesday night after he delivered that incredible, mind-numbing, mouth-melting kiss.

Stay in my room
Pros: Lots of time to try to remember what Nick's kisses are like. They're hot. I know they are. Not see Parker.

Cons: Be alone. Lonely. Living what my mother assures me are the best years of my life in isolation.

I was sitting on my bed, staring at the words I'd written in my decision-maker. After the park closed down at ten, there was going to be a special performance at the Summit Theater, open to all the staff, so we could enjoy the show that we normally might not be able to see because we were working during the performance time.

I really wanted to go. After all, Alisha would be performing, and everyone I knew planned to be there: Patti, Zoe, Lisa, Jordan. And of course, wherever Jordan was, Ross, Cole, and Parker were sure to follow.

Which was what originally caused me to pull out my decision-maker. Parker. I so did not want to see him.

I sat there trying not to relive the humiliation of not pushing Parker away when he latched his mouth onto mine. The humiliation of actually moving closer to him. I could still smell the rain mingling with his tangy scent. I thought I would never be able to smell rain without thinking of him.

When our mouths had finally unlocked, I'd been breathless and hot and shaking and terrified. And guilty. So guilty.

I kept telling myself that it was no big deal, that it was

just a kiss. But I knew that if I ever learned that Nick had kissed a girl the way that I kissed Parker, it would be so over between us. Would Nick know when he looked at me that I had kissed someone else? Would he be able to tell when he kissed me that another guy had branded his unique taste on my mouth?

I snatched up my phone and punched his speed-dial number. He answered on the second ring.

"Hey," I said, and thought I sounded guilty saying it.

"Hey, Megan." I heard him yawn. Had I woken him up? "What's wrong?"

"Nothing. I just wanted to hear your voice."

"That's cool." He yawned again.

"Did I wake you?"

"Yeah, but it's okay. I was out late last night."

"Doing what?"

Did I sound suspicious, like a jealous shrew?

"When I got off work, I went to Steak 'n Shake with some of the guys."

"Who?"

"Just guys from work. We got a lot of new summer help. I don't even know if you know them. Besides, what does it matter?"

"I just feel like I'm not part of your life right now."

"Because you're not. That was your choice."

"I don't want to fight, Nick."

"I don't either, but this is hard, Megan. I see guys with their girlfriends—"

"And I see girls with their boyfriends. Look, Nick, I don't want to get into this. I just wanted to hear your voice and know that you love me."

"'Course I do."

Not exactly a resounding endorsement.

"Can you say it?"

"I love you."

"I love you, too."

We talked a little more about nothing in particular, but I didn't feel much better than I had before I called. I stared at the pros and cons again.

There was a knock on the bathroom door and Alisha walked in. "So are you coming to watch the show tonight?"

She looked so excited, so hopeful, and maybe a little nervous as well. Tonight was a dress rehearsal. Tomorrow night would be the big opening for her. I wanted to be supportive, I really did.

Pro: Be a good suitemate.

Con: Be a jerk. Okay, be a coward.

"I wouldn't miss it," I said, giving her a smile that

threatened to unhinge my jaw.

And hoping I wouldn't live to regret it.

The afternoon and night seemed to take forever, probably because I spent so much of my time looking over my shoulder. I kept expecting Parker to show up and to suggest we take up where we left off the night before.

I was sure the slow progression of hours had nothing at all to do with the million and a half people who were wandering through H & G, unfolding T-shirts to look at what was on the front—even though we had samples displayed on the walls—picking up a stuffed toy to purchase, changing their mind halfway to the cash register and putting it on the shelf with the shot glasses. (I still couldn't figure out why any kid who visited Storybook Land would want a shot glass.)

There were bells and spoons and thimbles. Little collectibles. And we rotated between the cash register and cleanup, putting everything back so it didn't look like we'd been invaded by hordes—even though we had been.

So this particular day was going exceedingly slowly. I told myself that it wasn't because I was disappointed that Parker hadn't shown up. I wasn't disappointed. I was glad.

So why did I feel so let down?

It was usually close to ten thirty when we finished in the shop, because we had to undo the damage done by customers. I was still rearranging the miniature teacups when Nancy tapped me on the shoulder.

"We'll finish up in the morning," she said. "We have a show to catch tonight. You are going, right?"

"Wouldn't miss it."

Patti and I stood outside the shop while Nancy pulled down the iron gates that kept people out. A gingerbread house with iron doors. I guess it worked, though. Maintenance crews were already sweeping and cleaning and washing things down. Whenever I felt silly in my costume, I thought things could be worse. I could be scrubbing toilets.

Patti, Nancy, and I walked together to the Summit Theater.

"Giving us a special show is almost as good as what they do for us at the end of summer," Nancy said.

"What do they do?" Patti asked.

"Right after Labor Day, we go back to winter hours, so of course a lot of the staff will be leaving. So Tuesday, when they start closing the park to the public at seven again, they use skeleton crews on the rides and the park is ours."

"I think by the end of summer, the last thing I'd want is to ride another ride," I said.

"It's the camaraderie," Nancy said. "The free food and drinks don't hurt, either."

The camaraderie. That was the nice thing about working here. Meeting all the people, from all over the world. Although right now, it seemed like maybe most of the world was trying to file into the Summit Theater. It was crowded and I somehow lost sight of Patti and Nancy.

"Hey, roomie!"

I almost groaned. My worst nightmare realized.

I felt a tug on my arm and there was Jordan standing beside me, grinning like she'd discovered the world's largest diamond. It felt good that she was so glad to see me, but I was also extremely uncomfortable because the usual suspects were with her. Including Parker.

"You're going to sit with us, right?" she asked.

How could I say no?

"Sure."

We made our way into the theater. An usher was standing there saying, "Move all the way down, move all the way down, don't leave empty seats, move all the way down. . . ."

"Think they gave him a script?" Jordan asked beside my ear.

"I'm sure they did. Don't want to leave anything to chance."

I finally got to the row of seats we were supposed to sit in, grateful because Jordan was behind me. But when I edged my way down the row and took a seat, I looked up to find Parker moving in to take the seat beside me. How had that happened? Jordan had been right beside me, whispering in my ear!

And now Parker was sitting next to me, in uniform, his bare knee brushing up against my bare knee. I jerked my leg away. Short skirts and cargo shorts. Dangerous combination.

I didn't want to think about the pleasant spark our touching had ignited. All around us, people were talking, mumbling, excitement mounting. I wanted to enjoy the show, but I was so aware of the guy sitting next to me, distracted by his presence.

He leaned toward me and I froze, waiting.

"You mad at me or something?" he whispered.

I turned my head and there he was, his face close enough to mine that I wouldn't have to move more than an inch to have a repeat of last night's performance.

"You know what's the matter," I said. Had I been running? Why did I sound like I couldn't catch my breath?

"I'm not sure I do."

"You kissed me," I hissed.

"You kissed back," he said, lowering his voice even more

so the words were more intimate.

"Because you took me off-guard."

He grinned, he actually grinned. "So if your guard weren't up, you'd be kissing me all the time?"

"That's not what I meant. Do we have to discuss this now?"

The lights dimmed. Thank goodness. I turned my attention to the stage. Let the show get started. Give me a distraction.

"We do need to discuss it," Parker whispered, "because I haven't been able to stop thinking about it."

I slid my gaze over to him, and even in the shadows, I could feel the heat in his eyes.

There was a clash of cymbals that almost had me leaping into the row in front of me. I know my reaction was clearly evident because I heard Parker chuckling.

Then music started up, curtains were pulled back, and the show began. It was quite an elaborate production with a group of people dancing and singing.

I felt Parker's mouth brush against my ear and a shiver went down my back.

"Which one is your suitemate?"

"She's not on the stage yet."

"Tell me when she is."

Like he had to ask me and not Jordan? Give me a break. He was just looking for an excuse to get near me. I should have been angry, but instead, I was . . . flattered.

I hated to admit that, even to myself, but his attention made me feel special. I quickly told myself he was probably just looking for a summer fling.

The lights went out on the stage. Everything was black. And when a spotlight hit the stage, there was Alisha. She was dressed in a sequined gown. She looked beautiful.

I leaned over to Parker. "That's her."

"Wow. She's hot."

Was that a spark of jealousy I felt? Couldn't be.

Then Alisha began to sing. Wow indeed.

I just sat there, mesmerized.

"She's really good," Parker whispered, his voice a raspy rumble.

It was then that I realized I was still leaning against him, our shoulders touching like they'd been fused together. I told myself to move away, that I didn't need to be touching him, that I didn't *want* to be touching him.

"Yeah, she is," I said, staying exactly where I was, inhaling that scent that was him.

"Let's go somewhere after this."

I swallowed hard, shook my head. I felt like I'd felt at the top of the one roller coaster that I'd ridden with my dad. Terrified of what awaited me.

"We need to talk. There's an all-night pancake house. Ten minutes away."

I shook my head again. What was the harm in talking? The harm was that it might develop into another kiss. Just having his mouth this close was more temptation than I'd ever experienced.

This was insane!

Yes, he was hot, but so was Nick. Yes, he was nice, but so was Nick. Yes, he sent shivers of anticipation through me. But so did Nick. Okay, so they weren't this strong. But they were there. Parker terrified me. Nick didn't. Nick was safe, like a carousel.

Parker was the tallest, fastest, scariest thrill ride imaginable.

"I like you, Megan," he said so low that I barely heard. "I know you don't want me to, but I do. All I want is for you to go get some coffee with me."

"I don't drink coffee after dark."

"Tea, then."

I could have sworn I heard laughter in his voice.

"Water," he continued, "lemonade, milk. Some kind of

liquid. Sitting across from each other, not beside each other, where we're touching."

So he'd noticed, too, and hadn't moved aside. Why was I not surprised?

Alisha closed out her routine. The theater went dark again. I found comfort in the darkness when I turned my head and felt, but couldn't see, my nose touching Parker's cheek. "Okay."

The rest of the performances were a blurred haze, and I fought not to hyperventilate after I gave Parker my answer. When the show was over, we got up and walked out of the theater without a word.

Jordan was babbling about how talented our suitemate was, and yes, their dad really did need to come see her perform. Ross kept nudging her up against his side and planting kisses on her mouth. Maybe that was the only way he'd figured out how to stop her from talking.

"So what now?" she asked when we reached the gate of the park. "What should we all do? I'm totally pumped. Couldn't go to sleep if I had to."

"Megan and I have something to take care of. We'll

catch you later," Parker said.

I was afraid Jordan was going to ask for details. Instead she just looked at me and said, "Don't forget our signal."

I figured she was glad to know she'd have the room to herself for a while.

"I won't."

Parker and I took off in a different direction, toward the costume shop. He waited outside while I changed out of my costume—not nearly as interesting a costume as Alisha had been wearing. Part of me wanted to change slowly, hoping he'd lose patience and leave. Part of me wanted to change quickly so I could see him again, find out what he wanted to "take care of."

I settled for changing somewhere in between. Storybook Land and its fairy tales were starting to get to me—now I was thinking in terms of the Three Bears.

When I got outside, Parker was still there, leaning against a lamppost. He started walking without a word, and I fell into step beside him as we headed to the parking lot. I kept expecting him to take my hand or something, but we just walked, silence surrounding us.

But it wasn't uncomfortable. It was more like how the air feels right after lightning flashes and you're waiting for the thunder to rumble.

We got to his car and he opened the passenger door for me. Nick had never done that. Not that I expected him to. I mean, I was fully capable of opening my own door, but still, it made me feel . . . special. And I so didn't want to feel special around Parker.

I slid into his car. It smelled way too much like him. I stared straight ahead while he climbed in and started it up.

Only he didn't start it up. He just sat there. Out of the corner of my eye, I could see his arm draped over the steering wheel, the way he'd turned his body so he could look at me.

Okay, I was starting to think that my agreeing to get something to drink was a big mistake. I should probably get out of the car now, before he did turn it on and took me someplace that I might not want to be.

"Relax, Megan, I'm not going to jump your bones."

I shifted around and glared at him. "I thought we were going to a pancake house."

He reached over and tugged on one of my braids. "Can you undo your braids first, so it doesn't look like I'm sitting there with a kid?"

"I don't see what difference it makes," I mumbled, even though I began undoing them. My compromise between fast and slow. I hadn't bothered to fix my hair. Mostly because I hadn't wanted him to think I was doing anything special for him.

When I had the strands undone, I ran my fingers through my hair, shook my head, and wondered why he was grinning like the Cheshire cat.

"I really like it loose," he said.

I thought about grabbing my clip out of my backpack, but I liked the way he was looking at me.

Bad, Megan. Don't encourage him.

"Are we going to go?" I asked. It was so wrong to be attracted to this guy. I had Nick.

"Sure." He twisted around, started the car.

I breathed a sigh of relief.

We didn't talk during the short drive to the pancake house. And we ordered more than coffee and milk. I ordered a short stack of pancakes, and Parker ordered the International, which included pancakes, Belgian waffles, and French toast, plus bacon, eggs, and hash browns. The guy had an appetite.

The waitress poured him a cup of coffee and brought my milk. After she left, Parker stretched his arm along the back of the booth, reminding me of some lithe creature that was about to pounce.

"You wanted to talk?" I said.

"Like I said, I've been thinking about that kiss—"

"Well, I've been thinking about it, too, and it shouldn't have happened."

"I agree."

With a devilish grin, he reached across and nudged my chin up so my dropped jaw closed. His words were so not what I was expecting. I was thinking he was going to say that it should happen again. I was confused, mostly because—shame on me—I sorta wanted it to.

"That's . . . that's good," I finally stammered. "So it won't happen again."

"Won't happen again." Leaning forward, he crossed his arms on the table. "So there's no reason that we can't be friends, hang out, have some summer fun."

For some reason an old Elvis Presley song about suspicious minds that my grandmother played a lot was suddenly reverberating through my head.

"You want to be just friends?"

"Sure. Why not? We're here for the summer. I like you. I do a lot of stuff with Jordan. You're her roommate, and knowing Jordan, she'll invite you to join us. If I hook up with someone else, you'll always feel like a third wheel. If I stay unattached, then when pairing takes place, you have someone to pair with." He shrugged. "And so do I. Lot less work on my part. I'll have a partner for the summer that I don't have to impress. Just hang with. Who wants to spend the summer looking for dates?"

I furrowed my brow. "Why don't I trust you?"

He pounded his fist against his chest, over his heart. "I'm hurt. It's an earnest offer. Friends for the summer. Nothing more."

"Friends."

"Friends."

"Didn't think guys and girls could be just friends."

"Sure they can. I have lots of just friends who are girls. Kate Hudson—"

"You know Kate Hudson? *The* Kate Hudson?"

"Sure. She was in one of my dad's movies. You could have fun with me, Megan. I'm an interesting guy. Be *really* nice, and maybe I'll introduce you to Orlando Bloom."

My jaw tightened. "And what does *really nice* involve?"

He grimaced, realizing his poor choice of words.

"I didn't mean it like that. I'm not expecting anything other than friendship. Be a good friend, and maybe I'll introduce you to Orlo."

Orlo? Did he really know him that well?

"I don't get it, Parker. I mean, you hanging out with me, when I have a boyfriend, will mean that I won't be alone for the summer, but what do you get out of the deal?"

"The same thing. Not being alone for the summer. Look, Megan, it's a lot of work to try to develop a relationship, especially if you want it to go beyond friendship. With you, I wouldn't have to put forth any effort. Which works for me, because basically I'm a lazy guy."

I thought about how all Jordan's car had needed was a new battery, and he'd gone to the trouble to change her oil. Lazy? I didn't think so.

But if his offer was honest and sincere, while I had Patti and Lisa to hang around with, it would also be nice to have a guy around—especially when Jordan did ask me to join her for things. Because he was right. I would start to feel awkward, in the way.

"Okay," I said, nodding. "We can be friends."

"Great." He held out his hand. "Let's shake on it."

But when I slipped my hand into his, felt the strength and warmth of his close over mine, I couldn't help but worry that I was getting in over my head.

"So you and Parker, huh?"

I looked up from the glass shelf I was dusting at H & G to find Nancy staring down at me.

"Excuse me?"

"I saw you and Parker sitting in his car last night in the parking lot, so I just figured you and him . . ." She wiggled her eyebrows and gave me this I-know-what-you're-up-to-and-aren't-you-a-lucky-girl grin.

"No, we're just friends."

"Yeah, right. He's totally hot. And you're 'just friends.' Give me a break."

"Seriously. That's all we are."

"If you say so."

She walked off, but her skepticism hung in the air. We *were* just friends. After we'd made our agreement last night, I'd actually relaxed and enjoyed our midnight snack. The conversation had been pleasant. He'd told me all kinds of stories about his encounters with famous people. He knew everyone, and he talked about them like they were just regular people. I guess because to him they were. I mean, some of these guys were in his "media room" watching football games, cheering the same team he did. Amazing.

And no wonder Jordan's dad had given her a credit card. She often went shopping with the stars.

After I finished dusting, I went to my place behind the cash register. Patti was working the same shift as I was, but she'd been really quiet since I'd arrived.

"Everything okay?" I asked.

"I don't approve of summer flings," she said tartly without looking at me.

"Neither do I."

"Then why are you having one?"

"I'm not."

"We were going to sit together last night."

"I lost you in the crowd."

"I saw you sitting with Parker."

"Sitting. That's all we were doing."

"You looked pretty chummy to me."

I rolled my eyes. "You know, it's really not your business, but just for the record, we are only friends."

That seemed to become my mantra for the afternoon as one person after another dropped by during his or her break and said, "You and Parker, huh?"

The guy was Mr. Popularity, and suddenly I was his girl-friend.

By the time Parker actually stopped by to see if I wanted to take my break with him, I was fuming.

"Everyone thinks there's something going on between us," I said, as we sat at the miniature table outside the Gingerbread Man and munched on our peanut-butter cookies.

"What difference does it make what everyone thinks? We know what's what."

"How can it not bother you that people are talking about us and not even interested in hearing the truth?"

He reached across and laid his hand over mine where it rested on the table. "Megan, I grew up with gossip and tabloids. All that matters is that *we* know the truth. I'm not going to waste energy trying to convince everyone else that we're just friends. They'll see what they want to see."

"It probably doesn't help that you're holding my hand."

He grinned. "Technically, we're not holding hands."

I couldn't help but return his smile. "It's pretty darn close."

"Close only counts in horseshoes. Isn't that what they say in Texas?"

"Yeah, something like that." I knew I should probably pull my hand back, but I didn't. I left it there because his thumb had started to stroke the back of my hand and it just felt nice. Calming. Soothing.

"Jordan, Ross, Cole, Ronda, and I are going to spend next Monday out at the lake. So, friend, are you going to come?"

I narrowed my eyes, wondering if I'd been manipulated. "Why didn't you mention this last night?"

"It just came up this morning. The guy we're renting the cabin from has a boat. He asked me to take it out, keep the engine in shape. Just gonna do some cruising."

"Sure. Why not? *Friend*."

He laughed. It was a good laugh, a carefree laugh that made me laugh in return.

I thought it would probably start the gossiping going again. But I didn't care.

I liked being with Parker. We could keep our relationship as friends. I knew we could. Even if I felt a bit of loss when he finally moved his hand away from mine. Even if I wished our break would never end.

It was the work I was avoiding. Not the being with him that I wanted to prolong.

Or at least that's what I told myself.

Only 44, no 43 Nick-less days to go, and counting. . . .

CHAPTER 15

We couldn't have picked a nicer day

to go out on the lake. I was wearing black shorts and my red "Too Hot to Handle" halter. Which of course made Parker grin when he saw it. That he refrained from commenting surprised and pleased me at the same time. He was wearing swim trunks and a Hawaiian-print shirt. It was unbuttoned, the front flowing back as he drove the boat across the lake. I sat in the seat beside him.

I shouldn't have been impressed. My dad had a boat. It was green. Metal. Had a motor. Held two people. He used it when he went bass fishing.

This boat was a lot bigger, a lot nicer. Cole and Ronda sat in the two seats behind us. A padded bench ran along either side of the boat behind them. Jordan and Ross were sitting there. We probably could have accommodated a few more people.

Apparently, Parker and Cole had discovered a little cove last summer when they were out exploring with the guy they were house-sitting the cabin for. So we were headed there now for a little swimming, a picnic, and just general relaxation away from the hordes of people we dealt with every day. The wind and the motor created too much noise to talk, and I couldn't explain why I was having a great time. We weren't really doing anything. Maybe it was just getting away from it all.

I didn't want to contemplate that it was being with Parker. Since we'd made our agreement to be just friends, he always came to H & G during his break—whether it was his short break or his lunch break. He was always at the park when it closed and walked me back to the dorm. And he was always asking me to come with him at dawn when he took Magnum Force for its first run of the day.

He never used the word *test*, but that's what he was doing. Testing it to make sure that it was operating properly. If I didn't want to ride it after it was declared operational for the day, I sure didn't want to ride it *before* it was declared ready to go. He kept promising that it was safe. If it was safe, why did it need to be tested?

He looked over at me now and smiled. I loved his smile. It gave the impression that he was simply glad to find me there.

"We're almost there," he shouted, and I read the words formed by his mouth more than I heard them.

He slowed the boat as we got closer to shore. I could see the tree-lined cove. When he got near enough, he cut the engine.

"Let's go, guys," he said.

He, Cole, and Ross jumped into the water. There were ropes used for mooring the boat to a dock, but of course, there was no dock here. They used the ropes to pull the boat partially onto the shore and anchored it in the sand.

Ronda, Jordan, and I handed off all our gear to them: quilts, blankets, towels, ice chests. Then using the ladder on the side of the boat, we climbed down, dropped into water that went past our knees and waded to shore. It wasn't as cold as it had been the first night that I'd waded into it. But it wasn't Texas-warm, either.

We spread out blankets and set up the bucket of fried chicken and drinks because the guys were starving. I wanted to explore but figured that it would be better to do it on a full stomach. The place was amazing. Really secluded.

"I wonder why there aren't any houses around here," I asked once we were all settled and eating.

"I think it has to do with the ghosts," Parker said.

He was sitting beside me, his bare knee touching mine. I didn't know why, but there always seemed to be some part of him touching me: his knee, his hand, his foot. It was all very innocent, and I'd grown comfortable with it. It was just the way he was.

I swallowed the chicken I'd been chewing and looked around. "The ghosts?"

"Yeah. In the late eighteen hundreds, there was a big storm. A ship sank a mile or so from here. They say twenty-seven people drowned. And this is where they came to rest. A little bit farther down is a lighthouse. We can go look at it after we eat."

"A shipwreck?" I asked.

"The Great Lakes are huge. There have been a lot of ship-wrecks. Haven't you ever heard of the *Edmund Fitzgerald*?"

"My dad has a song about it that someone sings."

"Gordon Lightfoot. Yeah, my dad does, too. Anyway, div-ing expeditions are searching for the wrecked ships all the time. And huge cruise ships travel the lakes. Don't you think when you look out that it's like standing at the edge of the ocean? You can't even see the far shore."

I had thought that, the first night when I walked along the sandy beach.

"Okay, so there are shipwrecks. There has to be a more practical reason that no one lives here," I said.

"It's the ghosts," Cole said. "We saw one last summer."

"Get out!" Jordan, sitting between him and Ross, shoved his shoulder.

"Hey, watch it! You almost made me drop my drumstick," he said.

"You so did not see a ghost," she said.

"We saw something." He pointed behind us. "Right between those trees. Then it was gone."

"You're just trying to make us more cuddly," Ronda said.

"And how do ghosts do that?" I asked.

"Get us on edge and the next thing they know, we're clinging to them, like they're He-Men or something and will protect us from all harm."

"You know, there are definite disadvantages to having a girlfriend who's studying psychology," Cole said.

"So it is the cuddle factor and not real ghosts?" Jordan asked.

Strangely, I could hear the slight apprehension in her voice, like maybe the idea of ghosts really would make her more clingy.

Cole just shrugged. I peered over at Parker. He was study-ing his chicken thigh like he was trying to determine what it was. Was he hoping to make me cuddle with him? Was he not looking at me because he didn't want me to see the truth in his eyes?

"I don't believe in ghosts," I said.

"You will," he said in an eerie voice. "After we go to the lighthouse, you will."

As it turned out, only he and I trekked around the cove to where the lighthouse was. I've always been fascinated by lighthouses. This one was a typical tall cylinder shape, painted white with fading red around the top.

"It's not a working lighthouse, is it?" I asked as we approached.

"Nope. Hasn't been in years."

I saw the lighthouse keeper's house. It looked ramshackle, lonely, as lonely as the lighthouse. "It's kind of sad."

"Only a girl could think a building looks sad."

I peered over at him. "That is so chauvinistic."

"But true."

"You must find something interesting about it or you wouldn't have wanted to come here," I said, fully confident that the words were true.

"Haunting," he said. "There's something haunting about it."

I rolled my eyes. "You're not going to scare me with your ghost stories."

"I'm not trying to. I don't mean haunted like with apparitions. I mean haunted like . . . lonely, abandoned . . ."

"Sad?" I offered sarcastically, anything not to let on how it always rattled me when we were thinking the same thoughts. That never happened with Nick. We could be looking at an apple and we wouldn't see it as the same shade of red. Which I'd always thought was a good thing. Isn't it better to be different, so you don't bore each other?

Parker laughed. "Okay. Maybe sad does work."

We'd reached the lighthouse. Spider webs were laced at the top corners of the door. Thank goodness no spiders were in sight. It's not that I'm a scaredy cat. I just don't like spiders, or ghosts, or roller coasters . . . okay, basically anything with an ick factor or that creates the sensation of falling is at the top of my list of things I'd rather not experience.

Parker pushed on the door. The hinges creaked. All I could see was the darkness. He took my hand. I didn't object. As a matter of fact, I squeezed his hand hard, just in case he decided to let go. No way was that going to happen.

Once we were inside, my eyes adjusted to the shadows. Faint light was spilling down from the top where there were windows, and I could see the cast-iron spiral staircase that wound its way up. Without a word, Parker started up the stairs, with me following close on his heels, not only because he was still holding my hand, but because I didn't want to be left alone.

Our footsteps echoed a clanging sound. The wind was whistling up the stairs, creating an eerie howling. Or at least I kept telling myself it was the wind. I could barely feel it, but it was there. It wasn't those souls lost to the deep making the noise and sending chills along my spine.

And I looked up constantly, not down. It was that afraid-of-heights thing that I had. The cast-iron steps were a latticework of holes. Looking down meant seeing how far up we'd gone. Better to look up and see how close we were to reaching the top.

When we did reach the top, I couldn't imagine what I was thinking. Heights weren't my thing. Yet here I was, trying not to think about how I was going to get back down.

A hollow sound echoed around us as we walked the perimeter of the room. An emptiness. That sadness again. A crack in one of the windows was probably responsible for the shrieking of the wind. In the center of the room was where the light had once burned.

"It must have been so lonely living out here," I said.

"I think it would be cool to live away from everything," Parker said.

He was still holding my hand. I still didn't object.

"You wouldn't like living alone," I said. "At the park, you know everyone and everyone knows you. You're Mr. Popularity. Popular people don't do well on their own. They need others."

"Oh, so now you're the psychology major? Explain to me someone who won't go on a tall ride, but will walk up to the top of a lighthouse."

"It's not the height so much as it is the plummeting drop."

"So if I could find a roller coaster without the drop, you'd ride it?"

"Would it be a roller coaster without a drop?"

"Good point. Did you hear the ghosts?"

"It was the wind, coming in from the open door and through that cracked window there."

"Ah, come on, Megan, what's the fun in having a logical explanation for everything?"

"It's my practical nature."

"That practical nature is going to get you in trouble some day."

"What?"

He released my hand and walked to the lake side of the lighthouse. "Look how vast it is. Awesome."

I moved up beside him and couldn't help thinking that this was an incredible kissing place. I could see a lighthouse keeper's daughter sneaking up here with her boyfriend. I was glad that Parker and I had decided to be just friends, because this was the kind of place that made a girl think about passionate kisses. Especially when the sun started to go down.

"It really is nice to get away from the crowds," I said.

"Yeah, that's why Cole and I jumped on the chance to stay in the cabin, away from everything. The dorm is nice the first year or two because it gives you a chance to meet people, especially when you've never been away from home before. Eliminates that homesickness. But there are always people around. At the park all day. At the lake near the hotel. That's one of the reasons that I really like taking the roller coaster cars out first thing in the morning. It's like this. Quiet, peaceful. With the sun coming up." He looked over at me. "Even if you're not interested in riding, I wish you'd come to the park with me first thing in the morning sometime. It's a totally different place."

When he was looking at me like that, with those green eyes focused on me, I had a difficult time thinking. "I'm not much of a morning person."

"Neither am I. But some things are worth getting up for."

"You promise not to make me ride Magnum Force?"

"I wouldn't ever make you do anything you didn't want to do."

"You won't nag about it?"

"Nag is what my mom did before she and Dad got divorced. I simply ask."

"If you ask more than once, it's a nag."

He narrowed his eyes. "Okay. If that's what it takes to make you come with me in the morning, then I promise not to ask you to ride the roller coaster."

"You are a nag, but I'll go anyway."

"Great! You won't regret it. I'll come for you at six in the morning." Before I could protest at the ungodly time he'd suggested, he grabbed my hand. "Let's go swim."

CHAPTER 16

I loved Parker's enthusiasm as we

walked back to the picnic site. He pointed out different birds and plants and strange cloud formations.

"Tell me that you're not this energetic in the mornings," I said, as we walked along. Not holding hands.

I really couldn't figure out a pattern as to when he would hold my hand. When he thought about it or when he didn't? Was it reflex or planned?

Having never been just friends with a guy, I was walking an uncharted path. I mean, I knew what to expect in a boyfriend/girlfriend situation. But with Parker, I hardly ever knew what to expect.

By the time we got back to the picnic area, everyone else

was already in the water. I kicked off my sandals. I was wearing my bathing suit underneath my clothes so I took off my shorts and top. Parker was already in his swim trunks so he just tossed his shirt onto the blanket.

He ran into the water, then dove in, and came up sputtering a short distance away. Which left only me on the shore.

"Come on, Megan!" he called out. "There are no sharks."

"I'm not a *total* chicken," I said, as I walked into the water.

It was pretty chilly, and I thought about how nice it would be to lie in the sun afterward and warm up.

"It's easier if you just go under," Jordan said. "You'll get used to it faster."

Only I didn't want to get used to it faster. I was perfectly fine taking my time.

I was up to my knees in the water, had just stepped forward when pain sliced through my foot. I screeched, stepped back, lost my balance, my arms windmilling . . .

I fell backward, went under . . .

I felt strong hands grabbing hold of me, jerking me upward. I found my wet body against Parker's, skin to skin, as he held me in his arms.

"What happened?" he asked.

"I don't know. I felt something sting—"

"Omigod, she's bleeding," Jordan cried.

Parker carried me out of the water, set me on the blanket.

"Were you a lifeguard in another life?" I asked jokingly.

"Yeah, a couple of summers during high school," he said distractedly, while examining my foot.

"What do you think happened?" Ronda asked, kneeling beside Parker, looking at my foot.

"Broken glass maybe," he said. "I think it's going to need stitches."

"Stitches?" I practically shrieked. "You're kidding, right? I've never had stitches in my life."

I pulled my foot free of his hold, bent my knee, and tried to view the damage. But there was so much blood. "Oh," was the best I could manage. It looked ghastly.

Ross handed Parker a strip of shredded towel. Parker took my foot and began wrapping it.

"We need to get you to the hospital."

"It's just a little cut."

"You know you were swimming in a lake, not a pool. No chlorine to kill the germs. When was the last time you had a tetanus shot?"

When I was about two?

"I don't know."

"Come on. Everybody, pack up," he ordered. "We're going."

"Don't do that. It's not an emergency. We can go later."

"Now isn't the time to prove you're not a chicken," he said, and sounded seriously irritated.

I wasn't trying to prove anything. I just thought he was overreacting.

"Fine," I finally said. I wasn't really ready to go, but he was bigger than I was.

"See, I told you it wasn't that bad," I said, as we pulled away from the hospital emergency room.

When we'd arrived at the dock, Parker had left the boat for the others to put away and he'd driven me to the hospital. Since Jordan had her car there, she and the gang had a way to get home, so I hadn't been concerned about them.

"I don't call a huge bandage wrapped around your foot and a tetanus shot not bad," Parker said.

The tetanus shot was a precaution since I wasn't sure exactly what I had stepped on. Could have been an old rusty can or something. I couldn't remember the last time that I'd had the shot before tonight and I didn't want to call my mom and ask her. I didn't want her worrying. And for some reason, as silly as it seemed, I was feeling guilty for being out having a great time. I didn't want Nick to know that I was doing anything other than working.

Silly, I know. I mean, I was certain that he was doing more than working. He was going to movies and having fun. I was sure of it.

"You should call in sick tomorrow," Parker added.

"I'm not sick. I'm just limping a little." The doctor had told me to stay off it for a day, but it was wrapped up pretty tight. I was sure it would be fine. "Besides, how can I call in sick if I'm planning to go with you in the morning?"

He gave a quick glance my way, a smile tugging up the corner of his mouth. "You're still gonna come with me tomorrow?"

"Just to watch."

"Before the summer is over, I'll have you screaming on a roller coaster."

"In your dreams."

It was strange. He got really quiet. It wasn't so much that he wasn't talking, but this heaviness settled in the car, like he wanted to say something, but didn't dare, and I had this crazy idea that maybe he really *was* having dreams about me. But was too embarrassed to tell me.

He pulled up in front of the dorm. "Wait there," he ordered as he got out of the car.

I rolled my eyes, but watched as he hurried around the front of the car and jerked open the car door. Then he reached inside, slid an arm beneath my knees—

"Hey, what are you doing?" I asked, even though I knew what he was doing.

"I'm going to carry you inside," he said.

My arms wound around his neck as he lifted me out of the car.

"You're overreacting again," I said. "Put me down. I can walk."

Even though I didn't really want to. Even though I sorta liked the fact that he was carrying me. It wasn't really romantic. We weren't kissing or hugging or gazing into each other's eyes. It was just fun and silly and I realized that the pain medication the doctor had given me to help me sleep through the night must have kicked in, because I was feeling kinda giddy.

Laughing, feeling special, and wondering about kissing Parker. Wondering if I could use the medication as an excuse to do what I'd thought about doing a dozen times throughout the afternoon.

He walked through the doors and I protested feebly. "Put me down."

"When we get to your room."

"Oh, that's it," I said. "You just want to tell people you've been to my room."

He grinned and wiggled his eyebrows, still walking to the elevator. I laughed.

"Megan?" A voice called out questioningly—and tartly.

I froze. Only one person I knew could sound both ways at the same time. It was a commanding voice, and I guess Parker reacted to it as well, because he spun around with me still in his arms, clinging to his neck.

And standing there, hands on her hips, brow furrowed in disgust, was my older sister.

CHAPTER 17

"So how long have you been see-ing this guy?"

Sarah and I were at a Starbucks. I knew it was a big mis-take to drink coffee after dark, but I needed something to chase away the lethargy brought on by the pain meds. They weren't heavy duty or anything, just enough to make me not care too much that my sister had caught me in a guy's arms.

"We're not *seeing* each other," I answered.

She was wearing her judgmental, I-know-what-I-saw expression. I'd never been crazy about it.

"Sure looked like you were seeing each other to me," she said, and I could hear the disapproval in her voice.

"He was carrying me because he was worried about my foot."

"Geez, I guess all that giggling didn't exactly scream 'concern'!"

"You're not the boss of me."

How grown-up did that sound? Not very. But it was true.

"Does Nick know about him?"

Boy was that a low blow. It made me feel guilty when I had no reason to.

"There's nothing for him to know." I dumped three packets of sugar into my coffee. So now I would have a sugar *and* caffeine high. I'd be climbing the walls before I was done here.

Sarah laid her hand over mine before I ripped open another sugar packet. "Look, Megan, I know how it is to be away from home for the first time, with no parental control, no limits, complete freedom—"

I snatched my hand out from beneath hers. "It's not like that. Parker is my roommate's brother. We were all at the lake together. Just a big group, having fun. His carrying me meant absolutely nothing. We are *just friends.*"

She stared at me, blinked her eyes. "You really believe that," she said, like she couldn't believe I believed it.

"Because it's the truth," I stated emphatically.

She shook her head. "Maybe your truth, not his. He is definitely interested."

"He *was* interested, but he knows about my feelings for Nick. So we've agreed to be friends."

"Oh, God, Megan, tell me you aren't that naive. Guys can't be *just* friends with girls. It's biologically impossible."

"I didn't realize you'd suddenly become a biologist." She opened her mouth and I raised my hand to stop further commentary. "Let's agree to disagree on this situation. I'm more interested in what you're doing here and why you didn't tell me you were coming."

"I didn't tell you because I wanted to surprise you—which I did with resounding success."

"Okay. One question answered, one to go," I said, getting really irritated with her. "Why are you here? Don't you have a wedding to plan or something equally important to do?"

Sighing, she picked up a sugar packet and started flicking it like it was a miniature punching bag. "The planning is driving me crazy. I had to get away."

"I know Mom's been difficult—"

"Not Mom. Bobby."

"Bobby?" That wasn't good. "You mean, like you had a fight?"

"No." She shook her head. "It's like he doesn't care."

"He loves you, Sarah," I reassured her.

"I know that. It's not that he doesn't care about *me*. He doesn't care about the *wedding*. Every time I have to make a decision, I'll ask him for advice and he'll say, 'Whatever makes you happy.' "

She rolled her eyes, looking totally disgusted.

"What's wrong with that?" I asked.

"It doesn't help me make a decision. It just puts all of the burden on me. I don't know how to make him tell me what *he* wants."

Her constant hammering at the sugar packet wore it down. It tore and started sprinkling sugar over the table. She didn't seem to notice.

"So you came here to get away?" I asked, still not getting it.

"I came here to get advice."

"From me?"

She nodded.

"About handling Bobby?"

She nodded again.

I laughed. "Sarah, I've been dating for all of three months. I don't know anything about guys."

"That was obvious after I saw you with that guy tonight—"

"His name is Parker."

"—then you said you're just friends—"

My cell phone rang and I welcomed the distraction. I glanced at the display and thought about not answering. . . .

Decisions, decisions. Talk with Parker or talk with Sarah. No brainer.

"Hi."

"Hey, how'd it go with your sister?"

"It's still going."

"Good?"

"No."

"Bad, huh?"

"It's been better." I felt like we were talking in some sort of code, so Sarah wouldn't figure out exactly who was on the other end of the phone.

"Invite her to go with us in the morning," he said.

"She won't be interested."

"Try her and see. She looked majorly stressed. I know a great stress reliever."

"Magnum Force?" I asked. The other alternative was one of his kisses, which almost literally melted bones.

"You bet."

"Hold on." I moved the phone away from my ear and looked at Sarah. "It's Parker."

"I figured. Your short responses gave you away."

Ignoring her sarcasm, I said, "He wants to know if you

want to ride one of the roller coasters with him in the morning before the park opens."

"You mean, like, by myself?"

"And with him. He has to test Magnum Force every morning."

She got this look in her eye that I didn't quite trust, but I knew her answer before she even spoke.

"Sure, why not?"

Because the ride is scary. But I held the words back.

I told Parker the good news, and he did sound like it was good news. I hung up thinking he was really a nice guy. To want to do something for my sister while she was here.

"I can probably get you a free pass for all the rides," I told her.

"We'll see. I'm not really here to have fun."

"Are you saying that being with me is a downer?" I asked teasingly.

"I'm saying that I'm beginning to think that I came here to run away from my problems, and that's not really a grown-up thing to do."

A chill was in the air the next morning as Sarah and I stood outside the entrance to the park, waiting for Parker. The morning sunlight was glinting off the lake. It was totally peaceful.

Even Sarah didn't seem quite so uptight. She'd stayed in the park hotel and we'd had breakfast together. We'd talked about safe things: movies, music, TV shows, shoes. It had actually been fun.

"So where is this guy?" she asked. "I don't get up at the crack of dawn for just anyone, you know?"

I smiled. "He'll be here."

And just like that, I saw him walking up the path. I guess Sarah did, too, because she murmured, "He is a fine specimen."

"I hadn't noticed," I lied.

"Yeah, right."

He was decked out in his park gear: cargo shorts, red polo shirt, sneakers. He did look really good. So what was new about that?

Nothing, except I was thinking about how he'd carried me yesterday and how it had felt to be held by him and how I really shouldn't be intrigued by him at all . . . but I was.

He was grinning broadly.

"Hey," he said, when he got near enough that he didn't have to shout. "So glad you decided to come today."

He walked past us and Sarah and I followed.

"So you do this every morning?" Sarah asked.

"Every morning."

The guard at the gate let us in without asking for our identification cards. He and Parker greeted each other, so I figured it was a morning ritual for them.

When I worked during the day, I would get to the park just before it opened to get my costume on, but by then it was already buzzing with activity: the various vendors setting up, the cleanup crew getting into position, the ride crews preparing the equipment for the day. It was never like it was now: almost eerily quiet.

The park had shade trees here and there. I could hear the leaves rustling in the early morning breeze. And that was about it. Maybe an occasional clank as people began gearing up for the day.

"How long are you staying?" Parker asked Sarah as we wended our way through the maze of sidewalks that led to Magnum Force.

"Only until tonight. So, do you have a girlfriend back home?" Sarah asked.

I gritted my teeth, incredibly tempted to stick my foot out and trip her, but it was still sore from yesterday. I was still limping slightly.

Parker didn't seem offended by Sarah's interrogation. He just laughed and said, "Nope."

"I would think someone as good-looking as you would have lots of girlfriends," Sarah said.

"Sarah!" She was really going too far. "His love life is none of your business."

"It is if it involves you."

"We're *friends*," I said. I looked at Parker. "I'm really sorry. She has a problem with minding her own business."

"Doesn't bother me. I've got nothing to hide." He was wearing dark glasses, so it was hard to know exactly what he was thinking. "You gonna ride with your sister?"

I know my eyes got big. "No. I'm just here to watch."

"You sure?"

"I'm sure."

We got to Magnum Force and walked up the ramp. Parker had Sarah's undivided attention now as he explained all the stats: length of track, speed, highest point. You'd think he was responsible for building the thing the way he went on and the way she gushed over every detail. Had to be a roller coaster fanatic thing.

Not that I'd ever considered my sister a fanatic, but she was sure acting like it now.

Since there were no people, the chains that usually forced

the line to snake around the barriers weren't in place, so we were able to walk straight through to the set of cars that was waiting on the track. A guy was standing by the controls, punching a button here, a button there. When we got closer, I could read his tag: CHRIS (BELLINGHAM, WA).

He and Parker greeted each other. Parker helped Sarah climb into the first car. Then he looked back at me. "Sure you don't want to do this?"

I felt like such a wuss.

"Come on," Sarah said. "It'll be fun."

"If they're safe, why do they have to be tested?" I asked.

"So they *stay* safe," Parker said.

"Which means there's the possibility they aren't."

He tugged on my hair and grinned. "Can't argue with a phobe."

"I'm not a phobe."

His grin grew, revealing his dimples. "Whatever."

He climbed into the car beside Sarah, and for the first time in my life, I hated that I really didn't like roller coasters. Sitting that close to him would be . . . well, it would be nice. Except for the screaming and throwing up part.

They buckled up, then he pulled the bar down across them. He gave Chris a thumbs-up. Chris pushed a big blue button and the train of cars began the ascent. I moved to the edge of the platform and just watched.

I could tell that Sarah and Parker were talking. Great. What were they talking about? Not me, I hope. Gosh, don't let them be talking about me.

They got to the top and there was that one second of heart-stopping anticipation.

Then the park wasn't so quiet anymore.

It was echoing with Sarah's screams.

CHAPTER 18

"It was so awesome," Sarah said for, like, the hundredth time.

She slurped a strawberry freeze. We'd left Parker at Magnum Force and I'd taken her on a tour of the park, finally ending at Storybook Land. I was sorta delaying going to change into my costume to get ready for my shift.

I had nothing of interest to say to her roller coaster enthusiasm, so I kept quiet.

"I like Parker," she suddenly said.

I jerked my gaze up from my grape freeze and stared at her. She shrugged. "It's not a big deal."

"Last night you were on my case about hanging out with him."

"That was before he made me feel better about Bobby."

I arched an eyebrow. "When did this happen?"

"When we were on the roller coaster. It's a long way to the top and he said that he thinks Bobby does care about the wedding, he's just not telling me what he wants because he really does want the wedding to be the way that I want it. At least he said that was the way he would be if he was getting married. Then he looked kinda green and said he had no plans to get married any time soon." She was smiling, wistful, looking off in the distance. "I need to get home to Bobby, wrap up these wedding plans."

"Okay."

She peered over at me. "After I see you in costume."

I groaned. "He told you about that, too, didn't he?"

"He said you're cute in costume."

"Cute?" I shook my head. "It's embarrassing."

"I promise not to laugh, but I do want to see you decked out. I'll hang around the park today. Before you start your shift, we'll do dinner, then I'll head to the airport."

She did laugh when she saw me in braids. At least, I think she was laughing at my hair. She could have been laughing at the entire outfit.

"You're adorable!" she cried out, in between gasping for breath.

"Thanks a lot." I felt a little too old to be adorable.

But when she hugged me good-bye to head out to the airport and back home, I really started to miss her: her laughter, her complaining, her worrying about me. And her final parting words kept haunting me:

"Watch out for Parker. He could get you into a lot of trouble."

I was still trying to figure out how he was going to get me into trouble when my shift ended. I mean, he couldn't get me into trouble if I didn't let him, right? And I had no plans to let him.

My plans changed just a little when I came out of the costume shop and saw him leaning against the wall, arms crossed over his chest. He straightened when he saw me, and I really didn't like the way my whole body just seemed to smile because he was there waiting for me.

Just friends. Just friends. Just friends. We could be just friends. I was sure of it.

"Your sister get to the airport okay?" he asked.

"Far as I know." I kept walking toward the park exit.

"I like her," he said, as he walked beside me.

"I do, too," I admitted.

"You're supposed to say that she likes me, too."

I peered over at him. "She didn't say if she did or not."

He placed his hand over his heart. "I'm crushed. I thought a ride with me on Magnum Force would win her over."

He was being so melodramatically hurt that I couldn't help but laugh.

"Why was it so important to win her over?"

"I have this thing about not being liked. I want everyone to like me," he said.

"Don't let it go to your head, but I think she did like you a little."

"Yes!" He punched his fist into the air.

I laughed as I exited the park with him right on my heels. On the other side of the gate, he took my hand. It was dark, except for the occasional light along the sidewalk. I didn't figure he could see my cheeks turning red.

I thought I should jerk my hand free, but it was so totally innocent. Just holding hands. Just friends.

"Let's walk along the lake," he said.

Not waiting for me to answer, he guided us off the sidewalk and onto the sand. I didn't want to think about how romantic this would be if Nick was here, because it was romantic and Nick wasn't here and I wasn't supposed to have romantic thoughts around Parker.

Take your hand out of his. Take your hand out of his.

But my arm wasn't listening to my brain. It wasn't jerking away. It was leaving my hand snuggled warmly within his.

"You coming to the hump party tomorrow night?" he asked.

"Probably." I looked over at him. I could just make out his silhouette thanks to the distant lights and the moon. "It doesn't seem fair that you have to get to the park before it opens and you have to work until it closes."

"I don't work until it closes."

"But you're always at the park when I get off my shift."

"Not because I'm working."

I stumbled and he caught me. "Be careful with your foot," he said, and I could hear the genuine concern in his voice.

"My foot's fine," I said. "If you're not working till closing, then why are you at the park when I get off?"

We weren't holding hands anymore. We were much closer thanks to my lack of coordination and near stumble. We were facing each other, his hands on my waist.

"Why do you think, Megan?" he asked quietly.

"Because we're friends."

"Yeah, because we're friends."

"Sarah says that guys can't be just friends with girls."

"Sounds like a suspicious woman to me."

I thought he was going to pull me close. I thought he was

going to kiss me. Instead he let go of me, took my hand, and started walking again.

"What's your boyfriend have to say these days?" he asked.

"Nick? Nothing really," I stammered. "Working hard. Keeping busy." *Hardly calling.* I didn't know why I was reluctant to mention the last. Maybe because it had me a little worried. Not that I was calling him every five minutes, but my plans for keeping in constant contact through some form of communication seemed to be falling by the wayside.

I had so much to keep me busy. Like walking slowly along the shoreline with Parker. If I'd rushed back to the dorm, I could have called Nick before it was too late. Or I could have even talked to him on my way to the dorm. I had my cell phone. But no way was I going to call him when Parker was here. Even if Parker promised not to say anything, I was afraid that Nick might sense—

Suddenly my cell phone was ringing, I was screeching, and Parker was laughing. I reached into my pocket, grabbed my cell phone—

"Hello?"

"Hey."

Relief swept through me. "Hi, Nick. I was just talking about you."

"With who?"

We'd stopped walking, and I could feel Parker's gaze on me.

"Someone I work with. What are you doing?"

"Talking to you."

I laughed. "Where are you?"

"Driving home from work. Had a really bad night."

"I'm sorry," I said, like my being there would have prevented it when I knew it wouldn't. Out of the corner of my eye, I watched Parker walk to the water's edge. To give me privacy? Or because he wanted to get away from me while I was talking with my boyfriend?

"—a total pain in the butt."

I realized that I'd been distracted and hadn't been listening to Nick.

"I'm sorry. Who's a pain in the butt?"

"Tess. The new waitress I'm training."

Oh, yeah, he'd mentioned her before.

"Haven't you been listening to anything I said?" he asked.

"Yeah, but I'm really tired. Sarah showed up unexpectedly last night and we stayed up really late talking, then we got up early this morning . . . it's just been a long day. Why is Tess a pain in the butt?"

"She thinks she knows everything."

"Does she? Know everything I mean?"

"'Course not. You probably have to be here to really appreciate how hard it is to train someone who doesn't listen to what you say."

"Nick, I know you're upset that I'm not there—"

"No, Megan, I didn't mean it like that. I just meant it's hard to describe what a pain she is. You just have to see it."

"You can show me when I come home in"—oh, gosh, how many days was it?—"for the wedding," I finished, a little rattled that I couldn't remember the exact number of days I had left until I saw him. Knowing Nick, he'd pick up on it right away and it would hurt his feelings if I tried to fake it.

"God, I hope I've finished training her in thirty-nine days. She really bugs me."

Thirty-nine days. Whew. I'd thought it was forty-one.

"I'm sure you're a good trainer," I said, thinking how lonely Parker looked standing where he was.

"—you think? Cool idea?"

I grimaced. I'd stopped listening again. Was he still talking about the waitress or had he moved onto another topic?

"Totally cool," I said, unwilling to admit that I had again lost track of the conversation.

"So when do you want to do it?"

I dropped to the sand and buried my face in my free hand. "I'm sorry, Nick. What is it that we're doing?"

I heard him sigh on the other end. "Never mind."

"Come on. I'm really sorry. So tell me again."

"I was saying that we could both watch the same TV show at the same time and it would be like we were together."

"Oh, that would be nice, but I'm working nights most of this week. Guess we could watch a soap during the day."

He groaned. "No way."

I sat there wishing Nick was with me. Wishing he could hold me. Maybe Parker wasn't the only one who was lonely. "Do you miss me, Nick?" I suddenly asked.

"'Course I do. Do you miss me?"

"A lot."

Then there was the silence again.

"Guess I'd better go," Nick finally said.

"Yeah, me, too."

"Dream about me, okay?" he said, making me smile.

"Okay."

I hung up and just stared at my phone. This long-distance relationship thing was hard, harder than I'd thought it would be.

Parker crouched beside me. "Everything okay?"

"It sucks. Him, there. Me, here."

Very slowly, he tucked my hair behind my ear. "I bet."

"I don't know if it's a good thing for you and me to be friends," I admitted.

"Why? I'm behaving."

"Yeah, but it makes me feel guilty, like I'm keeping a secret from him."

"So tell him about me."

I laughed. "Yeah, me hanging out with a guy is going to go over really well with him."

He hadn't moved his hand from when he tucked my hair back. It was comforting to have his fingers against my head, his palm against my cheek. "Nick is my first boyfriend. I don't want to screw it up."

"You're not going to screw it up."

"I wish I was that confident."

"Come on. If Jordan can have a boyfriend for a couple of years, you can, too. You're way cooler than she is."

Only I didn't feel cool at all.

"Being with Sarah today, talking to Nick"—I shook my head—"I think I'm homesick."

"I get homesick all the time."

"Do you really?"

"Sure."

His thumb started to stroke my cheek. It was really nice. Nick held me and kissed me, but he never just comforted me. Then I realized that my thoughts were unfair. If Nick were here and I was homesick, he'd stroke my cheek, too.

I pushed myself to my feet, feeling even guiltier, because I'd wanted to stay there longer, with Parker being so close. And that was wrong. Totally wrong.

"I need to get back to the dorm," I said, like he didn't know that already.

"Let's go."

He didn't take my hand. Which was good because I wasn't sure what I'd do if he did.

Only 39, 39, 39 Nick-less days to go, and counting. . . .

CHAPTER 19

My foot healed nicely, and the days settled into a routine. Work. Eat. Play.

And always, there was Parker. Stopping by the gift shop about the time I was ready to take a break. Buying me Dippin' Dots. Waiting for me at the end of my shift. Walking me back to the dorm. Talking with me. Laughing. It seemed like we never ran out of things to talk about.

Which was so not the way things were going with Nick.

Whenever Nick called or I called Nick, it was a struggle to keep the conversation going. He'd always gripe about Tess. I'd listen, but I didn't really care. I didn't know her. He didn't care about the things going on at the park, all the rumors about all the various summer romances that had started up.

Alisha was apparently involved with the guy whose job it was to light up the stage she performed on. Lisa was hanging out with a guy who worked the Ferris wheel. Patti was seeing a guy who managed one of the lemonade stands. Everywhere I looked, I saw couples.

And so Parker and I just naturally seemed to always be together. Who else was I going to hang out with? Everyone had someone. Even Zoe the floor monitor was spotted seriously kissing a guy who worked at the House of Crazy Mirrors.

But Nick didn't want to hear about any of the summer romances. Not that I could blame him. He didn't know these people.

Which left us with very little to talk about. And that sometimes frightened me because I was afraid it would be the same when we were together again in nineteen . . . no, it was eighteen days. What would we talk about? What had we talked about before?

Homework, teachers, school, friends. What else? I racked my brain every night trying to grab on to some topic of conversation. Then it never failed. After I hung up with Nick, Parker would call. And we would talk. For more than an hour. About everything and anything: people we knew, favorite movies, actors he'd met, his family, my family. Why did I never seem to run out of topics with Parker, but I had such a hard time talking with Nick?

Those were my thoughts Tuesday night as I walked back to the dorm. Parker, of course, was walking along beside me. He was telling me about this woman he'd helped get into the first car.

"She has to be eighty, if she's a day," he said. "Uses a walker."

"Aren't there restrictions against frail people riding the roller coasters?" I asked.

"Hey, we post warnings. Ride at your own risk. She was willing to take the risk. This is the third year that I've seen her. She always comes to celebrate her birthday. This year I was ready. Gave her a 'I survived Magnum Force' T-shirt."

"That was nice of you," I said.

"Hey, gotta admire her, you know? I want to be like that when I'm old. Still searching out the thrills."

"I'll ride the carousels," I said.

"It's not an either/or option, you know. You can do both."

He was still trying to convince me to ride with him in the morning. Roller coaster fanatics seemed to have a one-track mind, which I figured made sense, since cars usually ran on one track. The thought made me smile.

"What's so funny?" he asked.

But I just shook my head. My cell phone rang. Of course, I answered.

"Hey!"

Silence.

"Hellooo? Nick?"

"I thought that was you," he said.

His tone of voice had a really strange undercurrent to it.

"What do you mean you 'thought'? You called me, so who were you expecting?"

"I'm also watching you."

My heart slammed against my ribs, while my gaze darted madly around.

"How can you be watching me?"

"I thought about Sarah surprising you with a visit and decided I'd do the same thing."

I stopped walking. "You're here?"

"Yeah. So who's the guy?"

Parker must have sensed my distress because he reached out to touch my face, but I backed up. "Where are you, Nick?"

Then Parker was looking around as well.

"Right behind you."

I spun around and watched in shock and amazement as Nick stepped out of the shadows.

"Nick, what are you doing here?" I asked into my cell

phone, which I realized was totally ridiculous. He was here! Here! We didn't need a cell phone to communicate.

"I wanted to surprise you," he said, walking toward me, close enough for me to see that he wasn't happy. Not happy at all.

I hung up. "You did surprise me."

"Yeah, I can tell." He was glaring at Parker while people from the park, heading to the dorm, tried to figure out what was going on.

Some people tried to be discreet, but most didn't care if I knew they were trying to get the scoop. It was pretty obvious something worthy of gossip was going on.

"This is Parker," I said. "My roommate's brother."

"You work together?"

"We work at the park."

"It's no big deal," Parker said. "We were just walking the same way. Look around. Lots of people walking this way."

I stepped closer to Nick. I'd fantasized about him showing up. It was always one of those romantic moments: running over the sand, straight into each other's arms. Shouldn't I hug him or kiss him or something?

"How did you get here?" I asked.

"Drove nonstop."

"Why?"

"Because I miss you."

"Oh, Nick."

Then my arms were around his neck and I was hugging him tightly and he was hugging me. And all the doubts about us that I'd been having melted away.

This was Nick. My boyfriend who had driven nonstop to be with me.

What could be more romantic than that?

I wanted to kiss Nick. I mean I really, really wanted to kiss him. I hadn't realized exactly how much I missed him until we were hugging. It just felt so good, so familiar, so the way it should be.

But a crowd of people were still walking to the dorm, and Parker was still standing there looking at us. I felt self-conscious and embarrassed. And relieved and happy and tired. Wound up.

I stepped out of Nick's embrace. "I can't believe you're here. I mean, I'll be home in a little over two weeks."

He shrugged. "I couldn't wait, Megan, but I can only stay a couple of days. Then I have to get back to Hart's."

"Where are you staying?" I asked.

"I hadn't thought that far ahead. I need my money for gas to get me back home, so I guess I'll sleep in my car."

"You'd do that for me?" I asked, feeling guilty for not missing him more, for not being willing to drive home to see him. Of course, not having a car could have factored into that decision as well.

"You can stay at my place," Parker offered.

Alarms rang in my head. No way did I want them comparing notes. Not that there was really anything to compare. Neither did I want them sizing each other up, which was sorta what they were doing now, looking at each other the way two dogs did before one decided he could take the bone away from the other.

"Who are you again, man?" Nick finally asked.

"Her roommate's brother. Megan's like my second kid sister. Just watching out for her, like I do Jordan. I've got a house up the way with a couch you can use. If you decide you want the couch, get directions from Megan. I'll leave the door unlocked. See you around."

Just like that, Parker was walking away.

"See you, Parker. Thanks!" I called after him.

He waved a hand in the air without looking back.

"What were you thanking him for?" Nick asked.

"Offering you a place to sleep, walking me home in the

dark." I shrugged. "Nothing in particular." Everything in general. "I can't believe you're actually here."

We'd been standing on the sidewalk long enough that there weren't any people around anymore. He looked like he might be embarrassed or was feeling awkward. Like maybe he just realized he was here, too.

"I missed you, Megan," he said.

"So you just got in your car—"

"Yep. And drove, after scheduling a few days off. Drove nonstop."

Territory we'd already covered, but it made me feel special and loved. We weren't long-distance anymore. We were right in front of each other. I was starting at zero Nick-less days!

I threw my arms around Nick and kissed him. He kissed me back. It felt right. It felt good. He'd driven all the way up from Texas just to see me for a few days. How cool was that?

"Don't guess I can sleep with you," Nick said.

We were lying together on one of the lounge chairs that the hotel set out on the sandy beach for the guests.

"I have a roommate and suitemates," I explained. "I'd be okay with you sleeping in the room, but I'm not sure they would be. Plus there is the whole sneaking-you-in-without-the-floor-monitor-seeing."

Not that I thought Zoe would chase him out or anything. Guys were parading in and out on our floor all the time. But as far as I knew, none stayed the night. Besides, it would be inconsiderate toward the girls I shared the suite with. They were used to walking around in their underwear.

"I can't believe you drove all the way up here without a plan," I said, surprised that I was actually a little irritated, which made no sense at all.

He was holding me close. "All I could think about was seeing you." He squeezed me tightly. "God, I miss you."

"I miss you, too, but gosh, Nick, I'll be home in eighteen days."

"I didn't want to wait."

I snuggled against him. "I'm glad you didn't."

"Do you work tomorrow?" he asked.

"Yeah. I can get you a pass into the park."

"What fun would that be, going on all the rides alone?"

"I don't go to work until the afternoon. We could hang out together until then."

"That sucks."

I rolled my eyes. "Nick, if I'd known you were coming I might have been able to switch days off with someone."

"It wouldn't have been a surprise if you'd known, and I wanted to surprise you."

"You certainly did that. And I'm not complaining. I was just explaining that I can't change my shift at the last minute."

"I know. When I started driving I wasn't thinking of anything except seeing you."

He sounded utterly defeated.

"So where are you going to sleep tonight?"

"Guess I'll sleep at your friend's, since he made the offer."

I still didn't totally like that idea, but really there was no other alternative. The dorm had a lounge, but I didn't think the management would appreciate him bunking down on one of the couches there. Besides, he needed more than a place to sleep. He needed a shower.

"What was his name again?" he asked.

"Parker."

"Parker? And he works in a park? How lame is that?"

"Nick!" I didn't know why but it felt like he'd insulted me. I felt a strong need to defend Parker. "I like his name."

"You gotta admit it's an unusual name. How many Parkers do you know?"

"It doesn't matter. Besides, he was nice enough to offer to let you use his couch."

"Whatever. I don't like the guy, Megan."

"You don't even know him."

"But apparently you do."

I sat up. "Did you see us do *anything* suspicious?"

"You were laughing."

"Oh, what? I can only laugh when I'm with you?"

He sat up and put his arm around me. It took all my will-power not to shrug out of his embrace.

"I'm sorry, Megan. I'm tired from the drive, and I guess a little disappointed that I have to sleep on some guy's couch."

I stood. "The dorm has a curfew, so I need to get inside. Guess you can sleep here if you don't want to go to Parker's."

"No, I'll go stay at his place."

"Come on, then. I'll get a piece of paper and draw you a map. It's easy to find."

"You've been to his place?"

"Sure. They have a party there every Wednesday night. We can go tomorrow."

"Thought you had to work tomorrow."

Why did he sound suspicious again?

"A lot of people work tomorrow. The party goes on late into the night so people can go over there when they get off their shift."

He followed me into the lobby, looking around, nodding with approval, like maybe he'd expected to find me living in the slums. I went to the front desk and asked Mary

(Baltimore, MD) for a piece of paper and a pencil. When I finished drawing the map, I walked back to Nick.

"So where's your room?" he asked.

"Sixth floor. If we have time, I'll show you tomorrow."

We were standing there, suddenly awkward. I thought maybe he was expecting me to cave in and invite him to my room.

"I'll walk you to the door," I said.

At the door, I offered to go outside with him. "Call me as soon as you get here tomorrow," I said.

He kissed me goodnight, and I watched him walk to the parking lot to get to his car. As I went back into the dorm, I couldn't understand why I wasn't more thrilled that he was here, why it felt like an intrusion on my space.

Maybe because I hadn't planned for his arrival. My countdown was ruined. I would be home soon anyway, so why come up?

Because he missed me, and I missed him.

So why was I sorta wishing that he wasn't here? And why did it make me so sad not to be more excited to see him?

The next day was the longest day of my life. It had as many hours in it as the day that had come before, but they moved along at an excruciatingly slow pace. That morning Nick had joined me for breakfast at the dorm cafeteria. They allowed guests and the food was cheap, and since Nick was seriously short on cash, it seemed to be the ideal place to eat. Then I'd gotten him a free guest pass to the park, and we'd spent the morning just walking around, hanging out on a few of the tamer rides.

That afternoon, he'd laughed hysterically when I'd come out of the costume shop. Which had sort of hurt. I mean, I knew my costume was embarrassing, but it wasn't *that* bad.

The strangest part of the day was having Nick join me

during my breaks instead of Parker. It wasn't so much that it was odd having Nick with me as it was weird not to have Parker with me. When had I started to look so forward to spending time with Parker? Why wasn't I doing cartwheels because Nick was here?

Maybe because he was being . . . difficult. That was the word.

We were at Parker's house for the weekly party, standing on the back porch, desperately searching for conversation. Anytime someone stopped by and talked to me, I'd introduce the person to Nick and he would act totally bored. I knew it was hard to feel comfortable when you didn't know people, but at least there was music and free food and drinks and the people were nice.

"I can't believe Mr. Hart hired her," Nick said.

"Who?" I asked.

He gave me an impatient look. "Haven't you been listening? I've been talking about Tess for the past couple of minutes."

"I was listening." Sorta. "Maybe you should tell him that you don't like working with her."

"It's not that I don't like working with her. She just has this attitude problem. Thinks she knows everything."

I had a vague memory of hearing this before. Why wasn't

I enthralled with our conversations lately? Why couldn't I remember anything that we talked about?

"How old is she?" I asked.

"Our age."

"Do I know her?"

"Probably not. Her family just moved to town."

"She'll go to school with us in the fall?"

"Yeah."

"Maybe she's just uncomfortable being in a new place. I can relate. It's hard not knowing anyone."

Nick looked around. "No kidding. I can't believe you know all these people."

"Not all of them. Just most of them. Even if I don't know them, we have the theme park in common. Can always find something to talk about."

"When I decided to drive up here, I thought I'd have more time with you."

"You're with me now."

"Yeah, and a hundred other people."

"You want to go somewhere else?"

"Where would we go?"

I shrugged. "I don't know."

Why was it so uncomfortable? He was my boyfriend.

Shouldn't we feel at ease, regardless of where we were or what we were doing?

"Walk down to the lake with me?" he asked.

"Sure."

The music and the din of people talking got fainter the closer we got to the lake. Surprisingly the night seemed warmer than it had since I'd arrived here. We were really heading into summer. Nick was holding my hand, and I tried to be glad that he was with me, not to feel like I had to entertain him. Usually I visited with people at the party and had a much better time.

It was so unfair to Nick for me to blame him because I was bored.

What had we always talked about?

When we got to the edge of the water, he dropped my hand and stepped away from me.

"I don't get it, Megan," he said.

I stared at his shadowy silhouette. "Get what?"

"Get what you think is so great about being here." He turned around and faced me. "Don't you miss me?"

"Of course I do, Nick. I can't believe you'd even have to ask."

"Then come back home with me."

I stared at him. "Nick, I made a commitment to work here for the summer."

"And what are they going to do if you quit? Arrest you? Be mad at you? So what? You're working in a freaking gift shop. Anybody can do that."

And anyone could wait tables. And it wasn't like Hart's was the only restaurant in town or the only place he could work.

"I like being here, Nick. I like the people I've met. They're all so different and so interesting. I've made new friends—"

"And forgotten about the old ones?"

I shook my head. We'd had a similar discussion before I'd left home. Had he really just come here to hash it all out again?

"Of course I haven't forgotten about the old ones. I know it's difficult with us being apart—"

"It's impossible! I'm alone, Megan. I've got no girlfriend to go to movies with or talk to—"

"We talk on the phone."

"Big deal. I can't kiss the phone. This long-distance relationship thing just isn't working for me, Megan. If you don't come back with me, then . . ."

His voice trailed off, like he was choking up. I wondered

if tears were burning his throat like they were burning mine. "Then what?" I rasped.

"Then I want to break up. I want to be free to date other people."

"Nick, I'll be home in seventeen days, and then it's just six more weeks."

I reached for him and he stepped back. "I can't do this anymore, Megan. Wondering about what you're doing and who you're doing it with."

"What are you talking about? I'm working at a theme park—"

"And hanging around with other guys—"

"Friends! Parker is a friend. I told you that. He even gave you his couch to sleep on. Do you think he would have done that if there was something going on between us?"

"You have to choose, Megan. Me or this stupid park."

CHAPTER 22

Decisions, decisions . . .

Go back home with Nick.

Pros: Nick and I stay together

Cons: Too late to get a summer job anywhere; no money; will miss my new summer friends; giving in to Nick's demands; no compromise (do I really want a boyfriend who says it's his way or the highway?); live at home while Mom and Sarah . . .

Stay here.

Pros: Weekly paycheck; playing on the lake with new summer friends; can get to know Parker better (Will he kiss me again if I don't have a boyfriend? Do I want him to?)

Cons: No complaining boyfriend.

I didn't remember choosing. I didn't remember giving Nick an answer.

It was like I suddenly woke up and found myself alone beside the lake, with his words *We're so over* echoing around me.

Just like that. A snap of the fingers. We were no longer together.

Why had he really come? Had he really thought that I would just pack up and go?

Everything was suddenly blurry, the lake seen through a mist of tears.

"You okay?"

Parker. I swiped at the tears that I didn't even realize I was crying until that moment. "I'm fine."

"Nick said he wouldn't need my couch tonight. That he was driving back home. Like, right now. That's crazy."

"As crazy as us breaking up."

"You broke up?"

"Am I in an echo chamber?"

Parker wrapped his hand around my arm and turned me. I guess I'd missed a tear or two because he ran his thumb along my cheek. "Is that why he came here? To break up with you?" he asked.

"How the hell do I know why he came here? He gave me

an ultimatum. Go home with him or break up. So I guess we broke up."

"And you're sad about that?"

Were all guys idiots?

"Have you never had a girlfriend? Have you never had anyone break up with you?"

This was a first for me, and I really didn't like it. I wrapped my arms around my stomach. I wanted to double over. "Why does my stomach hurt? Shouldn't the pain be in my chest, where my heart is?"

"You need some serious heartbreak intervention," he said.

"What?"

And even as I asked it, I thought I knew where he was going with his intervention plan. A kiss to take my mind off Nick.

Only I didn't want a kiss, not even one of the heat-seeking kind that Parker was so good at.

"I know just the thing to make you feel better."

"Nothing is going to make me feel better."

"This will. Come on."

We started walking back to the house. Parker pulled out his cell phone and called someone. I couldn't hear what he was saying. His voice was quiet, mysterious. I didn't care.

I didn't care about anything. I was devastated. I couldn't

help but wonder if my mascara had run. Would people look at me and know that I'd broken up with Nick? Would they think it was my fault, that there was something wrong with me?

Should I have gone with him? Should I have thought that he meant more to me than anything else in the world? When you loved someone, weren't you always supposed to do what made that person happy?

Did that mean that I didn't really love Nick? Had I ever loved him?

Could you fall in love then fall out of love? Did you have to be together all the time in order to stay together forever?

"I don't want to go into the house," I said, as we got nearer. "I don't want to see anyone."

Parker had finished talking with whomever he'd been talking to and put away his phone.

"We'll make a wide circle around the house," he said. "We're heading for my car. I'm going to take you somewhere."

"Where?"

"It's a surprise."

I wasn't sure that I wanted any more surprises tonight.

He took me back to Thrill Ride!

A security guard was waiting for us at the entrance. I was too numb to object when the guard opened the gate and

Parker nudged me through.

"Call me when you need out," the guard said.

"Thanks, Pete."

I guess when you worked here for three summers you got to know everyone.

"What are we doing here?" I asked.

"You'll see."

"I am so not riding the roller coaster." Although I was so lethargic, I might actually be able to ride it without feeling any sort of emotion at all. I was totally numb.

"Not the roller coaster," Parker said.

The park wasn't completely dark. A lot of the lights were turned off. All the lights in the buildings and a lot of the lights that lighted the path. But the lights that identified some of the more popular rides were still on. Just the signs, beaming out their names. Just enough light to see where we were going.

I supposed I should have been excited, or at least inter- ested, to see the park when it was closed down, but I couldn't work up any sort of enthusiasm about anything. I'd never broken up with anyone before. To use Nick's favorite term, *it sucked. Big time.*

It didn't help that the carousel came into view. My favor- ite ride. Nick had refused to ride it with me earlier in the day.

"A kiddie ride," he'd called it.

"What are we doing here?" I asked.

Parker dangled some keys in front of my face. "I have a master key that opens the control box for all the rides. Go get on your favorite horse."

I laughed, a strange sound when I'd thought I'd never laugh again. Or at least not so soon. "You're kidding, right? Won't you get in trouble?"

"Only if I get caught. I don't plan to get caught. And I don't think you'll snitch on me. Go on. Get on a horse."

He walked over to the control box, fiddled with some switches or something, and the bright lights on the carousel were suddenly shining. I was smiling when I stepped onto the wooden platform and climbed onto a horse. A prancer. Three of its legs were down, one lifted slightly and bent. Colorful, carved flowers adorned it.

Music began to play. The horse began to move up and the platform began to rotate.

I knew it was silly, but it made me feel good, made me happy again.

As I came around in a full circle, I saw Parker standing there. He grabbed the outside pole and leaped onto the platform. He stepped over until he was standing next to me, holding the cranking rod that moved my horse up and down.

"Carousels always seemed magical to me," I admitted.

"They are magic. The horses on this carousel were carved in the late eighteen eighties. They've been renovated. Think about how many people have smiled while riding them."

"Thank you for doing this for me," I said.

"No big deal."

Only it was a big deal. He'd known what I needed more than I'd known.

"I'm sorry Nick hurt you," he said.

I was sorry, too. Sorry that maybe I'd hurt him, too, by not being willing to choose him over the park.

"I was probably silly to think that our being apart for so long wouldn't change things for us," I said.

"People do it all the time, have long-distance relationships."

"It's harder than I thought it would be," I admitted.

"It always is, and my parents haven't set the best example, but I've seen a lot of relationships weather the storms."

"But we barely lasted a month apart."

"His loss," he said.

But it felt like mine, too.

CHAPTER 23

It was strange to check my e-mail and not find a daily message from Nick. Not to find any silly jokes or cartoons forwarded to me. Not to call Nick before I went to bed. To not have him call me in the morning. To dust shelves at H & G's and not pick up little things to send Nick. No postcards, no wish-you-were-heres. There was just this empty place in my life.

How could I miss him more now than I had before? Although I wasn't really certain that I was missing Nick. It was more like an absence in my life, an absence of habits, expected things. And I found myself wondering, had I ever really loved Nick, or had I just loved the idea of being in love? Of having someone to go places with, someone to e-mail, someone to text message, someone to instant message, some-one to call.

It had been two days. Shouldn't I be back on track by now?

Parker had walked me to the dorm after my shift. He'd pretty much carried on a one-sided conversation, telling me funny stories about different people who'd ridden the roller coaster that afternoon while he'd worked. I'd smiled but it had been an automatic reflex, trying not to be a downer.

He asked me if I wanted to catch a midnight movie some-where. I'd said no.

Did I want to go get something to eat?

No.

Hang out at his place?

No.

He'd walked away from me with his head bent and his hands shoved into the front pockets of his jeans. And I'd wanted to cry because I'd said no only because I wanted to say yes so badly.

I was racked with guilt. Guilt because I did want to be with him, maybe I'd always wanted to be with him, and now I was feeling guilty because I'd hurt Nick. It didn't make any sense.

I went to my room. Jordan wasn't back yet, so I just turned

out the light and lay on my bed in the dark, forcing myself not to e-mail Nick. Maybe I could e-mail him as a friend.

There was a knock on the door. I ignored it. It came again. I got up, turned on the light, and opened the door.

"Rescue party!" Zoe cried.

She was standing there with Jordan, Lisa, Alisha, and a couple of other girls who lived down the hall. They were all wearing bathing suits.

"What?" I said.

"Rescue party," Zoe repeated. "Heard you broke up with your boyfriend, luv. And you're moping around. Can't have that. Get your bathing suit on. We're going to the pool."

"The pool closed at ten."

"Only to the unimportant. Come on now, nothing like a late-night dip with friends to get you right back on track."

It was crazy. Everyone filed into the room and I had this horrible fear that they were going to watch me dress.

"Come on, Megan," Jordan said, as she pulled out a drawer of my dresser and scrounged around. She tossed me my bathing suit. "It'll be fun."

"You're all insane," I said, laughing.

But still I went into the bathroom and changed. I could hear the others giggling and talking on the other side of the door.

When I stepped back into the room, they were waiting for me. And was I ever glad. Wasn't doing things with people one of the reasons I hadn't gone back home with Nick? So it was totally stupid to be moping around about it.

"Let's go!" Zoe commanded.

We hustled out of my room and headed toward the pool. It was the pool at the hotel. We had the right to use it, although I'd always thought only during certain hours. But it sorta made sense that they would let us use it when it was closed to the tourists.

"Whose idea was this?" I asked once we were outside.

Jordan turned around and started walking backward. "Mine, of course. Can't have a sad roomie. I was starting to suffer from second-hand break-up. You know? Like second-hand smoke?"

"I got it," I said, laughing. I should have known it was Jordan's idea.

As we got nearer to the pool, I could see other people hanging around within the fenced area.

"We're not alone," Lisa said.

"Not to worry. Employee e-mail is a wondrous thing," Zoe said. "I just put the word out that we were all in need of some spirit lifting."

Zoe opened the gate and we all filed into the blue-and-white-tiled pool area. Ice chests were lined up against one side.

"Brilliant!" Zoe exclaimed. "Who brought the drinks?"

A few guys admitted they'd brought them.

"How much do we owe you?" she asked.

"We raided the concession stands," one confessed. "So let's keep that little fact to ourselves."

"We've got chips over here," Lisa said. "This is great."

And it was great. To be here with so many—

"Oh!"

I found myself being lifted into someone's arms. I threw my arms around his neck. Parker. I should have known. He was grinning, but he had a mischievous gleam in his eyes.

"You know you've been a wet blanket lately," he said.

I narrowed my eyes at him. "You wouldn't dare."

"Never dare me, Megan."

He yelled and leaped for the pool. I screamed. We hit the water. Went under. Came up sputtering.

"You idiot!" I cried. I put my hands on top of his head and pushed him under.

He grabbed my legs, lifted me up, and tossed me back.

I don't know how long we wrestled until we were both

laughing so hard that we were in danger of drowning.

"Feeling better, Megan?" Jordan asked from her crouched position by the pool.

I flung my hair out of my eyes.

Parker tickled my bare stomach. "Answer her."

I splashed water at him and moved out of his way. I was feeling better, so much better. I looked at him. "You know what would make me feel really better?"

He gave me a wicked grin and nodded. "Yep."

It was incredible, but I knew that he did know what I was thinking.

At the same time, we both lunged for Jordan. She screamed as we grabbed her arms and pulled her into the pool.

She came up sputtering. "No fair!"

"All is fair in love and war," Parker said.

"This isn't war, so does that mean it's love?" she asked.

I know it sounds strange, but it was like Parker suddenly got very still, very quiet.

I don't know if he was trying to come up with a witty comeback, or what it might have been. At that moment, Ross yelled "Cannonball!" and jumped into the pool, causing a tidal wave. That seemed to be the catalyst for the party to really get underway.

More people jumped into the pool. Someone turned on

music. We were far enough from the hotel that I didn't think it would disturb any of the guests, the wise people who were sleeping so they'd be rested for going to the park tomorrow.

I was standing in water up to my shoulders. Parker was watching me, studying me.

"I'm fine," I finally said.

"Good. Want something to drink?"

I shook my head. "Think I'm just going to relax here for a while. I can't believe how warm the water is."

After a while I swam across the pool, got out, and slid into the Jacuzzi. The water there was really hot, bubbling around me. I scooted over until I was sitting by Jordan, who was sitting by Ross.

She leaned over to me. "It was really Parker's idea. The party here."

"As Zoe would say, 'brilliant.' "

"Don't tell him I told you," she said, her voice low.

"Why does he want it to be a secret?"

"He worries that you're vulnerable. That you might think he's trying to take advantage of what you're going through right now." She shrugged. "Or maybe he's scared."

"Of what?"

"Of liking you and you not liking him."

"Did he tell you that?"

"Are you kidding? No way. But I see the way he looks at you. The way he's looked at you from the beginning. If you're not interested, just tell me, and I'll tell him. It won't be so hard coming from me."

"I don't know if I'm interested or not," I told her truthfully. "I just had one failed long-distance relationship."

"It's two months before we get to that part."

Yeah, but I'd had three months with Nick before ours went long-distance. We didn't even survive a month being apart. How could I build a strong enough relationship in two months to weather the long-distance part that would come? I didn't think I could.

So would it be better not to try?

CHAPTER 24

The pool party was a turning point.

I stopped worrying about my relationship—or lack of one—with Nick. I started living in the present, enjoying every day that came along. Enjoying every minute of being with Parker.

We ate meals together, went to movies, hung out at his place. And there was always the Wednesday night party, gearing up for the weekend. Only at this party, this week, I was gearing up to leave. To go home on Friday for the wedding.

Parker and I were sitting on the back porch. Just sitting there, enjoying the evening. The really strange thing was that since I'd broken up with Nick—or he'd broken up with me—Parker hadn't kissed me. Hadn't even tried. He'd made no moves at all.

At first I'd thought maybe the whole attracted-to-me thing had been because I'd had a boyfriend. You know: You want most what you can't have.

And once I was available, well, where was the challenge? But if that was the case, why would he have kept hanging around with me? Was he waiting for me to make a move? To show I was interested?

How could he not know I was interested? We were practically living together. Except for the sleeping part, of course. But we were doing everything together, with each other whenever one of us had free time.

I enjoyed every minute of being with him, but I thought I wouldn't mind at all if he broke his just-friends pact with me and took our relationship to the next level.

All these thoughts were going through my mind as the party began winding down. People were coming out to the porch to say good-bye. If we followed our usual routine, Jordan and I would help clean up, then she, Ross, and I would go back to the dorm. The last ones to leave.

I didn't know if that would be the routine tonight. Jordan had been downing piña coladas. Ross, too. I had designated myself as the driver.

When it got really quiet and the only sounds we heard were the insects chirping, I yawned and stood up. "I guess

I'd better start cleaning."

"I'll help," Parker said.

"It doesn't seem fair that you always help with the cleanup when you're the one who provides the place for the party," I said, as we walked into the house.

"I promised Mitch that I'd take care of the place," he said.

"That's right. Responsibility is your middle name."

"First name, actually."

I looked over at him and laughed. "You're kidding, right?"

"Yeah."

It was really, really quiet in the house. "It feels like we're totally alone here," I said.

"Can't be." He went to the front door, looked out. "Jordan's car is still here."

He walked back through the house. "This way," he said.

I followed him to his bedroom. And just like Goldilocks, Jordan was curled up on Parker's bed asleep. Well, not exactly like Goldilocks. Her boyfriend was snuggled up against her, both fully clothed on top of the covers.

"I *thought* she was hitting the drinks pretty hard," Parker said.

"Can you take me back to the dorm after I help you clean up?" I asked.

"Sure."

It didn't take us long. Paper plates and cups into the trash. There were never any leftovers. Put a few dishes into the dishwasher, wiped down the counters.

I was standing at the sink, staring out the window at the lake, having just rinsed out the dishrag, when Parker came up behind me, put his arms around my waist and rested his chin on my shoulder.

"I TiVo'd one of my dad's movies. Want to watch it with me?"

I looked back at him. "Now?"

"Sure. You can sleep late in the morning, right?"

"Yeah, but don't you have to get up early?"

"I don't need much sleep."

I shrugged, watched his head bob up with my movement. "Sure, I guess."

We went into the living room, sat on the couch. He put his arm around me, nestled me up against his side, turned on the TV, went through the TiVo menu, and selected a movie I'd never heard of.

"I've never seen this one."

"It's one of his better ones."

I watched the opening credits. "Sandra Bullock? I guess you know her, too."

"Yep."

"And she's just a normal person."

"They all are, Megan."

It was a romantic comedy. We were about fifteen minutes into the movie when Parker said, "You know, the thing about my dad's movies is that they're more entertaining when watched from a horizontal position."

I snapped my head around and looked at him. "Are you making a move on me, Parker?"

I thought he would smile, laugh. Instead he looked deadly serious.

"Yeah. Do you have a problem with it?"

Did I? I shook my head.

We laid down on the couch with me nestled against his side, my back against the couch so I could still watch the movie, but it suddenly wasn't making any sense to me. I'd lost the flow of the story, mostly because I was thinking about how nice it felt to be snuggling against Parker.

"I'll take you to the airport Friday," he said quietly, tucking my hair behind my ear, over and over, like it was attempting to escape from the place where he'd put it. It felt really nice.

"You'll be working. I can take the shuttle."

"I can take a couple of hours off. No problem."

"Okay. Thanks."

"When do you get back Sunday?"

"Late."

"Time?"

I smiled. "Around nine."

"That's not late, Megan. I never go to bed before one."

"It'll feel late to me after the busy weekend."

"You will come back, won't you?"

"Of course. I have half the summer left to go."

"Will you see Nick while you're there?"

"I wasn't planning on it."

He was still tucking my hair behind my ear, studying me. "You ever think about getting back together with him?"

"No."

"That's good. Look, Megan, I didn't want to rush you, I didn't want to push you. I know you were hurting, but I don't want you going home without knowing exactly what's waiting here for you."

He lowered his mouth to mine. Finally, after all this time, he was kissing me again. And I was kissing him back.

Glad that we were moving beyond the just-friends stage. Glad to know that what would be waiting for me was something that I desperately wanted.

Parker . . . and his kisses.

CHAPTER 25

"So have you slept with Parker yet?"

Sarah asked.

I was standing in front of a mirror, making sure the gown I was going to wear tomorrow fit properly, trying to see if it needed any last-minute adjustments. Her question took me totally off guard and I wasn't exactly sure how to answer it.

Had I slept with Parker? Yes. After an incredible kissing session on his couch Wednesday night, early Thursday morning, we'd fallen asleep. So yes, technically, we'd slept together. But I knew that wasn't what Sarah was asking.

"You know, Sarah, it's really none of your business."

"You have, then."

I rolled my eyes. "No, I haven't, not like you mean."

"Are you dating him?"

"We spend a lot of time together."

"I knew he liked you," she said. "And that you liked him."

"He's not the reason I broke up with Nick." I shook my head. "Or Nick broke up with me."

"It doesn't matter, Megan. I just want you to be happy, and you seemed really happy whenever you were around Parker."

"I do like him, Sarah. I like him a lot. It's just so natural to be with him. I can't explain it, but I'm so dreading the end of summer."

"That's weeks away. Don't sweat it. It'll work itself out. Besides, we have enough to worry about this weekend. What do you think of your gown?"

Her brow was deeply furrowed, and she was nibbling the French manicure off one of her nails. I couldn't tell her the truth.

"I thought the bridesmaid's gowns were supposed to be purple—"

"That's what I thought chartreuse was. I didn't know it was the color of puke."

"Let's call it green with a hint of yellow. Sounds better."

Although her description was pretty accurate. She'd ordered the gowns through a catalog. The gown shown had been blue, with the other colors available just listed. I couldn't believe she'd ordered what she hadn't seen. They'd arrived yesterday. No time to send them back. What had she been thinking?

"It doesn't look that bad," I said.

"I ordered purple irises for the flowers in the church. My bouquet has purple in it. Yours has purple in it."

"It's probably got green, too, right? Stems and leaves. So it'll match the gown."

Then she did the most unsettling thing. She started crying.

I knelt in front of her and put my arms around her. "Sarah, it's all right."

"It's hideous. Your gown is hideous. Everything is going wrong."

"I hear it's good luck for your wedding to go badly. It means the marriage will last."

She looked up at me. "You're just trying to make me feel better, right?"

"Yeah." I squeezed her hand. "Honestly, the gown isn't that bad. At least I don't look like Gretel and I don't have to wear my hair in braids."

She laughed. "That's true. I just wanted everything to be perfect, and instead, I'm just ready for it to be over."

"Tomorrow will be here before you know it."

"If we survive tonight." She scrunched up her face, and I knew she was about to deliver some really bad news.

"Tonight is just the rehearsal, then the dinner, right?" I asked.

"Right, except that the groom's parents handle the dinner and they've made reservations at Hart's. And I'm pretty sure that Nick is working tonight."

I figured my face had just turned the same shade of green as my gown. "Great."

"Yeah. I'm sorry. I just found out today—"

"Don't worry about it. Nick and I go to the same school. We're going to run into each other. I can handle it."

"Are you sure?"

"Absolutely."

I was proud of myself for sounding more confident than I felt. I wasn't sure that I was ready to see Nick again. Or if he was ready to see me.

The rehearsal went smoothly, which I'd always heard was bad luck. I didn't mention that to Sarah. She was so crazy in love with Bobby. Even though they were both totally stressed. Bobby was being a good sport, pretending to care about all the little details, but I could tell he was thinking *Let's get this over with already.*

I couldn't have agreed more.

I almost bailed out on the rehearsal dinner. I was really missing Parker, wishing I'd brought him with me so I wouldn't have to face Nick alone, which was an insane thought. I wasn't alone. There were at least two dozen people joining us in the private banquet room at Hart's.

And sure enough, our waiter was Nick. A girl with short black hair and dark eyes was assisting him. It was a little awkward when he got to me. We'd always had this private joke, because I'm so predictable. At Hart's I always ordered the chicken fried steak, extra gravy. And whenever Nick waited on me, he never actually took my order.

He'd just give me a wink and say, "I know what you want." Like the moon and stars were in alignment and we knew each other so well that we always knew what the other wanted.

But the truth was that we didn't really know each other that well. And I think that was part of the reason that our relationship didn't last. Our relationship was built on forwarded e-mail jokes and . . . convenience, if I was honest with myself.

"And what would you like?" he said, formally. Like he'd never hugged me, never kissed me, never told me he loved me.

I almost said "the usual." But in the end, I told him, "Chicken fried steak, extra gravy."

"Sides?"

"Mashed potatoes and salad with the house dressing. Sweet tea."

He moved on to the next person. I wanted to grab his arm, ask how he was. Ask if he was doing okay. If we could still be friends. But twenty-four guests were watching us, plus the girl who was following him around like a puppy on a leash.

I spent a lot of time talking to the best man, Bobby's younger brother, Joe. Probably the only guy I knew who was looking forward to school starting in the fall. He'd gone skiing last winter break and fallen in love with a girl named Kate. He couldn't wait for the fall semester to start because she would be attending the same college he was.

"Don't you think it's hard keeping a long-distance relationship going?" I asked.

"It sucks big time, for sure. But we talk every day and I've gone to see her a couple of times over the summer. She's come to see me. We make it work."

"I never thought of a relationship as being *work*," I said.

He grinned. "It's a good kind of work. I don't mind it at all."

"You just said it sucks."

"Being apart sucks. But when we're together"—I thought he was actually blushing—"she's terrific. I'm crazy about her."

"She's not going to come for the wedding?"

"No, she's traveling in Europe right now with her aunt. I get a postcard every day that says, 'Wish you were here.' I wish I was there, too."

Our conversation came to an end when Bobby's dad stood up to make a toast, to welcome Sarah into their family. Sarah looked radiant. Bobby looked so proud.

I realized that tomorrow no one was going to notice that I was wearing puke green. No one was going to notice me at all. All eyes would be on Sarah. The bride.

And that was how it should be.

When we got home, although it was late, I asked Dad if I could borrow the car for a while. I drove back to Hart's Diner and parked beside Nick's old Chevy Nova. I got out of the car and sat on the hood and waited.

Waited for most of the other cars to leave. Waited for the lights in the restaurant windows to dim and for the lights outside to go out. Only the streetlights remained on, but they were enough to see by.

I spotted Nick as soon as he came out of the building. Came out of the building with the girl who had helped him serve us. I hadn't heard her name, but I knew who she was. Tess.

He hadn't seen me yet. I watched as she wrapped her arm around his waist and he slipped his arm around her. Then he leaned down and kissed her. She laughed. So did he.

I thought maybe I should have felt a prick of hurt or jealousy or anger. But I didn't. I felt glad.

He must have finally seen me, because he staggered to a stop. Tess looked at me, looked at him.

"What's up?" she asked.

I slid off the hood. "Hi, Nick."

I walked toward them. "You must be Tess."

"Yeah, so?"

Talk about an attitude.

"Nick's told me a lot about you."

"How come?"

"This is Megan," Nick said impatiently. "What do you want?"

"I'm flying back out Sunday. I just wanted to visit with you for a bit."

He scoffed. "It's a little late, Megan."

"Yeah, I can see that. If I hurt you, Nick, I'm sorry. That's all I wanted to say. I'll see you around."

I got into my car, put the key into the ignition. A knock on the window nearly had me jumping out of my skin. It was Nick. I rolled down the window.

"Tess was here. You weren't," he said defensively.

"Were you seeing her before you drove up to see me?" I asked quietly.

He looked away, and I realized that he might have been struggling with his feelings toward Tess, just like I'd struggled with mine about Parker. That he'd driven nonstop to see me not so much because he was so desperate to be with me, but because he was afraid that he might be losing the battle to resist Tess.

"Not seriously," he finally said, before looking back at me.

"It's okay, Nick. I'm happy for you."

"I miss you sometimes," he said.

"I miss you, too. But summer will be over soon and maybe we'll be friends again."

He growled. "You know guys hate the 'let's be friends' comment."

I grinned. "I know. But I don't think we'll ever be more than friends again. So you'd better hang on to Tess."

"I will."

He reached his hand into the car, to touch my cheek, I thought, but at the last second he pulled back. "See ya."

He was gone before I could say anything.

I watched him get into his car where Tess was waiting for him. I thought about how nice it was to have someone waiting for you. Maybe that was what made long-distance relationships so hard. Because even if you had someone waiting for you, he had to wait so long.

"How's it going?"

Parker's deep voice rumbled in my ear in the dark. I'd just snuggled beneath the covers when my cell phone rang.

"Other than the fact that Sarah never learned a color chart, things aren't going too badly. My gown was supposed to be some shade of purple and instead it's after-a-roller-coaster-ride green."

He laughed. "It's not too late for them to get married here. I'll even put streamers on the roller coaster for them."

"It *is* too late. We've already had the rehearsal."

I told him about the toasts during dinner and talking with Joe. He told me about the design for the next roller coaster that he'd seen. It would be built over the winter, ready for operation next year.

We talked for over an hour, about everything and nothing. Just to hear each other's voices. And when I finally hung up, it was almost like he was there with me.

CHAPTER 26

When the plane landed Sunday evening, I was wiped out. The weekend had been an *emotional* roller coaster: seeing Nick; a lot of hand-holding with Sarah and reassurances that everything would go smoothly; staying up late Saturday night talking with Dad, who wanted to know everything about my job at the park. And dang it, I owed Jordan a day off, because I did get my dad to confess that he'd thought I was getting too serious with Nick and some time apart would do me good. I wondered how he'd feel about Parker? This morning I'd gotten up early to visit with Mom, who was still weepy over her firstborn daughter getting married and leaving home. I guess the weekend had been hard on everyone.

I wasn't looking forward to hauling my suitcase to the Thrill Ride! shuttle, but I figured as soon as I got to the dorm, I was going to crash. Big time.

I was thinking about the luxury of crashing as I walked from the plane to the gate. Not paying much attention to my surroundings. Suddenly someone stepped in front of me. I lifted my gaze. Smiled.

Parker.

"Hey," he said.

"Hey." I am such an amazing conversationalist that I astound myself sometimes.

He dipped his head and gave me a quick kiss. A welcoming kiss. That was the thing about Parker. I loved all his kisses. No matter how quick or how long or how slow. Each one was perfect.

"How did you get through security without a ticket?" I asked.

"I've got connections." He slipped his arm around me. "You got baggage?"

Have I got baggage. What a loaded question. Nick. The weekend with my family. Too much to unload right then and there.

"Yeah." I held up my ticket with my baggage claim

number. "I wasn't expecting you to pick me up."

"Why not? You're my girlfriend, right?"

I nestled my head in the curve of his shoulder. Was I his girlfriend? For how long?

We got my luggage from baggage claim, stopped for burgers, then drove out to his place. He didn't ask me if I wanted to go there, and that was fine with me. Because it was where I wanted to be.

Now we were sitting on the grass by the lake, my back to his chest, his arms around me. Watching the moonlight dancing over the lake. It was so peaceful. I thought I could stay here forever. But we didn't have forever. We only had about six more weeks and then . . .

"I saw Nick," I said quietly.

I felt him stiffen, then relax. I wondered if he felt threatened by Nick. Parker always seemed so confident, so in charge, and yet we'd both avoided actually defining our relationship. At the airport, when he called me his girlfriend, it was the first time that he'd hinted that we were more than friends, that maybe being "just friends" hadn't worked out for us after all.

"And?" he finally asked.

I turned around so I could look at him. Even though it was night, there was enough moonlight, enough stars that I could see his face.

"It was kinda sad seeing him. I mean, I thought we had something special, that what we had could survive being apart. And it didn't. It hurts that I couldn't make it work, that it didn't last."

"So you're completely over him?"

How could I explain that seeing him again had made me realize that, as much as I'd liked being with Nick, it didn't begin to compare with how much I liked being with Parker? With Parker, it didn't matter if we were talking, if we were doing anything. Simply being with him was enough. And that was scary.

Because not having Parker was going to hurt. And in less than a month and a half I wouldn't have him in my life anymore. And apparently I sucked when it came to long-distance relationships.

"I'm totally over him," I said. I could have told him that Nick had a girlfriend, that he was totally over me as well, but it wasn't really an issue. It wasn't important. The important part was that I had absolutely no interest in Nick anymore as anything other than a friend.

Parker, on the other hand . . .

He tucked my hair behind my ear, keeping his warm palm pressed against my cheek.

"I want to be more than just friends, Megan."

"Me, too." The words came out in a raspy whisper. "But I'm no good at long-distance relationships and that's what we'll have at the end of summer." I shook my head. Maybe I was presuming too much. "I mean, we'll either just have a summer fling or we'll try and take it farther and if it doesn't last—"

He pressed a finger against my lips. "Let's just worry about now."

He drew me closer and kissed me. Slowly. Provocatively. If he was working to make me forget about the future, he was succeeding, because I was thinking only about this moment in time. His lips on mine. His hands cradling my face. The way he smelled, crisp and spicy.

When he kissed me, my mind didn't want to list out the pros and cons. I wasn't thinking about making decisions. I was totally involved in the kiss.

He drew back, nipped my chin, then started kissing me again. I loved when he did that. He took kissing to a level that I'd never experienced before him. Was it totally Parker? Or was it the two of us together, the way we meshed?

When I was with him, I felt like I was part of him. Scary.

I didn't want to think about what waited for us at the end of summer. Saying good-bye. Maybe forever.

He stopped kissing me and pressed his forehead against mine. "I don't want to take you back to the dorm tonight," he said, his voice the low rumble that always shimmied through me, warming me and exciting me.

"I don't want to go back to the dorm tonight," I said.

He stood up and drew me to my feet, took my hand, and started walking back to his house.

Inside it was eerily quiet. I didn't know if Cole had already gone to bed or if he wasn't home yet. Maybe he was with Ronda. It didn't really matter. All that mattered was that I was with Parker.

The sun was just starting to peer in through the window when Parker woke me with a kiss.

"Come on, lazybones, I have to get to work," he said.

I groaned, rolled over, and buried my head beneath the pillow. "I'm not a morning person," I grumbled.

He pulled the pillow off my head. "I want you to go with me."

I peered up at him through a narrowed eye. "I'm not riding it."

"Hey! Did I ask? I just want you to be with me." He

combed my hair back from my face. "Come on. Morning is the best time."

The best time for sleeping, I thought, but didn't say.

"I'll even fix breakfast while you shower," he said.

How could a girl resist an offer like that?

When I walked into the kitchen after my shower, dressed in shorts and a tank, I couldn't help but laugh at the sight of the breakfast he'd fixed for me. A bowl of Raisin Bran.

Giving me a sheepish look, he grinned. I loved his grin.

After breakfast, we drove to the park. The sun was higher, but the day echoed that stillness that you feel before most of the world is up and moving about. We walked through the park, holding hands.

Parker seemed unusually quiet this morning, like he had something important on his mind.

As we got nearer to Magnum Force, he said, "Last night you were talking about what we'd do when we got to the end of the summer."

"Yeah."

"What do you see as our options?"

"Break up or stay together. I don't see us staying together, not long-distance."

"Why?"

"Because I'm no good at it."

"A relationship takes two, you know."

I looked over at him. He was watching me.

"It's hard, Parker. Not being with someone. Just having e-mail and phone calls—"

"I know it's not easy, Megan, but if you really care for someone, you can make it work. I really care for you."

I didn't know what to say.

He led me up the steps of Magnum Force and across the platform. He called out a greeting to the guy at the controls. "Hey, Chris."

Chris just waved.

Parker let go of my hand and stepped into the first car.

He turned back to me. "Come with me, Megan."

Shaking my head, I crossed my arms over my chest. "I can't."

He held out his hand. "Trust me."

He was more serious than I'd ever seen him, his steadfast gaze boring into me.

"Trust me," he repeated.

And I knew he was talking about more than the roller coaster. He was talking about total trust, that he wouldn't hurt me, like Nick did. That things would be different for us. That he would make them different. That *we* were different.

I was scared. My stomach tightened and my mouth got

dry. I took a deep, shuddering breath.

I put my trembling hand in his and his fingers closed around mine—sure, steadfast, secure. Symbolic of what he wanted me to know. That no matter what, he wouldn't let go. Even if we were no longer touching, he'd still be holding on. He'd be there.

I wish I could say that the little tremors of dread melted away, but they didn't. I was still terrified, not looking forward to the ride. But I wanted to be with Parker, and that meant conquering my fears.

I took another deep breath, stepped into the car, and sat on the cool leather seat. He buckled us in and pulled the bar down across our laps. I cringed at the clanking sound. Wrapped my hands around the cold metal.

"Ready?" he asked.

I swallowed hard again and nodded. He gave Chris a thumbs-up.

There was another clanking sound as the lead car began pulling the others up the track. Parker put his arm around me, leaned in, and kissed my cheek.

"It's totally safe, Megan."

I looked at him. "But it's so high and so fast—"

"Don't think about it. Just be in the now."

He kissed me, distracting me so I wasn't thinking about

the fact that I was traveling at a sixty-degree angle and after I reached the apex I was going to be plummeting almost straight down at a hundred and twenty-five miles an hour.

Okay, so I was thinking about it a little, but I was also thinking about Parker and the decision to trust him that I'd made without considering pros and cons. It hadn't even required my decision-maker. And maybe that said more about my relationship with Parker than anything else. That when it came to anything involving Parker, I didn't have to list out pros and cons.

The lead car stopped for only a heartbeat, but it was long enough for Parker to pull back, grin, and say, "You're gonna love it!"

Then we were speeding down the track, the wind whipping across my face. I was screaming and laughing and he was laughing. My stomach was queasy and my heart was in my throat—

It was so exciting. Thrilling!

And so totally not how I'd thought I'd spend my summer.

Me, carousel girl, on the tallest, fastest roller coaster that the park had to offer.

As we swooped up another incline, then dashed back down, I realized that I *was* loving it . . . loving Parker. Being with him was thrilling and exciting.

The ride of a lifetime.

It felt so right. Us. The two of us together.

At that moment, I knew we could last past the end of summer. That with Parker, I could make a long-distance relationship work.

That relationships were a lot like roller coasters, filled with highs and lows, terrifying split seconds, and awesome moments when you simply enjoyed the ride.

Want more Rachel Hawthorne?
Turn the page to sample

TROUBLE FROM THE START

Rachel Hawthorne

A companion to THE BOYFRIEND PROJECT

Chapter 1

AVERY

"You can't just stand here, Avery. You have to get out there and flaunt it."

I wasn't quite sure what Kendall Jones, my best friend since forever, thought I had to flaunt.

"It seems a little late for all that," I told her. "We only have a week left until we graduate."

"Which is exactly why we're here," she said, removing the clip from her red hair, retwisting the curling strands, and securing them back into place. "Jeremy and I had our pick of three parties tonight. I knew this one would have the most people."

Because it was totally without chaperones. Scooter Gibson's parents were out of town and he had the key to his family's lake house so here we were, standing out by a magnificent pool, catching glimpses through towering trees of the moonlight dancing across the calm lake waters. Laughter, screeches, the din of conversation, and raucous cheers as girls stripped before diving into the pool competed with music blasting from speakers on the patio.

"I feel like a party crasher," I told her. "It's not like I was invited."

"You're with us. It's cool."

"I shouldn't have come."

"You're never going to get a boyfriend if you just stay at home."

I had been staying at home more since Kendall and Jeremy Swanson hooked up over spring break. They invited me to go almost everywhere with them, but I often simply felt out of place.

Kendall wrapped her hand around my upper arm. "Look, Avery, I want you to have what I have. But if that doesn't happen, you still need to go on a date. You can't start college never having been alone with a guy. You'll feel awkward."

As though I could feel any more awkward than I did now, standing around, experiencing a rush of hope that I might find a boyfriend of my own every time a cute guy glanced my way, only to be disappointed when he turned back to his friends. I longed for some guy to think I was special enough to kiss.

At seventeen I wasn't kissless but my one kiss had happened at band camp sophomore year. I still shuddered when I remembered the tuba player pressing his puckered, chapped lips to mine. We'd gotten trapped with a spin the bottle game. I'd thought I would be perceived as cool if I acted like I was up for anything. Instead I discovered that some things just aren't worth it.

"You just need to get out there," Kendall continued. "Let guys know you're interested."

How was I supposed to do that? Wish a flashing neon sign? Not that I thought it would make any difference. I knew these guys, and they knew me. If we hadn't clicked after twelve years of being in school together, what made Kendall think it would happen tonight?

Jeremy was the newest kid in town, and it had taken six months for him and Kendall to start dating, although I noticed the sparks between them way before that.

"Yeah, okay," I said with far more enthusiasm than I felt. "I can put myself out there."

She gave me a quick hug. "You deserve to be as happy as I am."

"Here we go," Jeremy announced, rejoining us and handing us each a plastic cup.

Jeremy's family had moved here in the fall when his dad got a job transfer. He'd been bummed about not graduating with his friends. He'd started hanging around with us, and the three of us grew close. One night when we were all planning to go to a movie together, I'd faked being sick because I suspected he liked Kendall as more than a friend, and I was in the way. That night he'd kissed her, and the rest was history.

"Mmm," Kendall sighed, snuggling against him. "This tastes like an orange dreamsicle."

It did, but it also had a little kick to it. I had a feeling that it wasn't a melted ice cream bar. The two he'd brought each of us earlier had been strawberry something or other.

Jeremy slid his arm around her. He was tall enough that her head fit perfectly into the nook of his shoulder, like fate had made them to go together.

"Let's dance," he said in a low voice near her ear.

She looked at me, one brow arched. "He could be out there."

"Who?" Jeremy asked, clearly baffled.

"The right guy for Avery," Kendall said.

"Oh, yeah, he could totally be out there." Jeremy shifted his gaze to me. "Just avoid the house. It's make-out central in there. Don't want someone to get the wrong idea about what you're looking for."

"I'm not even sure what I'm looking for," I admitted.

"Someone nice like Jeremy," Kendall said. "And you'll have a better chance of meeting him if we're not here. Have fun!"

She handed me her drink and they wandered off. Self-consciously I glanced around. Everyone else was already separated into groups, based on common interests—which usually involved gossiping about someone *not* in the circle. I didn't really feel like barging in. But I also didn't want to stand here alone like a total loser.

I ambled over to the nearest group of girls. They were giggling hysterically. While I'd missed the joke, I laughed, too, and tried to look like I was part of their gab-fest. Melody Long stopped laughing, which caused the others to stop as well, because she was the alpha in the group. Flicking her long blond hair, she turned ever so slightly and looked at me as though she was considering tossing me in the pool.

"Hi, Melody," I said, plowing ahead, even knowing that I was about to ram into a brick wall. "Isn't this a fun party?"

She narrowed her eyes. "Are you wired?"

"You mean feverishly excited about being here?" I smiled brightly, refusing to let on how much her barb had hurt. It wasn't the first time someone had hinted that I might be a narc. "You bet."

Blinking, she stared at me blankly. It was the same look she wore when we had a pop quiz in history.

"One of the definitions for wired is feverishly excited," I explained, realizing too late that I was making the situation worse, doing my Merriam-Webster's impersonation. After drinking two fruity somethings-or-other I was finding that my mouth could work without any social filter.

Jade Johnson stepped in front of her. "She means wired like recording stuff for the cops."

"Why would I do that?" I asked, knowing exactly why they thought that and hating that they distrusted the police, that they distrusted me.

As Jade moved in, reminding me a little of a pit bull, she brought with her the fragrance of recently smoked weed, which explained why they were so paranoid. "Because your dad's a cop," Jade said, as though I didn't know what he did for a living. "I think you need to strip down so we know you're cool."

"Yeah," Melody said, brightening as though she'd finally figured out an answer on the pop quiz. "You need to show us you're not wearing a wire."

I thought about pointing out that my clothes—white shorts and a snug red top—weren't designed to hide much of anything. Instead, I just said, "Not going to happen."

Spinning on my heel, I walked away, their laughter following me, and this time I was pretty sure I was the joke.

I passed a group of three couples, but I wanted to avoid twosomes since I would stand out as someone no guy was interested in being with. I spotted two girls and a guy talking. They seemed harmless, but as I neared they began wandering off toward the house. Following after them would have made me appear desperate to be included.

Then I spied Brian Saunders leaning against a wooden beam that supported one corner of a cedar-slatted canopy. He was alone. I created a zigzag path to get to him because I didn't want it to seem obvious I was beelining for him in case he walked away before I got there. When I was three steps away, he was still there, drinking a beer. I noticed a few empty bottles at his feet and it occurred to me that he was still standing there because he was too unsteady to move away. But I was here now.

"Hey," I said brightly, moving in front of him so he blocked the view of the kissing couple stretched out on the lounge chair beneath the canopy.

For a moment he furrowed his brow, blinked, and I was afraid he didn't recognize me.

He blinked again, scowled. "I'll get to the problems tomorrow."

What was he talking about? Then I remembered that I'd given him an extra assignment to work on the last time I tutored him. "Oh, I don't care about that."

He brightened. "So I don't have to do them?"

"They're always optional, but if you work them out then you're more likely to learn the material—God, could I sound any more geekish? I'm sorry. I didn't come over here to talk algebra." Please don't ask me why I came over.

Eager to look like I belonged wasn't a much better reason.

But he seemed to have forgotten I was even there as he took another sip and shifted his attention away from me. "Do you think Ladasha likes Kirk?" he asked.

I turned in the direction he was looking. I was hardly the one to tutor him in love, although his question seemed to be a no-brainer. Ladasha—who actually spelled her name La-A—always got the leads in the school plays and was moving to New York after graduation to pursue acting. At that particular moment, though, she was in the pool with her legs wrapped around Kirk's waist like he was her life preserver. "Uh, probably," I finally answered.

"She is so amazingly beautiful," he said.

"Yes, she is." She was probably the most beautiful girl in our graduating class.

"I'm going to tell her," he said, and staggered away, leaving me feeling even more self-conscious, as though everyone would figure out that I couldn't hold a guy's attention for two minutes.

Sighing, I returned to the spot where Jeremy and Kendall had left me so that at least they could find me easily. No way I was going looking for them. I wasn't sure all they were doing was dancing. Their relationship had seemed to have gotten intense fast. I was happy for Kendall. She deserved a great guy like Jeremy. He was the one who got invited to the party, and he'd included his girlfriend's best friend. A lot of guys wouldn't be that thoughtful. I'd come because senior year was supposed to be memorable, although at that precise moment I felt stupid and uncomfortable standing all alone while holding two plastic cups filled almost to the top. I chugged down Kendall's. Maybe with a little more alcohol, I wouldn't be bothered by the fact that since I'd spent way too much time studying and not enough partying, I didn't know any of these people well enough that they were going to include me in their little circles.

It had been that way for most of high school. I had so wanted to fall in love, or at least in like, before I graduated. Now I needed to admit that wasn't going to happen, but that was okay. The sea at college would contain a lot more fish, and no one there would know my dad was a cop. He wouldn't be coming to the university to hold assemblies with the theme "Dare to Say No." I loved my dad, loved that he was one of the good guys, but my dating life sucked.

That would all change at college, I was sure. I'd meet someone fantastic and fall in love. That had always been my plan, what I'd dreamed of when no one invited me to dances. I was going to be a late bloomer but I was going to bloom spectacularly.

Glancing around, I spotted a trash can a couple of feet away. I crushed the cup and lobbed it—

Missed. For some reason it irritated me. I should be

able to hit a trash can. I wandered over, bent down to pick up the cup. The world spun and I staggered back a couple of steps.

"Whoa, brainiac. Careful." A strong hand gripped my upper arm, steadied me, and managed to send a shiver of awareness through me.

I jerked my head up to find myself staring up at Fletcher Thomas. Staring *up* at him because, at six foot three, he was one of the few guys taller than I was. The lights from the Japanese lanterns circling the pool barely reached him. It was almost as though he hadn't quite escaped the darkness from which he'd emerged. His black-as-midnight hair was shaggy, long. His dark brown eyes were almost invisible in the night. Stubble shadowed his jaw, making him seem unreasonably dangerous, although his reputation managed to do that for him.

I was pretty sure that he would eventually end up in prison. When he bothered to make an appearance at school, he was usually sporting bruises or scrapes, grinning broadly as he said, "You should see the other guy." He seemed to live for getting into trouble.

"Thanks, but I'm fine. I don't need help." Irritated, I worked my arm free of his grasp. How dare he mock my intelligence, which I doubted he had much of? As a member of the honor society, I was obligated to tutor at the school a couple of nights a week. I'd spent many a night waiting for Fletcher Thomas to show up for a math tutorial. He couldn't be bothered, so if he didn't graduate, he got what he deserved. "And there is nothing wrong with being smart. You should try it sometime."

"Hey now, retract the claws. I was just trying to save you the embarrassment of a face-plant."

"While insulting me at the same time. Or trying to. I'm actually quite proud of my academic record." Could I sound any more like a snob? There went my mouth again, social cues disengaged.

He didn't seem the least bit offended. His eyes were twinkling like he found me humorous, and that irritated me even more. I took a long swallow of my drink, hoping he'd take the hint and go away.

"You know that drink is about three-fourths whipped cream vodka, right?" he asked.

I licked my lips, savoring the taste. "So?"

"So the reason it tastes like candy is to get girls drunk."

"I'm not drunk." I took another long swallow to prove my point, even though I realized I was way more relaxed than I should have been standing in the presence of a guy who had a reputation for showing girls a good time in the backseat of a car. Although I'd never figured out the car part, since he rode a motorcycle. Maybe he took them to the junkyard and found some beat-up vehicle there.

"Isn't this party a little wild for you?" he asked.

"Figured read-a-thons were more your style."

"Guess you don't know everything," I said.

"Oh, I know plenty, genius," he said.

"I'm a few IQ points shy of being a genius. Your trying to goad me by referring to my intelligence is a little juvenile."

One side of his mouth curled up into a grin and his gaze swept over me as though he was measuring me up for something that was definitely not childish. My stomach did this little tumble like I was back in gymnastics class—which I'd left behind during seventh grade when I'd shot up to a ridiculous height of five foot ten, well on my way to the six feet I'd finally top out at. Gymnasts are usually small, but then so are most guys in seventh grade. And eighth. And ninth. It wasn't until tenth that some started catching up to me. I hated towering over them.

"You're graduating first in the class, aren't you?" he asked, surprising me with what seemed like genuine admiration in his tone. That and his smile made it hard to hold on to my annoyance with him.

"Third." The announcement had come a few weeks earlier. "Lin Chou and Rajesh Nahar are one and two."

"You got robbed."

Was he sticking up for me? It was kind of sweet, but I also knew that I hadn't gotten "robbed."

"Not really. They're way smarter than I am." Which

he would know if he was in any of our advanced classes. And I didn't mind coming in third. It meant that I didn't have to give a speech during the graduation ceremony, but my grades were still high enough that I could get into any state-funded college I wanted—and the one I wanted was in Austin. I'd been accepted a month ago. I couldn't wait until mid-August when I could head down there and be surrounded by people who cared about academics and grades as much as I did. I took another long swallow of the dreamsicle.

He narrowed his eyes. "You should go easy on that."

"I'm not a novice to alcohol."

"So that's not why you staggered earlier?"

"Just lost my balance."

He brought a brown bottle up to his lips and gulped down beer. I hadn't even noticed he had one until that moment. When I realized I was transfixed by the way his throat worked as he swallowed, I lowered my gaze and noticed how his black T-shirt clung to a sculpted chest, washboard abs, and hard-as-rock biceps. Suddenly I felt warm. Why was I noticing these things? I couldn't deny that he *looked* hot, and while I'd come here hoping to catch a guy's attention, I just didn't want it to be some guy with whom I had absolutely nothing in common. I knew he'd been held back at least one year, so studying wasn't a priority for him like it was for me. Fletcher tossed his empty bottle back into a bush.

"Don't you care about the environment?" I scolded him.

"You're not one of *those*, are you?" he asked.

Ignoring his question, I walked over to the bushes, crouched, and tried to see into the darkness, but I suddenly felt light-headed and dropped to my butt.

Fletcher hunkered beside me, balancing on the balls of his feet, his forearms resting on his jean-clad thighs. How did he manage that? I'd bet money he'd already swigged down way more than I had. "You okay?"

"Yes, just—" I realized that I'd finished off my drink. Everything suddenly looked far away, like I was viewing it through a tunnel. The cup slipped from my fingers and onto the grass.

"You need some fresh air," he said.

"We're outside," I pointed out. "It doesn't get any fresher than that."

His fingers folded around my elbow and I was struck by how large his hand was, how strong, how warm against my skin. With no effort at all, he helped me to my feet. "It's better by the lake."

He curled his arm around my shoulders, pulled me in just a little, and I had this insane thought that we fit together like pieces of a puzzle. I liked his height compared to mine. He made me feel normal, when I often felt like a giant. He guided me over the uneven expanse of land that led down to the lake. When we reached the bank, he didn't release his hold, and while I wouldn't admit it to him, I was grateful because suddenly nothing seemed solid beneath my feet.

Can't get enough?
Watch for the companion to
TROUBLE FROM THE START

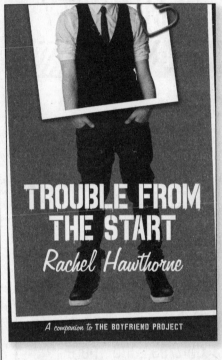